Breaking the Ties That Bind

Also by Gwynne Forster

When the Sun Goes Down
A Change Had to Come
A Different Kind of Blues
Getting Some of Her Own
When You Dance with the Devil
Whatever It Takes
If You Walked in My Shoes
Blues from Down Deep
When Twilight Comes
Destiny's Daughters
(with Donna Hill and Parry "EbonySatin" Brown)

Published by Dafina Books

Breaking the Ties That Bind

Gwynne Forster

Dafina
BOOKS

KENSINGTON PUBLISHING CORP.
http://www.kensingtonbooks.com

DAFINA BOOKS are published by

Kensington Publishing Corp.
119 West 40th Street
New York, NY 10018

All Kensington Titles, Imprints, and Distributed Lines are available at special quantity discounts for bulk purchases for sales promotions, premiums, fund-raising, and educational or institutional use. Special book excerpts or customized printings can also be created to fit specific needs. For details, write or phone the office of the Kensington special sales manager: Kensington Publishing Corp., 119 West 40th Street, New York, NY 10018, attn: Special Sales Department, Phone 1-800-221-2647.

Dafina and the Dafina logo Reg. U.S. Pat. & TM Off.

ISBN-13: 978-0-7582-4701-8
ISBN-10: 0-7582-4701-X

First trade paperback printing: October 2011

10 9 8 7 6 5 4 3 2

Printed in the United States of America

Acknowledgments

To my editor, Selena James, for her enormous respect for the creative process and for that perfect touch that makes writing a joy; to my husband and my son, who fill my life with joy; and to the memory of Jessica Ricketts. As always, I thank God for my talents and for the opportunities to use them.

Chapter One

Kendra Richards completed her ablutions, opened her sleep sofa, extinguished the lights, and crawled into bed. She had stood continually from three o'clock in the afternoon until eleven that night and she'd frozen a smile on her face as she checked coats, briefcases, canes, and umbrellas in a classy Washington, D.C., restaurant. A tally of her tips showed that, as balm for her tired feet, she had exactly sixty-three dollars.

"Oh, well, at least I have a job," she said to herself, fluffed her pillow, let out a long, happy breath, and prepared to sleep. Tomorrow, she would have lunch with her three buddies—The Pace Setters, as the four called themselves—a treat to which she always looked forward.

She heard the phone ringing, but she put her head beneath the pillow and willed the noise to go away. But it persisted, so she sat up and answered it. "Hello, whoever you are at half past midnight."

"What on earth took you so long? Don't tell me you were asleep."

She got comfortable and rested her right elbow on her knee. "What's the matter, Mama?"

"Nothing's the matter. Why does something have to be the matter?"

"Mama, it's almost one o'clock in the morning. I got off a

little over an hour ago, and I was just going to sleep. Why'd you call so late?"

"Oh, for goodness' sake. You're the only person in this town who thinks twelve o'clock is late."

Ready to throw up her hands, she said, "Yeah. Right," beneath her breath. Nobody had to tell her that Ginny Hunter was about to drop a bomb. Kendra cut to the chase. "What is it, Mama?"

"Don't be so frosty. Your mama needs a couple 'a thousand. I saw a nice little Lexus, and I need that money for the down payment."

Kendra stared at the receiver as if it were the phone that abused her patience. "You're not serious. You risked waking me up for this? And why would you buy a car? Your license has been revoked, and you can't drive it. Besides, you can't get car insurance if your license has been revoked, and it's against the law to drive an uninsured car."

"Oh, that's stupid. Nobody can get around in Washington without a car."

"Mama, I'm tired. Can we talk about this tomorrow? I'll call you."

"I don't want a phone call. I want the money. Getting anything out of you is like squeezing blood out of a turnip."

"That's hardly fair, Mama. For twelve years, I've been trying to save enough money to go back to Howard and complete the requirements for my bachelor's degree. And for twelve years, every time I get one or two thousand dollars in the bank, you borrow it, and you never pay it back. To make it worse, every year the cost of college is higher.

"I have two thousand dollars, but I saved it for my tuition. I hope you remember that you borrowed twenty-seven hundred dollars from me about six weeks ago and promised to pay it back in two weeks. You're acting as if you don't owe me a thing, Mama. So please don't say I'm stingy. I'll call you in the morning and let you know."

Kendra hung up wondering, not for the first time, about

her mother's spending habits. Hopefully, she didn't gamble or use illegal drugs. Kendra slept fitfully and awakened as tired as she'd been when she went to bed.

Ginny Hunter figured she'd done her duty when she gave birth to Kendra. She hadn't wanted any children, but Bert Richards, Kendra's father, threatened to hold her criminally liable if she had an abortion. She did her best to be a mother to Kendra after her own mother passed on and left the child rearing to her. She'd hated every minute of it, but she'd done her best, and it shouldn't be much of a stretch for Kendra to help her out when she needed money.

Ginny sucked in her breath. School. Always school. If Kendra would find herself a man with some money, she wouldn't have to work till nearly midnight. Damned if *she'd* do it. Ginny rolled out of bed, slipped her feet into her pink, spike-heel mules, and threw on her pink negligee. She glanced back at the long, brown male frame on the other side of the bed and frowned. Why didn't men realize that the sunrise shouldn't catch them in a woman's bed, unless the woman was their wife? She did not cook breakfast for any man.

She went around and whacked the man on his behind. "Get up, uh, Ed. It's time to go home."

He sat up, rubbed his eyes, and gave her a smile that was obviously intended to captivate her. She stared at him. "Listen, honey. What's gorgeous at night doesn't look so good in daylight. I got to get out of here and go to work."

"Don't I get some breakfast?"

"Baby, I don't even cook for *me*."

He got up, pulled on his shorts, and looked around for the rest of his clothes. "I can see why you're not married," he grumbled.

"No you don't. I just divorced my fifth husband, though the decree's not yet final. When a relationship starts to sag, I say *bye bye baby*."

"Don't you try to work it out?"

"What for? It'll sag again, and the second time it's practically unbearable. I don't pretend. If it ain't working, it ain't working."

Ed buttoned his shirt, pulled on his pants, narrowed his eyes, and shook his head. "I've never met a woman like you, lady. You're a piece of work. Be seeing you."

The door slammed. She went over to the night table beside her bed, looked in the drawer, moved the lamp and the phone. Son-of-a-bitch hadn't left her a penny. Her anger slowly cooled when she remembered that he wasn't a john, just a guy she'd wanted. Young and virile. It had surprised her that she'd gotten him so easily. She laughed aloud. The guy wasn't a player, only lonely and terribly naive. But the brother could certainly put it down! She didn't turn tricks, but she expected a guy to be generous if he had a nice time with her.

She answered the telephone, thinking the caller would be Kendra. "Good morning. Lovely day, isn't it?"

"This is Phil. I'd like to know what makes you so happy. You coming in today? If not, one of my other operators will take your all-day spa customer."

"Let her have it. I've just decided not to come in till tomorrow." She gave manicures, pedicures, and massages when she needed money, but she had no intention of working five full days a week every week. No indeed! "My head hurts."

"Okay." He hung up.

Ginny showered, changed the bed linens, made coffee, and waited for Kendra's call.

Ginny would have awhile to wait, however, for at that time, Kendra sat at her tiny kitchen table going over her financial affairs. She tried always to have as much money in her savings as she had debts, her reasoning being that, if she lost her job, she could still pay what she owed. From her childhood days of shuttling from her grandmother to her father and sometimes to her mother, she counted nothing as certain. She drained her coffee cup, sat back, and considered what she was about to do.

At times, her resentment of her mother nearly overwhelmed her, and it also gave her an enormous burden of guilt. But shouldn't she discharge her obligations to herself? She had two thousand and eight hundred dollars in the bank. If she could save all of her tips—an average of twelve hundred dollars a month—for the next six months, till the first of October—that plus what she had in savings, along with whatever part-time work she could find, would get her through school. After the first semester, she would apply for a scholarship, and she knew that as a straight-A student, she'd get one.

She went to the phone to call and ask her mother what she had done with the twenty-seven hundred dollars she'd borrowed six weeks earlier, which she'd claimed she needed to move to a better and safer neighborhood. She hadn't moved. However, before she could dial Ginny's number, the phone rang. She looked at the caller ID.

"Hi, Papa. How are you?"

"I'm fine. What about you? I just got in some nice spring lamb from New Zealand. I can bone you a couple of roasts and a few racks, wrap them up, and all you have to do is put them in your freezer. When can you come by for them?"

"My goodness, Papa, that's wonderful. I have to be at work a few minutes before eleven today. Put it in your freezer, and I can pick it up Thursday evening when you're open late. I always get the best meat in town," she said with pride.

"That's because your papa's the best butcher in town. When are you moving to your new apartment?"

"I'm off Sunday and Monday, and I thought I'd pack Sunday and move on Monday. I'm so excited! I'll have a real bedroom separate from my living room."

"And it's yours. Don't let Ginny get her hands on that co-op. She'll destroy it. You hear me? Your mother thinks money grows on trees. Don't let her stay with you, and don't let her get her hands on that deed."

"I won't, Papa. She called me after midnight last night asking for two thousand dollars to put down on a Lexus."

"What?" he roared. "Don't you dare! I buy you an apartment to get you out of that neighborhood, and you give your mother thousands of dollars in the course of a year. Don't you dare. You said you're trying to finish college, and I'm trying to help you."

"I told her I'd call her and let her know. Papa, do you think she gambles or that she's using drugs?"

"Ginny? Never! She's foolishly self-indulgent. I've known her to be on the way to the dentist with a bad toothache, see something in a store window that she liked, and buy it, knowing that she wouldn't have enough money left to pay the dentist. She told the dentist a lie, and he sent me the bill. Back when I was hardly making two-fifty a week, she'd spend the grocery money on cosmetics for herself, or treat herself to a fancy lunch at an expensive restaurant. She's not mean, Kendra. She just thinks of herself and nobody else."

Kendra thought about her conversation with her father for a long time after she hung up. She'd said she'd call her, so she dialed her mother's number. "Hi, Mama. I don't think I can lend you that money. I need it. What did you do with the twenty-seven hundred dollars? You haven't moved."

"I used it for something else. Twenty-seven hundred dollars is not a lot of money. I really need that two thousand. You're always complaining that I should work full time, but how can I? Public transportation in this town stinks. Yesterday, I stood up on the bus at rush hour from Georgetown to Fifth and P. I need a car."

"But Mama, what you're about to do is illegal."

"You let me worry about that."

"I don't know, Mama. Every time I lend you money, I'm shooting myself in the foot."

"If I don't get it from you, I'll get it, legally or otherwise. I want that Lexus."

What could she do illegally that would net her that much money? Kendra wondered. However, knowing her mother, she wasn't prepared to doubt her. "All right. I can let you have a thousand and five hundred."

"What about the rest?"

"I'm moving this weekend, and I need it."

"Well, if that's all you're willing to spring for, beggars can't be choosers."

"When will you give it back to me?"

"Soon as I can. I'll come by and get it."

"Never mind. I'll drop it by your place tomorrow morning." She hung up and kicked the edge of her sofa with such force that she hurt the toe of her right foot.

She looked toward the heavens. "Why can't I say no to that woman? She's using me, and she doesn't care how much she hurts me." She poured half a cup of Epsom salts into the bathtub, ran some hot water, and sat down to soak her bruised toe. An hour later, wearing Reeboks for comfort, she headed to work.

Her boss greeted her with what seemed to her a hopeful smile, for he rarely smiled. "I'm glad you got here early. Mo and Emily called in sick, so I'm short two waitresses. Think you could wait tables during lunch?"

"I'd rather not, Mr. White. I'm wearing Reeboks because I hurt my big toe."

"If you can manage it, you'll make a lot more in tips. Just for lunch today. I'll work the cloakroom, and you can have the tips."

She couldn't say no to that deal, no matter how badly her toe hurt. To her chagrin, midway into the lunch hour, Ginny walked into the restaurant and took a table. Kendra made her way to the cloakroom as fast as her feet would carry her.

"Mr. White, my mother just walked in here and sat down at table twenty-three. She's a deadbeat, and if she orders something and tells you to put it on my account, I'm telling you right now, I can't afford it. She'll order caviar, the most expensive entrée, and your best wine. I just promised to lend her fifteen hundred dollars on top of all the other money she's borrowed from me and hasn't paid back. I am at my wits' end."

Ray White left the cloakroom and headed for the table at which Ginny sat. "Afternoon, ma'am. Are you paying with cash or a credit card?"

"Is it customary for you to ask your patrons how they're going to pay before they've ordered?"

"When family members show up here, I do. I want you to know that I don't put anybody's check on my workers' salary. No exceptions."

"Well, I never!" Ginny said, got up, and strode out, as regal as a giraffe.

"Well, I'll be damned," Kendra said under her breath. "She didn't even glance toward the cloakroom where she'd expect me to be. I'm going to give her the respect she's due as my mother, but I am going to quit toadying to her. She doesn't care about me."

Ray White approached Kendra, his face aglow in a triumphant smile. "You got nothing to worry about, kid. She wasn't planning to pay. I got rid of her."

Kendra stared at the man for a minute, whirled around, and rushed to the ladies' room as tears cascaded down her face. She washed her face, pushed out her chin, and went back into the dining room. "Don't let it get ya, kid. She oughta be proud of you. If she's not, it's her loss. Pick up table seventeen."

Lunch hour ended, and Emily didn't report at five o'clock, so Kendra worked the dinner hour, too.

When she crawled into bed past midnight after having soaked her swollen toe again, she had counted nearly two hundred dollars in her own tips plus eighty dollars in tips left at the cloakroom. She didn't think the money she'd earned was worth the humiliation of seeing her mother attempt to pull a fast one, though, and of having had to report her to the management.

"Papa is right. She'll drag me down if I let her."

The following night after work, Kendra wrote a check and tore it up. Forgery might prove too tempting for Ginny to forego. She went down to the main post office near Union Station, bought a money order, and sent it to her mother. "The next time you need money, old girl, go to work," she said aloud, and dusted her palms across each other, signifying the end.

Sunday morning arrived, and Kendra arose early and began packing. The moving company had supplied more boxes than she expected to need. Carrying a big black plastic bag, she took the elevator to the top floor of the building in which she lived, and from the incinerator rooms on each floor, she collected for packing purposes all the newspapers and magazines she could find and stuffed them into the bag.

After packing her dishes, glassware, and other breakables, she sat down to rest. The telephone rang, and she approached it slowly, thinking that the caller would be Ginny. But when she saw her father's ID, she perked up.

"Hi, Papa. You're not in church today?"

"I thought I'd go over there and help you pack. I've done a lot of that in my day." He paused, as if waiting for her response. "That is, unless you've got a man friend to help you."

"It's just me, Papa. I don't have a boyfriend right now."

"That's a pity. But at least you're not man crazy. And I won't say more about that. I hope you haven't packed the coffee pot. I'll bring over some pastries."

"I can definitely make coffee, but not much else."

They finished the packing in a little less than four hours,

and she dropped herself on the sofa, exhausted. "That was a real workout."

"Sure was," Bert Richards said. "It's early for dinner, but I'll drive you to a good takeout shop, and you can get what you want, bring it home, and eat it here when you get hungry."

She'd be satisfied with a sandwich and tea, but she knew he wouldn't accept that, so she went with him, and he parked in front of Lena's Gourmet Shop.

"Papa, this place is too expensive."

"Child, I've tried to teach you that anything you put in your stomach should be the best quality. They get their beef from me."

She went home with a gourmet meal, but she'd never been lonelier or needed company more. She telephoned Flo, one of her three good friends.

"Hi, Flo. Papa helped me pack, and then he took me over to Lena's Gourmet Shop. This gourmet meal he bought me is more than enough for two. Want to come over?"

"Where would we sit? Haven't you packed?"

"Sure I packed. Papa was helping me. We can sit on the sofa and eat, and I've got paper plates and cups and plastic utensils. Bring a sharp knife."

"See you in twenty minutes."

Twenty minutes later, the doorbell rang. "Hi. First time you're late getting somewhere, I'll expect Armageddon for sure. Come on in."

"Nothing gets on my nerves like a person who wastes other peoples' time. You and your dad did all this today?"

"Yes, and we finished before four o'clock."

Flo sat down and crossed her long legs. She had a good inch on Kendra's five feet, eight inches, and she worked hard at maintaining her size ten, flat-belly figure. They spread out the food, and Flo reached for a crab cake and cut a thick slice of artisan-baked Italian whole wheat bread.

Kendra eyed her friend. "You must be hungry. Better watch that bread."

Flo chewed the crab cake, looked toward the ceiling, and shook her head slowly. "This is heaven. And don't you worry about my figure. When you're asleep, I'm in the gym suffering. Lord, this stuff is good." She served herself some roasted peppers and green bean salad. "No wonder you called me. You couldn't eat all this in two days. I'd better be careful or Ernest won't recognize me. He says I'm perfect." She pushed some long strands away from her face.

"Is he talking about making it permanent? It's been going on for a year now, hasn't it?"

Flo sipped some ginger ale and leaned back. "Yeah, but for most of that year nothing much was happening, and I was about to give up on it. Half the time, I was so frustrated I wanted to throw things."

"What do you mean?"

"Look. Like I said, nothing was happening. I liked everything about him, Kendra, but the sex was awful and I didn't have enough experience to fix it. About a month ago, I went to see a doctor. She said nothing was wrong with me, and that all we needed was technique. She made some suggestions, so I bit the bullet and told him that it wasn't working and that if we couldn't fix it, I was out of there. So we tackled it the way you'd go about solving any other problem. The formula that the doctor gave me took us right there as soon as we learned to use it. Oh, happy day!"

"If I ever have that problem, I hope you'll give me that formula."

Flo's laugh was deep and throaty. "You bet I will. Every animal, wild or tame, is born knowing how to do it, but we humans have to learn. Just another one of nature's lousy tricks. It's good with us now, and if it continues this way, I may see if we can make it permanent. What about you, Kendra? I wish you'd get out of Ginny's clutches, find a guy, and grab some happiness."

"Mama and I are nearing a parting of the ways, Flo. I understand her now, and I know what I mean to her. It hurts, but dissing your mother isn't easy, no matter what she does. Mama's like a leech."

"If you had a man you cared for, she'd be less important to you."

"This is true. You know, there's a man who comes to lunch at the restaurant every Wednesday. He's always alone, has a crab-cake sandwich, a green salad, and a glass of white wine. He's elegant and good-looking, and I can feel his masculinity from a distance of twenty-five feet."

"Why don't you try to meet him?"

"Because he wouldn't give me a second glance. That brother's got *CEO* written all over him. I wish I had my degree in communications and the kind of job that goes with it."

"Don't worry, you'll get that degree. A person who wants something as badly as you want that degree is bound to succeed."

"Yeah. But I won't get *him*."

Flo poured herself half a cup of coffee, drank it, and stood. "You never can tell. I gotta go, hon. Thanks for the goodies, and give my regards to your dad."

Kendra had to make herself go to bed. The next night, she'd be sleeping in a lovely two-bedroom apartment, with living room, dining room, kitchen, and one-and-a-half bathrooms, one block from Connecticut Avenue on Woodley Road. She longed to furnish it elegantly, but that had to wait till she finished school. She tossed in the bed until daylight, got up, and began counting the minutes until eight o'clock when the movers would arrive.

That afternoon, with the move completed, and everything in place, she stood in the middle of her new living room, raised both arms, and laughed. Laughed until she felt like dancing; then danced to the point of exhaustion. She didn't know when, if ever, she'd been so happy.

Monday was her day off, and she headed down Connecticut Avenue to buy a few essentials for her new apartment. She didn't own a bedspread, because her previous apartment hadn't had a bed. But her father's gift of a bedroom set had arrived that morning, and she wanted to dress up her new bedroom. She bought the spread and walked down near Calvert Street to her girlfriend Suzy's dress shop.

"Hey, girl. What's up? You look as if you just won the lottery. Did you move?"

Kendra hugged herself, twirled around, and spread her arms wide. "I am now residing on Woodley Road, friend. Ain't that some stuff?"

"It sure is." Suzy walked over to a tall shelf, selected a silk scarf, and gave it to Kendra. "I don't deal in home furnishings, so this is your housewarming present."

Kendra leaned down and clasped the petite woman in a hug. "Thank you. This is beautiful. I think I'll treat myself to a nice dress to wear with it." She selected a red, tissue-linen, knee-length sleeveless dress that flattered her tall, 36-28-40 figure.

"It was designed for you. And you always look great in red. Be sure and let your hair down when you wear it," Suzy said. "I wish I had your height."

"Don't make jokes. Haven't you noticed that these tall, handsome brothers love women like you? Count your blessings." She paid for the dress.

"Uh . . . Ginny was in this morning and bought the same dress, although it's not for her. I tried dissuading her, but you know your mother. She said you'd pay for it when you came in."

"Really? I had no idea that she was coming here or that she was going to shop any other place." She gave Suzy one hundred and seventy-eight dollars for her mother's dress.

"Don't give her anymore credit. If you do, the loss is yours, Suzy."

"Gosh, I'm sorry, Kendra. I didn't know she'd fabricate things."

"If only that was all. I'll see you this weekend. How's Kitten?"

"Biggest heartache there ever was. Last night, Rick confessed to her that he's gay. Didn't we tell her that?"

"I guess she'll believe it now. I'll call her. Bye."

Ginny opened the letter, extracted the money order for fifteen hundred dollars, threw the envelope into the waste basket, and headed for her computer. If she was in luck, Saks would have a sale on those five-inch-heel, red patent leather shoes. They'd be perfect for her red dress. They weren't on sale, but seven hundred dollars for a pair of Jimmy Choo shoes was a bargain; she'd seen them for well over a thousand dollars. A phone call resulted in disappointment—the shoes were no longer available in her size. She pitched the phone across the room and stamped her feet. If Kendra had given her the money when she first asked for it, she could have gotten those shoes. No, she wanted her mother to beg. Infuriated, Ginny dressed and phoned her friend Lucille.

"Hi, Lucille. Let's go to Bart's for a couple of cocktails, and then find a good restaurant nearby." She listened for a minute. "Never mind. It's on me."

When she got home several hours later, her earlier anger resurfaced and, having no one at whom she could direct it, she went to bed. She'd spent a lot of money, and to what end? She had no choice but to work the next day. Phil wouldn't tolerate an empty booth on Fridays when business was usually good. He got a percentage of what his operators earned.

At work, she told each of her customers the woeful tale of her thankless and ungrateful daughter and, as she expected, each one sympathized with her. Her four-thirty appointment arrived a few minutes early and she was grateful for that, because it assured her that she'd be able to leave at six.

"How's it going, Mabel?" Ginny said when the woman sat in her chair for a manicure and pedicure. "You always come on time," she added, without waiting for Mabel's response. "I want you to know that I appreciate it. Some people don't give a hoot about the way they treat other people. I asked my daughter for a loan of two thousand dollars, peanuts to her, and after equivocating and pussyfooting for days, she came up with fifteen hundred, and had the gall to ask what I did with the previous twenty-seven hundred she loaned me. She actually thinks her mother should pay her back."

"Where she work?" Mabel asked.

"She's a coatcheck girl in one of the most expensive restaurants in town. Nobody can tell me—"

Mabel interrupted her. "She lend you that kind of money and she working for tips? I wish I had a daughter like her. Mine couldn't lend nobody two dollars, much less two thousand. You blessed, and you oughta stop griping about her."

Ginny swallowed hard, controlling the urge to nip Mabel with the nail clippers. She pocketed the three dollar tip, but she didn't thank the woman for it, and if Mabel knew she'd made her mad, Ginny didn't care.

Her next customer, a handsome twenty-year-old college student, arrived five minutes late, sat down, stretched out his long legs, and presented for her care the most beautiful hands she'd seen in a long while. He had the kind of presence that she liked in a man, but she was too mad to process his effect on her attitude.

"What are you looking so sharp for? Or maybe I should say, who?" she asked, and added, "Nobody's going to look at your hands, pretty though they are."

He sat forward. "What do you mean?"

So he liked compliments, did he? She decided to be less

direct. "Surely you don't need compliments from me. I imagine you get so many that you're bored to death with them. You go to school?"

"I'm a junior at Morgan University. You think I have nice hands?"

"I don't think it. I know it, and I see hands every day and all day. But, like I said, nice as they are, I definitely wouldn't spend my time looking at *them*."

He narrowed his eyes and creased his face with a slight frown, and she wondered if she'd taken the wrong approach. He didn't know it, but before he slept tonight, she meant to have him.

"Would you mind explaining that?" he asked her.

She supported her answer with a slow upward movement of her right shoulder. "Listen, honey, you're a man. I don't have to paint a picture for you. A guy who looks like you has had his share of options, and don't tell me I'm wrong." She pushed her stool closer in order to give him a better look at her ample cleavage and the hard nipples pressing against her scoop-neck jersey blouse. She saw his Adam's apple working and smiled inwardly.

"How old are you?" he asked abruptly, annoying her with his blunt attempt to put her in her place.

She looked him in the eye. "Old enough to know what to do with you and how to do it. Anything else you want to know?"

"Yeah. What time do you get off, and how far do you live from here?"

"I get off when I finish with you. I live on Kalorama Road. Why?"

"Who lives there with you?"

"I live alone. You want to go home with me?" She let the palm of her right hand graze her left nipple a few times.

He swallowed hard. "Yeah. I'd like to see if your bite lives up to your bark."

She winked at him. "Don't waste time thinking about that, honey. You can't even begin to imagine what I'm going to do to you and how I'm going to make you feel." She got up, patted his shoulder, and smiled. "And you'll feel real good about yourself, too."

She knew she had a couple of bottles of white wine in her refrigerator, but what would she give him to eat? He'd have to be satisfied with a ham sandwich, apple pie, and vanilla ice cream.

"Let's go. I don't have a lot of time," he said, but she didn't answer. Once she got him in her bed, he'd stay there for as long as she enjoyed him.

"This is a neat place," he said when they walked into her living room. "It's very feminine."

"What would you expect? I'm a woman and proud of it. Sit in here while I get you a bite to eat. Sex and an empty stomach are incompatible."

"Good idea, because I didn't eat much lunch."

She made the sandwiches, warmed the pie, and opened the wine.

"You fixed all that?" he asked when she put the tray on the coffee table. "I love apple pie and vanilla ice cream."

She poured two glasses of wine and gave one to him. "I hope you'll enjoy your visit sufficiently to come back."

A grin spread over his face, and she thought, *This kid is a helluva looker.* When he'd drunk most of the wine in his glass, she picked up a sandwich. He ate his and followed that with the pie à la mode.

"That was terrific. Thanks."

She handed him another glass of wine, and when he'd finished it, she leaned over and loosened his tie. His gaze clung to her cleavage, and she put his hand on her breast and rubbed. "Want some? It's all yours."

"What do you mean, do I want some?"

Remembering his age, she put her hand behind his head,

released one of her breasts, and pulled his hair. "The quicker you get a woman's nipple into your mouth, the quicker you'll get her into bed. And you'll love sucking it."

He suckled her like a greedy baby, and heat plowed through her, but she didn't rush him, because the wait would be worth it. A glance showed that he was not only ready but well equipped. And his moans told her to head to the next stage. She put his hand on her thigh beneath her dress, and he didn't need instructions as to what to do next.

You shouldn't do this, Ginny, the weak voice of her ineffectual conscience told her. But she pushed it aside, as she usually did when mental remnants of her early teachings emerged. Nothing was going to prevent her from getting a taste of that pig meat. She doubted that he was a virgin, but if he was, so much the better. She unzipped his trousers, stroked and squeezed him, and when his head lolled on the back of the sofa while he moaned in pleasure, she bent over and tasted him.

"Don't stop," he yelled.

"I'm not crazy, honey. This is for both of us. You're going to give me my share, too. Come on." She relieved him of his trousers, and led him to her bed. For the next three hours, she worked him over, showing him that she did indeed know what to do with him and how to do it. His rapid recovery after every session reminded her of the value of youth in a man. She relished every minute of this man in her bed until, finally exhausted, she'd had her fill.

"Honey, you have to get up now," she told him. "I don't want my neighbors to see you leaving here in the morning."

"In the morning? What? Good Lord, I was supposed to pick up my date at eight-thirty."

"It's too late for that now. Does she have a cell phone?"

"What time is it?"

She looked at her watch. "Eighteen minutes to ten. I'll make you some coffee."

He swung off the bed. "Where's the bathroom?"

"Right across the hall." She watched him stride out of the room, tall, naked, and all male, and liquid accumulated in her mouth. Damned if he was going anywhere right then. She got the remaining bottle of wine from the refrigerator and a bag of Cajun-spiced Doritos, put them on her night table, and was back in bed before he returned. He sat on the side of the bed.

"Here," she said, handing him a glass of wine. "As fine looking as you are, she'll forgive you. Any woman would. Besides, the way you put it down, honey, you can get any woman you want." She opened the bag of Doritos and handed it to him. He ate them absentmindedly and drained the wine glass, which she quickly refilled. Like a zombie, he drank more wine.

Ginny eased her hand from his back to his genitals and began her assault on him. Figuring that, after so much sex, he wouldn't explode the minute she touched him, she said, "Lie down. I never did get you all the way into my mouth."

When the sunlight awakened him, his mouth was at her breast, and his right hand rested between her thighs. Abruptly, he separated from her, jumped up, and began dressing. "Good Lord! I've ruined my life. My girlfriend's an only child. Her father was going to give me a job at gradua-tion, and I would eventually have been CEO of a Fortune five hundred company. All that for a romp in the bed of a woman whose last name I don't even know and who's older than my mother. Shit."

Affronted by his reference to her age, she sat up, put on her pink negligee, and waited until he was looking straight at her. Then, with an elaborate shrug, she said, "That's life, honey. You like to screw, so this won't be the last time your penis gets you into trouble."

"I see it doesn't mean a damned thing to you. All you

wanted was a good lay. Well, you got that, and maybe more. Didn't you wonder why I didn't use a condom?"

She gasped, as fear settled over her. "You bastard." She jumped up to express her rage with her fists, but the front door slammed, and she dropped herself on the bed as tremors wracked her body.

Chapter Two

Kendra rushed along rain-spattered Sixteenth Street, Northwest, and turned into Dupont Circle with one eye on traffic and the other on the threatening clouds. She dashed into La Belle Époque Restaurant seconds before a torrent of rain exploded from the sky, and entered the cloakroom out of breath.

"I was hoping you'd get here a little early," Natalie, the blonde who she was replacing, said, "but it doesn't matter. I can't go anywhere in this downpour."

"You want to borrow my umbrella?" Kendra asked her.

"Thanks, but I don't think an umbrella would do much good. Just look at that."

"I hope you're not missing something important," Kendra told her. She liked Natalie, for Natalie had befriended her on several occasions.

"I have a doctor's appointment. You're such a terrific person, Kendra. Find a way to get out of this job. You're too smart for it. I'm here because I can go to school mornings, work afternoons, and I live in Laurel, Maryland. I don't get much sleep, but I'll graduate in June, and then this torture will be a thing of the past."

"I'm working here to save enough money to go back to Howard and finish my undergraduate degree. Considering the tips, it's the best job I've been able to find."

"I'm glad to know you have a plan, and I wish you the best."

"It's stopped raining, so you may still be able to make your appointment on time."

"Thanks." Natalie hooked her purse strap over her shoulder, started out of the cloakroom, and then turned and looked at Kendra. "If you pray, please pray for me. I think I may be pregnant."

"Oh, Lord no. If you are, what about the father?"

"I thought we had a good thing going, but when I told him what I suspected, he told me he was married. I wanted to kill him. Even if I find I'm not pregnant, he's history. How can a man pull such a rotten trick on a woman? We've been seeing each other for eleven months."

"If you are, are you going through with it?"

"Considering how much I hate that man right now, I honestly don't know. Well, thanks for listening. See you tomorrow."

Kendra adjusted her uniform, pinned her big "smile" button to the lapel, and then greeted her first customer. A man collected his raincoat and umbrella and gave her a one dollar bill. She thanked him warmly, for she knew that the next time he might leave her five dollars.

"Have a good day, sir."

"Thank you, miss. The same to you."

She said a prayer for Natalie and she wrestled with the sadness she felt for the twenty-two-year-old girl, who'd had the misfortune to meet and fall in love with an unprincipled man. Maybe her own trials with Ginny weren't the worst that could happen to her. The lunch hour wound down, and she could finally sit down for a few minutes.

As she sat, barefoot, to rest her feet, she saw an iPhone on the cloakroom floor. She picked it up, made a note of its description as the restaurant rules required, and was about to take it to her boss, when she remembered that the last time she returned a "found" item to him, he put it in his pocket.

The following day, the owner had come back for it, and Ray had told the man that none of his staff had seen it.

She saw an address and phone number on the back of the iPhone, took a chance, and dialed the number.

"Clifton Howell speaking."

"Mr. Howell, this is Kendra at La Belle Époque. I'm the coatcheck girl. I found your iPhone, sir. But please don't tell my boss I called you. We're supposed to give everything we find to him. But I wanted to be sure you got it."

"Thank you so much, Kendra. I was thinking that I dropped it when I got out of my car, and that I didn't hear it drop because it was raining. Don't worry. I won't mention this call to your boss. I'm very grateful to you. I'll be there in about an hour."

She wrapped the iPhone in a paper napkin, and when Clifton Howell—a man who appeared to be in his fifties—arrived, she handed it to him. "At least now I know your name," she said to him; he was one of La Belle Époque's regular patrons.

"It's really nice of you." He opened his billfold to remove a bill, but she held up her hands, palms out.

"No thank you, sir. I didn't do this for you to give me something. I know it's very expensive, and it probably contains very personal and important information. I wanted to be sure that you got it."

He looked at her for a full minute. "I can't tell you how much I appreciate your thoughtfulness." A slight frown creased his brow. "Uh . . . How far did you go in school?"

She wondered at the question, but he'd posed it in a matter-of-fact way, evidently without an ulterior motive, so she replied truthfully. "I've completed two years at Howard University. My major is communications, and I'm working to save enough to complete the remaining two years."

He rubbed the left side of his face absentmindedly. "Hmm. You carry yourself well." He reached into the breast pocket of his suit jacket, pulled out a business card, and handed it to her. "If you're ever looking for a job, give me a call."

"Thank you, Mr. Howell. I definitely will do that. Have a wonderful day."

A half-smile flashed briefly across his face. "The same to you. By the way, what is your last name?"

"My full name is Kendra Richards."

He wrote it on the back of another of his business cards, and put it in his pocket. "Good-bye, Miss Richards."

The dinner hour proved hectic and crowded, and by eleven o'clock when she could at last leave, Kendra felt that she couldn't stand for one more minute. She had learned that standing in that cloakroom was more tiresome than waiting tables.

Kendra got home at midnight, and after a half an hour soak in a tub full of warm bubbles, she got ready for bed thinking that at least she had an offer of a job if she ever needed one.

She crawled into bed, reached toward her night table to extinguish the light, and she accidentally turned on the radio and heard someone singing ". . . one chance is all I need."

She bolted upright. "Am I crazy?" she said aloud. "I can at least call Clifton Howell and find out what kind of job he can offer me. I don't even know the kind of business he's in. I'll call him in the morning."

With that decision, an attack of anxiety set in and she tossed and wrestled with sleeplessness throughout the night. When her clock alarm went off in the morning, she jumped up and began planning what she'd say to Clifton Howell.

Ginny stopped at a drugstore and bought the darkest pair of sunglasses available there. She'd never been so humiliated in her life. Imagine having to go to a doctor and ask for an STD or HIV test. And it would cost money that she'd rather not have to lay out. She'd chosen two gynecologists and two internists listed in the yellow pages, because she didn't want to go to her regular doctor.

She reached the gynecologist on Columbia Road first, took a deep, fortifying breath, and went in. By then, chills traveled through her repeatedly, and she had begun to break out in hives. Needing support, she sat down in the waiting room without stopping to speak with the receptionist.

The woman walked over to her. "May I help you? If this is your first visit to Doctor Elms, you'll have to fill out these forms." Ginny filled out the three pages as quickly as her shaking fingers would allow, leaving blank the question of whether she had HIV/AIDS. Half an hour later, a nurse appeared.

"Come with me, Ms. Hunter. Doctor Elms will see you now."

It didn't help that she had to pull off every stitch of her clothing, including her stockings. The nurse gave her a gown, took her temperature, and weighed her. "The doctor will be with you in a minute."

Ginny's jaw dropped when a tall, white, no-nonsense-looking woman walked into the examining room. "I'm Doctor Elms, Ms. Hunter. How are you feeling? What's the problem?"

A woman doctor was the last thing she wanted. "I think I ought to have some tests. I was with a guy who said he might have some kind of VD. Naturally, the bastard told me that after he'd done the damage."

"Let's see what we have here. Next time, protect yourself. If you're in the habit of doing things in a hurry, keep a condom in your pocketbook. The average single man keeps one in his wallet."

After examining Ginny, the doctor said, "I don't see any signs, but we'll get a smear and some blood. These pimples look like hives. Ever have them before?"

"Never. They started coming out when I got to your door."

"Anxiety. Here's a prescription. Take this if they persist."

"How soon will I know?"

"I'll have to send this to the lab. You should know in a couple of days. Meanwhile, avoid any sexual activity." *Sexual activity! She never wanted to hear the word* sex *again.* And she never wanted to see J. H. Elms again, either. The woman had the personality of a flea.

For the next two days, Ginny hardly ate and slept fitfully at night. She'd been so anxious to get that boy into her and enjoy sex with a strong, energetic man who was eager to learn, that she hadn't used her common sense. Just because he looked clean didn't mean he was.

Janet Elms finally called her in the afternoon of the third day.

"This is Dr. Elms. You're clean right now, but come back for another HIV test in six weeks. And don't forget to practice safe sex."

The bill from the diagnostic center arrived the next day. Eleven hundred dollars—for what? Well, they could wait till they got it. She called the owner of the beauty spa where she worked. "I'll be in tomorrow and all of next week, so you can fill my card."

She hated to let him know she was broke. But he'd already guessed that she only worked when she was desperate for money and hadn't been able to borrow any. Maybe if she worked full time for a couple of weeks. . . . She sucked her teeth in disgust. *Hell no. I'm not standing on my feet pampering vain women eight hours a day, forty hours a week. No, indeed. Kendra would just have to loosen up and let her have some more money.*

Kendra's life was about to change, and, along with it, so would her conception of herself. She got up that morning, and drank her usual two cups of coffee, but she drank them while walking from her kitchen to her balcony to her living room and back to the kitchen, over and over again. She put the coffee mug on the counter with a resounding thud.

"Time's up," she said to herself. "No more procrastinating." She glanced at her watch. A quarter to ten. Slowly, her fingers dialed the number on Clifton Howell's business card.

"Mr. Howell's office."

"I'll never get through that sister," Kendra said to herself.

"Good morning. This is Kendra Richards. May I please speak with Mr. Howell. He's expecting my call."

"Oh. Let me check my list. There must be some mistake."

Kendra bristled at that. "There's no mistake, Miss, at least not on my part. You only have to check with Mr. Howell to find that I'm right."

"Well, just a minute." Kendra couldn't help wondering why some people enjoyed exercising the power of the word no.

"Hello, Miss Richards," Howell said. "I didn't expect to hear from you so soon. Did you get fired, or did it occur to you that I might offer you a better job?" he asked with a tease in his voice.

"I didn't get fired, but I came home exhausted, and it occurred to me that you might give me something better to do."

"I definitely can. Can you get here by noon?"

"Yes, sir. Please tell your secretary that you're expecting me."

After she ended the call, Kendra inspected her closet and chose a Dior blue two-piece seersucker suit with short sleeves and a mandarin collar. She added the de rigueur white pearl earrings and beads. Couldn't get less sexier or less threatening, she assured herself. Besides, her father liked blue, and he claimed that it was a ladylike color. Maybe all men liked that color. Medium-heel blue patent leather shoes and a matching bag completed her outfit.

She remained in the building's lobby until two minutes to twelve, took the elevator to the ninth floor, and rang the bell at noon. Someone buzzed her in, and she walked into the elegant suite of offices.

Less nervous than she'd thought she'd be, she addressed the receptionist. "I'm Kendra Richards." The woman raised an eyebrow. "Please tell Mr. Howell that I'm here."

Kendra let her gaze take in the area—the original paintings of Edward Hopper and other American painters, the enormous Tabriz carpet, brown-and-gold velvet seating arrangements, and live plants. What a lovely environment in which to work, she thought.

"Mr. Howell will see you now."

A door opened, and Clifton Howell entered the lobby while putting on his suit jacket. "I didn't want you to wait," he said, extending his hand and ushering her into his private office. "You said you're planning to get a degree in communications," he began, making it clear that she was not there for small talk. "Do you like music?" From the way he scrutinized her, it was clear that he was not planning to judge her on her words alone.

"Yes. I like classical music, easy listening pop, blues, and jazz. I liked the country music of the 1990s, but these days, most of it sounds like misguided rock. I like opera, but that sounds better on TV than on records."

"What about hip-hop?"

"Well, I, uh . . . I hate it."

He laughed. "Don't worry. Honesty is a good thing. What kind of hours can you work?" He strummed the fingers of his left hand on his desk for a few seconds. "For the hours nine to five, you get forty-five thousand yearly, but if you work from five to one, you get fifty. However, I don't advise trying to work those night hours and going to school the next morning. That's harrowing. If necessary, you could switch to part time. Which hours do you prefer?"

"Either schedule works for me, since I'm not in school right now—though nine to five would be wonderful for a change." She couldn't hide her eagerness and sat forward. "Are you going to offer me something? Maybe when school opens and I get my class schedule, we can work something out."

"Would you work as a disc jockey? Not on open air, but playing the kind of music you hear in supermarkets, stores, and such places. I'm phasing it out and installing an automated system. But if you do well, I'll put you in a spot on live radio."

Her eyes widened. "I'd love to do that. Who would choose the music?"

"My program director. Incidentally, we don't play rap and hip-hop."

She let out a deep breath. "Thank the Lord for that."

"All right. Will two weeks notice do for White?"

"I don't know, Mr. Howell, but I'd like to give him at least that much. Now, we haven't discussed benefits."

"You get two weeks' sick leave, two weeks' vacation, full health coverage, and you can have a 401K account. I'll give you a two-year contract, but it will specify thirty days notice for any change you need to make or if you want to leave. I'd like you to start two weeks from Monday. I think this is a fair deal."

"I think so, too." What she didn't say was how impressed she was with a rich man who behaved with the utmost civility. Not even her own boss, a middle manager, seemed able to remain businesslike and completely impersonal with her.

"Then we'll give you a contract. Wait out in the reception room for a short while, please. Oh yes, and if there's anything I hate, it's to hear no sound coming from that mike. Got it?"

"Absolutely."

"This job ought to see you through college. So get moving."

"Yes, sir. Thank you. I promise you won't be sorry."

"I'm sure of that, Miss Richards. I'm a good judge of people."

Less than an hour later, she'd signed a contract that almost guaranteed she'd have an opportunity to complete her bachelor's degree. She felt like splurging on something frivolous, thought better of it, and decided to treat herself to lunch at a Chinese restaurant. She sat at a table near the front and was reading the menu when a familiar voice got her attention. A glance upward brought her mother's friend Angela into her line of vision. The woman seated herself without waiting for an invitation.

"Child, your mother took Violet and me to one spiffy lunch at the Willard a little while back. She said she was flush. I sure did enjoy that lobster. First I ever ate. Honey, when I have to eat out, and I'm paying, Chinese is my level. But not Ginny. Honey, your mother has style. She is *some* lady."

"Yes," Kendra said, her appetite for food of any kind or price range suddenly gone. "If you don't mind, I'd better run. This is my lunch hour." She hadn't lied. It would have been her lunch hour if Angela's story hadn't ruined it for her. *The idea of her mother taking her money—money she'd saved for college—and blowing it on her friends!* If she needed evidence that Ginny Hunter didn't care about her, that alone would suffice. She hadn't had her furniture reupholstered with the nearly four thousand dollars she'd borrowed, or used the twenty-seven hundred dollar loan to move to the apartment she said she had lined up. And she took the fifteen hundred dollars that she borrowed, ostensibly for a down payment on a Lexus, and treated her friends to an expensive meal at the Willard and to who knows what else.

A ten-block walk took Kendra to her father's shop. When he saw her walk in, he immediately washed his hands and removed his apron. "Now, this is a nice surprise. And you look so beautiful, too." He took both of her hands. "Tell me how you are. I hope Ginny isn't up to her tricks again."

She hugged him. "I haven't heard from her in two weeks,

but I'm sure that as soon as she wants something, she'll call. Papa, I've got great news. I just got a new job."

"Really? Wait a minute and let me get us a cup of coffee." He called to a man who was waiting on a customer. "Gates, I'm going back in the office with my daughter for a few minutes," he called to Gates, his employee since he'd opened the store. He turned to Kendra. "Have you had lunch?"

"No, sir." She told him why she hadn't eaten lunch.

"Well . . . I don't know, Kendra. For me, Ginny has one redeeming virtue: she gave me a wonderful daughter, and for that, I will forever be grateful to her." He took a baked ham shank from the refrigerator, sliced it, and made some sandwiches. "Let's have a bite."

Kendra waited until he poured their coffee and then took a seat. "Papa, not long ago, Mama told me that when she was pregnant with me, she wanted to have an abortion, and you wouldn't let her do it."

He nearly choked on his sandwich. "She told you *that?* She had no right to tell you that. One of these days, she's going to be sorry, and I hope I'm around to see it."

"Oh, it's okay, Papa. Ninety percent of the time, I feel as if I don't have a mother, anyway. The other ten percent, I know I have one that I don't like. I've tried so hard to have a mother–daughter relationship with her, but I know now that I never will. I think she's incapable of love."

"That's true, but she's damned good at pretending. I'm going to be one proud man when you finally wear that cap and gown. If I hadn't borrowed so heavily to open this shop and have my own business, you'd have finished long ago."

"And if Mama had been paying the mortgage on our house instead of spending the money on herself and her interests, you wouldn't have lost the house."

"I know," he said, his voice seeming to come from a distance. "I knew then that if I stayed with her, she'd drag me to a bottomless pit." He leaned back in his chair and sipped his coffee. "It's been killing me all these years, and I never discussed it with anyone, but talking with you about it, well, I guess I'm over it. You be sure you don't ever let anybody, man or woman, knock the props out from under you. You hear?"

"Yes, sir. I don't think you need to worry, Papa. I've learned my lesson. I'd better let you get back to work. I love you."

A smile creased his face and brought sparkles to his eyes. "Of course you do. I'm your papa, and I love you, girl. You take care." She kissed him good-bye and left, refreshed and feeling very good.

At work the next day, she told Ray of her plans, and because he seemed neither surprised nor inconvenienced, she gave him ten days' notice, and took a one-week vacation.

With her feet dangling in the Atlantic Ocean at Cape May, the ringing of her cell phone disturbed her calm, and even more so when she saw her mother's ID on the screen. She was tempted not to answer. But she did.

"This is Ginny." She never referred to herself as Kendra's mother.

Having heard that attack was the best defense, Kendra launched one. "If it's money you want, Mama, I don't have any. You're fifty-two years old and healthy. I can't support you and your habits, so you'll have to work."

"What?" She screamed the word.

"That's right, Mama. I can't afford to pay for expensive meals for you and your girlfriends at the Willard Hotel. And I don't appreciate your borrowing my next-to-last dollar under pretense of great need and then wining and dining your friends with it. I'm done. Finished. Period."

"Don't you even want to know that I hurt my back, and that I've been in and out of the doctor's office?"

She didn't believe it. "What's the doctor's name and phone number?"

"Are you saying you don't believe me?"

"If a doctor treated you for back problems, I'll pay him or her with a check, but I will not give you one dime."

When the dial tone droned in her ear, she sagged in defeat. It was as if she didn't have a mother. She put the cell phone away and walked back to her hotel. The only vacation she'd ever had, and Ginny's call would forever mark Cape May as the place where she finally severed emotional ties with her mother. She'd be courteous to her, but she would not care what Ginny did or where she was. If Howard University wasn't in Washington, she'd get a job in another city.

Three weeks after she found Clifton Howell's iPhone, Kendra took a seat in the control room of Howell Enterprises' Soft Music Studios, picked up a Buddy Guy CD, played "Early in the Morning," and became a disc jockey.

"What I need," she said to herself after the first hour, "is a job like this one and a mike on which I can chat with my listeners. If I get these controls right, and if I don't give him any silence, as he put it, maybe he'll transfer me to his FM radio station as one of his live disc jocks."

At lunchtime, she programmed an hour of music and went to the staff cafeteria, although fear that she may have programmed the CDs incorrectly spoiled her appetite.

"No need to get so uptight, doll," Tabor "Tab" Carter, her FM counterpart, said with a deep southern drawl she wasn't sure she liked. "The boss is a great guy. He'll give you at least a week to get used to the system. After that, he'll chew you out if you make a bad boo-boo. And let's hope he lives a long, healthy life. His wife is just as nasty as he is nice. He was born with money, but she married it, and she shows it."

"I've got a lot to learn," she said, careful not to say anything that she didn't want to hear again. "How long have you worked here?" she asked him.

"Four years. Best job I ever had, but I'm hoping he'll shift me over to TV. When Mr. Howell automates the canned music, you can move to live radio. I worked my ass off to lose forty-six pounds, and I hope he noticed that I look like a young George Clooney these days." He stifled a grin and patted himself on the back.

Thank God he's got a sense of humor. She laughed along with him. "I hope you get that break," she said.

"Of course you do, doll. When I move on, you can, too. That's the way it happened with me."

"Really?" She slapped his hand. "Then put that chocolate mousse down. I've got an interest in your calorie intake."

They enjoyed a good laugh, and as they walked back toward the studios, he said, "When I get off at three-thirty, I'll drop by and give you some tips on keeping the music flowing smoothly." She thanked him and hoped his offer didn't spring from a personal interest, because blue eyes didn't do a thing for her.

One morning, two weeks later, Kendra sat at her desk in the soft music studio staring at her first check. Seventeen hundred and fifty dollars for her first two weeks on the job. Ten days' work. At the restaurant, she'd averaged five hundred a week; that meant she could save at least the additional seven hundred and fifty she'd make here. However, an attached yellow note stated that her future paychecks would be minus estimated taxes. She didn't mind that, because she always got tax refunds.

Tab knocked and entered the studio. "How does your check look to you? He'll raise you from that in about three months if you don't make too many mistakes. See you later." She'd welcome that, but she was happy with her current salary.

After work, she went by her father's shop to get some of the sage rope sausage that he made on Fridays for his Saturday customers. She showed him her check.

Bert Richards wiped the tears that dropped from his eyes. "Thank God you've got a respectable job and a future.

Would you go with me to church Sunday? I'll drive by for you."

She'd rather paint her bathroom, but if he hadn't bought her that apartment, she wouldn't have a bathroom with a sunken tub. "Okay. What time?" He told her. "Papa, can I have about a pound and a half of those sage sausages?" An idea occurred to her. Her father hadn't been in her apartment since he helped her move. "Come at nine, and I'll fix us some breakfast."

"That's wonderful, but in that case, I'd better give you even more of those sausages."

As they left church that Sunday, it surprised her to see the man who always came to La Belle Époque alone for lunch on Wednesdays. She'd never seen him at the restaurant in the evenings. She wanted to ask her father if he knew the man, but several of the worshipers joined Bert and her, obviously to sate their curiosity about the young woman with him.

"This is my daughter, Kendra," he said proudly. "She's a disc jockey."

"Really?" One woman of around sixty gushed. "You must be so proud of her. What are the call numbers, Kendra. I'll keep my radio tuned in to your program."

"I'm sorry, ma'am," Kendra said, "but the music I play doesn't come over a radio station. You hear it in stores, on elevators, and in some restaurants. I'm hoping to work up to being a radio disc jockey."

"Oh. I see," the woman said in a tone that implied Kendra's work deserved less admiration than that of a radio disc jockey. Her father must have detected the put-down, for he said to Kendra later, "You didn't have to explain. Betty is a snob, and now she won't be able to say she met Kendra Richards, the disc jockey who's on station XYZ during such and such time on Mondays."

"Papa, years of living with and dealing with Mama have

taught me the importance of always telling the truth and of leaving no element of it varnished." She looked around, but the mystery man had evidently left. She let out a long sigh. What would be, would be.

"It's a lesson well learned," he said. "Thank you for coming to church with me today. When I was young, one of my dreams was having my wife and children around me in the evenings when I came home from work, and walking into church with them on Sunday mornings." He shook his head. "It wasn't to be."

"It's not too late, Papa. You're only fifty-four, and you're still very handsome. What woman wouldn't want a tall, handsome, unattached man who's hardworking, intelligent, and decent?"

"Thanks," he said with a strange gruffness in his voice. "The one's I've met want me to sell the shop and invest in something that more properly suits a gentleman, or maybe that suits *them*. I say the hell with them."

"Me, too," she echoed with a grin.

"Since when do you use such language?"

"I don't, at least not to you. I just agreed with you."

"Humph." He parked in front of her door. "I'll be happy when you finish school, find a nice man, settle down, and give me some grandchildren."

She kissed his cheek. "You won't be nearly as happy as I'll be. Thanks for a really nice Sunday. Bye."

At home, she walked into her bedroom and saw the red light flashing on her answering machine. "Hello?" She hated calls from people who blocked their caller ID.

"Hi, this is Kitten. Where were you?"

"I went to church with my father, and I almost didn't answer your call. I told you what I think of people who block their caller ID. What's up?"

"Whew! You on the warpath? Suzy and Flo are coming over. My dad's grilling everything he can find. By the time you get here, I hope you'll be starving."

"I was planning to paint my bathroom."

"Oh, come on, Kendra. Next Sunday, the four of us can paint it in less than an hour. I'll bring all the shower caps I've collected from hotels so we won't get paint in our hair. You coming over?"

"What time?" She wondered what life was like living in a house with a steamroller like Kitten.

"You can leave your place as soon as you change into a pair of jeans or something. I'll drive you home."

"Thanks. See you later." She readily admitted that she'd planned to paint the bathroom because she didn't have anything else to do. Seeing a movie or going to a museum alone only made her lonely, so she rarely did it.

When she arrived at Kitten's home, she found Flo and Suzy, the remaining members of The Pace Setters, as they called themselves, sitting in white wooden chairs on a green spring lawn at the house on Queens Chapel Terrace just off Michigan Avenue.

Kitten greeted her with, "Mom's gone to a concert, so my daddy braced these margaritas with his best rum. Come on, sit down."

They raised their glasses to Kendra, congratulating her on her new job. "When she tells me she spent the night away from home, I'll drink a whole bottle of Veuve Clicquot in her honor," Suzy said.

"Don't be too hasty," Flo cautioned. She leaned back and sipped the drink with great relish. "Kendra could spend the night with a guy and make the poor fellow sleep on the floor while she hogged the bed. Girlfriend's not ready yet."

"This time last year, neither were you," Kendra told her. "Besides, every chicken here's been plucked, so get off my case."

"Yeah. But there's plucking, and then there's *plucking*," Suzy, the eldest of the four, told them. Their laughter bespoke of the warm camaraderie among the four women.

"Well, I have some news, too," Flo announced. "I just

promised Ernest that I'd marry him, though I didn't say when." The other three women ran to Flo and hugged her.

"Are you going to move in with him in the meantime?" Kitten wanted to know.

Flo looked at Kitten as if she had just sprouted horns. "Do you think I'm some kind of nut? Why do you think he asked me to marry him? I'm not *that* accommodating."

Kitten made a face. "Well 'scuse me."

"It's ready," Kitten's father said. "We've got roasted potatoes, club steak, hamburgers, country sausage, corn, carrots, asparagus, onions, and zucchini. Beer and sodas are in that tub. Serve yourselves."

Kendra asked Kitten, "Your mom willingly goes off knowing your dad is putting on a spread like this?"

"Oh, she always does this. That's how my dad learned to clean up after himself."

When Kendra finally got in bed that night, she had concluded that, as much as she loved her friends, they were poor substitutes for a man with whom she could share her life. *But I can't have everything I want all at once. I'm going to be grateful for my new job, do my best at it, and get my degree. That man, whoever he is, will have to wait.*

Kendra was unaware that Ginny followed her one morning, evidently to discover where she worked. Shortly after she closed the door of the Soft Music Studios and began her day's work, Ginny walked up to the desk of June, Howell Enterprises' receptionist

"I'm Kendra Richards's mother, and I have an extreme emergency. May I please speak with my daughter?"

"She shouldn't be interrupted, madam. What is the emergency?"

"My little boy, my youngest child, has just had a serious accident, and I need Kendra's help."

The receptionist's jaw dropped, and she gaped at Ginny. "How can you be so calm?"

Ginny didn't bat an eyelash. "Years of dealing with problems and all kinds of trouble. You become inured to the pain."

"Have a seat. I'll be right back."

However, Ginny did not sit down. Instead, she followed June, who, in her hurry to get to Kendra, didn't look back. Ginny brushed past the receptionist and charged into the Soft Music Studios.

"I need some money, Kendra, and if you don't give it to me, I'm going to kill myself right here."

Stunned, Kendra jumped up. "What on earth are you doing here? Nobody comes in . . ." She saw the receptionist staring at Ginny. "Why'd you let her in here?" she screamed.

"But . . . but she said your little brother has had an accident."

"My what? I don't have a little brother. I'm her only child."

"But she said—"

"This woman is a pathological liar. I don't care what she said. Besides, she's my mother only when she wants to borrow money, and she never repays it."

"I'm only asking for a thousand," Ginny said, as if she hadn't disrupted the office.

"I don't have a thousand, and if I did, you wouldn't get it."

"Then, I'll kill myself."

"Before you do that," Kendra yelled, "stop by and see the priest."

Tab ran into the room. "What's going on? Mr. Howell is in a rage. There's not a sound coming out of here, and the phones are jammed with calls. Are you all right, Kendra?"

"No, I'm not. Get a guard to escort this woman out of here."

"But she said she'd kill herself," the receptionist said.

Kendra looked at Ginny and shook her head. "If she does, this will be the first time in decades that she's told the truth."

The guard rushed in. "What's the problem, Miss Richards?"

She pointed to Ginny. "Please escort this woman from the building and make sure she doesn't come back. Not now. Not ever. I can't stand it anymore."

She turned back to her controls, but couldn't make another move. Shaking uncontrollably and with tears streaming down her face, she felt as if she couldn't cope. June, the receptionist, ran to the controls and tried to start the music but, instead, she pushed the wrong buttons with a result that several wires were crossed.

An irate Clifton Howell burst into the studio. "What the hell's going on in here?"

Tab rushed to Howell. "I'll fix it, Mr. Howell. It's not Kendra's fault."

"You'll fix it? And who will be covering your station? She's responsible for this station, so why isn't it her fault?"

"I put my channel on automatic," Tab said.

June grabbed Howell's arm. "She couldn't help it, Mr. Howell. Honest. It was horrible."

Howell took a deep breath and looked down at June. "What was horrible?"

"That woman! You should have—"

Through the drone of speech and excitement, Kendra turned toward the voice of Clifton Howell. She wiped her tear-streaked face as best she could, and forced herself to look at him. "If you want me to resign, Mr. Howell, I will. I'd rather not be fired, because I've never been asked to leave a job. It was my responsibility. I'm terribly sorry."

Howell looked toward Tab, who was busy trying to regulate the controls. "Can you repair it, Tab?"

"Yes, sir. Stations two and five are already working, and I'll have the others up in a few minutes."

Howell stuffed his hands in his trouser pockets. "Good. Come in my office, Kendra." He had never called her by her first name, so she didn't know what to expect. She followed him. "Have a seat. Tell me why it was not your fault, and start at the beginning."

"That would take too long, Mr. Howell, because it started before I was born."

He stared at her. "Whatever do you mean?"

"It began when my father wouldn't let my mother abort me. That was my mother who created the fiasco." His face reddened, his eyes widened, and his sharp whistle split the air. Kendra repeated Ginny's transgressions ending with her threat of suicide in the studio. "Mr. Howell, I'm too upset to be embarrassed."

He leaned forward. "Do you think she'll commit suicide?"

"I don't believe anything she says, so why should I believe that? I'm no longer going to allow her to manipulate me."

"And you shouldn't." He flicked on the eight-by-ten screen on his desk and pushed several buttons. "I'm checking our security cameras. Lean over my shoulder and let me know when you recognize her."

She stood behind him. "That's Mama walking into the building."

Howell pushed a button on the intercom. "Bob, check out this picture on eight. You see it? Good. If that woman ever puts one foot into this building again, I want her arrested and charged with trespassing, and no deal for leniency. Got it?"

Howell turned off the screen. "Sit down, Kendra. I don't know how you made it this far in life, and I especially can't understand why you're such a principled person."

"My late grandmother and my father have been the stabilizing forces in my life."

"My hat's off to them. I admire you. When I think of what you've lived through, I'm humbled. My parents are wonderful people." A smile flashed across his face. "I've been a husband and father for two decades, and my mother still calls to tell me to dress warmly when it's cold, to take my vitamins, and to eat a hearty breakfast. I'm going to stop complaining about her mothering a fifty-six-year-old man." His phone rang.

"Yes, June."

"Tab said to tell you that everything's working."

"Thanks." He looked at Kendra. "Go back to work and forget what happened this morning, but be careful at home."

"Yes, sir. Thank you so much, Mr. Howell."

On the way back to her station, she met Tab walking out the door. "I don't know how to thank you, Tab."

"It's okay, doll. You'd do the same for me. I just don't see how you made it this far with that shrew for a mother."

"My dad and my grandmother. Ginny will keep trying, but she'll never stop me."

Chapter Three

Half an hour after Kendra got home from work, the doorman of the building in which she lived buzzed her intercom. "Ms. Richards, there's a lady down here to see you. She won't give her name."

"Thanks, John. Ask to see her identification, two pieces. If her name is Ginny Hunter, I'm not at home, and please don't *ever* send her up here."

"Thanks, ma'am."

"I have to check your ID," she heard him say over the speaker phone, which he'd flipped on obviously for her benefit.

"Oh, come on," she heard Ginny say. "I'm her mother. I'll just go on up."

"No you won't. You don't get on one of these elevators unless I say so. Show me your ID, something with your picture on it, or leave before I call the police."

"Oh, the hell with you."

"She refused to show me the ID and left, Miss Richards. I'm sorry."

"I'm not. That's what ID is for, John. Thanks."

Unhappy because of the measures she'd had to take against her mother that day, Kendra hung up the intercom receiver and telephoned her uncle, her mother's brother. Ed Parks owned an accounting firm that supported himself and his family very well, and he kept his sister far from his business.

"Hello, Kendra. Good to hear from you. How are you?"

"I don't know, Uncle Ed. I hope things are good with you."

"They've been better, and they've been much worse. I can't complain. What's going on with you?"

She told him about her trials with Ginny over the previous months and added, "I'm at my wits' end, Uncle Ed. I don't want anything else to do with her. She's trying to ruin my life. Imagine having a mother who has no feelings whatever for you. I can't stand it, Uncle Ed."

"I'm sorry, Kendra. When Ginny was little, three or four years old, she was as pretty as a human being could be, and everybody with whom she came in contact told her so. Daddy gave her whatever she wanted, and Mama dressed her like a fashion doll. Nobody said no to Ginny. By the time she was ten, she was a little monster, and as soon as she got a bosom, she began seducing men for the hell of it. I don't see how Bert stood being married to her for five years.

"I'll speak with her, and I'm going to tell her that if she doesn't stop trying to trash your life, I'll have her committed to a mental institution, because that's where she belongs."

"But Uncle Ed, she's not crazy."

"That depends on your definition of the word. Listen to me, Kendra, and listen carefully. A parent cannot abuse an adult child without that child's consent and cooperation. You don't owe Ginny anything, because she's already squeezed from you all that was ever coming to her. I want you to take stock of your feelings about her. Ask yourself why you feel you need her affection and good will, which you've obviously been trying to buy . . . yes, *buy* . . . when you know she's incapable of giving either one."

"But, Uncle Ed, I thought I was trying to be a good daughter."

"Then you were fooling yourself. The Lord tells us to

honor our parents, but He did not tell us to be their doormat. Do you understand?"

"Yes, sir."

"I didn't know you'd gotten that job with Howell Enterprises. I'm glad for you. Let me know when you've registered at Howard. Dot and I will take you out for champagne and dinner."

She thanked him, said good-bye, and hung up.

Did Ginny really think she was trying to buy her affection? Kendra thought about that for a long time, gave her uncle credit for being right, and felt a heavy weight slide off her.

Ginny was counting the number of days that had elapsed since her second visit with Dr. Elms. Nearly a week. She sat at her kitchen table and dialed the doctor's office. If she was clean of HIV/AIDS, she could have a decent date. She wouldn't have waited to appease her appetite, if she hadn't read that a man could trace the infection back to the woman who gave it to him.

A voice said, "This is Dr. Elms's office. How may I help you?"

"I'm Ginny Hunter, and Dr. Elms has a report for me."

"What kind of a report, Ms. Hunter?"

"Well . . . uh . . . I'd like to speak with Dr. Elms, please." Damned if she was going to give a receptionist personal information that could be used against her.

"And you may speak with her, but she won't talk with you unless she has your complete file in front of her. I need to check whether a test for you came in today."

Getting angrier by the moment, she took a deep, calming breath and asked, "Can't you check by name?"

The silence lasted a bit longer before the woman said, "I don't have time for coyness, Miss. Was this an STD or an HIV/AIDS test?"

"HIV/AIDS," she said, gritting her teeth.

"Hold on. I'll see if she's busy."

"You have the test?" Ginny asked the woman.

"Obviously."

A click told Ginny that the woman had her on hold. "If this test is clean," she vowed, "I'm going nowhere unless I have a couple of condoms in my pocketbook."

After about five minutes, she heard, "Ms. Hunter, this is Dr. Elms. Your HIV test was negative, but you have chlamydia, which is easily treatable." She told her the symptoms. "We treat that with antibiotics. It's the most common STD. I suggest you be more careful. A good quality condom will keep you clean. The fact that you won't get pregnant is not a reason to neglect use of protection. Come in tomorrow for a shot, and I'll give you a prescription for pills. If you neglect this, it will become serious, and you will infect your partners."

Ginny hung up. *Damned bastard. If she ever saw him again!* She sat back down, rubbing her chin thoughtfully. *It needn't have been him. Suppose she gave it to him!* Where was she going to get the money to pay that doctor? She had four hundred and sixty dollars, and she planned to put that on a gray Dior skirt that she saw at Saks. Oh well, at least she didn't have AIDS.

"Now who is that?" she asked aloud when the phone rang. "Hello?"

"Ginny, this is Ed. I hope you're well."

"Of course I'm well. I'm just broke, and I have a big doctor bill."

"If you're well, why do you have a big doctor bill?"

"Never mind. I have to come up with a lot of money by tomorrow."

"You have my prayers for the best of luck. I called you to tell you to stop trashing Kendra's life."

"What? That dreadful child won't even—"

She heard him pull air through his teeth, a sure sign that he was going for the jugular. "Cut the drama, Ginny. I've known you since you were born. If you ever behave again with Kendra as you did yesterday at that studio where she works, I'm going to court and petition to have you committed to a mental institution. And I have enough documented evidence to do it. Only an insane woman would do to her daughter what you're doing to yours. You're trying your best to ruin Kendra's life, but I'm not going to let you succeed. That's all I have to say to you."

He had some nerve, Ginny thought. "I'm the one who was *forced* to have those horrible pains. I'm the one who had that agony for sixteen hours, not you. And for what? She makes plenty of money and won't give me a few thousand when I need it."

"She owes you nothing. You are not too good to work a steady, full-time job and take care of *yourself*."

"Don't make me laugh. Your halo gets brighter with the years."

"If you won't earn a living honestly, you'll have to make it on your back, because I am not going to let you destroy that girl. Any other mother would be proud of her, but you're doing your best to drag her down. People who don't want children should either use protection or remain celibate. Remember what I said, Ginny. One more time, and I'll have you committed."

Ginny hung up and kicked the stove with all the energy she could muster. "Damn him! He'll do it, too. He's always been jealous of me." She limped to the bathroom, poured some Epsom salts into the tub, and turned on the hot water. After half an hour of soaking, the toe still hurt, so she limped to her bed and crawled in. But her thoughts were soon focused on choosing the next bar where she could find a competent and willing sex partner, one likely to reward her with some money.

If Ginny had erased from her thoughts the probable consequences of her behavior in the studio at which her daugh-

ter worked, Kendra had not. She had discovered that she enjoyed working as a disc jockey, and she longed to have the
pleasure of contact with her listeners. At lunch with June one
day, she told the receptionist of her goal to attain a degree in
communications and then to have contact with people.

"I've discovered that I like being a disc jockey," she said
to June, "but I would really love it if I had contact with my
listeners."

"Why don't you join an organization of professional disc
jockeys? You could probably learn a lot and make some con-
nections, too. There ought to be one here or in nearby Virginia or Maryland. Tab might give you some tips."

Kendra was certain that he could, but he might not want
her to move so fast. She found SRDJ, Society of Radio Disc
Jockeys, on the Internet and sent that organization an e-mail.

She attended the next meeting of the local club and, at
once, she noticed the paucity of women. She already knew
this was a field in which men ruled overwhelmingly, but she
didn't care. She'd make her listeners like her.

"You mean you work for Howell Enterprises?" a man
asked her after she introduced herself during the Saturday
afternoon meeting.

"Yes," she replied, "but I'm in the canned music studio,
and he's phasing that out."

"Yeah. It's old hat. But that's a beginning. He'll eventually move you to live music. Start now to read all the information that comes with each CD. Listeners like to know
everything past and present about the performers. If you tell
'em it was Carl Perkins and not Elvis Presley who wrote
'Blue Suede Shoes' or that Duke Ellington and Billy Stray-
horn worked so closely together that they sometimes didn't
know which one of them wrote a piece, they'll think you
know something. That's the way you get a following. If you
get a note or an e-mail from one of your listeners, answer it
when you're on the air. That's the way you get fans. But remember that you can't fool 'em."

"Thank you," she said, "for being so kind. Most of these fellows are downright rude to me. I was beginning to think I wouldn't come back."

"Don't let 'em get you down," he told her. "These young Turks come and go. Every one of 'em thinks he's the Latter-day Messiah. Next year, half of 'em will be looking for a job. I've been in this business for almost forty years. Do your job, treat people with respect, be honest and friendly, and you can't miss. You got a nice voice and a warm personality. That's what you need. By the way, I'm Charley Brighton."

She stared at him. "You? You're the man who promises to brighten my day?" A smile creased her face. "You have indeed brightened my day. Many times. I've been listening to you for years. I'm Kendra Richards."

"Glad to meet you, Kendra. Come with me. I see someone you'd like to meet."

He walked over to a man who seemed too relaxed and laid-back to be one of the chest-banging disc jockeys that she disliked. "Jack, this is Kendra Richards. She's a canned music DJ for Howell and working toward handling an open mike. Kendra, this is Jack Meriwether of WLLW. She may be just what you're looking for, Jack. Be seeing you, Kendra." The man shook hands with her and immediately began leveling a battery of questions at her.

"Mr. Meriwether," she said, "would you please slow down? Answers to some of your questions require careful thought, and I don't want to misrepresent myself by answering from the top of my head."

Jack Meriwether nodded in the manner of one grasping a fact. "At least you're honest. I've done that almost a dozen times today, well aware that I was moving too fast to be comprehensible. But you're the only person to stop me. How'd you like to do the six to twelve slot at WLLW?"

"You're offering me the—"

"If you didn't pass muster, Brighton wouldn't have introduced us. He knew I was here looking for a jock."

"Thank you for your confidence. Do you mind if I think about this and call you Monday?"

"No, I don't. But I can tell you it's a more rewarding job than the job you've got, and it probably pays more."

"I know. May I have your phone number, sir?"

He handed her his card. "I'll be out from twelve till two-thirty. I look forward to hearing from you Monday."

There was her opportunity. But could she take it? And should she? It occurred to her suddenly that Meriwether hadn't said whether she'd be working mornings or evenings and that he might not be amenable to her having flexible hours. Clifton Howell treated her and the other young people who worked for him almost as if they were members of his family. Yes, she'd have to give it a lot of thought, and she'd have to discuss it with Mr. Howell; he'd been kind and considerate, and she meant to be straight with him.

On her way to the Soft Music Studio the following Monday morning, she stopped at June's desk. "I need to speak with Mr. Howell for about five minutes if he has time."

"Okay. Keep a stack ready for automation. I'll call you."

About an hour later, she walked into Clifton Howell's office on legs that felt like rubber. "Thanks for seeing me, Mr. Howell. I need your advice about something that I think is important. I attended the local chapter of SRDJ Saturday to join and to attend the workshops. I want to be good at what I do. Those guys made me uncomfortable, and I felt out of place until an older man walked over to me and started talking. His name is Charley Brighton. I told him what I did and where and, without my asking or suggesting that I was interested, he introduced me to Jack Meriwether, who offered me a job.

"Since I've been here, I've realized that I enjoy being a disc jockey, and that I'd like it so much better if I had contact with my audience. That's why I'm trying to learn more. By the way, Mr. Brighton gave me some good tips. Do you think

I can have a career with Howell Enterprises? I know it's too soon for me to think about moving to radio here, but from what you've seen of me, do you think I have qualities that will enable me to move to radio after you finish automating the canned music and do well?"

With the butt of his hands on his desk, Clifton Howell made a pyramid of his ten fingers. Then, he flattened his hands and, just as she was feeling she'd like to disappear beneath the floor, he smiled. "You are the most disarming person I've ever met. Nobody in this business is as honest as you are. For that reason if no other, you'd better stay here, because I won't take advantage of you. I don't know what Jack is like to work for or what kind of terms he offered you, but . . ."

When he paused, she said, "He didn't mention terms, only the hours—six to twelve."

"Noon or midnight? I'll bet my house it's the morning shift, because that's the most difficult one to staff. As for your career prospects, are you telling me you'd continue to work for me, let's say, in radio, after you get your degree?"

"Why not? My major is communications, and I'm focusing on radio and TV rather than on print media."

"All right. In that case, I'll groom you, but if you want to switch to radio right now, I don't have a spot open. When Tab moves to TV, my six-to-twelve jock will take Tab's seat, and I'll put you in the evening slot. If that proves too much along with your studies, I'll switch you to the weekends.

"Now. Do you want to stay with me, or do you want to go with Jack?"

She laughed. His office seemed to swirl around at a dizzying pace, and she felt as if she were on a merry-go-round. "Excuse me, sir, but I don't often get a chance to feel this good. Thank you. I'll call Mr. Meriwether and tell him that I appreciate his offer, but the hours are not suitable."

"You're welcome. Any more trouble with your mother?"

"I spoke with my uncle, her brother, about it, and I don't think she can get around him. He won't tolerate her foolishness."

"Thank God for that."

She went back to her station, took out her cell phone and called Jack Meriwether. "I'm sorry, Miss Richards. I thought you'd be perfect for the morning spot. If you ever want to leave Howell, let me know. Thank you for getting back to me."

"Thank you for considering me, Mr. Meriwether."

On the way home that afternoon, she stopped at a bookstore and bought a book on the history of jazz and blues and their relationship to spirituals. "From now on, my reading matter will have to support my career goals," she said to herself as she left the store. "When I know what's in these books, I'll start on biographies of major musicians. Whoopee! For two cents, I'd dance right here on Fourteenth and F."

The following Saturday, she attended the local chapter meeting of SRDJ again, and Charley Brighton greeted her as if she were an old friend. "You've just learned one of the crucial laws of success," he told her, after she told him of her conversation with her boss. "If you've got a job, you can get a job, and if you want your boss to promote you, let him know that somebody else wants you. You made the better choice for you."

She'd learned something else, too: the jocks who had ignored her or refused to talk with her the previous Saturday sought her out. But she soon became aware that they didn't like or respect her more; they figured that if Charley Brighton knew her, she had to be someone important who could give them a lift up the ladder to success. She didn't bother to correct them.

She bought a book on the life of Louis Armstrong and told her girlfriends—The Pace Setters—to buy the book, read it, and be prepared to discuss it the next time they met.

"I'd love that," Flo said, excitement coloring her voice. "Why don't we become a book club?"

"Because Suzy isn't going to read anything about sex, and Kitten isn't going to read anything *but* sex. Let's stay as we are, four women on the loose."

Laughter poured out of Flo. "You say the funniest things, sometimes. Maybe you should have become a writer."

"No thanks. I'll have my chances when I become a radio disc jockey."

Kendra pursued her new life without interference from Ginny, developing a widening group of acquaintances among the disc jockeys in the local SRDJ, and polishing her craft through the Saturday workshops and conversations with her peers. But she had begun to feel that she had to have more in her life.

If I had a mother, I could discuss it with her, she thought, with not a little bitterness. Needing a kind of anchor, she went to her father's shop after work one evening just prior to his closing time.

"Hi, Papa." She hugged him and handed him a bag of Snickers, his favorite form of self-indulgence. "Want to have supper together? I can cook something, and we can eat at my place."

"Thanks for the Snickers. What would you cook? I'd welcome supper with you, if it doesn't take you too long to cook it. Or we could eat out."

"I can make a great *choucroute garnie*. What kind of German sausages and wieners do you have?" He told her. "I need two of each and a piece of smoked pork tenderloin. I have sauerkraut, onions, and potatoes at home. Let's go."

"How long will that take?"

"Twenty-five minutes in the pressure cooker. It's great with beer."

"Yeah," he said, his eyes lighting up, "and with some fine horseradish."

* * *

Bert Richards sat on a stool in her kitchen and watched her prepare the one-pot meal. She didn't try to explain to herself the reason for her contentment, the inner peace she felt, temporary though it might be. When the food was ready, she arranged it on a large turkey platter and put it on her dining table, which she had set earlier. Bert said the grace, and they ate in contented silence. At the end of the meal, he said, "This was wonderful. You can serve it to the most discriminating eater."

He made coffee, put two cups of it on the coffee table, and sat down. "Let's talk, Kendra. You're in the dumps. Has Ginny done something to you lately? What's the matter?"

She told him about her job and its prospects for her future, her efforts to hone her craft, her plans to enter Howard in the fall semester, her uncle's assurance that her mother wouldn't interfere with her again, and his reasons for doing so.

Bert had focused intently on her words and her demeanor as she spoke. "What you've been through these past few months would rattle anybody's cage, but you're a woman of iron strength, so none of it explains your demeanor when you walked into my shop. You came to me for comfort."

"I don't like to dump on you, Papa. I just felt like . . . like my ship is finally coming in, but it . . . it isn't giving me the happiness I thought it would."

"That's because you're missing something important. You need someone to love and who loves you. When you find that, you'll feel as if you've got the world by its axis."

"But, Papa, I don't meet any interesting men. There was one who came to the restaurant alone every Wednesday. I thought I could like him. I saw him the last time I went to church with you, and I still thought so. I don't think he would have gotten interested in a coatcheck girl, but—"

"Then come to church with me next Sunday. Maybe he'll be there. You're not a coatcheck girl anymore."

"I'll be in school starting late September. Then I'd like to find a way to meet him."

"All right, but don't set your heart on it. He could be married, gay, or a hard-nosed bachelor, in which case he'll string you along forever and never marry you." He sipped the coffee, musing over what she'd told him. "If your boss gives you evening hours so you can go to school during the day, I'll meet you when you get off, and drive you home. That's the least I can do. You sure you're going to have enough money for your tuition?"

"Yes, sir. I'm sure I'll get an academic scholarship after the first semester. But if I don't, I'll have enough for my junior year. I know I'll get one for my senior year."

"If you're short, I'll do what I can to help you."

When he rose to leave, she hugged him and walked with him to the door. "I can't imagine what I'd do without you, Papa." With tears in her eyes, she hugged him again.

He looked down at her, and she thought his eyes seemed to sparkle with unshed tears. "You're the joy of my life, daughter." With that, he opened the door and left.

He'd barely reached the front door of the apartment building, when Kendra sat down at her computer, accessed Howard University, and downloaded an admittance form for former students. Kendra didn't anticipate any problems, because she'd dropped out with a straight-A record and had no demerits of any kind. She completed the form before going to bed and mailed it on her way to work the next morning. Two weeks later, she received notification of permission to continue her studies there.

She got her wardrobe in order, mending and altering some things and shopping for needed essentials. With an income to cover her living expenses and a good part of her tuition and other school expenses and working hours from five

to eleven in the evening, she considered herself blessed and
at last on the road to achieving what she had longed for.

However, her life was not to be smooth no matter how
carefully she planned each move. The day before Kendra
was to register at Howard, she received a telephone call at
eight o'clock in the morning. She answered the phone while
puzzled at the unfamiliar number on the ID screen.

"Kendra, this is Ginny." She shrank away from the phone
as if it were on fire. "Did you hear me? This is Ginny and I'm
in jail. They don't allow me but one phone call, so you'll
have to come down here and bail me out."

She sat on the edge of her bed, and breathed deeply, in
and out.

"Say something. I only get one phone call."

"I heard you. I'm trying to figure out what you want me
to do about this."

"Get me out of here!"

"Really, Mama. What did you do?"

"I didn't do anything. They say I broke the law."

"Then, you probably did. You'd better tell me what
they're accusing you of. I may not want to get involved."

"How dare you! I'm your mother. I didn't do anything.
They said I was driving an unregistered car with a suspended license, and it's a lie."

"I'll tell Uncle Ed. Maybe he has some money. I'm registering at Howard tomorrow morning, and that will take all
that I have."

"Listen here you . . . you . . . Get me out of here! Damn
Howard University. I'm not staying in this place with all
these crack heads."

"I'll tell Uncle Ed to call that number. That's the best I can
do."

"He won't do a thing!"

"I'm sorry. I advise you to get a professional bondsman
and work out a plan to repay him."

"They charge an arm and a leg. I don't have any money to pay a bondsman."

"Then you don't have any money to pay me back, either. I can't do it. This is my last chance, and I'm taking it."

"Damn you. You're just like your father. Fit for nothing."

Kendra hung up, dropped her face in her hands, and let the tears flow. How could one woman be such a never-ending cross? She called her father, told him about the call, and, having second thoughts, she added, "Papa, I can't leave her in that jail."

"Yes you can, and you will," he roared. "If you bail her out, how are you going to register at Howard tomorrow? She won't even thank you, and you know it. I absolutely forbid it. Use your hard-earned tuition money to bail her out, and I'm done with you."

"Oh, Papa. I know this is the last straw for you, and I don't blame you, because I've had it up to here with her." She sliced the air above her head as if he could see her. "I don't really care about her discomfort, because she deserves that and more. It's the idea of my own mother being in jail."

"Humph. If she'd been a real mother to you, I'd bail her out myself. Let her go, Kendra. If you don't break that tie, you may as well tie thirty pounds of lead around your neck and jump into the Potomac. My last words on this subject! I refuse to let that woman stress me out and damage the quality of my life. That's why I divorced her. Call me when you have your class schedule."

"Yes, sir. I will." She'd promised Ginny that she would call Ed, and now she dreaded doing it. She dialed his cell phone number.

"Parks speaking. What can I do for you, Kendra? Your number just came up. Don't tell me Ginny has interfered with you again. I told her—"

"It's not like that, Uncle Ed. She called me from jail this morning demanding that I bail her out, but I can't. I'm registering for school tomorrow, and I need what money I have. Right now, she's probably mad enough to kill me."

"Forget it. I'll take care of it. What's she in for?"

"Driving an unregistered car with a suspended license."

"Well, I'll be . . . She's really done it this time. Forget about it and leave it to me."

"Thanks, Uncle Ed. I appreciate this." After she hung up, she realized that he hadn't said he'd bail her out. Oh, well. The chickens always came home to roost.

Kendra strolled across Howard's massive campus remembering the dreams she'd had as a teenager, thinking how she'd once run up that steep hill from Georgia Avenue to Rankin Chapel and Founders Library at the top of the hill. The early autumn wind pushed her hair away from her face and, for one moment, she spread both arms, embracing the wind and the future. Nothing was as she had remembered it, except the clock on top of the library. She wondered if it still gave forth popular music at one o'clock, announcing the end of lunch hour. The sun shone through the trees as her jaunty steps took her down the hill to the School of Communications, located in a building that had once been a part of the hospital.

"My Lord," she said to herself after passing a group of students. "Everybody is so young, so fresh looking." She didn't like that.

When Kendra entered the John H. Johnson School of Communications, she thought she'd take wing and fly. But for some minor and attractive refurbishing, it had barely changed. She headed to the office of her favorite professor.

"Well, well. I was expecting you," he said. "Seeing your application for readmission made me happy, indeed. I had feared that you'd fallen through the cracks. It's good to see you. Tell me about yourself."

She told him why she had dropped out. "I've been struggling ever since to get back, but one thing after another got in the way. I hope my work this semester will merit a scholarship."

"I wouldn't worry about that. How do you enjoy your work as a disc jockey?"

"I like it, but I won't begin working as a live radio jock until Monday evening."

"You'll do fine. You have the voice, the personality, and the intelligence. Did you register for any supportive courses?"

"Yes, sir." She gave him her schedule.

"Very good. I'll see you in class."

She went to WHUR-FM, the university's radio station, an important commercial radio station in Washington with a hefty share of the local listeners. Standing in one of the studios or control rooms and recognizing that it almost duplicated Tab's studio at Howell Enterprises, she hugged herself. She'd wager that she was one of the few students there who already had a job in radio.

"Well, what do you think?" a student asked her. "This sucker is state-of-the-art."

"It sure is," she said. "I'm a jock at Howell Enterprises' WAMA-FM, and I can attest to the fact that this is absolutely the crème de la crème."

"There you go," he said. "Are you graduate, undergraduate, or teaching?"

"I'm a junior returning after twelve years."

He held out his hand. "Cool. I'm Martin Epps. Notice any changes since you were here?"

"Yeah. Everybody's so damned young. I'm Kendra Richards."

His lusty laugh comforted her. "I'm gonna like you. This school is not loaded with down-to-earth people. These future image makers have highfalutin notions about their own images. I'm a grad student, and I'm in charge of the day shift. Drop in whenever you like."

"Thanks. I appreciate it. I have to meet one of my favorite professors now. See you soon."

He leaned against the wall and appeared to be examining his nails, though she knew he was about to ask a sticky question. "Which one and what subject?"

She answered truthfully. "Professor Hormel, Journalism 307."

"One of the best. My favorite, in fact. You'll enjoy it."

She decided to take a chance and see how much of a friend he'd be. "I'm assuming from this that I'm fortunate."

"Blessed would be more accurate."

She waved at him. "Thanks. Bye for now." Recalling the nature of campus gossip, she knew she would soon know what was at the bottom of Martin Epps's statement. If students considered a professor to be lazy, incompetent, or unduly harsh in judgments, they didn't keep their thoughts to themselves. Kendra had liked Mark Hormel on sight, and after a ten-minute conversation with him, she didn't doubt that she'd made a good choice.

She arrived at the Howell's radio station Studio One at five-thirty, half an hour before air time. Clifton Howell had given her an easy evening shift, from six to twelve, since her first class didn't convene until eleven in the mornings. About five minutes before she was to start, Tab got out of the chair, hugged her, and said, "You're on your way, doll. I'll sit back here for an hour in case you need me. You know the controls backward, so nothing can go wrong. But I'll stay to give you moral support."

She thanked him and sat in the chair that he'd just vacated. "I wish you were my brother," she said. "Every girl should have a brother like you."

Tab released a big roar of a laugh. "I know you meant that as a compliment, doll, but you're wishing my mother was dead." When her eyes widened, he laughed harder. "My bigoted daddy would've killed her as soon as he looked at you."

"But you're—"

He interrupted her. "Of course I'm not. My daddy is ignorant. I'm intelligent, and I'm educated. There's your light. One . . . two . . ."

"Hi, everybody. This is KT speaking, your jock for the next six hours. Stick with me and I'll fill your evening with beautiful music. You got a birthday, anniversary, lovers' reunion, or just a beautiful memory, shoot me an e-mail, and I'll play your song. Here we go with Buddy Guy's 'Feels Like Rain,' and if you think you hear Bonnie Raitt and that slide guitar of hers in the background, you are absolutely right."

She had thought that her voice would give out from the constant patter, but after an hour and a half, she had developed a modus operandi. Three records in succession gave her twelve minutes in which to rest her voice. Twenty minutes of a favored artist, such as Billie Holiday, Ray Charles, Aretha Franklin, Jennifer Hudson, or Rihanna, gave her twenty minutes in which to read her class material. The buzz of a small alarm clock brought her back to her reason for being there.

At ten minutes of twelve, she told her listeners, "Thank you for making my debut on WAMA so delightful. I've received far more e-mail requests than I could handle. Tell you what. They'll all get answered, so listen in tomorrow evening between six and midnight. KT will be back then with the music you want. Till then, walk gracefully and strut your stuff." She signed off with Buddy Guy's "Feels Like Rain," and decided that that would be her theme song.

When she approached the guard's desk at the building's entrance, the man stood and gave her a large bunch of red and yellow roses. "Courtesy of Mr. Howell. He heard the first three hours of your program. He's really pleased, Miss Richards."

"Thank you so much, Rocky, for telling me. I appreciate it."

"You did great, ma'am. I heard the whole show. I liked the music you played, too. There's a car parked out front there. I'll walk out with you."

At the door, she saw that it was her father's car. "It's okay, Rocky. This is my father's car. He's meeting me. Good night."

"Good. Some guy who likes your voice and knows what time you get off could cause problems. Good night."

She got in the Mercury Cougar, fastened her seat belt, and reached over and kissed her father's cheek. "Thanks for meeting me, Papa. It never occurred to me that I'd be tired."

"I heard your whole program."

"What did you think?" she asked him, and held her breath for one of his tart replies.

But he turned fully to face her, shaking his head as if bemused. "I couldn't believe I was listening to my little girl. It was smooth as a baby's bottom from start to finish. You were made for that kind of work. I'm proud of you."

She showed him the flowers. "Mr. Howell sent them to me tonight. The guard said Mr. Howell heard the show and that he said he was really pleased. Papa, I'm so happy."

"You're a good daughter and a fine woman. God takes care of those kinds of people."

She walked into her apartment at twelve-eighteen and, by one o'clock, was in bed. If she could maintain that schedule, she'd make it with ease.

An eight o'clock phone call the next morning sent her heart into a fast trot. Reluctant to answer for fear that it might be Ginny, she lifted the receiver only once she saw her uncle's caller ID.

"Good morning, Uncle Ed. How are you?" She hated the awkwardness of having to ask him if he'd bailed her mother out of jail, especially when she suspected that he hadn't done that. After all, he had not promised to do it; he had only said he'd take care of the situation.

"I'm fine," he said. "What was it like to be back in school after all these years of dreaming about it?"

"When I walked into John H. Johnson Hall, I felt like a little pig finally getting into hog heaven. I felt different, but not out of place. It's a wonderful feeling."

"When are you planning to study?"

"Mornings, at school when I'm not in class, and on the job while the music's playing. Of course, I have to talk sometimes. Daddy's driving me home nights, so I get here quickly."

"Bert's a good man. Dot and I want you to have dinner with us Saturday night. I can pick you up at seven. I promised you a champagne toast. Would you like me to ask Bert to join us?"

"That will be wonderful. Uh . . . Dot's got a guy she wants you to meet."

"Tomorrow night? Good grief, Uncle Ed, I haven't been to the hairdresser in a week."

"*Women!* She didn't say tomorrow night. If she had, I wouldn't have said bring Bert along. She'll tell you when she can arrange it. I'm proud of you, Kendra. Just as proud of you as I can be."

She thanked him and hung up. The man she really wanted to meet was the guy who ate lunch at La Belle Époque every Wednesday.

Chapter Four

During the dinner, Kendra's father and her uncle and his wife expressed admiration for the woman she had become in spite of trying adversity. But Kendra nonetheless felt a need for a catharsis in regard to her mother.

Lolling on the lawn near Rankin Chapel the following Monday, she found herself idly writing questions to Ginny, who remained in jail. She was about to shred the paper when she realized the significance of her questions and decided to phrase them impersonally in the form of a letter to an editor of general interest news at the *Washington Post*.

> *Dear Editor,*
> *I'd like to know what you and your other readers think a child owes a parent. I have in mind particularly a mother who tells the child that she bore it only because she was forced to, who refused to take care of the child until it was eleven and she no longer had anyone to whom she could shift her responsibilities, and who deliberately hampers the child's every effort toward a commendable goal.*
> *On the other hand, the child gives the mother material aid each time she requests it, and each time she receives such aid, the mother throws it away frivolously, wining and dining her girlfriends, buying*

expensive clothes and Jimmy Choo shoes, not caring
that she took something her child needed. Is that
woman sane? If so, what does the child owe her. Is
she insane? If so, should she be institutionalized or
forced into treatment? Is she a menace to her child? I
look forward to your reply and to the views of your
readers.
   Sincerely yours,
   K. Richards

She knew that she risked being identified as KT Richards, the disc jockey, and as Kendra Richards, the student at Howard University, but she needed the opinion of disinterested people; her father and uncle were biased in her favor.

The third day after she mailed the letter, she saw it unedited in the paper. The following day, she received a telephone call as she was leaving home for school.

"Could you call back later?" she asked without saying hello. "I'm about to be late for class."

"Sure. Do you have a cell phone?"

"Who is this?"

"Luke Unger, producer of Families in Crisis on WWLL radio."

"Oh." She gave him the number. "Please do not give it to anyone. You may call me at five after twelve."

"Thanks, Ms. Richards. I will. Good-bye."

What did he want with . . . ? Oh. Oh. He saw her letter. All right. She'd go on the show, but only if he paid her. "I'd better ask Mr. Howell," she said to herself. As soon as she was seated on the bus, she telephoned Howell's office.

"Hi, June. This is Kendra. It's urgent that I speak with Mr. Howell. I need his permission for something."

"Hold on. You're in luck. He's got a conference in five minutes."

"I only need a minute."

"Hello, Kendra. What's the problem?" Clifton Howell asked, as he came on the line.

She told him about her letter to the *Post* and Luke Unger's phone call. "If he asks me to go on the show, is it all right?"

"I see Unger's on the ball. That was a good letter. Sure it's all right. And use every opportunity to promote yourself. How much did he offer?"

"He hasn't asked me yet."

"After he offers to give you peanuts, tell him I said he should pay you at least twelve hundred and that if he says no, I'll put you on one of my TV shows."

"Thank you, sir."

After her eleven o'clock class, Kendra sat beneath a tree in back of Douglas Hall with her books, a thermos of coffee, two homemade ham sandwiches, an apple, and a candy bar beside her, waiting for Unger's call. Her cell phone rang precisely five minutes after twelve.

She propped up her knees and pulled her flared skirt down as far as it would go. Pants were more convenient for school and work, but she only had two pair, and both were at the cleaners.

"Kendra Richards speaking."

"Miss Richards, this is Luke Unger. I'd like you to be a guest on the radio show, 'Families in Crisis.' There will be two panelists, a psychologist, and a family counselor. Will you come?"

"I'm not an expert on anything, Mr. Unger. I'm studying communications."

"And you're a sophisticated radio jock. I catch your show regularly when I'm driving. Anybody who read your letter to the *Post* could see that you were either writing about yourself or you are very intimately familiar with the situation. I won't identify you beyond the way you signed your letter to the editor. And I assure you that whoever that child is, he or she should listen to the program. May I count on you?"

"When is the taping or airing, and what remuneration are you offering?"

"Interesting. Most guests don't ask that."

"I doubt that most of your guests are college students who're working their way through school. I'm not wealthy enough and don't have the leisure to do charity, Mr. Unger."

"Touché. Eight hundred."

"My boss said you should pay me twelve hundred, and that if you won't, he'll put me on a program on his TV station. He knows, because I had to get his permission to appear on your program."

"Okay. The program will be live Sunday at five and re-broadcast Sunday at nine. It's a one-hour show. Please be here at four o'clock."

"I'll be there, and please have my check ready at the end of the program."

"Of course. You drive a hard bargain."

"I've learned some hard lessons. Thank you for inviting me. See you Sunday."

"At least it's on radio and I don't have to buy anything to wear," she said to herself. She loved red, but didn't wear it often. Knowing that she'd be more at ease and more self-confident if she looked her best, she decided to wear her old standby, a light-weight silk dusty rose suit that flattered every inch of her. She loved to wear it.

She spent the next forty minutes eating her lunch and memorizing "Thanatopsis," a poem by William Cullen Bryant, which she had to recite in her four o'clock public speaking class.

Later, as she left the campus after what she considered a perfect school day, she stopped by the bookstore on Georgia Avenue and bought a four-by-six notepad to put in her pocket-book for use while on the panel. So far, none of the students seemed to associate her with the letter in the *Post,* if indeed they had read it. She had already learned that her ten years out of school had not been wasted; in some important respects, life's classroom had put her ahead of her classmates. But they had important advantages, too. Because of their youth and the years still ahead of them, they had time to sit in the coffee shops, exercising their minds by shooting the bull on both serious and frivolous topics. They had time to be young; she didn't.

After nearly a month in the local jail, Ginny received a call to the warden's office. "You're free to go, but you have to report for trial October seventeenth."

Ginny rolled her eyes and pulled air through her teeth. "Who paid the bail?"

The warden looked down at the paper in front of her. "Edward Parks. Here are your papers." She showed Ginny an envelope containing her release papers. "And you'd better do something about your attitude, or you'll be spending a lot more time in here."

"He could have gotten me out of here right away. I don't thank him a damned bit."

"If you'd like to stay longer, I'll be glad to accommodate you. Get your clothes on." Ginny reached for the envelope, but the warden covered it with her hand. "You'll get it when you leave. And you can stop looking down your nose at the other inmates; you're a jailbird just like they are."

Ginny headed back to her cell. After dressing, she pinned her stringy hair up as well as she could, put on some makeup, and waited for the guard, who escorted her to the warden's desk.

The warden handed Ginny the envelope. "If you ever come back while I'm here, I'll see that you catch hell. Your brother bailed you out." She looked down at the paper in front of her. "Or at least it says here that he's your brother. Thank him for his kindness. If you come back, I hope he lets you dry up in here. Take her out, Greta."

Ginny stood at Nineteenth and E Street, Southeast, looking for a way to get home. The battery of her cell phone had long since died, and she couldn't telephone anyone. She didn't see a taxi, so after nearly forty-five minutes of shivering in the late October chill, she flagged down a red convertible Mercedes.

The driver stopped, backed up, and opened the front passenger door. "What's the problem?" the man said. "You look as if you just lost your best friend."

"I feel like I have. My cell phone's dead, there're no taxis around here, and I couldn't call anyone. I was about to die in this weather."

"Where're you headed?"

"I'd like to go home, but that's all the way to Kalorama Road."

"You're in luck. I'm headed that way."

"I don't believe you," she said, "but I sure appreciate your wanting to put me at ease."

"Who's waiting for you there?"

"I have no idea, except that no man will be there."

"What kind of an answer is that?" he asked, as he turned into North Carolina Avenue and headed for Massachusetts Avenue.

"You don't want to know."

"I guess I don't. What's your name?" he asked. She told him. "I spent two years in that hellhole for sniffing coke. It was my first time, and I got caught. It was also my last time, but it ruined my life. You can't practice law with that kind of record. What were you in for?"

"How do you know I was in jail?"

"That's why I stopped. You were half a block from the jail. Only a desperate woman would have flagged down a strange man this time of morning. You didn't look like a streetwalker. What were you in for?"

"Driving an unregistered car with a suspended license. I couldn't make bail, and my brother decided I needed to learn a lesson and left me in that dump for almost a month. I have to wait till mid-November for the trial."

"I was about to say I hope you learned a lesson, but something tells me you didn't." They rode in silence until he reached the building in which she lived. "Here you are, Ginny. Have a good life."

She got out, looked him in the eye, and said, "Sure you don't want to come in?"

He grinned and shook his head. "My days of tomcatting are over, Ginny. I'm a man of the cloth. So long."

She stood there, dumbfounded, as he drove off. *A preacher, for heaven's sake!* Twenty minutes after she walked into her apartment, her doorbell rang. Maybe the preacher had changed his mind. She patted the loose strands of her hair and hastened to the door.

"Ed! What are you doing here?"

He walked in, headed straight for the living room, and sat down, giving her no choice but to join him. "Would you sign this, please?"

"I ain't signing nothing."

"Oh, but you will. If you don't sign it, I will have your bail revoked tomorrow morning."

She read the document:

> *I, Virginia Hunter, will have no contact of any*
> *kind with my daughter, Kendra Richards, for the*
> *next twenty months, or until she finishes Howard. If*
> *I break this signed agreement, I must pay Edward*
> *Parks eight thousand dollars (bail money) on*
> *demand or face a judge. I understand that if I am ar-*
> *rested again, Edward Parks will not give me any*
> *kind of assistance.*
> *Virginia Hunter*

She read it twice, signed it, and handed it back to him. "One of these days, I'm going to shake the dust of this town off my feet and head west. Then, all of you can go to hell."

Ed stood and gazed down at her the way one looks down

at the dead, pained and sorrowful. "What a pity. I'd give anything if I had a sister. When I was little, I wanted a sister to protect, to adore, to play with, and to show off to my buddies. But by the time you were four or five, you were so full of yourself that you didn't even want Mama to kiss you. At twelve, you were a monster, flirting and trying to seduce every man you met. You're still passable looking, but I can't wait for the day when your looks are gone, and you'll finally understand what it means to need people for themselves. Be seeing you."

She threw her keys at his departing back, crossed the room to pick them up, and decided that what she needed was a bubble bath. Then she'd call Phil and tell him she wanted to work full time the following week. She didn't need Ed or anybody else.

Looking her best, with her hair around her shoulders and her face reflecting the dusty-rose silk that she wore, Kendra stepped off the elevator and tapped on Luke Unger's office door.

"Come in."

What a voice! The man sounded as if he were angry. She opened the door gently and walked toward his desk as he rose and extended his hand. "Mr. Unger? I'm Kendra Richards."

"I'm glad to meet you. You're a surprise. On the radio, you sound like a jeans-clad teenager."

"Good Lord! I hope not. I'll correct that at once. But you shouldn't worry. I'm usually wearing jeans or something of that order when you hear me."

"That's not the point. In person, you look like the type who'd be emceeing an opera at the Met in New York."

"Thanks for the compliment. What are the other panelists like? Should I expect dialogue, argument, attempts at put-down, or what?"

"I expect this will be more academic. At least, I plan to

guide it in that direction. It's a very serious topic, to which I believe many people have needed an answer. And it's also a problem that people do not share readily, if at all." He answered another tap on his door, and a tall woman who appeared to be in her late forties or early fifties walked in.

"It's good to see you again, Luke," the woman said. "Thanks so much for inviting me. What an exciting topic! I read the letter in the *Post,* and when I received your call, I was planning to write a reply."

"Thanks for coming, Edwina. Dr. Prill, this is Kendra Richards. Ms. Richards, this is Edwina Prill."

The two women shook hands, and Kendra was relieved to note that the woman gave no evidence of competitiveness. They exchanged pleasantries, and it surprised Kendra that Edwina Prill made no reference to the topic they were to discuss during the show. A solid knock announced the arrival of the last panelist.

"Sorry I'm late, Luke," the man said, and a loud gasp escaped Kendra as the man strode to Luke Unger and shook his hand.

"Ms. Richards, this is Professor Samuel Hayes. Sam, you know Dr. Prill."

"Get yourself together," she told herself as the man she'd wanted so badly to meet walked toward her with his hand outstretched.

"I'm delighted to . . ." Sparks of electricity seemed to dance off their hands when they touched. She felt it, and she knew he did, too. Both withdrew quickly.

When Kendra realized that Unger and Edwina Prill were gaping at them, she joshed, "You must be a magician as well as a teacher, Professor Hayes."

He smiled, and she didn't miss the intimacy of it. "I was about to wonder if your radio voice came over the air on your own air waves. I'm glad to meet you. Your letter to the *Post* piqued my interest. I wouldn't have missed being here."

"Let's go to the studio," Luke said, shaking his head as if

bemused. "We have about twenty-five minutes for tea or coffee and some cookies."

Kendra noticed that Samuel Hayes maneuvered so as to
walk beside her. She glanced down at his left hand, but
couldn't see his ring finger. If she reacted that way to the
man only to discover that he was married, she'd swear that
Providence was against her.

"How long have you been a disc jockey, Ms. Richards?"

She loved his voice. It had a comforting quality, like a
warm blanket. "About three months. I began as a canned
music jock and Mr. Howell promoted me to live radio. He
took a big chance."

"He probably didn't think so; he knows his business. I assure you that I would never have guessed you were the jock
on that show."

"I hope that's a compliment."

"I don't know. You're . . . well, different from what I expected, but pleasantly so."

"Don't tell me you expected tight jeans with holes in the
knees."

"Not quite, but you're getting there."

Unger stood beside an open door. "We'll be in here for the
time being. Sorry I can't offer you margaritas, but a serious
topic requires clear heads."

"What about after the topic has been aptly aired?" Hayes
said.

"Same thing," Unger shot back. "One should use that
time for constructive reflection."

"Yeah. Right," Edwina Prill said. "I've done a lot of serious reflection with a glass of scotch whiskey and soda in my
hand." The four enjoyed a hearty laugh.

"What about you?" Sam Hayes asked Kendra after the
laughter died down.

"I've never tasted scotch whiskey in my life. By the time I
was old enough to drink, the stuff cost too much. My dad's

tastes run to bourbon, beer, and good wine, so he was an unlikely source. Have I missed much, Dr. Prill?"

"Pour yourselves coffee, tea, cocoa, or green tea. And I see we have a chocolate cake, oatmeal-raisin cookies, and some cheese puffs. We can drink tea or coffee during the show, but if you want to eat something, now's the time. We'll have a small audience of perhaps fifty or so. A lot of listeners have phoned in to verify the time of this program."

When they filed into the broadcast studio twenty-five minutes later, they had developed the warmth and camaraderie that Kendra realized was Unger's intention in asking them to arrive an hour early.

Unger introduced the panelists. "A letter to the *Washington Post* prompted me to have a discussion of a topic that many people wrestle with daily. What is our obligation to our parents, and when are we not obligated to them?" He read Kendra's letter. "Doctor Prill, what do you think of this letter, in general?"

"Thank you, Mr. Unger. First, I do not believe that the mother is insane or mentally deficient in any way. Even without knowing her childhood background, it is clear to me that she is extremely selfish and may be narcissistic. Her daughter owes her nothing, not even 'good morning.' "

Sam Hayes balled his fists and knocked his knuckles together in the manner of one anxious to get a crack at something. "I think this child is starved for nurturing, for the love we all naturally expect from our parents, and is attempting to buy the mother's affection and love. He or she is obviously an income-earning adult and, in borrowing money, the mother is taking advantage and giving nothing in return," he said. "Remember that she takes what she knows the child needs and squanders it. What do you think, Ms. Richards?"

Suddenly, Kendra wanted to be left out of the discussion. She suspected that Prill, Hayes, and Unger knew they were talking about her and her mother, and that they treated it as an anonymous matter in order not to embarrass her. Would they evaluate the problem differently if they knew more about Ginny and her life since early childhood, as her uncle had related it? She took a deep breath and thought of an appropriate answer to Sam's question.

"I'm not an expert on interpersonal relations, but from what you and Dr. Prill have said, it would seem that the mother thinks the child has no backbone and won't stand up to her."

"Hasn't that been the case so far?" Sam asked. "Was the child born out of wedlock?"

"No. The father foiled the mother's attempt to have an abortion, and because of her attitude toward the child, among other things, he divorced her."

"So the child has a father?" Prill asked. "What role does he play in the child's life now?"

"I think he is and always has been the stabilizing factor in that child's life."

Sam rubbed his chin reflectively. "Really? In my professional opinion, that child should cut ties with the mother. Otherwise, the mother will destroy the child along with herself."

No longer able to affect an impartial attitude toward the discussion, Kendra stared at Sam. "Suppose the mother becomes ill? Should the child just ignore that, or should he or she take care of the mother?"

Hayes let his quick shrug relate his personal feelings about that question. "Not if she experiences anger, hatred, or resentment as a result."

Prill questioned that. "But what about moral obligation?"

Unger seemed impatient with that viewpoint. "What about it? If I were faced with that dilemma, and if I had the money, I'd pay her sick bills and bury her when she died, but that's all she'd get from me."

Sam Hayes looked straight at Kendra when he said, "Consciously or unconsciously, that mother knows that the child is trying to make her love her, and that only puffs up her ego."

"Yeah," Unger said. "Too bad."

Edwina Prill offered a prophesy. "When that woman is old, alone, and looking back on her life, the word, 'daughter' or 'son' will finally have meaning for her."

The comments of Prill and Hayes became increasingly academic, exposing the cause of Ginny's selfish behavior and justifying Kendra's growing distaste for her mother. As they talked, she made notes on what she would one day say to Virginia Hunter.

At the end of the hour, the audience of about seventy people stood and applauded. Unger thanked them, and one man yelled, "Bring them back and let us ask questions."

"I'll try to arrange that," Unger said. "My thanks to Ms. Richards, Dr. Prill, and Professor Hayes for an enlightening and engrossing evening."

No matter how hard he tried, Samuel Hayes could not associate Kendra Richards with her letter to the *Washington Post*. And as he reflected upon her contribution to the discussion of her letter, he was convinced that she wrote about her own mother and herself. As a professor of family psychology with a dozen academic texts on the subject to his credit, he could not associate her with the woman she described in her letter. Scratch that. He didn't want to associate her with such a mother, because a woman with a mother like that one was likely to be cool, uncaring, and sexually frigid. And considering the wallop he got when he shook hands with her and his certainty that it happened to her, too, resolving it with her could be like trying to climb a mountain with bare feet and bare hands.

He walked beside her as they were leaving the building.

"Did you drive?" he asked her.

"No. I don't have a car."

"Dr. Prill drives. This is not a neighborhood in which you should walk alone at night. Will you ride with me?"

When she seemed to hesitate, he said, "Look, Kendra. I'm thirty-four, and that's too old to play games. I want to get to know you. Also, I haven't had dinner, and I'm hungry. Will you have dinner with me?"

She hadn't hesitated deliberately, but had been wondering how to prolong the evening, and to see him again. She hadn't thought that he might be a professor, and especially not a professor at George Washington University. She liked what she'd learned about him, and he wasn't wearing a ring.

"I'd like that. Thank you." Not every man wore a wedding band, so she'd better ask. "Are you married? If you are, I'd like to go straight home."

"I'm not married or engaged. I don't cheat, Kendra."

"Professor Hayes, I couldn't look at you and know your vital statistics, could I?"

Laughter streamed out of him, and her smile suggested that she liked laughter.

"I guess not," he said. "The women I meet these days don't seem to care about my marital status. I'm glad you do. And I'd be more comfortable and enjoy my dinner a lot more if you'd call me Sam. I haven't asked if you're married, because Unger introduced you as *Miss* Richards." He assisted her into his car and fastened her seat belt.

He stopped for the red light at Fourteenth and P streets and looked her way. Not even the dim light could hide the mischievous glints in her eyes. "Are you one of these chauvinists who rejects the title, Ms.? Come now, Sam."

"Hold it. You're not accusing me of . . . wait a minute. Are you married?"

"No, I'm not," she said with a grin. "I wouldn't cheat."

Hmm. So she liked to tease. He could certainly handle that; he wasn't bad at it himself. "I had in mind an Italian restaurant just off Dupont Circle. Do you like Italian food? If not, we can go to a steak house not far from there."

"I like your first choice, and I especially like the variety of foods and flavors in Italian cooking."

"Then that's the second thing we have in common."

"What's the first?" she asked him. They approached Dupont Circle, one of many circles in Washington, D.C., and he parked a few doors from it.

"Sorry we have to cross the circle, Kendra, but I can't pass up this parking space. I might not find another one."

"I don't mind walking. Are you going to answer my question?"

He walked around to the passenger side of the car, but when he got there, she was already getting out. "Next time, wait till I get around here, otherwise, how will you know I'm a gentleman?"

"You'll find other ways to let me know. About my question . . ."

He grasped her hand and, once more, he felt the sparks, and the energy from it traveled to his armpits. He stopped walking and stared down at her. "Did you feel that?"

She nodded. "I was wondering if you did."

"Absolutely. All the way to my armpits. And that's the answer to your question, Kendra. The first thing we have in common is our mutual attraction." She attempted to remove her hand, but he wouldn't release it. "If you'd rather not be attracted to me, let's settle that this minute."

"You think I planned it?" she asked him. "Being attracted to you means I'll spend a lot of time daydreaming when I should be studying or working. And I've . . ." She slapped her hand over her mouth.

"Finish that sentence, Kendra." He released her hand and put his arm around her waist as they crossed Rhode Island Avenue. "Drivers like to speed around here," he explained.

"What sentence are you talking about?"

"About your daydreaming. You said 'And I've,' and then you slapped your hand over your mouth."

She squeezed his fingers, and he tried to discern the

meaning of it. Then she said, "You'll get the answer eventually, but right now, you don't need to know."

They entered the little restaurant, and he headed to his favorite table in the back, overlooking a little garden, which the manager opened from May till early autumn. Sitting across from her, her face aglow in that soft light, he wondered if he'd just jumped overboard. He'd never met anyone like her. Self-assured, but neither overly assertive nor aggressive, and so soft. Yet, he'd be surprised if she didn't have a sharp tongue. He reached for her hand, and she let him hold it.

"You've got to explain these cryptic remarks, Kendra. And another thing: Twice you've indicated that you expect us to see more of each other. It's exactly what I want. You don't merely fascinate me; I feel as if there's something preordained going on here. When I saw you, something hit me with the power of a sledgehammer.

Her smile became a grin that seemed to caress her face. He wondered if she had a secret.

Kendra did indeed have a secret, and she'd begun to think that she'd better share it with him. After all, if he proved to be a snob, he wouldn't fit into her life anyway. Before she could reply, he said, "I noticed that Unger was careful not to divulge any information about you. How do you spend your days and nights?"

So he was covering all bases. "During the weekdays from eleven to four, I'm on Howard University's campus working toward a bachelor's degree in communications. As you're aware, I'm WAMA's evening jock. At all other times, I'm either asleep or studying. During weekends, I try to get in as much study as possible."

"I have a lot of follow-up questions, but I'd rather you enlightened me when you've decided you trust me. Don't you ever have time for recreation?"

"I take a little time out on Saturdays or Sundays, usually the latter, when I don't go to church with my father."

"Do you do that often?"

"Occasionally. But those Baptists spend a lot of time in services, so . . . well, you know. I love to swim and fence, and I'd enjoy fishing and boating if I had the opportunity. I adore being in and on the water. What do you do in your leisure time?"

"Same thing you do plus fish and enjoy my boat."

Her eyes widened. "You have a boat?"

"I had a choice between buying a boat and buying a house, and I decided to buy a co-op apartment and a boat, because I love the water."

"Where is your boat?"

"I dock it at Saint Leonard on the Chesapeake Bay. It's down for the winter. I secure it and cover it with tarpaulin, to prevent deterioration. In mid-March, I'll start getting her ready to sail." He glanced up at the waitress.

"Y'all so busy talking, I hated to disturb you. Would you like a drink?"

"I wouldn't because I'm driving." He looked at Kendra. "What would you like?"

"Iced tea with mint, please."

"We've got cioppino, a great fish stew tonight. It's a lot like bouillabaisse, except that it has saffron and the French stew doesn't. The chef only makes it when he's very happy, or that's what he says. We serve it with a green salad and some hot homemade Italian artisan bread. I recommend it."

"Then, that's what I'll have," Sam said, and looked at her. "What would you like? They have a great menu."

"I'd like to try the cioppino. I love seafood."

The waitress took their menus and left.

Why did he look at her that way? His facial expression, so . . . so intimate, unnerved her. "Sam, what is it? Why are you looking at me that way?"

"I'm sorry. I didn't mean to embarrass you. It's . . ." He locked his hands together and shook his head. "This is so unreal. I'm enjoying being with you as if we were . . . as if I'd been close to you for years." His countenance seemed to brighten. "You said you'd decided that you'd better tell me something. What is it?"

"I . . . uh . . ." Sam leaned back with the demeanor of a man prepared for anything. Kendra continued. "I didn't see you tonight for the first time, although we'd never met. Before I went to work as a disc jockey for Howell Enterprises, I had previously worked as a cloakroom girl at La Belle Époque." His eyebrows shot up. "Every Wednesday for lunch, you ate a crab-cake sandwich, a green salad, and had a glass of white wine with it. You were always alone. I wanted to meet you, but I knew you wouldn't cast a second glance at a coatcheck girl."

He leaned forward, his long frame shadowing more than half of the table. "You were not a waitress and you never waited on me or spoke to me and I never had a reason to go to that cloakroom. Yet you know what I ate and drank and that I only went there Wednesdays at lunchtime. Why?"

"I never consorted with any of La Belle Époque's patrons. Not once. I was there to earn enough money to pay for my junior semester at Howard. I knew that the men who ate lunch there were mainly wealthy and important. But only their tips interested me. Except for you. You . . . you were different and . . . I don't know . . .

"I'll tell you something else. One Sunday leaving church with my father, I saw you, and I was about to ask him if he knew you, when several women crowded around us. By the time I managed to get his attention, you were nowhere to be seen. I was so disappointed."

"Would it upset you if I told you that I want to kiss you? I am not impulsive, not by any stretch of the imagination, and I am not a gambler. But I'd wager my job that, a year from now, you and I will be together."

She'd proved to herself time and again that she had guts, but, with this man, Kendra didn't know whether to run from him or embrace him. Looking at her as if he knew the inside of her soul, she figured that she'd better run while she could. Her teeth chattered so badly that she put her elbow on the table and supported her jaw with the butt of her hand.

He reached over and grasped her hand. "It's all right, Kendra. I'm as flummoxed as you are."

"Confused is one thing. I'm scared to death."

"Not me. I've waited a long time to feel like this in a woman's presence. You are right to be careful, because you don't know me, but don't be afraid. If it will give you a greater sense of security and if you're willing, I'll take you over to Alexandria to meet my dad. We lost my mother two years ago."

"Oh, Sam. I'm so sorry. I'd love to meet your dad, but not because I don't trust you. It's just . . . Sam, life isn't like this. We don't get happiness tied up in neat packages. At least I don't. For me, it's rare and usually so flimsy that it has to be figured out, rather like a difficult mathematical equation. But you . . . I didn't even pray to meet you, because it was such a long shot."

A grin spread over his face. "Trust me, sweetheart, a long shot's better than no shot. Right? Let's give it a chance."

Before she could answer, the waitress arrived with their orders. He said the grace, surprising her. "Can you arrange it so that we can spend either Saturday or Sunday afternoon and evening together next week? Sunday would be better, because you would have gotten your assignments out of the way. If you have written homework, why not dictate it, insert it into the computer, edit it, and print it out, saving time with homework?"

"I would, but I don't have a suitable recorder."

He stopped eating. "Then we'll find other ways in which to ease your burden. I definitely don't plan to let weeks go by without seeing you. He pried a mussel out of its shell and ate it. "Kendra, this is really good stuff."

"It sure is. I was thinking of asking the waitress if that happy chef would give me the recipe."

"He's Italian, and he takes his reputation as a chef seriously. That means he is not going to create competition for himself."

"In other words, don't expect success."

"Don't ask, is what I was thinking."

"Well, I can't make this cioppino, but I could make this wonderful bread . . . provided I had a brick oven, that is."

Both of them refused dessert. "I'll have an espresso, though," she said.

He appraised her appreciatively. "So will I."

Later, he parked in front of the co-op building in which she owned and cut the motor. Something told her to wait until he walked around and opened the door for her. Doing so made her uncomfortable, but she sat there. He opened the door, reached in to unfasten her seat belt and help her out, looked at her face, and frowned. To her amazement, he closed one eye, the frown disappeared and a smile altered the contours of his face. Then, he laughed and laughed.

"Do whatever the hell you like," he said. "I don't enjoy making you miserable." He stepped back and allowed her to unfasten her own seat belt, get out of the car as best she could, and close the door.

"I'm sorry, Sam, but I honestly have never liked women who expect men to toady to them, to kill themselves making the woman's life queenly. That's why most survivors of marriage are women."

"I'm not going to question your logic, but I will certainly check your facts. If you're wrong, you will hereafter stay in that seat until I walk around, open the door, unhook your seat belt, and assist you in getting out."

She couldn't help laughing, although she suspected that he was serious. "It's a deal."

"Good. You can start right away to look for statistics on how this problem stacks up when both the man and the woman work eight hours a day in paid jobs. If men's death rates aren't lower than the rates of men in similar jobs and whose wives don't work, you're it."

"That won't be proof positive," she countered, "but I'll take it as the answer. Shake?"

He ignored her outstretched hand. "Come on, woman. I'm taking you to your door and leaving you there while I'm still ahead. I'll call you tomorrow morning at a quarter of eight."

At her door, he gazed down at her with such intensity that shivers raced up and down her arms.

"You're very special, Kendra. Good night," he said, surprising her with the seriousness of his mien. He opened the door with her key, handed it to her, and left.

Chapter Five

Sam walked away from Kendra's apartment door deep in thought. If he'd done what he'd felt like doing, he'd probably have sent her into shock. It had been a good ten years since he wanted a woman with the intensity that he wanted her. Not for anything would he have gone into her apartment.

After a lifetime of thinking through every step, plotting every move, and shoving aside any- and everything that didn't fit the mold of his ideals, he'd stepped in the quicksand of Kendra Richards's personality. What was more, he expected to be there for a while. And he couldn't say he was unhappy about it, either. He'd spent with her one of the most pleasant, most comfortable evenings in memory. But he knew that what he saw of her and what he'd heard her say merely scratched the surface of Kendra Richards.

When she wrote that letter to the *Post*, she'd been seeking a way out of her own dilemma. The woman about whom she wrote was obviously her own mother, and nothing would make him believe otherwise. Oh yes, and she was that "child." He hadn't brought up that matter when they were alone, because he didn't want to ruin the evening, and he didn't want to give the impression that he judged her. Indeed, any person who'd gotten as far in life as Kendra had, in spite of such a mother, could boast of his full admiration and respect.

He settled into his Buick Enclave, ignited the engine, and headed for Appleton Street, not too many blocks north of Kendra's apartment on Woodley Road.

"I've got some thinking to do," he told himself, and then laughed. Thinking be damned. He either accepted it and cultivated it to find out what it could mean to both of them, or walked away. He doubted he'd succeed easily in dropping the relationship. It had a preordained quality, and though he was neither overly religious nor superstitious, he had a feeling that she was for him.

His cell phone rang, but he didn't answer it, because he didn't use it while he drove. He parked in the garage beneath the condominium building in which he lived, took the elevator to the ninth floor, and was soon inside his two-bedroom, den, living room, kitchen, and dining room apartment. He'd bought it with an eye to marrying Giselda Darden. But that was another story, one that he refused to unearth.

He checked his cell phone, saw that the call was from his father, made himself comfortable, and telephoned Jethro Hayes, who lived in Alexandria, Virginia.

"Hi, Dad. You called me?"

"Yes I did. You usually call me every Sunday. You hadn't called today, so I was checking to see if you were all right. No problem, and especially not if you were out with a nice girl."

Hmm. This was one man you couldn't fool. "Did you catch the radio show this evening?"

"I did indeed. You were articulate as usual. I've heard Prill before. What's she like?"

"Why? You want to meet her? I can certainly arrange it."

"I think we met about twenty years ago, but at the time, we were both married. So . . . well, you know."

"She hasn't been married for quite a while, I don't think. Maybe I'd better have a dinner party. Lettie's always after me to give her a reason to cook."

"Nice idea."

Coming from his father, that was tantamount to saying, please hurry up and do it. "I'll make a note of that," Sam told him. "I'd rather plan it for a Saturday or, if necessary, Sunday evening."

"Any time is good for me."

Well. I'll be damned. Who'd have thought it? To his father, he said, "What do you want Lettie to cook?"

"Anything she cooks is good. The food won't be my main interest."

He didn't laugh, but it cost him not to. "Thanks for straightening me out. How'd you like the program?"

"It was one of Unger's better offerings. That Richards woman has a beautiful, soothing voice. If she looks like she sounds, she must be a knockout."

"She looks like she sounds, and she is definitely a knockout."

"Really? Are we getting close to the reason I didn't receive a call from you tonight?"

"You could say that."

"Well, well! I hope you're going to invite her to the dinner party along with Edwina Prill."

"I'll ask her, but you must remember that I met her this afternoon for the first time."

"Don't worry. I'll remember that you've just met her. But I'm curious. You don't usually veer from your routine commitments, and that's another reason why I want to meet her."

"I hope you're not saying that I'm inflexible."

"I definitely am not. If you were, I'd pity you. I'm saying that for you, a promise or an obligation is sacrosanct, as it should be. Did you have dinner with Ms. Richards because she's intelligent and affable or because you're attracted to her?"

"All of those."

"Interesting. I hope you arrange that dinner soon."

"I'll do my best, but I'd like to make it convenient for Kendra."

"Any special reason why that may prove difficult?"

"She's in her junior year at Howard, and she works at night as a disc jockey at radio station WAMA."

"How old is she, for goodness' sake?"

Sam treated his father to a hearty laugh. "She's thirty-two."

"All right. For a minute, I thought you may have become attracted to a teenager. Just joking. If you have time, call me for lunch."

"I'll do that, Dad. Have a pleasant night's rest."

He hung up, slid down to the floor, maneuvered himself into the lotus position, and closed his eyes. Edwina Prill? His dad once wanted Edwina Prill? The world wasn't only small, it was damned crazy. He got ready for bed, crawled in, and told himself to sleep. But instead, thoughts of the life Kendra must have suffered with an uncaring and unfeeling mother plagued him. What kind of woman could do the things reported in Kendra's letter, and what impact would it have on that woman's daughter?

He awakened more tired than when he went to bed. And both his common sense and his professional training told him that he shouldn't wait too long before he discussed with Kendra her relationship with her mother.

To Kendra's mother, it was not she who represented the problem. She meant to get even with Kendra for letting her stay in jail with common criminals. She didn't expect more from her brother, Ed. But Kendra was going to rue the day she turned her back on her.

"I'm in no hurry," she said to herself as she sat in her kitchen mending a half-slip. Imagine Ginny Hunter mending something that should be pitched into the trash. She got up, went into her bedroom, picked up the land-line phone, and dialed a friend, one on whom she'd spent a good deal of money.

"Hi, Arlena. I'm so bored I could die. How about going to Rooter's in time for happy hour."

"Great. You want us to meet there?"

Arlena's eagerness suggested that she expected Ginny to pay. *But I got news for you, sistah, I always pay every place we go. This time, the bill will be on you, and I intend to put it down.*

"Good," Ginny said. "Meet you there at five. And bring some money, 'cause I won't have any till Friday when I get paid." She thought she heard Arlena gasp, but it was time that deadbeat spent some of her own money.

Feeling both vulnerable and reckless, Ginny put on the red woolen dress that exposed enough cleavage to assure her that if Arlena didn't pay her bill, some man at the bar would. She added a pair of fishnet stockings and five-inch-heel shoes.

"I may be fifty-two," she preened, "but I can still pin the tail on the donkey."

At five o'clock, she stepped into Rooter's and saw Arlena leaning against the bar talking to a man. *Hmm. She works faster than I thought. I'll have to find another woman to slum around with.* In order not to be the second woman in a threesome, she decided to talk with the first man who indicated that he wanted company.

"I haven't seen you in here before," the bartender, a reasonably attractive man of about forty, said to Ginny. "You live around here?"

"About five blocks. I'm on Kalorama Road. When did you start working here?"

"A couple of weeks ago. This place has the most loyal regulars of any bar I ever worked. But this is the first evening you been in here." Of course it was; she'd spent the three previous weeks in jail.

"How do you know that?"

"I would have remembered you, lady. What are you drinking?"

"Margarita. The original."

"Lime only," he said. "You got it."

He put the drink in front of her. "Don't drink too many of these things. I like my women cold sober."

She gazed into his eyes for a long time and then pushed the drink back to him. "Make it a tonic on ice with a twist of lime."

He nodded, understanding her perfectly. "It's on me."

Tonic water was the last thing she wanted, but it served her purpose, so she sipped. She didn't care for the nuts and trail mix in front of her, so she ordered some miniature quiche, each one not much bigger than a thumbnail. To her surprise, the bartender said, "You're not only an eyeful, you've got class. Plenty of it. I get off at eleven. Are you still awake?"

She chewed with care and let him wait, giving him the impression that she was both weighing his suggestion and mindful of her decision. She finished her third quiche, dabbed at the corners of her mouth with a paper napkin, and said, "Not as a rule."

"What about tonight?"

With her facial expression, she conveyed to him the idea that he was being scrutinized for more than the width of his chest. "I can manage to stay awake, considering what I'm anticipating." Slowly, she ran the tip of her tongue over her top lip and then her bottom one. "Yeah. I can stay awake for that. I wouldn't even be able to sleep."

He stared at her so intensely that she began to wonder if she'd overdone it. Then, proving that he could equal or better her as a player, he half smiled and said, "Just be sure you get some rest."

Figuring that she'd better quit while she was ahead, she fumbled in her pocketbook as if searching for money, until she heard him say, "Forget the money. See you later." She didn't say thanks, but wrote her address and phone number on a napkin, pushed the napkin in his direction, and got up.

She approached Arlena, who, to Ginny's surprise and irritation, was still deep in conversation with the man she'd seen her with earlier when she first entered the bar, a man who appeared to be of a more appropriate age for Arlena than the bartender was for Ginny. The bartender. What the hell was his name? Her shoulder jerked up in a shrug. She hadn't asked him, and he hadn't told her.

"See you another time, Arlena," she said, as she passed her friend, knowing that Arlena had her evening cut out for her and that the woman welcomed the opportunity to avoid paying for Ginny's drink. Oh, but she would pay. Arlena owed her plenty.

The sound of an alarm clock awakened Ginny at two o'clock the following morning. She tried to sit up and turn off the offending thing, but the weight of an arm across her belly hampered her movements. "What's that noise?" she asked the man sleeping beside her as the ringing continued.

"Sorry," he said after a few minutes. "That's my watch." He turned it off.

Angry and suspicious, she asked him, "Why do you need an alarm clock? You said you're not married. So what's the rush?"

"Take it easy, Ginny. I live in Columbia, Maryland, and a man will be there at nine in the morning to cover the pipes in the basement of my house."

"You own a house, and you're not married? Is that what you're telling me?"

"Right, and I'm thirty-six years old, work ten hours a day, six days a week, and don't answer to anybody."

"Well, 'scuse me."

He got out of bed. "You throw a great party, but let's get this straight. I punch a clock at Rooter's, and I'm well paid for it, but nowhere else and for nobody. If you can handle that, I'll see you tonight. Otherwise, it's been nice."

She didn't like the sound of that. Sex was easy to get; if the guy didn't know what he was doing, she delighted in teaching him. And she liked strong men, but tough guys didn't appeal to her. She wouldn't go to bed with a man unless she figured she could handle him. But this one was a pistol. The problem was, he knew it.

"Did you tell me the truth when you said your name was Asareel?" she asked him, figuring that was a reasonable question.

He fingered the stubble on his cheeks as if deciding whether to answer her. Then he said, "I don't lie to anybody about anything, babe. My mother loved the sound of that word. She combined two names of old friends, but I don't know who they were. Everybody calls me Asa. I gotta get moving, See you tonight."

"What if I'm busy?" she asked, testing him.

He didn't turn his head, but looked at her from the corner of his eye. "You aren't going to be busy. If you get your kicks from variety, I can certainly provide that, but you're not getting it on with any man but me. Get it?"

Figuring that she wouldn't get another chance to let him know she didn't take stuff from a man, and still keep him, she slid out of bed, wrapped herself in her pink peignoir, walked over, and caressed his chest with both hands.

"Honey, tough doesn't cut it with me. Nice and gentle like you were last night, and baby, you get whatever you want whenever you want it and just the way you like it." From his facial expression, she couldn't figure out his reaction.

"I'll be here tonight as soon as I get off. Cook something. I get tired of sandwiches and junk food."

"Honey," she began, resorting to her old line, "I don't even cook for me. I never learned, and I don't own a cookbook. Stop by a takeout place and get enough for both of us."

He stared at her. "You and I are going to have an under-standing. Or this is not going to work. A seven-year-old can fry chicken. What do I want with a woman who can't cook? I can teach any female past puberty how to please me." He zipped up his leather jacket, and as he headed for the door, he threw over his shoulder, "See you tonight."

"Now what?" Ginny asked herself after she locked the door. This brother was used to having women fawn over him and worship at his feet. "I'm not doing that. Not me." Minutes later, remembering the previous night, she said aloud, "But Lord, he can put it down. Hell, if sucking his toes would get him going, I'd suck his toes."

So at eleven-thirty that night, the smell of chicken and dumplings perfumed Ginny's kitchen, and if Angela's recipe and step-by-step advice didn't produce a first-class dish, she would repay the woman for her treachery in giving her a lousy recipe. She looked at herself in the hall mirror and wished she were twenty years younger. If she were, she wouldn't be cooking chicken or anything else. Men like Asa didn't appear every day, and she meant to keep him for as long as it suited her.

Asa walked into her apartment, and it did not escape her that he sniffed as soon as she opened the door.

"Hi. I see you've been taking cooking lessons. Good girl."

She didn't offer to hug him. If he wanted a kiss, he'd have to make the first move. "A hungry man isn't worth two cents in bed or out of it, so I'm looking after my own interests," she said, hoping to give him the impression that she had cooked for him only to ensure her own pleasure.

"What kind of work do you do?" he asked, surprising her, as he dropped his jacket on the back of a chair and fol-lowed her to the kitchen.

"I work sometimes when I get bored," she said, telling a lie, "and then, I'm a beauty consultant."

He opened the pot, sniffed, and smiled. "How'd you know I love this stuff?" he asked, as if pleased with himself.

She didn't plan for him to feel as if she was giving him special treatment. "First time I meet a man who doesn't like chicken and dumplings, I'll know I'm on Mars."

"Okay, if that's the way you want it," he said, reading her correctly. He opened an overhead cabinet, got a plate, served himself, sat down, and ate.

Kendra had just begun her second cup of coffee that morning when her house phone rang. She checked the ID screen, didn't recognize the phone number, and was about to ignore the call when she remembered that she didn't know Sam's phone number.

"Hello. This is Kendra."

"And this is Sam. I hope you had a restful night."

"I rested beautifully after I got to sleep."

"Kendra, I promised my dad that he could have dinner at my place next Saturday or Sunday evening. Which evening is better for you? You can see where I live, and if you think you need a chaperone, who'd be a better one than my dad?"

His laughter wrapped around her like warm sunshine on an early April morning. "Are you sure I'm the one who'd want a chaperone?"

"Touché. You'll get a chance to meet my father in an informal setting, and maybe you'll be more secure in whatever you feel for me."

She liked his style, although she wondered if he'd planned the occasion precisely so that his dad could check her out. "I'd love to see you in your home environment and to meet your father."

"You aren't bubbling with enthusiasm about this."

She wasn't and she was not going to pretend. "That's true, but I want to meet him, because he'll help me to understand you quicker than you will."

"What do you mean?" Did she sense a bit of hostility in his tone?

"I'll get from him the kind of home training you received. Am I right?"

"Absolutely," he said, apparently backing away from his negative attitude. "And it won't take half an hour, either."

She did not want to continue talking about his father. She wanted some evidence that he was anxious to see her. "What time Saturday?"

"I'd like to come to your place for you at six-thirty. I'm on Appleton, a ten minute drive from you. By the way, you'll see Edwina Prill here."

Kendra hoped that he didn't hear her gasp. She wouldn't have thought that Sam and Edwina socialized, but there was a lot that she didn't know about Sam Hayes.

Saturday evening arrived, and Sam rang Kendra's doorbell at six-thirty. When she opened the door, he greeted her with, "You really are one good-looking woman. You look . . . well, stunning."

"Stunning in a ten-year-old bell-bottom dress?" she asked him.

"It looks new to me. I don't care how old it is. This dress was designed for you."

"Thank you. I wanted to look nice for your father."

"For my *father!* I'm not playing second fiddle to him. What about me? I'll be there, too."

"He's getting the respect due him as your father," she said, with a hand on his arm, "but you're the man."

A grin lit his whole face. "Keep it up. That's what I like to hear."

They walked to the elevator with his arm snugly around her waist. When they were seated in his Buick, he held her hand, squeezed it gently, and then drove off.

At his house, he hung her coat in his foyer closet, and immediately the doorbell rang. Her heart skipped several beats and then seemed to drop to the bottom of her belly. As if he'd received a signal as to her sudden anxiety, he leaned down and kissed her mouth, electrifying and disconcerting her. But as if he'd done nothing of importance, he turned around and opened the door.

"Hi, Dad. How are you?"

His father embraced him, silently telling him that, as always, his only son could count on him. "Dad, this is Kendra Richards. Kendra, this is my father, attorney Jethro Hayes."

He watched his father closely, for his demeanor would reflect his thoughts and attitude more accurately than his usually carefully chosen words.

A smile altered the contours of Jethro's face, and his white teeth sparkled as he extended his right hand to Kendra. "I'm happy to meet you, Kendra. In fact, I've had a hard time waiting for Saturday to get here."

"Thank you, sir. From the time Sam told me you'd be here, I've been scared to death that Saturday *would* come."

Jethro laid his head back and enjoyed a deep, throaty laugh. "Never waste anxiety. Life gives you too many opportunities to put it to good use." He looked at Sam and winked.

Sam released a long breath and let himself relax. "You two go in the living room and find a seat while I . . ." The doorbell rang, and he knew that his father was about to face a moment of truth when, after many years, he would see Edwina Prill and judge whether what he felt for her so long ago had survived. He opened the door, intending to tell Edwina that his dinner guests would consist of her, Kendra, and his father.

His eyebrows shot up. Who was this elegant and feminine woman in spike heels, and with her hair loose below her shoulders. "Hi, Edwina. I'm glad you could come."

"Thank you for inviting me. Is . . . uh . . . is your father here?"

"Yes. He just walked in."

Although he'd told her that he'd invited his father, he

hadn't mentioned his dad's name. He hung her coat and walked with her to the living room. As they entered the room, Jethro stood and walked toward them.

"Hello, Edwina," Jethro said, extending his hand. "It's good to see you after all these years."

"Yes, it is. I've been out of my mind ever since Sam told me you'd be here. You've hardly changed."

Jethro didn't smile. "You've changed, but you're more beautiful."

Sam stopped gaping and looked at Edwina as if seeing her for the first time. "Until I was speaking with my dad after the radio program last Sunday, I had no idea that you two knew each other."

At Jethro's urging, Edwina sat close to him. "I never told you, though I knew you had to be Jethro's son. You look exactly as he did twenty years ago. I knew him then, but only for a brief afternoon."

Awed, Sam shook his head. "Really?"

"Yes indeed," Edwina said. "I didn't think he'd recognize me as a blonde. I was born a redhead."

"I'd recognize you if you dyed your hair green," Jethro said. "But you ought to be able to ease it back to red."

Sam had never heard Edwina laugh aloud, though he'd been in her presence on numerous social occasions as well as at professional events. Her laugh had the sound of a coloratura at her peak.

"If it's worth my while, I can definitely do that," she said.

Sam could hardly believe his eyes. Stiff and always professional, Dr. Edwina Prill was flirting with his dad. He went to the kitchen thinking that he needed to focus on Kendra and not on Edwina and his father. Jethro was way ahead of the game, and Sam had barely begun with Kendra.

Lettie, his cook and housekeeper, met him at the kitchen door. "Is everybody here? I'm going to serve some hors d'oeuvres right now. Dinner'll be ready in about twenty minutes. Was that your sweetie pie who came in with you? I caught a glimpse of her, and I sure hope she's as nice a person as she is pretty."

"Thanks, Lettie." He patted her affectionately on her shoulder. "When you finish one of your monologues, I'm always out of breath. Yes, we're all here, and the woman who came in with me is my date."

"I don't know why I'd ask. You're a genius at talking without saying anything." She brushed something off the lapel of his jacket. "People will think I don't look after you properly."

He humored her as he usually did when she treated him the way she treated her grandchildren. Years earlier, she had retired from teaching in a rural Alabama school without a pension and was forced to find, at the age of sixty, a job as a housekeeper.

"I don't know how anybody could think that. You do everything for me but part my hair," he said, and grinned to soften the brunt of the remark. He didn't feel guilty, because she knew he loved her.

She reflected that, when she lowered her lashes and smiled. "Oh, you go 'way from here, Mr. Sam. I do declare." She placed in a tray tiny broiled bacon-wrapped liver kabobs and arranged among them grilled jalapeño-wrapped jumbo shrimp.

"I'll take that in," he said, and reached for the tray.

However, Lettie was as conscious of propriety as she was of status in refusing to call him Sam. "And have 'em thinking you're the cook? No, sir. You bring whatever glasses you want to use." After six years, he'd grown comfortable with Lettie. She was devoted to him, and he cherished her.

"The glasses are at the bar. I'll get some ice."

In the living room, Sam introduced Lettie to his women guests and enjoyed a good laugh when, seeing Edwina sitting so close to Jethro, Lettie didn't hang on to Jethro as she usually did. Back in the kitchen, Lettie met Sam with both hands on her hips.

"What's Mr. Hayes doing with that blond woman? Isn't she white? We don't have enough good-looking black women that he can't find one?"

Sam lifted first one shoulder and then the other in quick successive shrugs. "Lettie, as far as I know, she's white. Now, your hair is almost naturally straight, so one of your recent ancestors, probably one or two grandparents, was either white, Native American, or some of both. Right?"

"Yeah. But that white man never acknowledged my grandmother. And one of my grandfathers was a Creek Indian, or so they say, Mr. Sam, but that does not make it a good thing."

"At least you know two personal cases in which race did not stand in the way of physical attraction. Nature doesn't give a hoot about peoples' prejudices."

She was not convinced. "If you say so, Mr. Sam." He didn't try to convince her. She was seventy years old and grew up in the era of Alabama lynchings.

When Sam returned to his guests, his father had served the drinks. He took a seat on the sofa beside Kendra and, as much as he longed to envelope her in his arms, he didn't. "What are you drinking?" he asked her.

"Your dad suggested that I try a vodka comet. I like it. I can hardly taste the vodka."

"He probably didn't put much in it, but it's there." She smiled, and his belly turned somersaults. The heck with propriety. He put his arm around her and hugged her. But he couldn't get his thoughts off his father and Edwina.

He managed to get Edwina's attention. "Where did you meet my dad?"

She smiled as if savoring a pleasant memory. "In court. I was a witness for the district attorney. Jethro got pretty hot with me, questioned my integrity, and almost lost his temper. After the jury gave him his comeuppance, he met me in the courthouse hallway, apologized, and invited me to lunch. I didn't see him in person from that afternoon until tonight, but I never forgot him." She looked at Jethro and lowered her lashes as if embarrassed.

Sam tried to relieve her of the moment's discomfort by letting her know that he did not disapprove of a relationship between her and his father. "This is fantastic," he said. "You and I have known each other for at least seven years, and I never dreamed that you knew my dad."

"I always knew you were his son. How'd you find out that he knew me?"

"He heard the program last Sunday and told me he wanted to see you and to meet Kendra."

"Interesting. I thought Sunday that you and Kendra had something going, so I wasn't surprised to see her here tonight."

Sam glanced at Kendra before staring at Edwina. "You did? I met Kendra Sunday when I walked into that radio station. It's true that she hit me with the force of a sledge-hammer, but I didn't realize it was so obvious."

Lettie walked in, putting an end at least temporarily to that conversation. "Dinner's ready, Mr. Sam."

"Thanks, Lettie."

They made their way through a seven-course gourmet meal that consisted of smoked salmon pâté, cream of mushroom soup, filet mignon with marsala wine sauce, lemon roasted potatoes, asparagus, green salad, and assorted cheeses. When Lettie presented the dessert, crystal bowls of crème Courvoisier, Jethro joshed, "Lettie, if I had known you could turn out this kind of meal, I'd have stolen you from Sam long ago."

Later, as they sat in the living room, sipping liqueurs and espresso, Sam reflected that Kendra seemed perfect in his environment. But the thought that she was the child to whom she referred in her letter to the *Post* cast a pall over what had been for him a perfect evening. It was also the first time that his sprawling apartment had seemed truly like home. He looked at Kendra and found her watching him before she quickly glanced away, but he had seen her feelings of affection and more for him mirrored in her eyes. Damn the luck. If he were alone with her, he'd light her fire.

Jethro went to the kitchen and thanked Lettie for the dinner. "It was wonderful. Your talents are underused," he told her.

"That's what I tell Mr. Sam. It won't hurt him a bit to have nice company like tonight once in a while. I'll lose my touch."

"Stay after him," Jethro said. "He loves to eat."

Sam couldn't resist following his father to the kitchen. "Are you glad to see her again?"

A frown marred Jethro's face as he looked at his son. "Where've you been all evening? You mean you can't tell? I was enchanted with her back then, but it gave me a guilty feeling, and by sheer willpower, I closed my eyes and my heart to it. I loved your mother, and I refused to let demon libido ruin our lives. But I never forgot her; I simply lived with it."

"But after Mom died, you could have found Edwina. Why didn't you?"

"I didn't know that she wasn't still married, and I didn't feel up to dealing with fresh feelings that I'd have to get over later."

Sam moved closer and patted his father on the shoulder. "I'll be damned. You're quite a man."

They returned to the living room, and Jethro shook hands with Kendra. "I'm looking forward to seeing you again and again." Then, he walked over to Edwina and grasped her hand. "I'd like to leave now. May I take you home?"

She stood at once. "Thank you. I'd like that." She looked at Kendra. "Good-bye. I hope to see you again soon."

Sam walked with them to the door, waited while Jethro

got them into their coats, and then he said, "I'm happy for both of you, and I hope this is the beginning of something good."

"Thank you," they responded in unison, and Jethro added, "If I'm lucky, it's a dream come true."

Sam left them at the door, shaking his head in bemusement as he went back to Kendra. Lettie had left, and his libido kicked up the minute he realized that he and Kendra were alone. When he reached her, he saw that her facial expression reflected her awareness of that fact.

"I've had a wonderful visit, and I'm glad I met your father. It's . . . I think I'd better be going."

He wondered if she didn't trust him or whether she couldn't rely on herself to follow the dictates of her own mind. "We'll leave as soon as you're ready," he told her, "but we've hardly had a minute to ourselves. I've been trying to adjust to my dad with Edwina, and that is not easy."

"Because she's white?"

"Oh no, not that. I grant him the right to a woman of his choice, and I demand the same for myself. Because she's Edwina. I've known the professional, always businesslike woman, but this Edwina was as soft as a kitten. Talk about a chameleon!"

"It was a dramatic change, all right," Kendra said, "but I liked this soft Edwina. She wants your father, and she's letting him see her without the armor of her Ph.D. Do you think it will work out?"

"I'll bet on my dad any day. What did you think of him?"

She leaned her head against his shoulder and stroked the back of his hand. "Sam, you know your father is an impressive man. He's also handsome and self-possessed, and . . . well, he's also gentle. I like that. In fact, I like him. You resemble him a great deal."

"Thanks. I hope I'm as much of a man as he is. When will we see each other again?"

"I'll study until around three tomorrow."

He played with the fingers of her left hand. "And after that?"

"Do you really want to see me again tomorrow?"

He wanted to shake some sense into her, but he settled for placing a hand on each of her shoulders and looking her in the eye. "I want to see you as often as I can and for as long as possible, and don't tell me that surprises you. I'm strongly attracted to you, and I want you. That's normal."

"I know that," she said. "Can we go?"

He stood, grasped her hand, and walked with her to the foyer. After helping her into her coat, he buttoned it. "The next time you're here, I'll give you a tour of the place."

"I like what I've seen."

He stared down at her for a few seconds, then leaned over and kissed her cheek. "You make the nicest promises," she said with a wicked glint in her eyes.

He wasn't sure he liked that, and he didn't know the source of his uncertainty. "Are you laughing at me, Kendra?"

A grin formed around her lips. "Kind of."

"What's amusing you? Let me in on it so I can laugh."

The grin became a laugh. "I'm not trying to ring your bell," she said, seeming to plead for his understanding. When she managed to control the laughter, she said, "It's . . . you're trying so hard not to give me the wrong impression. If I didn't trust you, Sam, I definitely would not be here." She eased her arm through his. "Come on. Let's go."

He locked the door, and with her hand snug in his, walked down the short hallway to the elevator. He stopped himself as he was about to whistle a song from the summer of his sexual awakening. He rarely whistled and never in a public place, but at the moment he had a need to express the gaiety and the freedom that he felt. He couldn't explain the feeling, but he knew it sprang from the hand he held, from the evening that was about to end, and from the way he hoped it would end.

Chapter Six

Sam parked a few doors down from the apartment building in which Kendra lived, helped her out of the car, closed the door and—

"You got change for a cup of coffee, buddy?"

Sam swung around. He hadn't seen the man approach, and he would have if he hadn't been so absorbed in what could happen when they got into Kendra's apartment. He took several steps backward and maneuvered so that Kendra was behind him.

"I don't have any change."

"Then give me your wallet."

Looking the man in the eye, he felt something hard at his right side.

"I've got a few dollars," Kendra said. "Just a minute till I find it." Sam could not imagine what her motive was, so he remained still and focused his attention on the man.

"If she's being funny, you'd better tell her to zip it while she can."

"Thank goodness, I found it." She stepped around Sam and extended her left hand in which she held several bills.

The thief grabbed the money. "What else you got in there? *Ow!*" he yelled, jumping up and down, rubbing his eyes and screaming in discomfort.

"What the hell happened?' Sam asked Kendra, who was calmly dialing a number on her cell phone.

"Don't worry. He'll be useless for a good while. I'm calling the cops."

Sam stared down at the man, who writhed on the pavement with an open switchblade knife lying beside him. After dealing with the police, who arrived within minutes, they continued to Kendra's apartment.

Kendra had a feeling of bravery while confronting the man, but as they approached her apartment, she became aware that Sam hadn't said another word and that he was not holding her hand.

He took her key, opened the door, and closed it behind them. In the dimly lighted foyer, he turned to her, and she saw from his demeanor that kissing her or any other affectionate exchange with her was not on his mind.

Staring into her face without an iota of warmth in his expression, he said, "You're going to tell me why you're carrying pepper spray on a date with me."

So that was it. She had offended his masculine pride. "My father meets me at night when I get off from work. He gave me this a few nights ago to use in case he couldn't meet me some time and I had a problem such as we had tonight. He made me promise never to take it out of my pocketbook. My money was in my coat pocket, but I had to fish around in my pocketbook to find the pepper spray. I saw the movement of his hands and, after years of living in high-crime neighborhoods, I knew he'd reached for either a gun or a knife."

He walked with her into her living room. "Come over here and let's sit down. I need to digest this thing. I didn't expect that in this neighborhood, but I suppose I should have. Thieves know where to get the bigger haul, and it isn't from the poor. You upset me when you walked up to that man holding out that money. My first thought was that I couldn't protect you, and that he might use you for a hostage. I was horrified."

She didn't want him to dwell on it. She knew that most men prided themselves on their ability to protect their woman and she'd taken that role from him.

"Can we put it behind us, Sam? If he had hurt you, I don't think I would ever have gotten over it. I was afraid, but I would never stand by like a shrinking violet and watch anyone hurt you. I couldn't do that."

He leaned against the back of the sofa and closed his eyes. "This has been a very eventful night, filled with surprises."

"Bad ones?"

"Except for the incident with that unfortunate thief, I certainly wouldn't say bad."

"Does this mean you aren't going to kiss me tonight? I mean *kiss me.* Not one of your safe little cheek smacks."

Laughter poured out of him, and she thanked God that he could laugh about it.

"You are precious, Kendra, more precious than you could realize. Walk with me to the door."

He reached for her hand and, needing the physical connection to him, she leaned into him in a bodily caress and rested her head against his shoulder. He slid his arm around her and turned her to face him.

"I told you, Kendra, that I don't want to make any mistakes with you. That doesn't mean I don't want you. God knows I do. Kiss me?" Her hands moved past the lapels of his jacket to his shoulders, and as she gazed up at him, her eyes must have portrayed her vulnerability and her trust in him, for a strange turbulence leaped into his eyes. He lowered his head.

She had thought that she wanted him to kiss her, but when she looked into his eyes, eyes that mirrored such tenderness and caring, everything changed. She knew for the first time in her life what it meant to need a man. And as if he saw and understood the change in her, he lifted her to him with an urgency that excited her and, with parted lips, she took him in. Feeling him inside of her, she clutched him to her in a frenzied passion. But when his hand pressed her buttocks, she stepped back.

He opened his arms to her. "It seems unreal, but I care deeply for you," he said.

"This is awful, and it's so wonderful," she said. "Considering the life I've had, this seems like something in a novel."

"Yes," he said. "It seems to have an agenda of its own. When we meet tomorrow, I want us to talk. We're both in this deep, and we need to know more about each other. I'll be here tomorrow at four, and we can spend the afternoon and evening together if you're willing."

"I'd love that."

"Dress casually." His lips brushed hers sweetly and gently. She'd never felt so cherished, protected, and cared for. He gazed at her for a second. Then, he was gone.

Kendra didn't know whether to be happy or scared. Maybe it wasn't real and Sam Hayes had supernatural traits that drugged her into a hypnotic state whenever she was in his presence.

"I'm being silly thinking such things," she told herself. "I just haven't known a man who made me feel as he does. I'm going to stop second-guessing him and my feelings for him. After all, he's only a man." She made a pot of strong coffee, changed into comfortable clothes, and sat down to study.

At eight o'clock Sunday morning, four hours after Kendra went to bed, her phone rang, awakening her. She lifted the receiver, saw a blank ID screen, and said hello. Hearing no response, she said hello again and again. "Whoever you are, I don't like you. Not one bit." She slammed the receiver into its cradle. Ginny. No one else who knew her would do such a thing. "That woman causes me more pain than I'd have if she stabbed me."

* * *

Ginny was not thinking of the pain she caused her daughter or anyone else. Fate was chasing her and seemed to be closing in. She had decided that she wanted Asa on a more permanent basis than she had originally thought. But the brother considered himself king of the hill, a godsend to womankind, and he didn't do anything unless he wanted to. To make it worse, she had, at age fifty-two, sixteen years on him, and she knew she'd better do something and soon. Maybe Kendra would let her have a few hundred or a thousand if she could come up with a good story. She'd even offer to do Kendra's hair and manicure at no charge. Ginny Hunter was not going to stand on her feet all day, five days a week, working on a bunch of ridiculous women. Period. She dialed Kendra's phone number hoping to catch her before she went to church.

"Hello?"

Ginny opened her mouth to speak, remembered the agreement she'd signed with her brother, Ed, and hung up. As sure as she appeared before that judge for having broken the agreement, she'd go to jail, and she'd had it with jail. She hung up, sat down on a chair near her bed and, for the first time in her memory, tears cascaded down her cheeks until they wet her gown.

Damn Ed. Damn Kendra. Damn the whole bloody lot of them. She had to have some money, and she'd get it no matter what she had to do. She meant to keep Asa happy. He was not going to get away from her.

When Sam rang Kendra's doorbell precisely at four o'clock that Sunday afternoon, she answered the door wearing a pair of brown corduroy pants and a burnt-orange turtleneck sweater.

"Hi. You said dress casual," she said, in effect apologizing for her appearance.

He pressed a quick kiss to her lips and handed her a small package. "Hi. Did you manage to study?"

"I got a lot done. In fact, I caught up. What's this? Can I open it now?" She imagined that her eyes sparkled like those of a child at Christmas as she opened the package without waiting for his reply. "Sam! What's this? It looks like a recorder."

"That's what it's supposed to be. Now you can take notes almost anywhere, dictate your assignments, and let the computer print them on the screen. It's very handy, and it will save you a lot of time."

She pressed the recorder to her breasts, not so much because of its usefulness, but because he'd thought of her and wanted to make her life easier. Reminded suddenly of her rule about not accepting gifts from men, but wanting to keep it, and still holding the precious gift, she looked at him with a sad expression on her face. "I don't think you should be giving me presents, and I shouldn't accept this."

"You need it, Kendra. I couldn't offer to help pay your tuition, and I need to be there for you. Can't you accept such a small thing from me?"

His facial muscles worked furiously in what she realized was an effort to control his emotions. She'd hurt him. With her arms wrapped around his waist, she attempted to undue the damage.

"Sam, my father and my grandmother are the only people who ever gave me anything without expecting something in return. I'm sorry if I made you feel badly. I didn't want to."

"Will you keep it?"

"Yes." She hugged him. "Thanks. I love it."

"It's chilly outside, so perhaps you should put on a scarf and some gloves. I thought we'd drive over to Alexandria. There are nice places to walk and to explore, to eat and to watch people," he said with an apparent enthusiasm for the little things of life. "Would that be a waste of your time?" he asked, and she wondered if he was judging her.

"I don't consider the time I spend in your company a waste." Her chin went up when she said it.

"I love chili dogs, and I haven't had one in a long time. A tavern in the old town sells some of the best I've eaten. Could you eat that for dinner?"

She rested a hand on his arm. "You and I have surely led different lives, Sam. I've eaten hot dogs and coleslaw for dinner more times than I could ever count. You've never been poor, but I've never had money. My father has made certain that I didn't want for anything important. But until the last couple of years, he was poor. He owns and operates an upscale butcher shop now that caters to the moneyed classes, and he's doing well, but he's seen very hard times."

Sam didn't want to get into her background—for that was what he wanted to know about—until they were seated in a comfortable and quiet place. Who was she really, and what could she tell him that would enable him to understand her and to know whether he'd developed such strong feeling for the right woman?

He found a place to park and walked with her along Queen Street in Alexandria's "Old Town," enjoying the light breeze and the pleasant late-autumn Sunday. He stopped at an old building.

"Two decades before the Civil Rights movement, an African American attorney named Samuel Wilbert Tucker staged a sit-in here because African Americans couldn't use the library."

"Way back then? What happened?"

"The five men were arrested, but the case was dropped. A year later, Alexandria built a library for blacks. That was in 1940. Common decency in this country is a very recent thing. This town is replete with history of African Americans' journey from slavery to where we are today."

"Yeah, but some of it, like that horrible Bruin 'Negro

Jail'—where enslaved people were held while waiting to be purchased—fills me with hatred."

"I know," he said, easing his arm around her, "but bitterness is a festering sore that only hurts the one who is embittered. Let it go. This is where we eat," he said, opening the door of King's Tavern. "It's quiet and cozy, and we can talk." He guided her to a rear corner not far from a fireplace. "I like to sit here and watch the flames."

A waiter approached and gave them menus. "I'm having chili dogs and a bottle of Heineken beer. Have whatever you like."

"I want two chili dogs and some lemonade," Kendra told the waiter.

The waiter seemed skeptical. "Madam, the chili dogs are big."

"Thanks. I'll risk it."

The waiter brought their food at once, and to Sam's delight, she bit into a chili dog, closed her eyes, and moved her head from side to side as she enjoyed it.

Should he begin a serious conversation while they ate, or should he postpone it until they'd finished? She solved the question when she said, "This is fantastic, but think how good it would be if the chef got his beef from my dad."

"I gather you're very close to your father, because you speak of him often and with such pride. You've never mentioned your mother. Why is that? Isn't she living?"

She stopped chewing and swallowed with difficulty, or so it seemed to him. Instead of rescuing her with some meaningless words, he decided to say nothing and see how she'd handle it. She took a few sips of lemonade, put the glass down, and gave him a level look.

"I hate to shock you, Sam, and I hope this doesn't change your opinion of me. My mother does not love me, and I'm not one bit crazy about *her*. Any contact with her gives me pain, but she is oblivious to anybody's feelings but her own. My father divorced her when I was six. She didn't want to work, so she stayed home. And it was she whose job it was to write checks for the bills for utilities, house mortgage, car payments, etc. But she spent the money on herself and her friends, which my father discovered when he faced foreclosure on the mortgage, the utilities were cut off, and his car was repossessed. According to him, when confronted, she merely shrugged and said she should have married a man with money.

"I lived with my grandmother until she died when I was eleven. Thereafter, I lived with my mother until I went to college, though my father supported me. It was pure hell. She spent the money my father sent her for child support, on herself, including that for my clothing, everything. He finally opened an account at a clothing store with the stipulation that only I could shop on his account, and she tried to force me to buy things for her."

Sam hadn't thought it was so bad, but as he reflected on what he knew of her, she bore the marks of parental neglect. "How did you manage those first two years at Howard University?"

"I had a full four-year academic scholarship. My dad was paying my living expenses, but at the end of my first year at Howard University, Mama sued my father for increased child support, and he countersued for full custody, which he won. But that battle was so costly, that he didn't have money left to support me while I went to school. He kept me there for my sophomore year. Then, I dropped out, originally for a year, I thought, and went to work to save money for the next two years."

"I see. So the letter you wrote to the *Washington Post* was about you and your mother?"

"Yes. I thought you had guessed that. Anyway, I've been trying to find an opening to tell you. I had thought it presumptuous of me to assume that, after knowing me for such a short time, you'd be interested in that aspect of my life."

"I considered it a ninety-percent probability, but I couldn't be certain until you told me. You have no idea how much I admire you. It takes a strong and determined person to surmount the obstacles you've faced. Where are you now with your mother?"

"She leaves me alone right now because her brother demanded it and forced her to sign an affidavit to the effect that she wouldn't contact me by any means until after I've finished Howard. If she breaks the promise, he may let her go back to jail."

His eyes widened, and he was sure that he gaped. "Jail? What was she doing in jail?"

"Driving an unregistered car with a suspended license. She begged me to use my tuition money to bail her out, but this time I refused. My uncle bailed her out after letting her stay there for nearly a month. I was so close to getting back in school. Papa had just bought the apartment for me and filled my freezer with meat and said he'd meet me every night at eleven o'clock when I got off from work, but she was storming and raging because I wouldn't let her take it all from me.

"Not long ago, she told me that she got pregnant with me accidentally and didn't want to have me, but Papa forced her to do it. I think she's been making me pay ever since I was born."

"She told you that? I hope to hell I never meet her." Anger furled up in him, and he told himself to take a deep breath and calm down. "How have you managed to live with this . . . this constant destructiveness? I hurt for you."

"It's always been with me, Sam. I try not to think about her unless she contacts me, but, sometimes, when I need a friend, knowing that I can't count on *her* hurts."

As she said the words, he saw pain etched in her face, and the sparkle in her eyes dimmed. He took her hand and held it. "You can depend on me. Did your father remarry?"

"No. He's had a hard time paying off those debts and getting his business started, but he's doing well now. I wish he'd find someone who's loyal and kind to him. What about you? Do you have any siblings?"

"I wish I did have, but when I was born, the doctor advised my mother not to try to have anymore children. She died nine years ago."

"I hope you don't mind my asking this. Were you surprised that your dad had been attracted to Edwina?"

He had barely answered that question for himself. Drumming the fingers of his left hand on the table, he let a smile move over his face. "Surprised hardly covers it. He unloaded that one on me without a single preliminary. Funny thing is that she knew I was his son and never alluded to it. Amazing."

Kendra supported her chin with the palm of her hand and rested her elbow on the glass-top table. "Edwina meant business. I'm happy for her. For both of them."

Sam thought of the previous evening, of the wonder and joy of their being together and conceded, "Sure she does, and my dad means business, too. You'd better believe it." Considering the fire that he saw burning in both of them, it wouldn't surprise him if they'd spent the night together. And bully for them!

Kendra leaned toward him, stroking his fingers as she did so. "How would you feel about having her for a stepmother?"

Damn! What a wild idea!

"Whatever makes my dad happy will make me happy," he said truthfully. "He's a great guy. I've always come first with him, and it's time I took second place." His answer seemed to please her. "You liked my father a lot, didn't you? Mind if I ask why?"

She bunched her shoulders in a slight shrug. "Simple. He looks like you. He talks like you, and he acts like you. How could I not like him?"

For a moment, he stared at her. Then he couldn't contain the laughter. "I guess that puts me in my place."

"I think I ought to tell you something, Sam."

He leaned back in the chair and gave her his full attention. "Do I want to hear it?"

"That depends. I'm planning to enter the journalism school's competition for hard news reporting. We'll all be given the same assignment. There will be three prizes for overseas travel and study next semester. If I win, I want to go to Egypt or Italy." The cold hand of disappointment squeezed his heart, but he didn't want to discourage her.

"What about the language difficulty?"

"In Egypt, I could get along well enough without Arabic, since English is so widely spoken. I'm prepared to take a crash course in Italian."

"I'd suggest Rosetta Stone, but it can be expensive. It's also exactly what you need. I used it to learn German."

"That's a good idea. Thanks."

"How long would you be away?"

"Six weeks, and before leaving, I'd have to enroll in all my classes, and catch up before the end of the semester."

"And you'd do it, too. Think you'd miss me during those six weeks?"

"I'd miss you if I were away only one week."

"You deserve a kiss for that."

"I think I'd better make a list of the things I can do that will assure me of getting one of your mind-blowing kisses."

"Mind-blowing, huh? You only have to be close by. Incidentally, when it's convenient, I'd like to meet your father."

She seemed pensive for a moment. Then, a grin spread over her face and her eyes sparkled. "You sure? Papa believes in cutting to the chase. He'll ask you straight out what your intentions are."

"And you think that'll frighten me? I'll tell him straight out what my intentions are."

Her stare was worth good money. "You *would?* Maybe you should meet him for coffee at some place like Starbucks, when I'm not around."

She had the appearance of sincerity, so he decided to shake her up. "Which one of us don't you trust, your father or me?"

"If you're as candid as he is, I'd rather be somewhere else. Simple as that," she shot back.

He decided to let up. "Let's you and I meet him for supper one Saturday or Sunday evening."

"Okay, but Sunday would be better, because Saturday is a very busy day for him. I'll arrange it and let you know."

"Then that's settled. Good." He looked at his watch. "It's only eight o'clock, and I'm not ready to end the day. Want to go to Treasure Island and see the puppet theater? Last time I was there, the show was hilarious. The current play is a political satire."

"I'd love to, as long as they're bashing Republicans."

"Trust me, sweetheart, they spare nobody."

Shortly after they took their seats in the fourth row of the small theater, Kendra noticed that a man sitting on the aisle of the third row continuously glanced back at them. Eventually, he smiled at her. She averted her gaze and focused on the puppet named Jimmy, who raised his nose in disrespect for Ronald, his rich-thespian next-door neighbor. They sat on their respective back porches, talking across their fences.

"I never could abide no-good actors," Jimmy said in his rich southern drawl. "Anybody who's worth a dime can act. Nothing to it."

"I suppose you'd know," Ronald replied. "Trouble with you is that you did your acting while residing at 1600 Pennsylvania Avenue."

Jimmy shelled a peanut and rocked in his old-fashioned rocker. "At least I could act, friend," Jimmy said. "Nobody ever accused y'all of acting anywhere."

Ronald shook his head sadly. "You're a cruel man,

Brother Jimmy. At least I was a good enough actor to get elected twice."

"That's nothing to brag about, Brother Ronald. The same people who elected you twice also voted for vice president of this great country a fellow who couldn't spell potato."

"I know, Brother Jimmy, and that was a terrible shock to me. Let's go down to Jake's Tavern and down a couple of beers."

"I'd love to commune with you, brother, but two beers don't sit well with my conversion. How about a margarita? That seems fairly benign."

Ronald raised an eyebrow. "It's named for a woman, Brother Jimmy, and that ought to tell you it's lethal."

Jimmy released a long, tired sigh. "Maybe we'd better have our usual."

"You're right," Ronald said. "Alcohol and rheumatism are like oil and water. Why don't we go over to Zach's and get our usual decaf and scones?"

Sam's laughter mingled with that of others in the audience. Lost in the merriment, he draped his arm around Kendra and hugged her to him as if he'd done it regularly for years. "That little guy playing Jimmy is so funny," he said. "Imagine a puppet eating peanuts. Do you want to stay for the second act?"

Even if she hadn't been enjoying it, and she had, she wanted to stay just to be with him. She had never been to a puppet theater or seen any other live acting by professional actors, and the magic of it captivated her. During intermission, they drank coffee in a little bistro off the theater lobby.

"I was hoping I'd find you here, Sam." Kendra looked up and saw the man who had attempted to get her attention earlier. "Haven't seen you for a while. Who's this lovely lady?"

The smile vanished from Sam's face. "Ms. Richards, this is Leonard Chasten, a former classmate." She noticed the lack of warmth in Sam's voice and the absence of enthusiasm for the man's presence.

"Hello," she said, omitting the customary graciousness.

"Just my luck that you should be with this guy," Chasten said. "Women take to him like ants to sugar."

Kendra cast a censuring glance at the man, but she didn't share her thoughts. Sam was more than capable of handling the intruder. And he did. "Some other time, Chasten. As you can see, I'm very busy."

As if they had not been interrupted, he said to her, "It's all right with me if you don't want to stay for the rest of the show. Frankly, this intrusion has taken the fun out of it."

She understood that he wanted to leave, so she said, "I'm sorry. If you're ready to leave, so am I." He paid the bill, helped her into her coat, and, with an arm snug around her waist, they left. She noticed that Sam didn't look back, but with her peripheral vision, she saw Leonard Chasten standing with both hands on his hips not far from the table they had occupied. Hmm. So it was not Sam's first unpleasant experience with the man.

Outside, a brisk and refreshing breeze announced the early arrival of winter, and she tightened the collar of her jacket. "I would have left you in the lobby while I went for the car," Sam said, "but Chasten would have pounced like a cat on a mouse."

"I was about to suggest that we walk for a while," she said. "The sky is clear, and the moon is so beautiful, even if it does seem cold and lonely. This time of year, I like to stroll around Dupont Circle eating roasted chestnuts and window shopping. I'm not much of a shopper, and certainly not a compulsive one. Observing my mother at that turned me off shopping. But I like to look."

"I've got an idea. Would you like us to have a picnic at

Rock Creek Park next Sunday, provided of course that the weather permits? Maybe your dad could join us. I'll bring everything."

"That's a great idea. You bring everything but the meat. Papa will definitely bring that. Can you get a grill?"

"There are plenty of grills in the picnic area. Let me know whether your dad likes the idea."

"Look at that," she said in awe as little clouds seemed to chase the moon. "I know it's an illusion, but the moon seems to be running from the clouds."

"Watching the evening sky can use up a lot of your time," he said. "As a teenager, I spent a lot of time doing that." They got into his car, and he drove several blocks, double-parked at Timothy's, and asked her, "What kind of ice cream do you like?"

"Anything lemony, caramel, or black cherry."

He returned a few minutes later with lemon custard ice cream for her and strawberry for himself. "You hold these," he said. He drove on and after parking in front of the building in which she lived, he reached for the bag.

"Are we going to eat it here? Why can't we go inside and eat it in my apartment?"

"That's certainly better than eating it here. I wanted some ice cream, but I didn't want to impose on you."

Inside her apartment, she put the ice cream in bowls, and they sat together on her living room sofa, quietly eating. She finished hers first, and rested her head on his shoulder, because it seemed so right. He finished, took the glass bowls to the kitchen, and put them and the spoons in the dishwasher.

Sitting beside her with his arm around her, he was quiet for a while, and she waited for his cue. "You will encounter Chasten again, Kendra, because he and I frequent the same places, and we have some mutual friends. That's to be expected, since we were classmates throughout college. Morehouse is known as much for its arrogant men as for its leaders, and Chasten was an ass when he was a freshman. By the time he graduated, he'd become unbearable, at least to me. If you don't want his company, nothing short of rudeness will work."

"I gathered as much." She did not want to spend precious time talking about Leonard Chasten. "Oops! Did you call your father today? I forgot to call mine."

"I did, too. It's ten-twenty. I'll leave now, and you can make that call." He stood, extended his hand to help her up, and gazed down at her with such intensity that shivers plowed through her.

"Sam, you've got to stop doing this to me. When you look at me like—"

He locked her body to his, parted his lips over hers, and possessed her. "Walk with me to the door, and don't forget to ask your dad about next Sunday. This time with you has meant a lot to me. My first class is at ten tomorrow, so I'll call you at eight." His lips brushed hers. "Sleep well." With that, she was alone.

After taking a few minutes to calm her emotions, she dialed her father. "How are you, Papa?"

"I'm fine. I called you earlier, but I didn't leave a message. I hate talking to a machine. I'm glad to know you weren't at home on a Sunday evening. Today was beautiful, something special, but it's getting colder."

"Uh . . . Papa, I was out with a friend. He's real nice. Next Sunday, he and I are going to picnic in Rock Creek Park, and he told me to ask you if you'd join us."

"Did I hear you right? You met a guy who's willing to drag your old man on a date with you? Times have changed more drastically than I thought."

"I met his dad, so he wants to meet mine. I didn't know anyone who knew him, so he said if I met his dad, I'd be more comfortable with him."

"Are you?"

"I was already comfortable with him, and I was a nervous wreck till I met his father. I liked his dad a lot."

"All right. If he wants to meet me, you bet I want to meet him! What does this fellow do for a living?"

"He teaches at GW, and his father is a lawyer. They're both down-to-earth. You'll like Sam."

"Is that your fellow's name?"

"Yes, sir. Samuel Hayes."

"Say! He was on that radio program with you. So that's how you met. Okay. Sunday's a good day for me. If he's got a good grill, I'll bring along some porterhouse steaks, serrated knives, a bottle of red wine, and a six-pack. We'll have a feast. What time?"

"He didn't say. I'll let you know tomorrow when I get off from work."

"Right. I'll be there at midnight as usual."

"Thanks, Papa."

As faithful as the sunrise, Sam called at eight the next morning. "Papa said if you want to meet him, you bet he wants to meet you. He's bringing porterhouse steaks, serrated knives, a bottle of red wine, and a six-pack; I don't know what kind," Kendra told him.

"He likes beer?"

"He rarely drinks anything. I suggest you bring whatever you like to drink. What time shall we meet?"

"I'll be at your place around eleven. Is that okay?"

"Great. Kisses."

"Kisses to you, too. Talk later."

At school, she glanced at the bulletin board on her way to her class in Vocabulary Building and saw a notice that caused her to stop. She had two more days in which to apply for the reporting competition prize which, if she won, could mean six weeks in Egypt or Italy. Making a mental note to speak with Clifton Howell about getting leave from her job if she won, she rushed on to class.

It seemed to her that she rushed to school, rushed to work, rushed home, rushed to bed, and then got up hurrying to get in as much study as possible before rushing to school and starting the treadmill all over again. Six weeks in which to roam a country she'd never seen before could be a stress remover as well as an education.

She met Clifton Howell in the hallway as she rushed to her studio. "Good afternoon, Mr. Howell. I have to ask you something one day soon when you have time."

"One day soon when I have time? This is as good as any. What do you want to know?" Too bad! She hadn't planned how she'd ask him, so she said to herself, *Out with it*, and explained about the competition.

"I can find a temporary replacement for you," he said, giving her a steely look, "but what will your fans think? And what if the listeners decide that they prefer your replacement? Never throw away the ball just because you scored a goal. The game continues, and if you want to play, you'll still need a ball. Let me know what you decide."

Well. He couldn't have been more pointed. He liked her, but if the circumstances warranted, he wouldn't hesitate to replace her. Lesson for the day: A bird in the hand is worth two in the bush, and nobody is indispensable.

At her eight o'clock break, Clifton Howell walked into the studio. "You've done well as host of this radio program, Kendra," he said without preliminaries. "Advertising is up and so is the number of listeners. I'd let you go for a month, but six weeks is pushing the envelope. If you win, tell your adviser to call me. Maybe I can work out a deal for one month. Would you object to that?"

Her concern about keeping her job was on par with her feeling about leaving Sam for a month, when their relationship had barely begun. "That would be a better deal for me, sir. You have been more than considerate and helpful. If it wasn't for your kindness, I wouldn't be in school, and I am not going to throw this away for a prize that makes me look good, and which I do not need in order to graduate."

He nodded. "You've got a good head on your shoulders. My offer stands. Good night."

"Good night, sir."

When she walked out of Howell Enterprises' building a few minutes past midnight that night, her father stood beside his car waiting for her as he usually did.

"Hi, Papa. Why didn't you wait in the car? It's cold out here."

He went around the car and opened the door for her. "A lot can happen before I can get out of this car. I'm a little older than I used to be."

She couldn't help laughing. Her father seldom owned up to thoughts of getting old. "So am I, Papa. A few more years, and I'll be as old as you are." His laughter always comforted her, for his happiness gave her a sense of well-being.

"Mind you don't get fresh with your papa. How did it go at school today?"

She told him of her chance to win a trip abroad and of her conversations with Clifton Howell.

"Seems to me that if you leave that job, you can lose a life-time career, and if this man, Sam, is worth your time and your affection, you're taking a chance with him, too. Six weeks from a guy you hardly know, and six weeks from a career-building job . . . I don't think I'd do it. Howell's a decent guy, and, after I meet Sam, I'll have a better notion about him. You said that if you did well in radio, after you graduated, Howell would promote you to television news. I'm wondering if winning that competition and wandering around Egypt or Italy—and you'd better make it Italy—are worth what you stand to lose?"

Chapter Seven

Sam rang Kendra's bell at eleven o'clock the following Sunday morning, and it occurred to him that always being precisely on time might not be in his favor; circumstances could arise in which he'd be late, and she'd think he wasn't coming. He waited impatiently for the moment when the door opened and she would smile up at him.

Women were usually closer to their mothers than to their dads, but. . . . He didn't finish the thought. If she loved her father so much, he couldn't possibly be a washout as a man, so Sam had no misgivings about spending an afternoon with him.

The door opened, and Kendra greeted him with a smile. "Hi. Do you think we'll be too cold out there?"

"No. We'll have a fire for warmth. If we're lucky, we'll get one of those grills inside of a brick oven. Is it possible to get a warmer greeting?"

She reached up and placed a quick kiss on his lips. "My papa is due here any minute, so I'd better appear circumspect. Come in." He resisted telling her that he didn't see a damned thing about a kiss on the mouth that wasn't circumspect.

Not long after she closed the door, the doorbell rang. "That must be my papa." Sam hoped that she had anticipated his own arrival there with as much happiness.

"Hi, Papa. Sam just got here."

"That means he's punctual. You look good. How are you?" he asked, standing with her in the foyer.

"I'm feeling great. How about you?"

"I'm not at church, but I expect the Lord understands. Where's Sam?"

"In the living room."

Sam stood and went to meet Kendra's father, a tall, handsome, and seemingly very fit man. Somehow, he had expected a butcher to be stocky. "I'm Sam Hayes. Glad to meet you, sir." He extended his hand and received a strong and honest handshake.

"Sam, this is my father, Herbert Richards."

"Please call me Bert. I've been looking forward to meeting you, Sam. Thanks for asking Kendra to bring me along on your picnic. I don't get out of doors often enough. I brought some steaks and a bottle of red, a six-pack of Pilsner, and some kindling. What part of the park are we going to?"

"We'll be near the creek. I've seen people fishing there, but I expect it's too cold for that today," Sam said.

"Cold? It's perfect weather for a picnic. The sun's shining, the air is dry, and the wind is calm. What more could we want?"

Nothing grumpy about this guy. Bert Richards was youthful, well kept, and very sure of himself. So far, he liked him. "Thanks for bringing the kindling. I was counting on finding some dry sticks. We'd better get started, sir."

Sam put an arm around Kendra's waist, then remembered who walked behind them and removed it at once. They stepped outside the apartment, and he opened his hand to Kendra for the key. "I'll lock it," he said. He considered it his duty to make certain that they left her home secure, and he meant to discharge it. Damned if he was going to relinquish his status to Kendra's father or any other man.

"I'll lead, if you don't mind," he told Kendra's father when they reached his car. "I'd rather take Connecticut to

Nebraska, exit Nebraska into Northampton Street, and take that into the park. That's a good area for what we want."

"I'll be right behind you."

With the traffic light all the way, they reached the park in less than twenty minutes and, almost at once, Sam found the brick-oven grill that he preferred, laid on it the potatoes, asparagus, and onions. Bert lit the kindling, and Sam added the coals. By the time they finished unpacking, the fire had begun to provide heat. Bert left them and returned with three folding chairs he'd put in the trunk of his car.

"Roughing it is fine when you're a teenager, Sam, but I like my comforts. Have a seat while the coals heat up. The steaks and drinks are in that cooler. It's your party, so you do as you please with it."

"Thanks for confusing me," Sam said. "I love red wine with steaks, but at a picnic, I love beer."

Bert laughed. "Moral of the story is not to bring steaks on a picnic."

"With charcoal-grilled porterhouse steaks the issue, I certainly wouldn't use that solution," Sam said. "Moral or no moral. Nothing's wrong with drinking beer before the steaks are done and wine while we're eating them." He went over to the cooler, got three cans of beer, opened them, and passed one each to Kendra and Bert.

"I never drink beer," she said.

"Then drink wine," Bert advised. "Or you can make this the first time you drink a beer."

She looked from her father to Sam, and Sam waited to see what she'd do. It did not displease him when she got the bottle of wine and handed it to him. "Would you open that, please?"

"My pleasure." While opening the wine, he noticed her father's careful attention to the way in which he and Kendra interacted, and he'd seen the day, years earlier, when he'd have given the man something to look at. But Sam knew that he would probably need Bert Richards's support one day, so he didn't want to make an enemy of him. He looked at the coals and then said to Bert, "Do you think those coals are hot enough?"

"Five or ten more minutes and they'll be perfect."

Sam had a few questions that he wanted to ask Bert Richards, but since the answers to none of them were any business of his, he kept his questions to himself. How had a decent, straightforward man like Bert married the woman that Kendra described her mother to be, and how had he lived with her for five years? And it wouldn't hurt to know in what ways, if at all, Kendra was like her mother. So far, what he'd seen of and experienced with Kendra suggested that she and her mother did not have the same DNA family. He'd have to be patient, because any allusion to that matter would probably ruin his relationship with Kendra.

He heard Kendra talking to her father and focused on her words.

"Papa, it would have been nice if you'd brought your guitar."

"You play the guitar?" he asked Bert, although it was obvious from Kendra's comment that he did.

"Whenever I have time, I do. When I get home at night, I'm too tired to practice, and on Sundays when I'm off, I have so many other things to do that I don't get to my guitar. Too bad. I was once pretty good at it. It's in the trunk, but there's no telling what it will sound like in this weather."

Kendra got the guitar out of the car and brought it to her father, who tuned it and plucked a few strings. Bert looked at his daughter. "What would you like to hear?"

"How about Mendelssohn's *Songs Without Words*?" She looked at Sam. "Papa transcribed that for guitar, and I love it."

"I like it, too, but I've only heard it for piano and violin."

Sam sat enraptured while Bert Richards played the guitar like a professional, and he couldn't help wondering about the man's youthful dreams and goals and what had torpedoed them. This man had not reached maturity intending to be a butcher, and Sam wouldn't demean his accomplishments by asking him how it had happened. It occurred to him that Kendra's drive and tenacity might have had its seeds in what she knew of her father's life. The music ended, but he remained under its spell.

"Thank you," Sam said, looking at Bert. "I could listen to you play like that forever. I'm surprised you don't make your living as a musician."

"I appreciate the compliment. It's a long, long story. We can put the steaks on now. Anything I can help with?"

"You've done more than your share. As soon as the steaks are ready, we'll eat." Sam turned the asparagus, halved Vidalia onions, and slices of small red potatoes on the grill beside the steaks. He spread the tablecloth on a picnic table, opened the wine, and tasted it. Not bad. The man knew something about wine. Bert Richards did not add up. Since this wasn't a fancy sit-down dinner, Sam stacked the plates and utensils on the table, poured three glasses of wine, and checked the grill, turning the steaks and the vegetables. He poured blue cheese dressing on the arugula and Belgian endive salad, tossed it, put the potato salad on the table and looked at his handiwork. Not bad. "It's ready."

They consumed most of the food, including a large porterhouse each, and drank the wine. Bert slapped Sam on the back, sat down with his second glass of wine, and said, "At least you'll be able to feed her well."

Sam glanced at Kendra, who stared at her father with eyes wide, and her lower jaw dropped. He regarded Bert's sanguine and smug expression and Kendra's barely leashed fury and couldn't control the laughter that rolled out of him. But he collected his wits when Bert said, "You think that's funny?"

"No, sir, I don't. But the difference between your facial expression and Kendra's is the funniest thing I ever saw. She's about to explode."

Bert emptied his wine glass. "This was a fine meal. Kendra was taught from childhood to control her temper, and I see she's doing a good job of it."

"Papa, how could you say that to him? We've practically just met."

The quick rise and fall of Bert's shoulders expressed his attitude toward that reasoning. "Sam understands me perfectly even if you don't."

Sam saw the first snowflake of the season and almost immediately silvery flakes began to fall silently all around them. "I didn't check the weather forecast, so I don't know how much of this we can expect," he said. "From the looks of it, though, we ought to pack up."

"My thoughts exactly," Bert said. "This has been wonderful. I hope we can get a chance to do it again soon. If the weather won't permit, I've got a nice place that's warm, and my stove has a wonderful grill. You don't have to be out of doors to have a picnic."

"Thank you. I'll remember your offer. I don't know where you buy your steaks, or what's different about your steaks, but that was the best steak I remember eating. Thanks for your company."

"It's been my great pleasure, Sam. And to know that my daughter has a man like you for a friend gives me a lot of satisfaction. I'll drive straight home. You two have a nice day." He put the cooler in the trunk of his car and kissed Kendra. Then Bert walked over to Sam, shook his hand, gazed into his eyes, and smiled. "Good-bye and thanks again." He strode back to the car, his steps quick and lithe.

"Your father is quite a man, and you were wrong, he did not ask me about my intentions."

"No. What he said was much worse. You wait till I tell him what I think about that."

"Really? I imagine your reprimand will be short, sweet, and gentle. Your father is not a man anybody yells at, and he is not used to reprimands. So, I'm not impressed with your threat. We'd better go; this stuff is getting heavier by the minute."

Sam stopped on the corner near the building in which she lived and put the car in park. It didn't surprise him when she said, "Does this mean you aren't coming in?"

He stroked her cheek with the back of his hand. "I'm debating that with myself right now. If the snow continues to fall at this rate, an hour from now I won't be able to see to drive, and in two hours, the streets will be nearly impassable."

"In that case, you go home with my blessings."

"How will you get to school tomorrow morning?"

"If the streets are really bad, classes will be cancelled. It's getting to the station that will be a problem."

"By that time, the streets will have been cleared. I hadn't planned for the day to end this way, but man proposes and God disposes. I'll see you to your apartment."

They dashed through the blinding snow, and when they entered the building, he brushed a heavy layer of snow from her coat. At her apartment, he opened the door with her key and gazed down at her, certain that his eyes reflected what was in his heart. But he didn't put it into words, for when he reached that stage, he wanted plenty of time in an appropriate place.

"I like your father. If he had asked my intentions, I was planning to tell him that I wanted you for myself. I'm glad he didn't ask, because having met him, I imagine that he wouldn't have liked that."

Her scent furled up to him, the smell of her rising heat sending him the message that if he was planning to leave, he'd better go right then.

He gripped her body to his, covered her lips with his own, and possessed her as surely as if he were dancing inside of her. "I'll call you in the morning," he said in a voice that he barely recognized.

Minutes later, he ignited the engine of his Buick Enclave and headed for Connecticut Avenue. He had some thinking to do, although he wondered if he'd gone so far that, for once, thinking would be a waste of time. Nothing could be done about one of his principal reservations, which was Kendra's mother and their relationship.

Kendra's mother was busily contriving to create a problem for Kendra, a serious one. On Monday morning, following one of the largest snowfalls in Washington, D.C., since records had been kept, Ginny telephoned the bank at which Kendra had an account, and in a soprano voice that camouflaged her usual alto register, she said, "This is Kendra Richards. I can't get to the bank in this weather, and I have an emergency. I need to withdraw fifteen hundred dollars from the nearest ATM and you didn't send me my debit card."

"Just a minute, Miss Richards. Let me check. We can get a card to you by mail tomorrow. What is your address?"

"I moved last week." She gave her own address.

"What are the last digits of your social security number, Miss Richards?"

She'd just looked that up from Kendra's college entrance papers. So far so good.

"And your mother's maiden name?"

"Virginia Hunter."

"Thank you, Miss Richards. I hate to ask all these questions, but we are only protecting your account. You have a security question here. Who is your favorite author?"

Just when she thought it was going so smoothly. "My favorite . . . My goodness, I have so many, I don't remember which one I put down. Gosh, I don't know what I'll do. I've got to have that money. This is an emergency."

"I'm sorry, Miss Richards. Maybe you wrote it down somewhere. When you remember, call us. In the meantime, because of this . . . uh . . . glitch, your account will be locked for twenty-four hours, but we can open it earlier if you remember the answer to the security question and call us back. Thanks for banking with Westwood."

Ginny hung up, slammed the phone against the wall, and paced from one end of her bedroom to the other, back and forth, back and forth. Talking aloud to herself, she said, "Damn her. She does everything she can to make me suffer. But I'll be damned if I'll kill myself standing on my feet all day when she's got a plumb of a job making good money. She's just like her damned father. I'll get it yet. A security question. I'll bet she's the only person in this city with a security question. What am I going to do when Asa gets here? He thinks I'm socially and financially well-placed. I've gotta get tickets to the Kennedy Center jazz series, and I need an evening dress. That means money."

She made a second pot of coffee and sat down at the kitchen table to drink it. Maybe if she sued Bert for letting their house go into foreclosure, she'd get a chunk. It would be her word against his as to why they lost it. A smile floated over her face, but it quickly vanished when she recalled that he'd won the divorce on the grounds that she'd squandered the money he gave her monthly to pay the mortgage.

Anger began to boil up in her. Damn that Asa. He should be giving her money. Being able to out-screw the man who invented screwing didn't make him worth more than Fort Knox. Besides, she wasn't bad at it herself. And maybe she'd manage to change things.

Kendra was in the midst of dictating her mid-term paper on the recorder that Sam gave her when the telephone rang. Sam had already called her, so she was not in a hurry to interrupt her homework. When the ringing persisted, she lifted the receiver.

"Hello?"

"Is this Kendra Richards?"

"Yes. This is Kendra."

"Ms. Richards, this is Westwood Bank calling. Have you phoned this bank today?"

Her antenna shot up. "No. I don't think I have ever phoned your bank. And how do I know it's the bank calling me or if you're a scammer?"

"Hang up. Call your bank and ask for Ms. Marris."

"I will." She hung up, dialed the bank's number and asked for Ms. Marris.

"Thank you for calling back, Ms. Richards, and for being careful. We suspect that someone has stolen your identity. The woman knew your social security number and your mother's maiden name. I'm not sure about your address, because she said she moved a week ago. We tripped her when she didn't know the answer to your security question."

A chill seeped into Kendra's body and she began to shiver. "Did you say *she?* What did she want?"

"She said she hadn't received her debit card, and asked if we would mail her a new one. She spoke of an emergency."

By now, Kendra was standing and breathing hard. "To what address did she want you to send the card?"

"The woman gave an address on Kalorama Road."

"Thank God for that security question. She would have cleaned me out and thought nothing of it."

Ms. Marris gasped. "You know who it is?"

"I sure do, and I'm going to decide what to do about this latest attempt to ruin me."

"If you'll tell me who she is, I'll take care of that for you."

"Thanks, but I'd better get some advice about this. I may call you back."

"All right, but as soon as you can, stop by the bank and give us a second security question and answer because she knows what the question is, and she may wheedle the answer out of you."

"Thank you. I'll be by as soon as this snow clears. She won't learn the answer, though I suspect she'll ask everybody who knows me. At any rate, she doesn't know the PIN. Thanks again."

"You're welcome, and thank you for banking with Westwood."

Kendra knew she wouldn't be able to concentrate on her mid-term paper, so she put away her notes and called her father. Ginny needed psychiatric counseling, and if she didn't get it and soon, she would eventually get a stiff jail sentence.

"Hello, Kendra. Couldn't you get to school this morning?"

"Classes were cancelled, Papa, so I was catching up on my homework. Then the bank called me. Guess what Mama's done now?"

"I'm not sure I want to hear it."

She related to him the details of her conversation with the bank's officer. "Papa, if I let them, they'll probably indict her."

"Of course they will. She attempted to commit a felony."

"What should I do?"

He was silent for a while. "You'll do nothing. I'll call Ginny and let her know that we know what she tried to do and that if we identify her, the bank will indict her for an attempted felony. I'm also going to tell Ed, because she'll run to him for help. Add a second security question to your account, but forget about the rest. One of these days, she's going to meet fate face to face, and fate will not back off. What time will you leave home for work?"

"Considering what's on the streets, I'd better leave no later than three o'clock."

"I have a buddy with a tow truck. We'll be at your place at three this afternoon, and we'll pick you up tonight."

"You sure he won't be busy?"

"He doesn't do snow removal. Besides, he's got lots of those trucks. He's my chess-playing buddy, and I know I can count on him. I meant to tell you that I like Sam, and I like him for *you*. He's a man who knows where he's going and how to get there, and he cares a lot for you. I mean, *a lot*."

Her father didn't go overboard for people, and his praise for them was almost never effusive. When he said he liked Sam, she had to listen. "Why do you say that?"

"I watched him as closely as he watched me. He couldn't keep his eyes away from you, and when he thought I wasn't looking, he managed to touch you. But the way that he looked at you, with his heart in his eyes, told me all I wanted to know. Sam Hayes knows exactly who he is, and he's full of self-pride. He's got good manners and a great sense of humor.

"I'll tell you this: You'd better not get on his wrong side, because he's straight, and he demands that of anyone close to him. That man is not single at his age because he hasn't been able to find a woman. If I was a betting man, I'd put a lot on his having ditched a faithless woman or lost a good one in a tragedy. He can have his pick."

She tried to remember another time when her father had spoken that long on any subject, but she couldn't.

"Papa, you discerned all that after being with him for four hours?"

"It took me less time than that. I know people, and unless you do something foolish, I'm expecting him to be the father of my grandchildren."

She wished that he could have seen her reaction to that, for her eyes felt as if they had doubled in size. "Papa! For goodness' sake! Is that why you insinuated that he was going to marry me? I could have sunk through the sod in that park. I was so embarrassed."

"You were also mad as the devil. But did you hear him object? I didn't. If it wasn't a possibility, he'd have straightened me out. A man isn't anxious to meet a girl's father, unless he feels a lot for her and wants to know what he's getting into. And he can learn a lot about her from what he sees of her parents."

She had yet to win an argument with him. "You must be busy, Papa, so I'll—"

"Busy with a foot of snow on the ground? I'm getting a chance to catch up on orders and accounts. I'll see you at three. Meanwhile, I'll get Ginny straightened out. Love you, girl."

"I love you, too, Papa."

She hung up, went to her living-room window, and looked down at the snow. She didn't see five people and not a single automobile. The scene reminded her of stories she'd read as a child, and she decided she would put a birdhouse and a birdbath on her balcony in the hope of attracting the little creatures. The snow made fancy patterns on the tree limbs, designs that might have originated on an artist's palette.

She had an urge to walk in the woods among the snow-burdened trees. On an impulse, she telephoned Sam, who was also at home because his university's classes had also been cancelled.

"Hi, Kendra," he said in a voice that reflected his surprise. "How nice to get a call from you."

"I was looking down at the snow. It's so beautiful that I had an urge to walk in the woods. I can't do that, but I could at least tell you how breathtaking the scenery is from my balcony."

"You're right. This isn't a good day for strolling among the trees, but it means a lot to me that when you wanted to take that walk, you wanted to do it in my company."

She wouldn't have phrased it that way, but it was an apt description of her thoughts. "It would be nice. Papa told me that he enjoyed being with you."

"I'm glad I met him. I understand you better, but he's a paradox, at least he seems that way. He's a first-class butcher, plays the classical guitar like a pro, he's educated, youthful, handsome, and vigorous. He's alone, yet he loves company. Have you figured him out?"

"It isn't difficult. He married my mother when he was twenty-two, right out of the university. She did a number on him, and it took him almost thirty years to recover fully from it financially. Because of her, he lost our home, and everything we owned. She ruined his credit, and if you can't get credit, you can't have a house, car, business, or anything else that costs more than a few dollars. You can imagine how badly he wants to remarry or even to develop close ties with a significant other. He had intended to be a classical guitarist, but she couldn't stand to hear him practice. She said it gave her a headache.

"He worked his way through school as a delivery boy for a butcher, from whom he learned about meat and other foods. Later, when Mama's antics indirectly cost him his job and we were almost penniless, the butcher took him on and taught him the trade."

"What a pity. I'm sorry. Does your mother do these things deliberately?"

"Occasionally she does, but mostly not. She thinks only of herself and never of the consequences."

"I didn't mean to pry, but I . . . well, I like your dad."

"I don't mind, and neither would he. If you play chess, he'll tell you all about it. That's one way to get him to talk."

"I'll give him a call, and maybe we can have a game of chess. Are you going to try and get to work?"

"Yes. Papa has a friend with a tow truck. They'll take me to work and bring me home. I'm sure Mr. Howell won't appreciate it if I don't go in. The show must go on."

"So I heard."

"I'd better get back to studying. Call in or fax a request."

"Great idea. Listen for me around nine. Bye for now, sweetheart."

"Bye."

"Now who can that be?" Ginny asked aloud as she rushed to the phone, hoping that someone at Westwood

Bank had found a way to send her that debit card, and praying that Asa was not the caller.

"Hello," she said, annoyed that the number didn't show in the caller-ID screen.

"Ginny, this is Bert. Westwood Bank called Kendra. To shorten a story that you know well, they want the name that goes with the address you gave them, so that you can be prosecuted for an attempted felony."

Perspiration beaded her forehead and dampened her bra and her thighs. "What are you talking about?"

"Try that or any other trick aimed to get into Kendra's bank account again, and I'll see that you spend a good long time in jail. If you had succeeded, you would have committed a felony. If Kendra won't expose you, I will, and it won't cost me a drop of sweat. You've got it coming."

"I never heard of such nonsense."

"Go ahead. You're like lemmings headed for a cliff and for self-destruction. If your shenanigans didn't affect my child, I wouldn't give a damn. As it is, I don't care what you do, but if you hurt Kendra, you'll deal with me. And I will be merciless."

He hung up before she could tell him what she thought of him. Damn Kendra. She had to go and tell him, and who knows what she told the bank. Washington was such a small place. She couldn't afford to get into anymore trouble with the law, and she definitely couldn't expect anything from that bank. Damn everybody!

Feeling defeated, she telephoned Asa. "Hi. Stop by here on your way to work."

"For how long?"

"Long enough," she said, not caring how he took it.

"What's the matter? You can't wait till tonight?"

His arrogance irritated her, and she wished she hadn't called him. But when he got into her, he made her feel that she was the only person in his world. "When are you going to learn to be a gentleman," she said, striking where she knew he was vulnerable.

"What does being a gentleman have to do with you wanting me to come over there and fan your hot coals."

"You're hopeless," she replied, avoiding answering him and, at the same time, taking care not to rankle him.

"I'll see you at twelve o'clock." He hung up without saying good-bye.

She stared at the receiver in her hand and with the quick movement of her right shoulder, she dismissed her problems and any affect that they could have on her life.

"You're what I call a loyal employee," Clifton Howell said to Kendra when she arrived at work. "Tab called in saying he couldn't get here, and June has a cold. It's a damned good thing I know how to operate these controls and play these CDs. How'd you get here?" She told him. "You get double pay today, and give your father my thanks. A radio station can't go off the air, but I don't think I could have carried this thing for twenty-four hours. So, I'll sleep in my office until eleven, and if Arnold doesn't come in, I can keep things going until two, when we sign off. See you later."

With the program director freaking out at home because of the snow, Kendra had to select the music. So she decided to make life easy for herself and make it a night of jazz and blues. She loved Frank Sinatra and Luther Vandross, but with two straight hours of Billie Holiday and Ella Fitzgerald interspersed, she could get a lot of studying done. To her astonishment, callers loved the program, proving that the greatest mix of performers didn't always meet with viewer approval.

When her direct phone rang at nine, her heart raced. "This is WAMA on a cold, snowy night. Feeling the blues? Some coming right up. What can I play for you?"

"Hi, K. This is Sam. Your show is wonderful. I'd like to hear a golden oldie, 'Everything I Have Is Yours' by Billy

Eckstine, and I should appreciate your dedicating it to my special girl, who loves to walk through the woods in the snow."

"Th . . . Uh . . . coming right up. I'm sure that special girl is listening with both her ears and her heart. Have a good night, Sam."

"Thanks. The same to you."

She found a re-mastered CD of the old recording and listened carefully as the great voice sang the intimate love song of a man who wanted to give everything to his beloved.

"I guess he just likes Billy Eckstine," she said to herself, "because I don't believe he feels that way about me." She put on some blues interspersed with Louis Armstrong, and her automatic answering machine recorded numerous calls applauding her selection. At ten-thirty, Howell walked in and sat beside her in the other chair.

"We've had a good response tonight. Here are some tickets to the Kennedy Center for a performance by Clarissa Holmes and The New Jazz Trio. They're great. I catch them whenever I can."

"Thank you, sir. I'll let you know how it went."

"You're welcome. I'm going to tell Josie to pep up our programs with more jazz. Thank you again for coming in tonight. Arnold can't get here from Silver Spring, so it's good that I could get some rest." She told him good night and got outside just as the big red tow truck pulled up.

"I was listening when Sam called you. He's a brave man," Bert said. "Never would I play that song for a woman. You're my daughter, but the chance that you're different from the rest of your gender is nil. Be sure you don't disappoint that man."

"It surprised me, too, Papa. We haven't gotten anywhere near that far, but I'm not saying we can't get there. Anyway, he made me feel good. Mr. Howell told me to thank you and Mr. Grayson for bringing me to work and coming back for me."

"Tell him I'll look after my daughter for as long as she needs me." The truck stopped at the building in which Kendra lived. "I see they cleaned off your sidewalk. See you tomorrow. Let me know if you need help getting to school."

"I will." She kissed his cheek. "Thanks a lot. Thanks, Mr. Grayson. Good night."

As soon as she closed the door of her apartment, she dropped her bag on a table in the foyer, turned on the light, and opened the envelope that contained the tickets. Four tickets for second row center at eight o'clock Saturday night. And at the Kennedy Center, yet! What would she do with them? Her papa couldn't go, because he closed at nine on Saturday nights. She told herself that Sam would have a suggestion. Another thought floated through her mind. She could invite her friends, The Pace Setters, but there wouldn't be a ticket for Sam, and she wanted to be there with him. She put the tickets on her night table, got ready for bed, crawled in, and quoted Scarlett O'Hara, *Tomorrow is another day*. She didn't have to decide about those tickets right then. Humming "Everything I Have Is Yours," she soon fell asleep.

Sam telephoned her at eight the following morning, as he usually did and, after they spoke for a while, she told him about the tickets and asked if he wanted to go.

"Absolutely, I do. I love that velvet voice of Clarissa Holmes, and her trio is one of the best. Did you ever hear her?"

"No, I haven't, but if I like her, I'll try to get an interview for my show."

"If you manage that, Howell will stand on his head."

"Would you believe I hadn't thought of that? And I'm hoping to be a reporter. I'd better start thinking of myself as one. The recorder you gave me has multiple uses, I see. Sam, what am I going to do with the other two tickets?"

"If you don't want them, my dad would walk all the way from Alexandria to your house to get them."

"Okay. It's all set. Tell him to meet us there at a quarter of eight next Saturday."

Hmm, she thought, after hanging up. *This is going to be interesting. I can't wait to see who Mr. Hayes brings with him.*

As soon as he hung up, Sam telephoned his father.

"Hi, son. What's up?"

"Hi, Dad. Everything's great. Would you like to see Clarissa Holmes and The New Jazz Trio Saturday night?"

"Would I *what?* Of course I would, but those tickets have been sold out for weeks."

"Maybe, but Kendra has four tickets, and she said you can come and bring whoever you like. She and I will meet you in the lobby at a quarter of eight."

"She's got four tickets? Are you sure?"

"So far, I've found her to be very reliable."

"You bet I'll be there. I'd like to know how she got them. I've tried every way I knew for the last few weeks."

"She was the only one of the staff of WAMA who managed to get to work yesterday, so her boss, Clifton Howell, gave her the tickets, plus a bonus."

"If she went to work last night, she deserved them. Give her my thanks. Aren't you going to ask me who I'm bringing?"

Sam smothered the laugh that seemed bent on pushing itself out of him. "I figured that if you didn't tell me now, I'd certainly find out Saturday night. Are you bringing Edwina?"

"Things are going well with us, son. We picked up right where we left off all those years ago. I never touched her that day, except to shake hands with her, but you can say a lot without opening your mouth."

"I suppose that answers my question. I'm happy for you. See you Saturday."

"I'll be there, and thanks."

Sam hung up and mused over his father's admission that

he'd fallen hard for Edwina when they met earlier, and had done absolutely nothing about it. He wondered if he'd have the strength to live up to his own guidelines for integrity and honor as his father had done. He couldn't imagine never making love with Kendra, never holding her and feeling her warmth and feminine softness. "I hope I've got half as much strength as he has," he said to himself. "I never want to do anything that I'm ashamed of."

Chapter Eight

On her way to work, two days after the big snowfall, Kendra stopped at Suzy's dress shop. "I need something to wear to a jazz concert at the Kennedy Center," she told Suzy, aware that she'd probably have to tell her friend more than she had planned.

"If you were going by yourself, you'd wear something that you already have," Suzy said, "so let's go for a soft suit that's appealing to a man, but won't overdress you. Okay?" Kendra tried on several, and liked each of them.

"I see you're keeping this guy a secret. When are you going to let us meet him?"

Getting around Suzy was no mean feat. "You think I'm buying this for a date?"

"Sure as my name is Suzy Monroe. No point in hiding him. These days, if a guy has all of his teeth, stands up straight, and isn't hung up on weed, he's a catch."

"He's a university professor, and I fell for him as he was walking toward me."

"You go, girl. He must be *something*."

"He is, Suzy. He's wonderful."

Suzy reached up and put her arms around Kendra. "You've got my blessing, friend."

She left the store with a burnt-orange wool crepe suit that

had a rounded collar on the short, fitted jacket and a straight skirt that flared slightly at the bottom.

On Saturday night, with her hair curled around her shoulders and gold hoops in her ears, Kendra looked at herself in the mirror and said aloud, "Who is this woman? When I get my next paycheck, I'm going to splurge and buy a nice perfume." She didn't think she'd ever looked that good before. Even her eyes seemed larger. The intercom buzzed.

"Mr. Hayes to see you, Ms. Richards."

"Thanks. Please ask him to come up."

Minutes later, the doorbell rang, and she tingled all over as she rushed to the door and opened it.

Sam stared down at her for a second. "Wow! If it wasn't bad manners, I'd whistle."

Happiness suffused her. "And if I knew how to whistle, I would, too," she said. "Come in."

He handed her a long-stemmed American Beauty rose wrapped in cellophane and tied with a red ribbon. "Thank you. It's beautiful," Kendra said.

"But not as beautiful as you are."

She swallowed the lump in her throat. No one had ever said she was beautiful. She gazed up at him with a question in her eyes that asked if he was serious, not about her being beautiful, but about *her*. And, as if he understood her, he enclosed her in his embrace.

"You are precious to me, Kendra. Don't forget that."

When she tightened her arms around him, he pressed his lips to hers, and the electriclike sparks that united them when they first met shocked them both. He gripped her to him, ran his tongue over the seam of her lips until she opened to him, and loved her until she trembled in his arms.

"I think we'd b . . . better g . . . go," she stammered, got her coat from the closet and handed it to him.

He helped her into it, locked her door, and walked arm in

arm with her to his car. As he drove out Woodley Road to Sixteenth Street, she noticed the still-glistening snow on the lawns of many homes and the icicles that had formed on trees. "Sam, can you see how beautiful this is? It's breathtaking in the moonlight."

He reached over and squeezed her hand. "Yes, and I just said to myself, damned if I'll let it get to me. Kendra, as soon as you felt the tension growing between us back there in your apartment, you cut it off and pushed me away. Don't you think we'll eventually make love?"

"Not when we're on our way to meet your dad."

"I know that, and it is not the answer to my question. You can be candid when it suits you. What about being candid right now?"

"I know how I feel about you, Sam, but you haven't told me whether you want us to be more than friends. I mean—"

"You definitely do not mean that. At your age, you know when a man cares for you, and you definitely know when he wants to make love with you. Be straight with me, Kendra. It isn't like you to be coy."

"Sitting here in the front seat of this Town Car with you and telling you bluntly that I want to make love with you is not something I'm going to do. If you want the answer, there are other ways you can get it, and *you're* old enough to know *that*."

She had not expected his chuckle. "You certainly know how to say what's on your mind. If I could park somewhere right now, I'd get the answer. You're the most provocative woman I've ever known."

He slowed to a stop for the red light, and she slid a little closer to him and rested her hand on his knee. "I'm sorry you can't park anyplace."

"Are you messing with me?"

"Of course not. Why would you think that I don't want you to kiss me till I'm practically out of my mind?"

The light changed and he turned onto New Hampshire

Avenue and headed for their destination. "Sweetheart, I think that big snowstorm must have fogged up my mind. Thanks for clarifying this thing. I consider myself well-advised."

"Now you're pulling my leg."

"Am not. Just don't want you to get a big shock."

"I forgot to tell you that I received by messenger this afternoon a note from Clarissa Holmes granting me an interview after the show. She included with the note a pass to her dressing room. I want you to come with me." She showed him the recorder that he had given her. "This is all I need."

"How'd you contact her? Did Howell make the connection?"

"He won't know a thing about it till I broadcast it. I wrote her a letter, telling her that I knew her story from a novella I read several years back, and asked her for an interview, so that my listeners would know how far she's come. I'd thought she wouldn't answer. I wonder if she'll let me introduce her to your dad."

"When we get there, you can ask her. Tell her he doesn't want to come in, only to meet her and shake her hand. If she says no, it's not a big loss."

"How am I supposed to introduce you, other than by your title, I mean?"

"Tell her I'm your lover."

"But you aren't."

"But I will be soon," he said, not bothering to control the laughter.

"Okay. Miss Holmes, this is Professor Samuel Hayes, my soon-to-be lover. How's that?"

"Your sense of humor is going to cause me to wreck this car. Switch to another topic."

"Who's your dad bringing to the concert?"

"You'll find out in about eight minutes when I get my suspicion confirmed."

"Sam, I'm excited."

He didn't need to know that this was her first really big date. She had had lots of dates, some of them at interesting places, but not with a man like Sam Hayes. Their being with his father, a prominent attorney, made it even more special. Or maybe it was special because of the way she felt about Sam. She leaned back, closed her eyes, and began to hum "Everything I have Is Yours."

When the car stopped, Sam got out, gave the car keys to a parking attendant, walked around, and took her arm. It did not surprise her that he didn't need directions. She stepped into the red-carpeted grand foyer—illuminated by at least a hundred hanging chandeliers and dominated by Robert Berks's three-thousand-pound bust of John F. Kennedy— and reached for Sam's hand. The pace at which her life had changed since the day she found Clifton Howell's iPhone suddenly made her dizzy. They went down to the A level where Sam checked their coats.

"We're meeting here," he told her, and immediately she saw Jethro Hayes coming to meet them with Edwina Prill close to his side.

To her amazement, Jethro stepped forward and hugged her before embracing Sam. She said, "I'm so glad you could come, Mr. Hayes and that you brought Edwina with you. I was hoping to see her." She and Edwina embraced, and she knew that she was seeing a different Edwina. *This woman was not with a stranger she'd seen once twenty years earlier. She was with her lover and proud of it.*

Sam explained the evening program, including Kendra's interview with Clarissa Holmes. "If you can wait for us in one of the lounges, we'll get together for a drink or something later," Sam said.

"I'm glad to hear this, Kendra. Of course, we'll wait. This is a day in which you can do no wrong," Jethro said. "You won't believe how much I love to hear Clarissa Holmes sing. And that trio is a great one."

"We're in the KC Jazz Club tonight, Dad, so we can get a

sandwich or something there, but I suspect we have to finish eating before eight-thirty when she comes on. Fortunately, clubs have to serve food if they sell drinks."

"I'm too excited to be hungry," Edwina said, "but I don't know how long that will last."

They took their seats at table three, second row on the center aisle. "A ham and Swiss cheese sandwich on whole wheat for me," Jethro said to the waiter, and looked at Edwina. "What do you want?"

"I'll have the same."

Sam looked at Kendra. "What would you like, sweetheart?"

He'd called her sweetheart within earshot of his father. "I'd like ham on focaccia bread."

"Great idea," Sam said. "I'll have the same with Swiss cheese and a Vodka Collins." He looked at her.

"Me too."

Jethro ordered bourbon and water for himself and a dry martini for Edwina.

"Thank you," the waiter said, tearing his gaze from Sam with great difficulty.

"Well I'll be damned," Kendra said to herself. "Poor fellow!"

"Have you written out your questions for the interview?" Jethro asked her.

"No, sir. I memorized them, and I'll use the recorder Sam gave me. It's really a gem."

They finished their sandwiches minutes before the band walked out on the stage to resounding applause. A man standing at the center mike smiled broadly and said, "That's Oscar at the piano, Konny with the bass, and I'm Raymond, the old man among these young Turks. I play the guitar and the dobro. We're gonna warm things up for Clarissa Holmes."

For the next thirty minutes, The New Jazz Trio drew from the audience sounds of whistling, applause, and stomping to tune after tune of classical and modern jazz. Then, Raymond stepped to the mike, bowed, and said, "You've been a great audience. Let's give some love to the first lady of jazz, Clarissa Holmes."

The audience stood and applauded the tall, elegant woman. When they finally sat down, Clarissa said, "Thank you so much. I always begin with this love song that I first sang to the man who is now my beloved husband, Brock Stanton." The spotlight shifted to table three on the first row, and the man half stood and waved at his wife. When Clarissa finished singing Duke Ellington's "Solitude," Sam took his handkerchief from his pocket and wiped the tears from Kendra's eyes.

She looked at him and whispered, "I didn't know I was crying. She sang it so movingly." His arm eased around her waist, and she let herself settle into the comfort that he offered.

"You're such a tender person," he whispered, "yet you're so strong. I'd like to have you all to myself for a few days. In fact, I think that's what I need with you."

"Be careful over there," Jethro said. "Her face is reflecting every word you say."

"Yeah? In that case, it's a good thing her face can't reflect what . . . Oh, never mind."

Clarissa finished a fast, rocking number and announced, "This next song was written by my super-talented bass player, Konny Patterson. It's a song for new lovers, 'Another Kind of Blues'" She sang it with soul-rending intensity. After three encores, she begged the audience to release her. "I have an appointment for forty minutes ago, and the band and I have to catch an early flight. See you next time."

Sam got the attention of an usher, and told him of Kendra's appointment with Clarissa Holmes. He asked to see Kendra's backstage pass and ushered the four of them to Clarissa's dressing room.

"I'm Brock Stanton, come in," the tall, handsome man who opened the door said. But Jethro remained at the door with Edwina. "Come on in," Stanton insisted. "Have a seat. Clarissa will be here in a second."

Kendra stepped forward and extended her hand to the man. She hadn't expected such a cordial greeting. "I'm Kendra Richards, Mr. Stanton. This is Professor Hayes, my uh—"

"Significant other?" Stanton finished for her.

"And these friends are Jethro Hayes, an attorney, and Dr. Prill, who only want to shake hands with Ms. Holmes."

"Who only wants to shake hands with me?" Clarissa Holmes breezed into the room wearing a silk caftan splattered with a dusty rose and lavender abstraction, that flattered her flawless skin and elegant features. "Y'all have a seat. Which one is Kendra?"

"I am. This is Professor Hayes; his father, Attorney Jethro Hayes; and Dr. Edwina Prill."

"I'm glad to meet y'all. Kendra, honey, that was just about the nicest letter I ever received, so warm and down-to-earth." She looked at her husband. "Honey, can't we offer them something? I think some guy sent some champagne that's in here. I don't drink, but I can toast these friends. What do you teach, Professor Hayes?"

"Psychology."

Clarissa winked at Kendra. "Honey, you have to watch it. He can zoom right in on our little feminine tricks."

She couldn't help scrutinizing the woman. "You think he's with me?"

"Child, I know he is."

"And don't ask her why," Stanton said. "Clarissa will answer any question you ask her." He poured champagne for the six of them, raised his glass, and said, "We meet many people, but none who've seemed like old friends, as all of you do."

Jethro stood. "I've met many celebrities, but none with your warmth, kindness, and down-home friendliness. I've been your fan since your first CD came out, and I always will be." He drained his glass. "Now, Edwina and I will leave so that Kendra can get her interview." He looked at Sam. "We'll wait for you in the Chinese Lounge." Stanton walked with them to the door.

Anxious to begin the interview, Kendra said, "Ms. Holmes, I appreciate your doing me this honor. I've brought my recorder. It's very powerful and will give excellent sound for the radio. Do you mind if I use it?"

"No indeed. Since you won't have to write, we can just sit here and talk."

"How much of your story published in the novella, *The Journey*, is true?" Kendra asked.

"Everything but those little details in the story. Even the parts about the band members is fairly accurate."

They talked for more than half an hour. "I've taken up so much of your time that I'm sure I've tired you out, especially after that long program you gave tonight. Thank you for the interview. I'm going to have a two-hour Clarissa Holmes program one night next week when I'll broadcast the interview and all of your CDs. I need a few nights to advertise it, so I can't tell you which night, but I'm gunning for Thursday. Thank you again." She stood to leave.

"Thank you, Kendra. I appreciate your interviewing me and giving me a spot on your program." She shook hands with Sam. "You the spittin' image of your daddy. He must be real proud of you. Next time I'm in Washington or anyplace near here, I'll send Kendra four tickets. Give my regards to your daddy and Dr. Prill. You Hayes men know how to pick your women." She and Stanton walked to the door with them. Clarissa and Stanton embraced them, and they left.

Kendra saw a ladies' room. "Excuse me a minute, please," she said to Sam. She opened the door, gasped, and stepped back, shaken.

Sam rushed to her. "What is it? What's the matter?"

"Come. Let's get away from here right now." She brushed his hand away and quickened her steps toward the grand foyer. Sam pulled her into a telephone booth. "Tell me this minute what's wrong."

"Ginny. She was in the ladies' room. My mother."

"What? Are you afraid of her?"

"No. But if she saw me, she'd make a scene in front of everybody, and spoil one of the most beautiful nights of my life."

He pulled her into his arms and rocked her. "What kind of ogre is she? If she finds you, don't say a word to her. I'll take care of it. Try to be calm, take a few deep breaths, and tell yourself that you're not alone, that I'm here for you. Smile. If you're miserable, Dad will detect it in a minute."

"I'm okay," she said after a minute or two. "Let's go." Sam held her hand as they walked the nearly empty hallway that led to the grand foyer and the Chinese Lounge. "It's been a fantastic evening," Kendra said. "I may never get over this." She wanted to ask Sam how he thought the interview went, but decided to wait and let him volunteer his thoughts about it.

"I was beginning to think you two were so excited that you'd forgotten we were waiting," Jethro said when they entered the lounge. "How'd it go?"

"She's a genius at it," Sam said. "I was flabbergasted. You'd have thought she'd spent her life doing nothing but interviewing. And she made it so intimate. I was really impressed."

Jethro regarded him with laughing eyes. "You must have been. I'm ready for a very late-night supper. Edwina knows a good place."

"Congratulations on the interview," Edwina said. "I'll be listening for it."

The valet brought Sam's car, and they were soon headed for Treadwell's, a supper club in the Southwest section of the city.

Later, Sam stood with Kendra beside the closet in her

foyer helping her out of her coat. "You gave me a shock tonight. Is there any way that you can get your mother to straighten out her life and stop damaging yours? That interview was a triumph, a big coup for you—and a glimpse of her demoralized you. Do you want us to talk to her together, to get some kind of understanding with her? I can't bear to see you the way you were after you saw her. You deserve better."

She took a deep breath and, shaking her head slowly, she said, "You can't reason with her, Sam. And you can't rely on her promises. She does and says what suits her at the moment. I don't think she's mean, though Papa disagrees, but I still can't deal with her."

"She's counting on that, Kendra. What's keeping her under control these days?"

"My uncle. Her older brother. If she contacts me, he'll have her bail revoked, and she'll have to serve out that jail sentence for driving an unregistered car with a suspended license."

"You told me about that. Why was her license suspended?"

"She had numerous traffic violations, and didn't pay any of her fines. Then, she drove down a one-way street the wrong way, and when the police caught her, she was rude. She lost her license."

"I see. She's antisocial."

"That's one way of putting it."

It was not the time for what he wanted and needed with her, although it would have been perfect if she hadn't seen her mother. "Can we be together tomorrow after you finish studying?"

"Great. That heavy snow made it possible for me to catch up with my studies, so any time after one will be fine. I'm going to church with Papa, and I'll be home by eleven-thirty. Say, why don't we come back here for dinner? It won't be as fancy as I'm capable of making it, but it will be nice."

"I like that." And he did. He wanted to know if he could be comfortable in her environment, and so far he wasn't sure.

"Okay, dress casually and comfortably, but not in sneakers or jeans."

"All right." His jaw nearly dropped when she looked up at him and said, "I love being with you so much. I'm never ready to leave you."

Quickly gathering his aplomb, he said, "I thought it was only I who felt that way." He got no warning for the unprecipitated and uninvited stirring in his groin.

"We'll be together tomorrow," he said, as much to himself as to her.

"I'm looking forward to it. By the way, I think your dad and Edwina are on a one-way trail. They're like teenagers."

"Yeah. They're not letting any grass grow under their feet. But that's the way my dad moves. He studies a problem, decides what course he'll take, and doesn't look back. I think he's fortunate, and I like her more each time I see her."

"I guess you do. She's besotted with him. I like her too, very much."

He sprinkled kisses over her face and on her lips. "I don't care what you cook tomorrow. I just want us to be together."

"I do, too, but if I was home all day before you got here, I'd present you with a first-class meal."

"You mean you can cook?"

"Do cats like mice? What a question!"

"See you at one o'clock. Give my regards to your dad. Good night, sweetheart."

"Good night, dear."

Sometime Monday, she would know whether she won one of the prizes for travel abroad. She would be disappointed if she didn't win, but she suspected that her life would be less complicated if she stayed home.

She went into her bedroom, saw the red message light

flashing on her phone, walked over, and was about to pick up the receiver when she saw Ginny's phone number. That was one call she did not plan to return; her mother must have glimpsed her from the washroom mirror. When would it end?

It was time she found out where she was headed with Sam. As natural as it seemed to be with him, she held back, as she knew he did. For her, it wasn't a matter of trust; she trusted him. But you didn't wade shoulder-high into the ocean waters if you couldn't swim. If she let herself love Sam, she didn't know whether she'd sink or swim. She hadn't wanted him to leave her tonight, but her reaction to seeing Ginny had killed their joy. She meant to do her best to make up for it.

She took a filet mignon roast from her freezer and put it in the bottom of the refrigerator to defrost. Then, she got ready for bed and called it a night.

"You're looking very nice this morning," Bert told her when he came by to take her to church with him the next morning. "You're just shining. Seen Sam lately?"

"I saw him last night." She told him about the previous evening, how she got the tickets and the interview. "If it hadn't been on Saturday, I would have asked you to come."

"Thanks, but Saturday is my busiest day. We were still taking orders at eight o'clock. I sure would have loved to hear Raymond Feldon play that dobro. He's a master at it. I'll be listening for your special program with that interview. Howell's going to like that. Don't put it off too long. Some other radio jock might beat you to it."

"I didn't think of that. Clarissa gave me her card, so I think I'll call her."

"Well . . . If you think she won't mind."

They left the church around twelve fifteen. "Do you want to have lunch somewhere?" Bert asked her.

"I'd love to, Papa, but I'm spending the rest of the day with Sam."

"Glad to hear it. Give him my regards."

"Thanks. I will."

She jumped out of her father's car and raced into the building, but it seemed ages before the elevator arrived. She got off at her floor, sped down the hall, and came to a sliding stop in front of her apartment. "I'm losing my mind," she said when she couldn't find her key at once. She found it, went in, and began undressing as soon as she closed the door. Ten minutes later, she had on a pair of beige pants, the burnt-orange turtleneck sweater, and her gold-plated hoop earrings. She stuck her feet into a pair of loafers and raced to the kitchen. She prepared two pots for steaming vegetables, put tiny red potatoes in one and shallots in the other. Then, she washed cremini mushrooms and laid them on a towel on the counter to dry.

"He can sit here in the kitchen this evening while I clean the asparagus and make the leek soup," she said to herself. She found a package of frozen raspberries in the back of her freezer, and relaxed; raspberry sauce on vanilla ice cream was good enough for the president. She would have been happier if she'd had two packages, but one would suffice. She didn't have any wine. Too bad. Next time, she'd cook him a decent meal. With six minutes to spare, she brushed her teeth, combed her hair, and put on the jacket that matched her beige pants.

Sam looked at his watch. Right on time. He rang the doorbell.

When she opened the door, he flung his arms wide, lifted her, and hugged and kissed her. "I can't say why, but I feel great, and I hope you feel the same. How's your dad?"

"Whew! Let me recover from your mind-blowing greeting. He's fine."

A grin spread from his lips to his eyes. He winked at her.

"Think that was mind-blowing? Sweetheart, I've got enough stored up to blow a race car off its course. Nothing is going to derail me today."

As she thought back, she knew that her reaction to Ginny had derailed them last night. She didn't reassure him and congratulated herself for having the presence of mind—or was it an understanding of men—not to do it. He kissed her again, a fleeting, sweet thing that caused her to gaze at him with a question in her eyes.

Caution be damned. "You're so sweet," she said.

He stared at her for a long minute. "Where's your coat? Let's get out of here."

"We're going to a matinee," he told her. "It's kind of like Comedy Central, maybe a little cleaner. There's nothing like laughter to banish the stress. Besides, this guy is good. Reminds me of Bill Cosby in his younger days."

"I like witty stuff."

"Oh, I would never pay to expose myself to slapstick, and I can't stand pie throwing."

She slid down in the leather seat of the Enclave and made herself comfortable. She'd never thought that luxury could be so appealing. "Dick Gregory uttered one of the funniest lines I ever heard from a comedian. With a nonchalant demeanor, he said he knew a lot about the South—'I spent twenty years there . . . one night.' That's what I call wit."

"What would you like for lunch?" he asked her. "There are a lot of restaurants near this little theater."

"Any pizza nearby. I haven't had a slice of good pizza in ages. That's one thing I'm going to learn to make."

"You're on. I'm told the difficult thing about making pizza is the crust."

"I imagine so. I've seen guys stretching that dough. At least right now, I don't have to worry about that."

"You don't, and we're in luck. Here's a parking space half

a block from the theater and the restaurant. I'm going to have half a bottle of beer with my pizza," he said. "Think you can drink the rest?"

"Beer should be good with pizza." This man was bringing so many new and wonderful experiences to her life. It was becoming increasingly difficult to recall precisely what her life was like before she knew him, but there was one thing she didn't want to recall, and that was the loneliness. A loneliness that neither her friends, coworkers, nor her father filled, but which she hadn't felt since their first evening together.

Throughout the show, they held hands, laughed, clapped, and enjoyed the fun. "Maybe next time, we can stay for the second show," he said as they left, "but we're not far from the Corcoran Gallery. They have a new show. Dad went Saturday before last, and he said it's spectacular. Half an hour would be long enough."

"I'd love to go with you." She knew very little about art, so whatever she learned there would be a plus, and she might even enjoy it. "I haven't studied art, so I'm not good at appraising it. I rely on my gut instinct. Let's go." They walked hand in hand four blocks to the gallery. As they approached it, he said, "Music and art are two things I'm glad I don't have to live without."

They passed works of some American painters, and she liked what she saw, but she didn't understand it. Most modern paintings didn't speak to her. "Don't they have paintings by African Americans?" she asked him.

"Of course, but not in this particular show. The National Gallery has wonderful paintings by Romare Bearden, Jacob Lawrence, William H. Johnson, and others, and works by the sculptor, Elizabeth Catlett. We can go there next weekend, if you'd like."

"That would be wonderful. I'm learning that we have to feed the soul as well as the mind and the tummy. Speaking of tummies, if we don't head home, yours will be paining you before I put food in front of you."

His hand tightened almost imperceptibly on her arm, but it touched every nerve in her body. "You wouldn't starve me, would you?" It struck her as significant that he didn't smile.

Her fingers stroked the back of his cheek while, without trying to make a statement or to send a message, she searched his eyes. "I wouldn't intentionally do anything to hurt you, Sam. In fact, I'd take great pains to avoid it."

He stared at her. Then, his face brightened in a smile. "Right. I forget that we don't eat until after you cook."

Wanting to clear away anything that might cause a misunderstanding or otherwise put a damper on their evening together, she decided that she'd better warn him about the travel contest. "I haven't been able to make myself tell you that tomorrow's the day I turn in my assignment for the travel abroad prize."

"Why is that?"

"Maybe you would welcome not seeing me for a month, but I'm not sure I want to be away that long."

"A month? I thought you said six weeks. And what about your evening job?"

"Mr. Howell said that if I win, he'd ask my professors to allow me to go for only a month. He doesn't want me to be away for six weeks."

"Of course he doesn't, but after he hears that interview, I'll bet you can call your shots."

"I wasn't aiming for anything like that. My goal is to get through school and to do my job well."

He parked the car, helped her out, then opened the trunk, and removed a package. With an arm around her waist as they walked, he said, "I know what it means to reach a coveted goal, and I'll do all that I can and all that you allow to help you achieve yours. I'll be routing for you to make the highest score on that assignment."

She stopped walking. "Sometimes . . . like right now, I could . . . Oh, nuts! You've got me bamboozled. I have to watch it with you."

Inside her apartment, she hung their coats. "Want to pull off your jacket? I'm going to put you on a stool in the kitchen while I cook."

"That ought to be interesting," he said under his breath, but she heard him.

"All right. I will *invite* you to sit there."

She lit the gas caps beneath the potatoes and the shallots, and then went to her room and changed into a red, three-quarter sleeve, nylon jersey caftan with just the right amount of décolletage and went back to the kitchen. It pleased her that he'd gotten an apple from the refrigerator and was eating it.

After wiping the filet mignon roast with a damp towel, she seasoned it, covered it with butter, and put it in a roasting pan. She peeled and diced a potato, cleaned the leeks, cut them, and put them in a saucepan with two cups of fat-free chicken stock.

"What's that going to be?"

"Leek soup. I hope you'll like it," she said, and turned on the oven.

"I love leek soup, but until now, I had no idea what was in it other than leeks. You know, my mother used to make wonderful cornbread and biscuits. Lettie's an excellent cook, but her cornbread is for the birds."

"And you like cornbread?"

"I love it. Biscuits, too."

While she cleaned the asparagus, she wondered at the wisdom of adding another half hour to their wait for dinner. She looked in the pantry to see whether she had enough cornmeal. She had barely enough, but she'd use a smaller pan. She put the frozen raspberries and sugar in the blender, processed it, and poured it into a strainer to remove the seeds.

"How many things are you doing at once? And how do you keep it all in your head?"

"It's not difficult, Sam. I have in mind the way I want the table to look after I put the food on it. I forget sometimes, because I don't do this often, usually for my three girlfriends, or for Papa and me. And I'm nervous, because you're sitting here, and I don't want to mess up."

She mixed the cornbread and put it in the oven to bake. "Want me to set the table?" he asked her.

She stopped sieving the raspberries. "You know how to set a table?"

He winked at her. "I'm as good as Oscar of the Waldorf was when he started."

She put her chore aside, removed the potatoes from the flame, and went with him to the dining room. The flower that he gave her the night before sat on the white linen tablecloth. "It's all in there," she said, pointing to the cupboard against the wall. "Napkins and flatware in the drawers. Thanks. You're a real sweetie pie."

She turned to leave him, but he grasped her arm. "You keep telling me that I'm sweet. If I am, why don't you act like it?"

She gazed up at his face, the picture of petulance, and impulsively grasped the back of his head, stood on tiptoe, parted her lips above his, and pulled his tongue into her mouth. But immediately, she pulled away from his quick and fierce reaction.

"Set the table, honey. Another minute and everything in and on that stove would have gone to waste."

"Yeah. And while you're cooking, remember how you look to me in this thing you're wearing."

She walked away slowly, giving him a good look at her back action. Quickly, she prepared the dinner, cleaned the kitchen counters and put out the serving dishes. *Where was Sam? He hadn't said a word to her in the last fifteen minutes.*

* * *

Sam stood by the living-room window wondering why a woman's priorities so rarely seemed in harmony with a man's. He had observed that incongruity in his parents—as much as they had loved each other—among his friends, and in his own relationships. Kendra was hell-bent on feeding him a good meal, when he'd have been content with a hamburger, if only he could get into her arms.

He enjoyed the many differences between them, not the least of which were her softness, sweetness, and gentleness. And when she'd look at him, smile, and tell him he was sweet or that she never wanted to leave him, the world was his oyster, and all he wanted was to bury himself deep in her until she couldn't think of another man. He knew they began near the top, enchanted with each other the minute they met. Learning each other's personalities, dreams, goals, and needs had brought them close, but they hadn't crossed that all-important bridge of intimacy. He needed that. Badly. But was it right?

"Sam, can we eat now?" She walked up behind him and touched his shoulder with the tips of her fingers. "You're so quiet. Are you all right? Thanks for setting the table."

"Don't thank me for that. I wanted to do what I could to help you. And yes, I'm all right."

She walked him to sit opposite her, and he did.

"Do you mind if we say the grace?"

"No, I don't mind. We always said it at home." He said it and immediately sampled the leek soup. She cut the cornbread and offered him a piece.

"This is . . . When did you make this cornbread?"

"After you told me how much you like it. It extended the wait for dinner by about half an hour, but I figured it was worth it."

"It definitely was." He finished the soup and bread. "If you hadn't cooked anything else, I'd consider this a gourmet meal. Both were wonderful. And since you made the corn-bread for me, is there a reason why I can't take what's left home with me?"

"No, there isn't. I'm so glad you enjoyed it." Pride radiated from her when she served the main course. He looked at the roast, evenly browned and lying in a bed of roasted potatoes, shallots, and cremini mushrooms.

"If there is a weakness in this meal, Kendra, it's the absence of wine, and I brought a bottle each of red and white burgundy. Which would you like? I'll get it. The red goes best with our meal."

"Then red it will be," she said. He opened the wine, and they finished what he considered an excellent meal.

"We have dessert," she said, "and I'll make some coffee."

As he sat with her later sipping coffee in her living room, and pondering the evening, he realized that although it was clear to him that she wanted them to make love, and he wanted that probably more than she did, it was too soon. In the past few days, his strong physical attraction to her had begun to take a backseat to something inside of him, and if he was reading it right, he'd better be careful. If she met his physical needs, considering all of her other attributes, he'd no doubt be hooked.

Giselda had hooked him with sex and getting out of those chains had not been easy. He had to find a way to cool the pace of his relationship with Kendra without hurting her. He didn't want to ruin it, he only wanted it to proceed at a normal pace. But would she understand and help him?

Chapter Nine

Sam felt that if he could only be straight with Kendra, as he needed to be, they would be able to develop the deeper relationship that he'd just realized he wanted for them. He pushed the cup aside, got up, and sat facing her. Sensitive woman that she was, her entire demeanor changed at once.

"Don't jump to conclusions, sweetheart. But you and I have to talk. We've been moving like two thoroughbreds headed for the finish line, because we're deeply attracted to each other, but it's been based on this powerful physical attraction that we share. I'm feeling something else now that is apart from sex, and I want to nurture that in me and in you. I fully intended for us to make love this evening if you were willing, and I've been so keyed up about making love with you that I couldn't appreciate what you did since we got here. When I realized that you'd baked that cornbread, the best I've tasted in years, simply because you want me to be happy, I was humbled.

"This could be the most important thing that has happened to us, or we could exploit it, and it would be an affair, nothing more. I want to try for more, but I want to know what I'm doing. How do you feel about this?"

She thought for a while. "I'm pretty much stunned. You're right; we've traveled fast and far in a few weeks. You've said a number of times that you want us to get to know each other, and that made sense to me. Still, things sort of set their own course. I've never had this kind of relationship with a man, so I don't know the dangers. I understand that you want to pull back. Just tell me how far."

He leaned forward and looked at her intently, willing her to understand him. "I don't want to pull back. I want to slow down. In addition, there are strings that need to be tied and some that must be untied. I'm asking you, does any man have a right to demand anything of you?" She shook her head. "Good. I have no ties to any woman. I was engaged, but that died a bitter death almost three years ago. I've been over it almost as long."

"Does slowing down mean that you won't call me at eight o'clock mornings anymore?"

"Yes. It means that I'll call you when I need you or if I feel the need to talk with you, and that's more honest than a call the same time every morning. And I want you to call me whenever you need me or feel that you want to talk with me, even if it's three times a night. I want us to be open with each other. Can we sit here, play some music, and talk about our childhoods or whatever comes to mind?"

She put on some Louis Armstrong and Ella Fitzgerald CDs, lowered the volume, and went over and sat beside him. She put her head on his shoulder. She didn't know it, but she'd won more points with him in the last ten minutes than she needed. He put an arm around her shoulders and closed his eyes, contented.

"When I courted as a teenager, we spent Sunday afternoons in an ice cream parlor. Alexandria, Virginia, had a slew of them. What did you do?"

"My mama always had a boyfriend around, so I stayed in my room with the door locked. I started dating when I was in college."

"Why did you lock the door?"

"Because Mama's boyfriends didn't know what to do with their hands, and Mama didn't seem to notice."

The more he learned about that woman, the less he liked her. "I probably don't have the right to say what I'm thinking. At least you had some sense."

They talked until after eleven. "I'd better leave. We both have to get up early. My dad and I always spend Thanksgiving together. I suppose you spend it with your father. Let's try to work something out. I'm sure Dad is going to be wherever Edwina is, and who can blame him. Kiss me good night, sweetheart."

She walked with him to the door, and he could see that she was unsure of herself. He opened his arms, and she walked into them. With both arms around her, he urged her lips apart, and when the hard nubs of her breasts pressed against his chest, he wondered how long he could live according to his own sermon.

As he drove home, Sam acknowledged that Kendra's mother represented a problem for him, and that he had to be careful to put the blame and punishment where it belonged.

If Ginny had begun to represent a problem for Sam, Asa was about to become one for Ginny. She had borrowed five hundred dollars from her friend Angela claiming that she was due a new bank card, and that she should have it by Monday. Of course, she didn't have a bank card because the bank had rescinded her last one. She answered the telephone thinking that her caller was Asa.

"Hi, lover. What time—"

"This ain't your lover. This is Angela, and my husband is raising hell with me about that five hundred dollars you were supposed to give me this morning. Ginny, you better straighten up, 'cause my husband's 'bout to blow a gasket. If you got it now, I'll be there in a few minutes to get it. If you hadn't said it was a matter of life and death, I wouldn't 'a loaned you my husband's money."

If Angela came there, she'd run into Asa, who'd be there on his lunch hour. She sucked her teeth in disgust. Angela should have known that if she didn't have five hundred dollars Saturday morning, she wouldn't have it by eleven o'clock Monday.

"Don't come over here. You'll get me killed. I'll call you soon as I get it." She hung up and disconnected the telephone. If Asa called and got a busy signal, his temper would propel him to her that much faster. She borrowed the money from Angela because she'd promised to take Asa to see Clarissa Holmes on his one Saturday night off for that month. But she had to take him to dinner, too. That, with drinks and taxis had taken all but thirty dollars of the money she'd borrowed from Angela.

She'd called Kendra for help, and risked Ed's ire, but her precious daughter—the wretch—never returned her call. Now, Asa wanted to see the Giants play the Redskins that night, his night off, and she'd told him she had promised to get the tickets—but where was she going to get the money? Damn Angela.

She had other things to worry about. A good-looking, young man like Asa, who could put it down every time, could get any woman he wanted. She gazed at herself in the mirror, reached in the cabinet for a piece of black chalk, and colored the newest strand of gray that grew near her temple. A hundred dollars for a hairdresser to color her hair! She didn't have it. With an oath, she swore that Kendra or somebody would give her some money. If she got it from a man, Asa would have a piece of her. She paced from the living room to the kitchen and back. *But did he have to know it?*

Using her cell phone, she telephoned the one person she could rely on. She couldn't stand him, because she had to do things she didn't like doing, and she got no pleasure from it. But he was good for a thousand, and he would be anxious to see her. But she'd be half-dead after hours of his sucking and stroking every orifice she had with his tongue and demanding that she return the favor.

She phoned Asa. "I have to leave now to get the tickets,

and there'll probably be a long line. I sure hope they have some left," she said. He didn't catch the fact that she'd told him she had the tickets.

"All right, babe. See you at about six-thirty."

She got into a taxi to keep her rendezvous with the old man, seconds before Angela and her husband parked in front of her building in which Ginny lived.

Morning found Kendra somewhat less accepting of Sam's wish to temper their fast-moving relationship. After fretting about it, she telephoned Suzy. "If I had a real mother, I could discuss this with her," she said after they talked awhile. She gave Suzy a brief summary of Sam's conversation with her. "What do you think? At first, I didn't take exception to it, but he's been leading me to believe that I'm . . . that he's practically in love with me."

"Hold on there, Kendra. Until a man uses those three words, don't think he loves you. I think Sam just moved from wanting you badly, to really caring, and he has now defined for himself what he feels. You mean more to him than you did before, and he's trying to protect that. Remember that he knows himself a lot better than you do."

"That's a fact. Thanks, Suzy. We'll talk later; I have to get to class."

From nine to eleven, she sat in an auditorium with thirty other students, widely separated, and wrote a journalistic account of her high school graduation day. She hadn't known what the topic would be, and she was at a disadvantage, in that she had been out of high school twelve years compared to an average of two-and-a-half years for her competitors. But she remembered it well, because the rain had fallen in torrents all morning, and the sun had shone early in the afternoon during the commencement exercises. She gave the valedictory address looking like a wet rat, and in the evening, she had neither a date nor a dress—thanks to her mother's forgetfulness—to wear to the graduates' ball. She gave the tale the poignancy that she felt as she looked back to that day, turned in her paper with her fingers crossed and left the auditorium.

Shortly after she entered the broadcast studio that afternoon, Clifton Howell walked in. "How'd you like the concert? I hear it was over the top. Did you find anybody to go with you?"

"It was wonderful, and I took three friends with me. But I've got a present for you, Mr. Howell."

"Really? What is it?" His eagerness surprised her.

"Well, I got to thinking that I'm a journalist, and Clarissa Holmes is news." Howell's face lost its eagerness and took on an expression of anticipation. "So I e-mailed her for an interview, and she granted it and sent me a pass to her dressing room."

He sat down. "Tell me you're not making this up."

"After the show, which was very long, my friends and I went backstage. She and her husband greeted us, served us champagne, and after two of my friends left, she and I sat and talked for half an hour." She showed him the recorder. "I've got it right here, and I'm planning a two-hour show of her CDs around this interview. I thought Thursday would be a good night."

"Thursday? You serious?"

He hadn't said he appreciated it, and she was becoming apprehensive. "I . . . uh . . . thought we'd spend a few days advertising the program."

"A few days. Kendra, you strike when the iron is hot. Air it tomorrow night. We'll advertise it beginning tonight both on radio and television, and I'll have it in the papers tomorrow morning. Let's make it from eight-thirty to ten-thirty, so people can call in their comments before you leave. This is absolutely wonderful. You'll have a substantial bonus in your pay this period."

"You haven't heard the interview yet."

"I'm not worried about that. You don't half-do anything."

He examined the recorder. "It will play over the air perfectly. This is a first-class recorder. I'll get to work on the ads, and don't forget to announce it every fifteen minutes. I'm proud of you, Kendra. You have far more than justified my faith in you."

A bit more than an hour later, he put his head in her studio. "Can you read the news? I think Marcie is going into labor. I'm taking her to the hospital, Roane is out on dinner hour, and Quincy's full of bourbon. Today's his fortieth birthday, and he hasn't made his first million. Put forty-five minutes of CDs on." He handed her the news copy.

"Yes, sir. I'll do my best." She had a minute to read over the copy and correct the grammar. She wished she knew how to pronounce *Erkowit*, a place in Sudan, but her listeners probably didn't know how to pronounce it, either. She switched channels, read the six-thirty news, and congratulated herself on not having stammered or otherwise embarrassed herself.

Her phone rang. "Ms. Richards, this is Sam. I heard you read the news, and it was a very smooth job."

"Thanks, Sam. I'm surprised that you were listening. I'm not on an open line."

"I wasn't sure. You sounded like a true pro. What did Howell say about your interview with Clarissa Holmes?"

"After he got over the shock, he was delighted, even excited. He said we'll air it tomorrow night at eight-thirty." She told Sam of Howell's advertising plans. "And he said I get a bonus in my next pay."

"You may have changed the course of your career when you got that interview."

"Maybe. I kinda hope my career will be with Howell Enterprises."

"You'll have even more to offer after you receive your degree. I'm happy for you. My dad wants to know if you and your father can join us for Thanksgiving dinner at his place in Alexandria."

"I'm sure Papa will agree. Thank your dad for inviting us. I'll—"

He interrupted her. "My dad invited your father. I'm *bringing* you. That is not the same."

"Sir, I stand corrected."

"I'd better not keep you. There's nothing like dead air to make your boss furious. Can I pick you up at school tomorrow? If so, we'll get a bite somewhere and I'll take you on to work."

"Don't you have classes on Tuesday?"

"I do, but only in the morning."

"I'm free at one tomorrow. I'll be at the John H. Johnson School of Communications on Bryant Street."

"I know where that is, and I'll be there at one. Oh. How did the exam go today?"

"We had to report on the day of our high school graduation. I'll never forget standing in front of all those people and delivering the valedictory address with my hair, shoes, and clothing sticking to me after one of the heaviest downpours I can remember. It was June, and I was freezing. I did my best on that test."

"I'm pulling for you. Kisses. Bye."

"I kiss you, too, Sam." She hung up wondering how long their careful behavior would last.

Ginny didn't get as much from the old man as she usually did, and she spent all that he gave her on the football tickets and transportation for her and Asa to and from the game. Asa's appetite for limousines rather than taxis had raised the cost of keeping him happy.

She stood beside one of the big square columns that flanked the entrance of the building in which Kendra lived and waited. Fortunately, a steady rain insured that the minute a woman stepped out of the door she would be distracted while she opened her umbrella. As she had anticipated, Kendra came out and opened her umbrella, and at that second, Ginny snatched her daughter's pocketbook. But she had not considered Kendra's athleticism—her excellence at track, basketball, and fencing. Before she could escape with the pocketbook, Kendra tripped her up, and she went sprawling across the sidewalk.

Kendra bent to retrieve the pocketbook and gasped. "Mama, for goodness' sake! How could you!" The doorman had phoned for the police, but Kendra didn't wait. She spun around and went back to change her wet clothing. Before she returned, the police arrived.

"You'll have to come with us, ma'am," the policeman said.

"Come with you? Get your hands off me. I haven't done anything."

"This doorman said you attempted to steal a tenant's pocketbook. You're coming with us."

"I want to call my lawyer."

"You do that after we book you."

Kendra changed her clothes as quickly as she could, blow-dried her hair, and forced it into a knot at the back of her head. If she could get a taxi, she'd make it to class.

The doorman waylaid her. "Ms. Richards, the police want you to go down and press charges against that purse snatcher."

She cringed, but the man didn't know that he was referring to her mother. "I don't want to press charges," she said. "She didn't get away with it, and that's all I care about."

"Yes, ma'am. If you're sure."

"I'm sure. Could you please help me get a taxi?" He called a cab company, and while she stood at his desk waiting for the taxi, the full measure of what her mother had attempted hit her with the force of a sledgehammer, and she groped her way across the lobby and sat down. The doorman brought her a paper cup of water.

"I think you don't feel well. Should you go out in this weather?"

"I'll be all right, thanks. I'm going to class." The taxi arrived, she got in, and, in spite of the traffic, she took her seat in class a minute before the professor closed the door. At the end of the fifty-five-minute lecture, she could not recall one word that the instructor had uttered.

When one o'clock arrived, the rain had ceased, but the sky remained overcast, and the rising wind signaled the imminent arrival of colder weather. When Sam drove up, her spirits revived, and she fairly skipped to the car. He got out to greet her.

"Hi." He kissed her cheek, opened the door for her, fastened her seat belt, and closed the door. "You're not your usually ebullient self. Is there something wrong?"

"You could say that, but it can wait till we're at the restaurant or wherever we're going."

"We're going to have a proper lunch. I hope you don't mind that I ordered it in advance, but you don't have time to wait forty minutes while a cook hones his skill."

"I don't mind. Sam, you're such a thoughtful and considerate man. I like that about you."

"That's a sweet thing for you to say. Any news about the test?"

"Not yet. Three professors have to grade all of the papers. I'm not nervous about it. If I win, I win. If not, not."

He parked a short walk from the Howell Building. "We're close by, so you won't have to rush." He had reserved a table, and as soon as they sat down, the waiter brought them lobster bisque.

"Oh my gosh, Sam. I'm crazy about this. I've been promising myself to learn how to make it. It's delicious."

Midway through the second course, Sam said, "I'm having a hard time waiting to find out what upset you since we spoke last night."

She stopped eating. "Brace yourself." After taking a deep breath, she told him about Ginny's latest trick.

He didn't speak until he'd finished eating. "What's her address?"

"No. You don't want to get involved with her."

"I *am* involved with her. She's trashing your life. Give me her address." She shook her head. "All right. Don't. I can get it in five minutes."

She shook her head as if rejecting the inevitable. "Last I heard, she was in jail. But since I refused to press charges, she may have been released by now."

"She deserves permanent residence there. Are you airing the Holmes interview tonight?"

"Yes, at eight-thirty. Goodness, I forgot to tell Papa, and I'm not sure I'll have time."

"Don't worry. I'll call him when I leave you."

He had asked her to slow down, but even though he wasn't touching her, she was seeping deeper and deeper into him. She was so vulnerable, and he had a deep-seated feeling that she needed him.

"Have you told your father about this morning's happenings?"

"No. I try not to mention such things to him when he's working. I'll tell him when he picks me up tonight."

They finished the meal, and he walked outside with Kendra, kissed her cheek, and watched her go into the Howell Building. He had the feeling of one suspended over a precipice. As much as he cared for Kendra, he could not allow himself to become involved with a woman who would do what her mother did that morning. And to have such a woman as the grandmother of his children was unthinkable. He walked toward his car, passed a Starbucks, turned back, and walked in. After ordering a cup of coffee, he found Bert Richards's card and telephoned him.

"I hope I'm not disturbing you, sir. This is Sam Hayes."

"How are you, Sam? Good to hear from you. What's up?"

"Kendra wants you to be sure and tune in on her program tonight at eight-thirty. She forgot to tell you that she'll be broadcasting her interview with Clarissa Holmes and playing Holmes's recordings. She asked me to phone you."

"Thank you. I wouldn't have missed that for anything."

"She did a great job. I hope I'll see you soon."

"Same here."

Sam threw the remainder of the coffee into the wastebasket and walked back to his car. He realized that he'd parked in front of a florist and, without giving it much thought, he went inside, bought a dozen long-stemmed red roses, and had them sent to Kendra. On the note, he wrote, "Thinking of you. Sam." *I don't know why I did that, but I did, and I feel good about it.* He was not confused about his feelings for Kendra; far from it. His problem was what he'd do about them.

At his father's suggestion, he ate supper with Jethro and Edwina, after which they sat in Jethro's living room sipping liqueurs and espresso coffee while they waited to hear Kendra's program. At eight-thirty, Clarissa's sultry voice began the soulful words of "Sophisticated Lady" and immediately faded into the background.

"Hey, all you Holmes fans, this is KT. Tonight is Clarissa Holmes night, and for the next two hours, we're going to celebrate her in her own words and her own music."

"This interview sounds as if it's live," Edwina said. "What kind of recorder did she use?"

He didn't miss his dad's knowing look. "Probably the best small recorder available. She said Sam gave it to her."

"I'll have to ask her to let me see it."

"That won't be necessary," Jethro said. "I'll ask Sam about it."

It looked to him as if Edwina and his father were living together, but until his dad told him, he wouldn't mention it. He closed his eyes and let the smooth tones of "When a Woman Loves a Man" flow over him. Listening to the famous singer express the meaning of that song got to him. He opened his eyes to see Jethro and Edwina locked in a torrid kiss and wished there was some way that he could give them the privacy that they needed. He doubted that they knew he was in the room.

At the end of the program, he was more than ready to leave them. He wanted to see Kendra, but her father would meet her when she left work, and he had no role to play. But whose fault was that? He went home, not merely disgruntled, but irritated at himself. Yet, he knew that where Kendra was concerned, he'd done the right thing. They were headed for a relationship in which sex was the end-all and be-all, and he'd realized—barely in time—that he wanted more with her. Something on the periphery of his conscience told him that he was ready to build a family, but he had two good reasons not to build it with her. *And at least two good reasons that favored her,* his niggling conscience reminded him.

He headed home. Maybe what he needed was a dog. He laughed at himself. No dog could substitute for the way her breasts felt against his chest the last time he held her close.

Clifton Howell flung open the studio door, his hand outstretched. "Kendra, you hit a home run. It was off the chain. The phones are ringing constantly. Do you have her address? I want to drop her a note, thank her, and tell her she has a home at WAMA Radio and WAMTV. You're a wonderful interviewer. I can see you a few years down the road with your own TV show." He sat down. "I can't tell you how proud of you I am. And for WAMA to pull off a tour de force like that . . ." He beamed. "Let 'em eat humble pie."

Kendra left the radio station feeling as if she walked on clouds. Howell had as much as told her he'd eventually shift her to his television station, but she didn't want to be an overly made-up pretty face asking inane questions of the latest popular celebrities; she wanted to collect and report the news.

Her father parked as she walked out of the building. "Hi, Papa. Did you hear it?"

"I did, and it was great. You are a wonderful interviewer. You made that woman respond to you as if you were her best friend. I wish I could have seen that on TV. Your boss had to be pleased with it."

"He was, and he came in and told me so."

She waited until he parked in front of the building in which she lived. "Papa, I have something to tell you." From his silence, she knew that he was preparing himself for the worst. She told him of her mother's attempt to steal her pocketbook. "I think she's losing her mind. Why won't she work a steady job?"

"She's done some awful things, but I would have thought that was beneath her. I'd like to know why she's so desperate. She's too self-centered to take care of a man . . . but, well, you never know. Is she in jail?"

"I don't know. I refused to press charges."

"When you finish school, get a job in New York or someplace where she can't find you. It's bad enough that you can't depend on her and that you don't have a mother–daughter relationship, but for you to have her as an enemy is horrible, and it's painful for me to watch."

"I'm tough, Papa, and I can thank her behavior for that. She isn't going to drag me down. I won't let her." She hugged her father and went inside.

The doorman stopped her. "How are you, Ms. Richards? I have something here for you." He handed her a vase of red roses wrapped in clear cellophane. She thanked the doorman, and when she got into her apartment, she unwrapped the flowers, thinking that Clifton Howell had gone overboard.

She opened the little envelope and read: "Thinking of you, Sam."

Kendra sat down. Holding the crystal vase in her lap, she leaned her head against the back of a chair and let the tears cascade down the sides of her face. She had needed someone, and he was there for her. It was twenty minutes after twelve, but she had to talk with him. She went to her bedroom, put the roses on her night table, sat on the bed, and dialed Sam's number.

"Hello, Kendra. I'm glad you called. Your show was great. I listened at my dad's house along with him and Edwina."

"Thank you, Sam. Your verdict is important to me, but I'm calling because these beautiful roses and the sentiments on your card are what I needed tonight. Thank you."

"Did your father hear your show?"

"Yes, he did, and he enjoyed it. Well, I just wanted you to know that what I got from you tonight lifted me up at a time when I needed that."

"Say, wait a minute. After the success of your show, you should have been happy. Oh, no. What happened to you this morning finally set in. Baby, do you want me to come over there?"

"I won't lie and say no, but if anything ever happens between you and me, Sam, I want it to happen naturally. But knowing that you would come to me this time of night is one more reason why you're dear to me. Good night."

"You're dear to me, too. Good night, sweetheart."

She hung up feeling better. He may have slowed things down, but he cared for her and wasn't loath to express it. She made up her mind to seek psychiatric help for Ginny, but she didn't want any direct contact with her, so she would probably need the assistance of local authorities. She made a note to speak to a psychiatric social worker. There was no point in allowing her mother to destroy herself.

When Kendra entered Professor Hormel's class the following morning, he called to her. "Ms. Richards, may I see you after class?"

"Yes, sir." She took her seat and tried to focus on the lecture, but her mind insisted upon trying to guess what Professor Spam—the students' nickname for him—wanted. At the end of class, she stopped at his desk.

"We've read the papers of our nine best students, and I don't see anybody catching you. We've taken Egypt off the list of countries for the winner to visit and added Kenya and The Gambia. This is confidential."

"Thank you, sir. I wouldn't dare mention it. Is Florence, Italy, still on the list?"

"Italy is on the list. The winner can choose where to go in a particular country."

"If I win, would you have a suggestion?"

"You'll find plenty to write about in each of these countries, but no country compares to Italy for variety. I could write books on the experience of just eating in Italy. Do your research and choose well."

She dashed into the ladies' room and nearly knocked over an obviously pregnant student. "I'm sorry. Are you all right?" she asked the woman.

"Fine except that I keep tripping over my shoe strings."

Kendra looked down at the untied shoes. "Can't you tie them?"

"I've tried everything but a robot. Maybe I'd better take out the strings."

"I'll tie them for you," Kendra said, put her bookbag and pocketbook on the floor, and tied the woman's shoes. "Won't the baby's father do that for you?"

"He can't stand responsibility, so I sent him packing. I'm in this by myself, and I'm dealing with it."

"Good girl. If you're right here tomorrow morning at nine, I'll be glad to tie them for you."

"You're an angel. I'll be here. Thanks."

Kendra waved her on, but suddenly she remembered Natalie, her coworker at La Belle Époque who feared that she might be pregnant by a man who had lied to her about his marital status. During her lunch period, she telephoned Natalie at home, got no answer, and left a message. She had been so caught up in her rapidly changing world that she'd forgotten her former coworker who had encouraged her and been a friend to her on several occasions.

"It's a lesson, and I won't forget it," she said to herself.

With about half an hour at her disposal, Kendra went up to Founders Library on the main campus, and began her search for information about the kind of caregiver who could help her mother. She didn't expect to succeed overnight, but she had to begin, because each one of Ginny's escapades seemed more desperate and more outrageous than the last.

She didn't mention her search to her father when he picked her up from work that night, but she might have if he hadn't brought up the matter of Thanksgiving Day dinner. "I got a phone call from Sam's father. He said he and Sam always have Thanksgiving dinner together, but that he's sure Sam intends to have dinner with you and that you'd want to have dinner with me, so we should all go to his house. He asked if I had allergies or if there was something I didn't like, which was real thoughtful of him. I told him I hated brains, kidneys, liver, or anything from the inside of a pig. That drew a big laugh from him. He sounded like he wants you and Sam to make it permanent."

"He's a man who scrutinizes a thing until he practically singes it, makes up his mind, and doesn't waver thereafter. I like him a lot."

"That's because he likes you."

"Did you tell him you'd go?"

"Of course I did. That means you and I will entertain at Christmas."

"He's involved with a very nice lady. I'm anxious to see how it works out."

"If the way you described him a minute ago is accurate, it will work out. Any more nonsense from Ginny?"

"No, sir, and when I don't hear anything from her, I begin to get nervous."

"If you like, I can take you to school mornings. If she sees me, she won't tarry. Does she know what you're studying?"

"Not unless she followed me to the communication school. If she doesn't lay off, I'll have to get a restraining order, Papa. But you and I both know she would ignore it. I don't want to be the reason my mother goes to jail."

"You wouldn't be the reason; she'd be there because of her attitude and behavior."

"I know you're right, but all the same . . ." She reached over and kissed his cheek. "Good night, Papa, and thanks."

"Don't thank me. If you need me to take you to school, call."

Ginny dragged herself out of bed, went to the kitchen, and checked her refrigerator. With what she had in her freezer and in the pantry, she could eat for the rest of the week. After that, she'd have to beg Phil to take appointments for her. She hated having to pamper women who weren't as good as she was and accepting the measly tips they offered. With Angela's husband's car parked in front of her building every day for a miserable little five hundred dollars, what else could she do? She couldn't leave the building as long as he sat there. But she'd find a way. If necessary, she'd leave by the back alley.

She'd lied to Asa and told him that she had a viral flu, but she'd noticed that the bastard hadn't been there to check. He hadn't sent her any flowers, either. She used her cell phone to call Phil.

"This is Ginny. I'm just getting over that awful flu. Damned thing nearly took me out of here, but I'm fine now. Haven't had a fever in four days. Could you put me down for some appointments?"

"You're good at what you do, Ginny, that is, when anybody can get you to work. I'm putting you down for Tuesday to Saturday every week. The holidays are coming up, and that's when we make the money. The first day you don't show up here, that's the day I'm putting an ad in the paper for your replacement. You could make over a thousand a week if you'd get off your lazy ass and work. I'll see you Tuesday or not at all."

"I'll see you Tuesday, Phil." A thousand a week! He thought that was money? She kicked the ladder-back kitchen chair halfway across the dining room. "I'm not standing on my feet forty hours every week for nobody." She made a pot of quick grits, steamed a hotdog, put some butter on the grits, poured boiling water over instant coffee, and ate her breakfast. As she was putting the dishes in the dishwasher, she remembered. And recoiled. Her postponed hearing had been rescheduled for the day before, and she had forgotten it.

She phoned the court clerk. "I've been in bed sick, and I just remembered it."

"If you're smart, you'll get here before the cops go to your house to get you, and they could be on their way."

She looked out the window, didn't see Angela's husband's car, brushed her teeth, dashed into her clothes, powdered her face, put on some lipstick, and headed for the elevator. She put on her dark glasses, took the elevator to the basement, and left by the back alley.

"You're a lucky woman, Mrs. Hunter. In another minute, I would have signed this warrant for your arrest," a court officer said when she walked in.

Chapter Ten

Sam walked out of his classroom that afternoon feeling out of sorts. He'd made it to the university in spite of the second late-autumn blizzard of the year, a weather pattern with which Washington was unfamiliar and for which it was unprepared. His normal trip to work took him from fifteen to twenty minutes by car, but after more than an hour of trudging through the wind and snow, and standing on corners trying to thumb a ride, he'd entered his classroom practically frozen. His hands were so cold that he was unable to write. But with eleven of his twenty-three students present, he was glad he'd made the trip.

"Do you have an hour to spare, Professor Hayes?" a colleague, James Enders, called to him.

He stopped and waited until the man was walking along with him. "What's up, Jim? If it's important, I can take the time."

"You live in my direction. What do you say we stop at Rooter's or someplace like that, get a cup of coffee, or a beer and a sandwich or something? I've got a problem with one of my students, and I think she has a class under you. I'd suggest the faculty lounge, but, considering this weather, I want to get as close to home as possible before the rush hour begins."

"If it's convenient for you. I didn't drive."

"I drove my four-wheel-drive jeep," Enders said, "so this snow won't be a problem."

Sam had a feeling of satisfaction. An hour of his time in exchange for a comfortable trip home didn't require a second thought. "Sure. Do you live near Rooter's?"

A sheepish expression settled on James Enders's face. "Six or so blocks. I confess to being addicted to those little hors d'oeuvres they serve during happy hour."

Sam laughed. "You could be addicted to worse."

"Yeah. That's what I tell myself. Fortunately—or unfortunately, depending on how you look at it—my observations of the effects of alcoholism as a child were sufficient to ensure my devotion to sobriety. One drink of anything is as much as I'm comfortable with."

"You're a wise man. You may be genetically predisposed to alcoholism. These are things we can't predict, though it seems to me that if you were, you'd know it by now."

It was Sam's first ride in a jeep, and to his way of thinking, it wasn't bad. They walked into Rooter's, where four or five men, two women, a bartender, and a uniformed messenger conversed as a group. Jim ordered gin and tonic in order to get a tray of free hors d'oeuvres and, since he wasn't driving, Sam ordered a vodka comet.

"I've passed here plenty of times," Sam said to Jim, "but never been in this place before. It's rather pleasant."

"That's because the snow has kept most of the regulars at home. It can be very noisy." Sam glanced at the mirror behind the bar and frowned. A woman was gazing at him as if she wanted to get to know him. She was decent-looking, but near the age his mother would have been if she were still alive. She smiled at him, and a strange sensation shot through him. When the woman smiled, she reminded him of Kendra. He motioned for the bartender.

"What's the name of the woman who's wearing the gray tweed coat?" he asked the bartender.

No one had to tell him that he'd asked that man the

wrong question. "What's it to you, buddy? No pick-ups allowed in here. If that's what you're looking for, you can leave right now."

"No offense meant," he said. "She looks so much like my girlfriend that I'm curious about her."

"Looks like your girlfriend, huh?"

Sam looked the man in the eye. "Yeah. She does. They could be mother and daughter."

He could see that he'd piqued the man's interest. "Her name's Hunter, Ginny Hunter, but if you try to pick her up, buddy, you're gonna be in big trouble." Sam's lower jaw dropped. The woman looked at him, lowered her lashes and winked.

"What's your problem?" the bartender asked.

"That's my girlfriend's mother. That's her name."

The bartender narrowed his eyes. "I gave you information, so you give me some. How old is your girlfriend?"

Aware now as to the reason for the bartender's interest and behavior, Sam looked him in the eye. "She's thirty-two years old. I hope I haven't created any problems for anybody."

The bartender brought him another drink. "No, you haven't, but you've answered some questions. The drinks for you and your friend are on me."

Sam stirred the drink, looked at Jim, and said, "Were you following my conversation with that guy?"

"Only snatches of it. As soon as we sat down, I figured he had something going with that woman who's wearing the gray coat. He looked at her as if . . . as if she dances to his tune, but she's looking for an opportunity to meet you."

"In that case, I just screwed things up for her."

"That, too. I'm waiting to see what his reaction is."

Sam didn't look at the woman, but gazed at her reflection in the mirror as the bartender spoke to her in what appeared to be a less than friendly manner.

"That's a lie."

"No, it isn't," the bartender said. "You're over fifty, if you're a day, and you've got a daughter who's only four years younger than I am. You're almost old enough to be my mother, and you were lying when you said you were forty. I knew I'd catch you. And another thing. That lie you told me about being independently wealthy. I'd like to know how you manage your lifestyle."

She jumped up from the bar stool and glared at him. "No two-bit gigolo of a bartender is going to look down his nose at me." As if she didn't need to make another point at the man's expense, she shoved the drink toward him. "Here. Dump it out. It didn't cost you a penny. Old man Dunner puts you in the shade."

"If saying that makes you feel good, fine with me," the bartender said, "but if you're smart, you'll shut up. I've had it up to here with you." He sliced the air above his head.

She tightened her coat, headed toward the door, and stopped when she reached Sam.

"You don't believe what that ridiculous man was saying, do you? Why don't you and your friend come by my place for a drink? It's not far, and it's very warm there."

Sam stared at Ginny Hunter, feeling his lips curl into a snarl. "You're not my type." He turned his back to her as raw pain seared his insides. What kind of life had Kendra suffered during the years that she lived with her mother?

"I'm sorry, man," James said. "I wish I'd suggested some other place."

"Actually, you've done me a favor. I can't imagine how I would have gotten home if you weren't taking me there in your jeep."

"I'm glad you feel that way," James said. "Anyway the problem concerns a student who's got two-year-old twins. She's an A student, left her husband because he's non-supportive, abusive, and cheats. I suspect she doesn't even get enough to eat and that she gives what she has to her children. But her concern doesn't seem to be with her health, only with getting her degree."

Sam put the glass down, dragged his attention from Kendra's mother, and frowned. "You mean Melody Jenkins? Yeah. I've been concerned about her, and I've been wondering if I should ask the Dean of Women to check whether she's getting adequate food and health care."

"That's an idea. The university has money for helping needy students."

"Yeah, but they have to ask for it. I'll speak with the dean tomorrow. You do the same." He drained his glass. "It's getting dark."

"So it is. I don't suppose they give doggie bags full of these goodies," James said.

Sam couldn't help grinning. "Next time, bring a big plastic Ziplock bag."

"Right," James said. "Wonder why I never thought of that."

The bartender walked over to Sam. "I'm called Asa. You helped me out of a hole I've been telling myself I had to get out of. It made no sense, and I was taking advantage of her. I hope your girlfriend is not a chip off the old block."

"No, she isn't, and as you may imagine, her life has not been an easy one."

"I wish you luck, man," Asa said.

"Thanks. I suspect I'll need it."

As James drove the jeep through snow and ice, the two men hardly spoke. Sam had locked his mind on Ginny Hunter and her brazen invitation to bring his friend to her home for a threesome sexual romp with her, a complete stranger. He had refused to give her the satisfaction of knowing that she had propositioned her daughter's boyfriend. And he did not doubt that she would have rejoiced in having done it, that she would delight in any pain she could inflict on Kendra.

He thanked James for getting him home in comfort. "Don't forget to contact Dean Watkins tomorrow."

"I'll get it done before noon. Thanks for your support in this."

"I'm glad you brought it to my attention. The woman needs help, and it's our duty to see that she gets it. You can't let a straight-A student fall through the cracks. See you tomorrow."

He wanted to talk with Kendra; indeed, he had a driving, gnawing need to protect her, but something was eating at him that he suspected wouldn't let him have a normal conversation with her. He wished he hadn't gone to Rooter's Bar and Grill and that he hadn't encountered Ginny Hunter. His estimation of her had not been high, and now, he didn't feel that he could comfortably be in her company for even five minutes. Any man with the tiniest of brains would know that if he continued the relationship with Kendra, both of them could be miserable as a consequence.

Because of the weather, Lettie hadn't been able to get to work. He prowled around the kitchen looking for something to eat. Exasperated after half an hour of searching, he telephoned his housekeeper.

"Lettie, this is Sam Hayes. I'm starving. What can I find to eat?"

"I called you a couple 'a times, Mr. Hayes. Who'd 'a thought you went out in this weather. Look in the freezer. You'll find quiches, pizzas, beef pot pies, and chicken pot pies. All you have to do is select one, turn the oven on to four hundred, shove it in, and wait twenty minutes. I made all of 'em and froze them for just such times as this. There's cold beer on the bottom shelf of the refrigerator in the back. And you can have apple pie à la mode for dessert—but warm the pie. It's on the top refrigerator shelf. I'll be in tomorrow, 'cause my son said he'll bring me. He couldn't get his car out of the garage this morning."

"I didn't expect you here today, Lettie, and with all that

food in the freezer, stay home tomorrow if your son can't bring you."

"Thanks, Mr. Hayes, but he's good as his word."

This was one thing that Sam did not want to discuss with his father. On the other hand, Bert Richards would understand, but what man wanted to be reminded that he'd made such a gargantuan mistake with a woman? "Suck it up, fellow," he said to himself.

He finished a delightful meal of beef pot pie, Pilsner beer, warm apple pie, and vanilla ice cream, made a cup of coffee, turned on the television, and sat down to watch the news and sip coffee. "This won't due," he said to himself. "What if she needs me?" He dialed Kendra's home phone number, got no answer, and dialed her number at the studio.

"WAMA, KT speaking."

"Hello. How'd you get in?"

"The show must go on, as they say on Broadway. All lines are open tonight, because only three of us were able to get through this weather. How are you, friend? We're doing everything tonight, manning the phones, reading the news, even reading the commercials. I'll get to you as soon as I can."

"Nice going, KT," he said. "You're absolutely number one. If you get a chance, please play 'Everything I Have Is Yours.' "

"You bet I will. Any way you cut it, you're the greatest, friend."

He thanked her and hung up. He felt a little better after talking with her, but now he worried about how she'd get home. Why the devil had he given her the impression that he wanted to cool down their relationship? Granted, it had been moving too fast, but what had he solved? Nothing. In fact, he'd interjected unnecessary complications. He looked at his watch. Bert should be home, if indeed he'd left in that blizzard. He dialed Kendra's father's telephone number.

"Richards speaking."

"Mr. Richards, this is Sam Hayes. Kendra is at work tonight, but all of her lines are open, and I couldn't ask her how she'll get home. Do you know?"

"Good to hear from you, Sam. One of my customers has a towing service. He took her in this afternoon, and he'll take her home tonight."

"I take it you trust this guy."

"If I didn't, you bet I wouldn't have called him. I've known him for fifteen years. He's as straight as they come. Thank you for your interest. And it's all right if you call me Bert."

"Thanks. Kendra is important to me, and I care about everything that concerns her."

"I know that, Sam, and I hope she does, too."

Immediately after he hung up, his cell phone rang. "Hello, Kendra. Thanks for calling me back. I wanted to know how you'll get home, but I called your dad, and he told me. I'm impressed that you're practically running the station tonight."

"It's not too bad, but I wouldn't like it as a steady job. I'll play your request in five minutes. Let's get together someplace this weekend."

"I'd thought we might explore Alexandria. We hardly saw the old town and, except for the cotton picking, plantation slavery of the Deep South, it's a living history of African American life from the early eighteenth century onward. What do you think?"

"I'd love it. If I had a car, I think I'd spend my free time getting acquainted with the nearby historical places. Would you believe I've never been to the Chesapeake Bay?"

"Then I'm going to have a wonderful time introducing you to Maryland's Eastern Shore. I've got my boat docked over there, but it's down for the winter. I may go to my place over there around the first of the year or for a quiet New Year's Eve."

"My papa said that your family is to spend Christmas Eve with us. He has a really nice apartment in Silver Spring. But he'll tell you about that when he sees you next week at your dad's house."

"I'm looking forward to that. From the time Mom died, Dad and I are usually alone at Thanksgiving, and it's been a rather sad occasion. But this year will be different, and I'm going to enjoy celebrating the holiday."

"At least you miss your mother. I'm not sure I'd ever miss mine."

He didn't want to think about Ginny Hunter. "Let's not dwell on anything that hurts you right now, Kendra. You'll reflect it in your tone when you're on the air."

"You're right, and the five minutes are about up. Here's your song. Bye for now." He'd have her understand that it was *their* song, but time enough for that.

Ginny struggled home through the thick snow, unable to feel her heels or her toes. Once home, she filled the bathtub with hot water, sat on the side of it, and let the water bring her feet back to life. She had been almost oblivious to the discomfort as thoughts of Asa and his cruel remarks pained her. She'd like to know who told him about Kendra and how he found out about her situation. For two cents, she could maim him. He was hell in bed, but other than that, he wasn't much of a man. She rubbed her tingling left foot against her right instep in an attempt to get rid of the numbness.

Now what was she going to do? If those men had come home with her, she'd have gotten at least fifty dollars from them, maybe more since they looked prosperous. She took her feet out of the tub, dried them, and padded barefoot to the kitchen. She had to go to that awful salon the next morning or lose that means of getting a few dollars. Her untidy refrigerator contained milk, half a loaf of bread, three eggs, and butter. She knew that in her pantry she'd find a can of corn, a box of oatmeal, a sweet potato, four white potatoes, and a small can of Vienna sausages. She hated Vienna sausages, but it was meat, and it filled her up.

Luckily for her, the clerk at the court house had accepted her plea of a cold and high fever as reasons for not being at her court hearing at the scheduled time, and she'd been let off on probation. But that meant she had to toe the line for the next five years, considering her past offenses. Damn him! Damn everybody! She washed a cotton uniform, hung it up to dry, and went back to the kitchen to cook her supper.

Scrambled eggs, toast, Vienna sausages, and a baked potato. She sat down to eat, realized she'd put too much salt in the eggs, and a tear trickled down her cheek. She wanted to call someone, but she hadn't paid Angela back, and neither Bert nor Kendra wanted to hear from her. Nobody had to tell her that she'd been with Asa for the last time. If only she hadn't lost her temper and said those things to him.

Desperate, she phoned the old man. "Hi, Mr. Dunner. This is Ginny."

"Ginny? You were just here. What's the matter? You must be needing money. Sorry, I can't accommodate you tonight. My daughter is here, and it looks like she's gonna have to spend the night. Call tomorrow afternoon. If the coast is clear, you can come over."

"All right. Call you tomorrow." She hung up, disgusted. She hadn't wanted a session with him, and if he thought she was strapped for money, he'd make her do everything he could think of, the depraved old coon.

She put her dishes in the dishwasher, cleaned the kitchen, and went to the living room to watch television. One of these days she'd shake the Washington, D.C., dirt off her shoes, take the first train north, and never come back. Damn! She couldn't even do that, because she had to stay in Washington for the next five years. The court had been ready to throw the book at her. Everything she'd ever done wrong was there in front of that judge. One false move and she'd go to jail. She shrugged first her left shoulder and then her right one. "I'll deal with it when I get to it."

Kendra looked out of her bedroom window the next morning, saw that much of the snow had been removed from the sidewalks, and prepared to get ready for school. After turning on the radio, she learned that school was open and that students were expected to attend class.

Her phone rang. "Hi, Papa."

"What time do you have to be at school?" She told him. "Fine. Be downstairs in about forty minutes. We'll take you in one of the tow trucks, and from the looks of things, we'd better pick you up after your classes and take you on to work. It's not snowing, but it's bitterly cold, and it's icy underfoot."

"Thank you, Papa. I have a nine o'clock class. I don't know how I'd manage this without you."

"You would. Incidentally, Sam called me last night to see if I was bringing you home. I have a feeling that you are not playing your cards right with him."

"It takes two to tango, Papa, as you well know."

"Yeah. This is true. See you in about forty minutes."

She hung up and released a long, deep sigh. If her mother were half as supportive as her father, how much easier her life would have been. Well, it was too late to try repairing that damage.

Her first class was with Professor Hormel, and she was one of the few among his students who attended that morning. Hormel entered the room and closed the door, but not tightly. "I expect we'll have a few stragglers," he explained, "and on such a day, that's considered normal. Thank you all for coming. First, let me say that names of the winners of the journalism writing trip are on the bulletin board in the dean's outer office. We are all very proud of the winners."

At the end of the lecture, Kendra tore out of the classroom

and raced down the hall to the dean's office like a teenager. At the door, she marshaled sufficient self-control to open the door and walk in.

"Where's the list?" she asked the secretary.

"Right in front of you."

"Hot dog!" she said aloud.

"Congratulations," the dean's secretary said. "Have you decided where you want to go?"

"Italy."

"Professor Hormel said you'd choose Italy. You have three weeks in which to map out a travel and research plan, a loose one. Just indicate the place you want to go and what you'd like to write about. The department will assist you in making at least two good contacts. They must all be reachable entirely by train and bus. Then we'll get a travel agent to help you firm things up. You're lucky. First prize got first choice. Third prize gets what's left of the three locales."

"Thanks so much. I'll see you in a couple of days." She sat on the steps leading down to the first floor and dialed her father.

"I won. I won," she shouted when he answered his cell phone. "Papa, I won first prize, and they're going to send me to Italy."

"You can't imagine how happy I am for you, Kendra. Somehow, I knew you'd do it. When are you going and for how long?"

"Next semester, but I hope it's not for six weeks. If Mr. Howell can negotiate a shorter period with the chairman of my department, I'd prefer that."

"I wish him luck."

That remark surprised her.

"You bet I do. I want you to have interesting and fulfilling experiences, but I don't want you to stay away from Sam indefinitely."

She phoned Sam who greeted her with loving words.

"I thought you wanted us to slow things down."

"Dammit, Kendra, they've already wound down to a snail's pace. How did you get to school this morning?"

"Papa and his friend with the towing business took me to school and they plan to chauffeur me for the remainder of the day."

"What's the name of the guy who owns that tow truck?"

"Grayson. When I got into the truck that first time, Papa just said, 'This is my daughter.' "

"He didn't intend for you to be friends with the guy."

"I don't even know what the man looks like, because I only see the back of his head. Papa sits in the front seat with him. When are we going to Alexandria this weekend?"

"If the weather's good, I suggest we leave your place Saturday at noon. Shops and museums will be open, and you'll get a better feel of the place. Would that suit you?"

"Fine. I can study Saturday morning and Sunday."

"It seems like years since we spent any time together. I'm looking forward to Saturday."

She took a great deal of satisfaction in that. Perhaps his plan was having a good effect on him. "I'm looking forward to it, too," she told him. And as far as she was concerned, that was an understatement. But she was growing up by the hour, and he didn't need to know that she was dying to be with him.

At work that evening, she went directly to Howell's office and asked to speak with him. Her status was now such that Howell's secretary gave her immediate access to her boss. "You did a great job here last night, Kendra, and Tab held down the TV station. I hope we don't have anymore snow emergencies this year."

"That may be too much to hope for, sir. It's only just past mid-November. I have some news, Mr. Howell." He cocked an eyebrow, put his right elbow on his desk, supported his chin with the ball of his hand, and waited.

"I passed the competition with the highest score, and I can do the research for my journalistic paper in Italy."

His eyes widened. "No kidding. Italy, huh? If you want to write something fresh and interesting, stay away from Rome, Florence, Venice, and Milan. But you don't speak Italian." He paused. "Do you?"

"No, sir. I was planning to get along with English and modest French. You said you'd contact my Professor in the communications department. He's Professor Hormel."

"Yes, I did. I'll try to reach him tomorrow and see if he'll settle for a month."

"Thank you, Mr. Howell. I need that experience, but I also need to pay my bills."

"You'll never be the same after you come back from Italy," her father told Kendra as they drove her home that night. "You'll feel freer there, and you'll be where the finest things in life—the best foods, great music, and the greatest art—are ever-present and revered everywhere."

"I'm getting excited, Papa."

"Good. Order your passport now so you won't have any last minute hang ups."

She wished that Sam was going with her, but she didn't voice that thought to her father. He liked Sam, and she wanted her father to continue liking him.

Sam's feelings about his relationship with Kendra had begun to perplex him. He was not a wishy-washy person. He considered a problem—or what he thought was a problem—worked out a solution to it, and applied that solution. He'd done that in regard to his relationship with Kendra, but it hadn't satisfied him. Indeed, he thought at times that he'd done the wrong thing and sometimes he believed he'd been foolish. He had deprived himself of true intimacy with her and certainly of any rights. It should be he and not her father who took her to and from work or school when necessary, and he gave up the right to advise her. He certainly couldn't expect her to follow his suggestions now. He was not a man who wavered, and he was far from fickle, so why had he demanded that Kendra accept a proposal by which he no longer wanted to abide? As with anything else, repairing that damage would be more difficult than creating it.

He'd walked with Kendra through two blocks of Alexandria's "Old Town" feeling that he might as well have been miles away from her. But as they stood facing the old Bruin "Negro Jail" on Duke Street, where slaves had been housed in brutal conditions while awaiting purchase, Kendra stepped closer to him and took his hand in hers. He looked down at her as she stared at the remnants of their ancestors' wretched past and shivered visibly. He put an arm around her. She looked up at him, squeezed his hand, and walked on. Maybe she had decided to fix the mess he'd made of their relationship. He hoped so, and he intended to follow her lead.

Farther up Duke Street, with map in hand, she stopped at Franklin & Armfield Slave Office & Pen, former location of one of the largest slave trading companies in the country. Enslaved black Americans were housed in "pens," large walled areas with males kept on one side and females on the other.

"I'd rather not linger here," he told her. "This place has always taken the starch out of me."

She squeezed his fingers. "I didn't know it existed. When I can afford it, I'm going to buy a car and see what this country is like."

"I've seen a lot of it, Kendra, and sometimes ignorance is bliss."

"I can imagine. Even then, African Americans supported their churches."

"When you look at the past, it's easy to understand their hope for a world beyond and their ardent faith in it."

"I know," Kendra said. "When I was little, I used to pray that my mother would love me. I don't remember when I stopped. I still pray, but not for that."

If they had been alone with privacy, he would have

showed her what she meant to him. As he saw it then, his effort to temper their relationship could only have undermined her trust in him and her belief that she was important to him.

He tightened his arm around her. "Aren't you hungry?"

"I'm beginning to feel a pinch in my tummy," she said, put an arm around his waist, and walked with her head resting against his shoulder. She was not a clinging woman, and he wanted to ask why she held onto him. But he couldn't, because she might have taken it as a criticism, and he wanted her close to him.

"Let's go over near the Potomac. I know a couple of good restaurants there."

"I'd like that," Kendra said. "My papa once took me to a great fish restaurant right on the river. I forgot the name." Sam drove across the town, parked in the restaurant's parking lot, and entered the restaurant tying his tie. The maitre d' seated them, gave them menus, and stood by wringing his hands.

Sam looked at the man. "What's the problem?"

"We're fresh out of salmon and tilapia, our most popular entrées."

Sam looked at Kendra. "What are you having?"

"I'd like some bouillabaisse, if there's any left."

"I'll have the same," Sam said to the maitre d'. "So you worried needlessly."

"You've chosen well, sir. You can't find a better fish stew than ours in all of France."

"I think I've had enough African American history for today," Kendra said. "Can we see a silly movie?"

"Sure. Most movies made these days are silly. If you mean something light, how about that remake of *The Shop around the Corner?*"

After leaving the restaurant, they left Alexandria and went to see the movie in an F Street theater. He didn't care what they saw, as long as she was close to him.

As the love story heated up and it seemed as if the lovers wouldn't get together, she snuggled closer to him, and he leaned down and kissed her.

She amazed him when she said, "When you take me home, remember how you did that."

He wanted to laugh aloud, to spread his arms and let all of the uncertainty, pain, and loneliness seep out of him. "You're fresh, but you please me, and I hope you can say the same about me."

She wrinkled her nose and caressed the side of his face. "You've had some shortcomings lately, but none that can't be repaired."

He could feel the grin forming around his mouth and spreading over his face. "And I'll get to work on that immediately."

She smiled up at him. "I'd almost forgotten what it meant to feel like this." Her fingers tightened around his and she rested her head on his shoulder and closed her eyes.

"You can't see the movie if you close your eyes," he said.

"Doesn't matter. I'm in my own movie."

It had been years since she shared Thanksgiving with her mother, yet Kendra had a hollow, empty feeling spending Thanksgiving in a friendly and loving environment when her mother might not only be alone, but conceivably without food, if she hadn't worked or if she hadn't been able to swindle an unsuspecting person out of money.

However, Kendra need not have worried about Ginny; her mother had paid several visits to old man Dunner, who had rewarded her more handsomely than he realized. In addition to the few hundred dollars he gave her, she had robbed him while he slept from sexual exhaustion and from the wine she had inveigled him into drinking.

She sat on the edge of her bed counting her money—five thousand, six hundred and eighty dollars. *If it wasn't for that miserable judge, who insists that I get a job, I could skate awhile on this since I'm not keeping Asa happy. He's the last man who's ever going to get a penny from me.*

But what would she do evenings after she left the salon? She couldn't go to Rooter's, and she couldn't call Angela. Maybe she ought to pay Angela the five hundred dollars. She recounted her money and put it away. Angela wasn't expecting her to pay back that money. Besides, she needed it. Angela had a husband to take care of her. When she left work the next day, she bought a capon and other makings for a Thanksgiving dinner. "It beats eating by myself in a restaurant," she rationalized.

Sam rang Kendra's doorbell at two o'clock Thanksgiving Day. "A punctual woman is a treasure," he said, when she opened the door, evidently ready to go. "You look wonderful, and I especially like you in this color," he said of her burnt-orange wool crepe dress. "I offered to bring your dad, but he wanted the freedom of driving his own car. Can't say I blame him."

"I'm glad you like it," she said. But she wore it because she already knew he liked her in that color. She'd bought a bunch of multicolored calla lilies as a house gift for Sam's father.

"What's that?" Sam asked her.

She told him, and added, "Since I don't know whether your father and Edwina are still together, I couldn't bring anything for her, so I just bought a house gift." He locked her door, and they left the building walking hand-in-hand.

"From what I saw the night you aired the Clarissa Holmes program, I doubt they would willingly sleep anywhere but together. I just can't see how my dad managed to be away from that woman all these years and remain sane. They're crazy about each other," he said, seating her in his car.

"He could do it, because he had to and, especially, because he had never even kissed her. Once he got a taste, and found her willing, he let himself love her. You can understand that."

"Maybe. Dad lives on the edge of Alexandria. We'll be there in a few minutes."

"Did you ever live there with your father?"

"From the time I was born until I got my doctorate and a job. My dreams still echo off those walls."

"What did you dream?"

"I dreamed of reordering the world so that there would be no rich–poor, well–sick, enslaved–free, talented–untalented divisions among us, that we would all be equal. At the age of nine, I was very naive. But I still want equality and justice and, at the least, common decency among people."

"You're a wonderful person. Getting to know you is the most precious experience of my life."

"I hope you mean that, and I'd appreciate if you'd save such declarations for a time when we're someplace private and both of my hands are free."

"I can't promise. If I had known I was going to say that, I probably wouldn't have."

When they arrived at the brown-brick, two-story house, Bert Richards's car was the first thing she saw. "Papa's already here."

"Good. I don't have to worry about his having gotten lost." Sam turned to face her. "Can I have a kiss?"

"Sure. But make it a little one. I don't want to walk in there looking as if I've had too much to drink." From the way his lips settled on hers, she figured he'd decided to explore their relationship fully.

"Are you sure?" she asked him.

He stared at her, surprised that she'd read him so well. "Yes. I'm sure."

But was he? When she'd nestled close to him in the movie theater, he'd reached for that peace and contentment that he needed to feel with her, but it wasn't there. During the early days of their relationship, he knew that sex and his over-whelming attraction to her prohibited feelings of peaceful contentment. But he'd dealt with that and maneuvered them to a different plane, one in which they could learn about each other, in which their assessment of each other wouldn't be conditioned by the ravages of demon sex.

She was everything a man should want, but. . . . He put the car in park, got out, and walked around to open her door. She smiled her thanks, and in his mind's eye, he saw Ginny Hunter smiling at him and inviting him to her home for a threesome tryst. It had nothing to do with Kendra, but he could not get it out of his head. He took her hand and walked with her to the door of the place where he was born and raised.

If his mother were alive, what would she say about it? Kendra dropped his hand, and he looked down at her, saw the frown on her face, and wondered if he had communi-cated his misgivings to her. He took her hand back and squeezed her fingers, but she didn't return the gesture. She was too gracious to put a damper on the holiday feast, but she'd find a way to let him know that he had vexed her.

Chapter Eleven

Sam pasted a cheerful expression on his face, opened the door, and walked into his father's house. He relaxed a bit when he realized that Kendra was not going to drop his hand. He walked with her into the living room where Kendra's father sat with Edwina.

"How are you? Edwina? Bert? Good to see you both," Sam said. "Where's my father?"

"He went to the kitchen for some ice," Edwina said. She seemed to him a bit sheepish, and he wanted to know why.

"Have a seat," he said to Kendra. "I'll be right back. Maybe I can give him a hand."

"How's it going, Dad?" he said as he walked into the kitchen and embraced his father. "Can I do that for you?"

"Everything's fine, and thanks, but slicing a lemon doesn't take much grit. I like Bert Richards, but I don't get it. Nothing about that man says he should be a butcher."

Sam leaned against the stainless steel refrigerator, stuffed his hands in his trouser pockets, and crossed his ankles. "He's the victim of a rotten marriage with a self-centered woman. How are things with you and Edwina? Do I get the sense that she lives here?"

Jethro dropped the knife on the counter and looked at his son. "Do I get the sense that you think you've got a stupid father?"

Taken aback, Sam closed his eyes, drew a few deep breaths, and sifted the comment around in his mind. "You think that would be stupid?"

"Absolutely. For a man with integrity, the next step would be marriage, and that's not on my mind right now."

"But I thought—"

"At every age, marriage is a serious step. I think Edwina is a wonderful woman, but neither of us knows the other well enough for marriage. Time will tell."

"Are you still attracted to her?"

Jethro's grin exposed a set of perfect white teeth. "Does the sun set in the west? You say Bert Richards made a bad mistake when he married. I'll bet he'll tell you that he was insane crazy about the woman. I had a happy marriage, but as I look back, it was through no wisdom of mine. I was lucky and very blessed. I tell myself daily that the postman does not ring twice. So this time, I'm not depending on luck or good fortune." He shaved off a few thin pieces of lemon peel and put them in a little dish beside the lemon slices. "It's too bad that I didn't meet Edwina's mother."

"Why?" Sam asked him.

Jethro rinsed the knife, dried it off, and returned it to the knife block. "Oscar Wilde once said that the tragedy of women was that they all become like their mothers. I'm not sure I'd dispute him; my mother was certainly like my grandmother. Here. You take the ice, and I'll bring these glasses and the lemon."

Sam walked back to the living room feeling as if he'd had a kick in the throat. "Where's the turkey, Dad? I didn't smell a thing in the kitchen."

"The dinner is catered. I didn't want Edwina to prepare it, and my cleaning woman says she can't boil water. This way, we eat and repair to the living room as if we're in a restaurant. The caterer will clean the kitchen."

Feeling as if he'd had the air sucked out of him, Sam sat beside Kendra, put an arm around her shoulder, and left the serving of drinks to his dad. He wondered if his gesture of affection to Kendra was genuine or if it was generated by his guilt. He'd withdrawn from her in response to his father's quote of Oscar Wilde—though God knows Wilde was anything but a paragon of virtue—and he was covering it by putting his arm around her shoulder.

Some weeks earlier, he hadn't withdrawn, but after a logical consideration of their relationship, he had purposefully slowed it down. However, this was a gut reaction aided by the solid distaste he already had for Kendra's mother. If Kendra noticed, she didn't let it show.

Almost as soon as he and his father returned to the living room, the doorbell rang, and Jethro went to answer it. "How are you? Thanks for coming a little early and sparing me a fit of nerves," Sam heard his father say, and figured that the caterer had arrived.

"You know I always keep my appointments in good time, Mr. Hayes," a female voice replied. "Bring that on in, Allen."

Jethro returned to his guests. "My caterer and her assistant are here, so we'll have some hors d'oeuvres in a few minutes."

Sam got up and walked over to the piano. He couldn't stand hypocrisy, and he was, at the moment, living it. "Dad, when did you last have this piano tuned?"

"About a month ago. It should be in tune."

Sam beckoned to Kendra, pulled out the bench, and sat down. "Do you sing?"

"Not unless I want to clear out this place. Do you?"

"I've been known to carry a tune. What's your fancy—pop, blues, jazz, or classical?"

"Whatever you'd like to play. I love music."

"How about some Ellington?" He didn't especially want to play jazz, but he figured he'd better keep it light, and after letting his fingers dance over the keys in a warm-up, he played "Sophisticated Lady," because he knew she liked it.

"Sing something," Jethro said. "It's been ages since I heard you sing."

Sam didn't want to sing, because he preferred to sing ballads, and he did not want to sing a love song. So he sang "I Still Suits Me," a playful song that Paul Robeson made famous in the movie, *Show Boat*. He loved the song, and it suited his rich baritone.

"That's quite some talent you've got," Bert Richards said. "I'd like to hear you play something from an older classical composer. Ellington wrote classical music, but you know what I mean."

"Do you know 'Rite of Spring'?" Kendra asked him. He did, and he was happy to play it for her.

"Thank you," she said when he finished. "You're really talented."

He thanked her. "My dad will tell you he had to ride herd on me to make me practice, but after I saw some real progress, I enjoyed practicing." He got up and turned to Bert.

"I bet you didn't bring your guitar, but there are at least two guitars here."

"Let's wait for that till after dinner," Jethro said. "Mrs. Watkins is about to give us some hors d'oeuvres. I've heard that you're very skilled at the guitar, Bert, and I want to hear you play when I'm in a relaxed mood." He turned the radio on, and soft, easy-listening music surrounded them.

At the dinner table, the conversation turned to art and travel. "The day after I graduated from college, I went to France on a tramp steamer," Bert said. "If I'd been smart, I would have stayed there for a few years."

"But in that case, you wouldn't have had me," Kendra said.

"Oh, I don't know about that. You might have had a differently shaped nose or been a half inch shorter or taller, but you would have definitely come along."

Sam watched the interplay between father and daughter and surmised that their relationship was much like his with his father. If only he hadn't stopped at Rooter's with James Enders, he wouldn't have that awful taste in his mouth of seeing Ginny Hunter in his mind's eye, propositioning him, or making street-level remarks to the bartender. How could he have an honest relationship with Kendra and not share with her what he now knew of her mother?

"Kendra just won a nice scholarship to do research in Europe and write a journalistic account of it," Bert said, beaming with pride.

"I'm going to Italy in January," Kendra said, and it was the first Sam had heard of it.

"That's wonderful," Edwina said. "Italy's lovely when it isn't filled with tourists, though you may need to speak Italian."

"I'm going to take a crash course."

Sam looked straight at Kendra, his expression cool and unfriendly. Why hadn't she told him? They rode together from upper Northwest Washington to Alexandria, Virginia, and telling him about an event so important to both of them didn't occur to her?

"She won the trip by coming out on top in some stiff competition at Howard's School of Communications where she's a student," Sam said, his tone as impersonal as if he were lecturing in Psychology 101. He was proud of her, but he'd be damned if he'd show it right then. He wanted to ask how long she would be gone, but if he did that, he'd tell everyone present that they were not as close as he had thought they were.

His father asked the question for him. "Will you be away for the entire semester?"

"Only for a month. The scholarship is for six weeks, but my boss at the radio station called Professor Hormel and prevailed upon him to allow me to go for a shorter period. I wouldn't have had the nerve to ask that, but I'm happy for the change, because I still have to pass all of my classes that semester. And I prefer it also for personal reasons." With a shy smile, she glanced at Sam, and then lowered her gaze.

At times, she was so soft that he wanted to protect her from everyone and everything. He told himself not to give in to it, that caring for Kendra meant dealing with Ginny Hunter, and he didn't want that woman cluttering up his life.

"No thanks," he said to his father's offer of a martini cocktail. "I'll stick with gin and tonic. A martini is suicide for anybody who plans to drive a car within the next five hours."

Bert declined a drink. "I'll have something during the meal, and that will be aplenty for me."

Sam nodded appreciatively. The more he saw of Bert Richards, the more he liked him. Here was proof that a sensible man did not always make sensible choices in women.

Dinner was served, and as they headed for the dining room, he said to his father in hushed tones, "I'm surprised you didn't invite one of the unattached women in your office as a date for Bert."

"It never occurred to me. I believe in letting a man choose his own poison. It keeps things a lot less complicated."

Jethro said grace, and Sam noticed that Bert mouthed the words along with him. He asked him, "Do you attend church regularly, Bert?"

"If you mean every Sunday, yes, I manage that, but I don't participate in the many weekly activities and services. Occasionally, Kendra attends with me, and that's always a pleasure."

"You're fortunate," Jethro said to Bert. "My only son has to sleep late at least once a week. You'd think a big-shot medical specialist prescribed that his great sleep-in should take place on Sunday mornings."

"Dinner is ready, Mr. Hayes."

The caterer served smoked salmon pate; corn and oyster chowder, followed by raspberry sorbet for a palate cleanser; roast turkey with dressing and gravy, wild rice pilaf, asparagus tips, and cranberry relish; Port du Salut and St. Andre cheese; and for dessert, she presented the brandied baked Alaska to a rousing applause.

Jethro uncorked two bottles of Moët & Chandon champagne, explaining that the champagne was a gift from Bert. He raised a glass to the caterer.

"Thank y'all," she said. "Catering for Mr. Hayes is always a pleasure. I'm happy that you enjoyed it. I'll serve the espresso in the living room. Would anyone prefer regular coffee?" No one did. Along with the espresso, Mrs. Watkins and her helper served toasted pecans, mints, and grapes.

"This is the way to go," Bert said. "To enjoy a meal like this in your own home with not even the slightest scent to tip off the menu." He raised his glass, "Jethro, you're a man of class and imagination. I've enjoyed this tremendously."

"So have I," Kendra said, "and to spend such a wonderful Thanksgiving with both my papa and Sam makes this very special for me."

Sam looked at his father—who sat comfortably among his guests, with his arms around a woman who he'd wanted for years before he finally got her—and told himself that his own life was going to be smoother, that he was not going to spend years missing and wanting *any* woman. He glanced down at Kendra, pulled her closer to him, and a grin spread over his face. *His dad at least knew what he wanted.*

Except for occasional banalities, Kendra was silent during the ride home with Sam. She couldn't say that she hadn't enjoyed Thanksgiving dinner at Jethro Hayes's home, because she had. Seeing her papa in the company of men with whom he belonged and watching him hold his own with them was an experience she didn't have often, and one that she would not soon forget. Sometime between leaving her apartment and arriving at Jethro's home, Sam had changed. Further, she figured that while in the kitchen helping his father, he must have had an epiphany. Oh, he tried to act as if nothing had changed, but throughout her life, she'd lived with on-again off-again affection from her mother, and she had become a master both at detecting it and at living with it.

When they arrived at her apartment, it did not surprise her when he indicated that he didn't want to come in. "I want you to come in, Sam. I want to talk with you."

His quick shrug told her that he was ready and able to take whatever came.

She led him to her living room, took off her coat, and waited for him to let her know whether he planned to remove his. He took it off, and she draped it across a chair along with hers. She sat down in a side chair.

"Sam, what happened from the time we were at the movies until now? You told me you were sure, but you weren't. I don't like being on a seesaw. It's very painful. I thought we had everything going for us, and you've led me to believe that you care for me, but something has derailed this relationship. What have I done? I'm not asking how I can repair it. I just want to know."

He leaned forward and looked her in the eye. "Why didn't you tell me that Howell succeeded in shortening the time required for you to stay in Europe? Hell, you didn't even tell me you'd chosen Italy and that you'd be leaving in January."

"That is not the reason for your icy treatment today, and you know it. We'd been at your father's house over an hour when I told that. I didn't tell you earlier, because I'd planned to reveal that to you about now when we returned from dinner. In fact, I bought my first bottle of champagne for that purpose. It's in the refrigerator," she said, the finality of her voice saying that it would remain there. "If Papa hadn't needed to preen," she went on, "I wouldn't have mentioned it in that group." She folded her hands and waited for his explanation.

"I've been moving too fast, Kendra. And every time I tell myself to slow down, the advice only works for a short while. I don't want to make a mistake with you, and I don't want to create a problem for myself. You're important to me. I know it and I feel it. But it came so easily and with such resounding power, that it stunned me."

"I see. So you don't believe in it. Well, if you want to go your own way, I don't promise to wait for you to change your mind. I've learned from you the sweet contentment to be found in a loving companion, and I hope never to be without it."

"Just like that, you're willing to say, it's been nice and so long?"

"Don't misunderstand me, Sam. What I've been saying is that I refuse ever to beg any man to be with me, no matter who he is or how I feel about him. If he wants to go, he can walk. If I cry all night, he'll never know it."

"Well, I'm not ready to finish it. I don't know that I'll ever be. I told you the truth when I said you're in here." He pointed to his heart.

"Then what's wrong? Something is not right. Is there someone else?"

"I haven't looked at another woman since I met you. But you're right; I'm having trouble giving my whole self to this. It—"

"You mean you're having trouble giving your whole self to *me*. Let's call a spade a spade."

"There's something I have to resolve. I hadn't thought it would have significance for my relationship with you, but in spite of myself, it does."

"And if it wasn't for that something, whatever it is, you would be able freely to express your feelings for me? Is that what you're telling me?"

"Yes. You see, I still need your warmth and affection, your presence, your company. I . . . I still need you."

She closed her eyes, tried to digest his words and to understand them. "You think you're still capable of kissing me the way you did in that movie theater?"

"Of course. If I were guided by my feelings for you, I could kiss you with as much genuine passion as I ever did."

"I see. So the change is in your head." She didn't think she could handle that. Standing, she picked up his coat and handed it to him. "In spite of this downer, I don't remember having spent a more pleasant Thanksgiving."

He stood, put on his coat, and walked with her to the door. "Please don't make a date for Christmas Eve and New Year's Eve that doesn't include me."

"Are you asking me for those dates?" From then on, she didn't intend to assume anything in respect to Sam.

"Yes, and some between now and then."

"Like what?"

"Like my frat dance. Don't push me, Kendra. From the minute I met you, I vowed to be absolutely straight with you about everything. Please don't reward me by being picayunish."

She didn't need to comment on that. "Is your fraternity dance black-tie or tails?"

"Black-tie, and please let me know the color of your dress so I won't clash with it. If there's time, I'll have the cummerbund made to match it."

"Then, I'll decide what I'm wearing this weekend. Thank you for the gesture."

"Don't. I want every man there to know you're with me."

In spite of the dull feeling around her heart, she laughed. She couldn't help it. "Sam, you're a professor of psychology, so the word schizophrenic must occur to you with some frequency these days. Mind you, I'm not making a diagnosis, but your recent behavior is rather peculiar since I saw no evidence of it earlier."

"I know. I've been inconsistent with you. Kiss me?" He'd phrased it as a question. He'd been honest, and she owed him the same, so she reached up and kissed his cheek.

He stared down at her. "Is that as much as you can give?"

"It's as much as I feel right now."

His gaze seared her, deep and penetrating as if he searched for something beyond his grasp. "I'll be in touch."

She didn't watch him as he walked to the elevator, and that was just as well, for he didn't look back.

It was his fault, and he'd better do something about it. If anybody should understand how a person's behavior affected others, especially intimate friends, it was a professor of clinical psychology. Truth was admirable, but sometimes it was out of place. Kendra had just showed him how tough she could be when she hurt. And he didn't doubt that she hurt. He got into his car, ignited the engine, turned it off, and took his cell phone out of the breast pocket of his jacket. He dialed Bert Richards's number.

"Richards speaking."

"Bert, this is Sam. I've just left Kendra. I need to talk with you. It's early yet. Can you and I meet somewhere? It's very important." He knew he'd taken the man aback, but he also knew that Bert Richards loved his daughter and that the man would meet him halfway.

"Sure, Sam. It was clear to me at your father's house that you and Kendra have lost something since we were together in Rock Creek Park. I live on Colorado between Kennedy and Longfellow. Most coffee houses are closed now. We can talk here, if it isn't too far out of your way." He gave Sam the address.

"Thanks. I appreciate this. See you in about fifteen minutes."

He hadn't thought about the kind of home Bert Richards would have; in fact, he tried not to judge a man by his possessions. Yet, when he entered the charming foyer of the six-story building in which Bert lived, his eyebrows shot up. Blue and rose Persian carpets covered the hardwood floors; soft-white sconce lights against dusty-rose walls gave the area a soothing and inviting appearance.

"I'm Samuel Hayes. Mr. Richards, please," he said to the uniformed man seated behind a horseshoe-shaped desk.

"He's expecting you, Mr. Hayes."

Bert waited for him at his door, which stood slightly ajar, a gesture that assured Sam of the man's cordiality. "Come in, Sam. You look oppressed," Bert said. "I gather this has to do with Kendra. Otherwise you would have talked it over with Jethro."

"You're right."

Bert took Sam's coat, hung it in a nearby closet, and walked with him into the living room. "I can't decide how best to handle this," he continued.

"I made us some coffee, and that's about all I can offer. I don't drink except for wine in a restaurant or as a dinner guest at someone's home." He poured coffee for each of them. "What's eating you?"

Sam sipped the coffee and nodded appreciatively. "When Kendra first told me about her mother's antics, her selfishness and self-centered behavior at her own daughter's expense, I figured it made no difference to my relationship with Kendra.

"But when she attempted to steal Kendra's pocketbook, it shook me up, and I still told myself that I could deal with it."

"*And now?*" Bert asked him, leaning forward with his hands gripped tightly in front of him.

"You remember that second heavy snow storm?" Bert nodded. "I went to class that day, and a professor with whom I talk from time to time asked me if we could discuss one of our students. He lives in my direction and suggested that we stop at Rooter's Bar and Grill, after which he'd drive me on home in his jeep. I saw a woman sitting at the bar and asked the bartender her name, because she looked so much like Kendra. That nearly got me in trouble with the bartender; the woman was Ginny Hunter and the bartender was her man. She'd been ignoring him and casing me over.

"I explained to him that she looked like my girlfriend, and after I confirmed her identity, the guy asked my girlfriend's age. I told him. He went back to Ginny, and they had a row, during which she used some street language and stalked out. When she passed me, she invited me and my colleague to come home with her.

"Bert, I can't seem to get over that. I know it has nothing to do with Kendra, but she's Kendra's mother, and she invited me and my colleague to a sexual romp with her. If I tell Kendra about this, it will hurt her terribly, but if I don't tell her and keep this disgust inside of me, I may hurt her even more. Right now, we're in partial limbo. Kendra wouldn't even kiss me good night. I didn't level with her, but she questioned my behavior, and I told her I had to resolve something.

"You can understand why you are the only person with whom I could share this."

"I know Ginny is reckless, but I didn't realize that she had developed such loose morals. She loves money, but she does not like to work and avoids it to the extent possible. The money I gave her to pay our mortgage, she spent on designer perfumes and clothes. The bank foreclosed, and she did little more than shrug. It took me almost thirty years to get out of the rut she left me in. I opened a butcher shop because I couldn't pay those bills working for a salary, and I'd worked in a butcher shop while in college. It was the only trade I knew.

"If you'll trust me, I'll try to talk with Kendra about this. She can be hardheaded, but she'll listen to me. It will take time, because I imagine that every time you put your arm around Kendra, you see Ginny. Kendra is the image of her mother at that age."

"I know it's best you talk with her, but I feel as if I'm

shirking my responsibility. She may think that I don't trust her."

Bert looked to the ceiling, shaking his head. "It's as if fate had ordained that Ginny destroy Kendra. Thwart her at one trick and she pulls off another one. Kendra wants Ginny to love her, but the woman is incapable of love. Kendra refused to appear in court against her for attempting to steal that pocketbook, explaining that Ginny didn't actually steal it. I'll think about it, Sam. Maybe I should prepare her for what you have to say, and you tell her yourself. But I agree with you that if you don't tell her, your relationship will suffer irreparable damage."

"Bert, I'm indebted to you for your help and understanding. I don't want to hurt Kendra. I want to protect her from hurt and pain, but this news will hurt Kendra no matter how she gets it."

"And if she isn't told, she will hurt far worse," Bert said. He shook his head slowly as if perplexed, and his next words held a tinge of sadness. "I'd hate to see the two of you lose that magical spark that you had—and which I've never experienced—but man proposes and God disposes. It's the way of life."

"One problem is that a relationship between a woman and a man either goes up or down; it never stands still."

"I know, so it's best we get to this as soon as we can."

They said good night, and Sam headed home, in one sense relieved, but in another, more heavily burdened. He cared deeply for Kendra, and as he talked with her father, reflecting on what her life had been like, he remembered telling her that he'd always be there for her. Perspiration beaded his forehead, dampened his shirt, and made him want to pull over and take off his jacket. He kept driving. He'd gotten out of some tough spots and done it without compromising his honor and integrity. And he'd deal honorably with this.

* * *

Sam couldn't know of Kendra's decision to take her cues from him. If he called, they would talk; if he didn't, they wouldn't. She had been rejected by her mother more times than she could count, and it had yet to kill her. "That's not a good comparison," she said aloud. "I don't really know what having a mother is like."

Figuring that she could get in two or three hours of study before bedtime, she opened her notes from a class in public speaking, but as she began to review them, the telephone rang.

The caller ID didn't appear on the screen, so she hesitated to answer. Well, it could be Sam, she thought.

"Hello."

"Miss Richards, I'm sorry to call you on Thanksgiving night, but Mrs. Ginny Hunter was in an accident, and she said you should be notified."

Kendra blew out a long breath, rested her elbow on the desk, and said, "Now what?"

"I beg your pardon, ma'am."

"Oh, sorry. Where is she and who are you?"

"I'm head nurse on this ward at Freedmen's Hospital. She said you'd take care of the bill."

"How is she, and what happened to her?"

"According to the report I have, she was riding with someone who was speeding up Georgia Avenue at seventy miles an hour and totaled the car, crashing it against a wall. In the crash, Mrs. Hunter got a sprained left wrist."

"I see. Who was driving that car?"

"She says that a man named Dunner was driving it, but he can't speak for himself. He was thrown outside of the car, and she jumped out before the police came. The police think she was driving, because they found Dunner's watch on the floor by the front passenger's seat."

Kendra didn't doubt the police evaluation of the situation. It was just like Ginny to break the law—as she'd done if she was driving—and put the blame for the accident on someone else. "What is the situation with the man named Dunner?"

"He was thoroughly banged up, and he's just regained consciousness. We expect he'll survive."

"Thank God, he's alive." She gave the nurse her uncle's number. "Call this man. He may be able to help. I don't have any money." She had barely enough to meet her expenses and buy what she needed for her trip to Europe. Further, she did not believe that her mother had no health insurance; Ginny was too afraid of death to neglect a way of circumventing it. And she wouldn't miss an opportunity to make Kendra feel guilty and spend money on her sprained wrist. She was not being unfair, just clearheaded.

"But she gave *your* name," the nurse said.

Kendra bristled at that. "So what! I can give Michael Jordan's name, though he doesn't know I exist. In a similar situation, would you argue that he should be responsible for me on the strength of my having given you his name?"

"Somebody has to pay this bill."

"Sure, and I imagine it's a sizeable one, since hospitals are known to gouge so skillfully that they're even able to get blood out of a turnip."

Kendra hung up, refocused, and, within an hour, wrote a paper on women in front of the TV cameras. But the night was not to be hers. When the phone rang again, she knew someone was calling her about Ginny. Maybe her papa was right when he advised her to move from Washington as soon as she graduated.

She couldn't see the caller's ID. "Hello."

"Kendra, this is your uncle Ed. Did you get a call about Ginny tonight?"

"Yes, sir. A little over an hour ago. I told the nurse to call you. I don't have money for a hospital bill, Uncle Ed."

"I'm sure you don't. Here's the problem. Ginny is on probation for driving an uninsured car with a suspended license. She was clearly driving this car, because the old man's daughter swears that he doesn't know how to drive, has never attempted to, and has never owned a car."

"So who's car was that?"

"It was a rented car."

"Both of them were thrown clear of the wreckage, because they didn't have their seat belts fastened, so Ginny thinks she can swear she wasn't driving and get away with it, but she can't."

"I know. The man's watch fell in front of the front passenger seat."

"Right. And she'll discover that her fingerprints are on the steering wheel, but the man's prints are not. She could have killed someone. That car was going seventy-some miles an hour on a city street."

"What will we do?"

"I put up ten thousand dollars for her bail last time, and I'll never get it back. I'm not poor, but I plan to be able to say that years from now. Ginny is like an addicted gambler, and if you support a gambler's habit, you'll soon be as destitute as the gambler. I've finished."

"But doesn't that mean she'll go to jail?"

"Kendra, I have three children to feed, clothe, house and send to college. Should I mortgage my children's future for a woman who doesn't give a damn what happens to anybody but her? Should I?"

"But Uncle Ed—"

"If you want to let her ruin your life, I can't stop you, but I'm not going to tear my family apart on account of Ginny, and that's final. Half of what I have legally belongs to Dot, and she doesn't want to hear the name 'Ginny' again. Further, I don't blame her. We've given Ginny enough of our money."

Uncertain as to what to do next, Kendra let her mind drift back over the fourteen years since she had reached legal age and got her first job—summer work at the Hot Shoppes. Ginny badly needed a hundred dollars of her first paycheck—one hundred and fifty dollars for two weeks—swore she would repay it in a couple of days, and still hadn't repaid it or the thousands of dollars she had borrowed subsequently.

Kendra telephoned her father and informed him of her mother's latest caper and subsequent predicament.

"I see," Bert said, when she finished the story. "So Ed has finally washed his hands. I can't tell you how to behave with regard to your mother, and I can't protect you from her exploitation; you have to protect yourself. But if you continue to support her when she breaks the law and violates normal civility, I'll have to distance myself from you, because it's too painful. I won't want to know about it."

"I've been planning to try and get professional help for her, but she won't stay out of trouble. Psychiatric social workers for the city are not going to counsel her unless she gives them her court records, and she's not going to do that. She's on probation right now, and if this case goes to trial and she loses, she's had it."

"You listen to me, Kendra. No kind of professional is going to straighten Ginny out until she sees firsthand what it means to be in jail a couple of years as punishment for her crimes. And what she did tonight was a crime. How will you feel if she kills an innocent person after you put your life in hock and bail her out of this?"

"If you put it that way, I'd feel responsible for that person's death."

"And you would certainly share that responsibility. Look, Kendra, I'm tired of this. If you can't see the necessity of allowing her to pay for her crime, there's no use talking to you. Have you told Sam about this?"

"No, sir."

"Well, you'd better, but for heaven's sake don't let him think you've been agonizing over whether to bail her out. That reminds me. Can you come to the store tomorrow around twelve-thirty? I want to talk with you, and we can have a really nice lunch in the office."

"Yes, sir. I don't have classes tomorrow. I'll see you then."

That reminds me, he'd said. She went over the conversation, but nothing rang a bell. But she'd know what it was when she left him the next day, because it had to be what he wanted to talk with her about. Eleven-thirty and too late to call Sam. She wasn't even sure that she wanted to.

She got ready for bed, but she didn't feel like sleeping. Standing at her bedroom window looking out at the cold Thanksgiving night and the perfectly rounded moon hanging in the clearest and coldest-looking sky she could remember, tears splashed her cheeks. She wiped them away, impatient with what they symbolized.

That probably won't be the last tear I shed, but I'll be damned if he'll ever know how much I hurt.

Chapter Twelve

Kendra dashed into her father's store seconds before a torrent of freezing rain swept the streets of Northwest Washington. She braced her strength against the gust of wind blowing in from Dupont Circle and managed to close the door. Bert was taking an order by phone and hadn't noticed her predicament.

"Papa, you have to do something about that door. It weighs a ton. Your canopy is elegant, but what good is it in a storm like this one?"

"Not too much," he agreed, walking to her with arms outspread. He hugged his only child with more affection than he usually displayed. "I hope you're hungry."

She gazed at him with a frown. "Of course, I'm hungry, Papa. It's lunchtime. Besides, my mouth waters when I'm anticipating your fantastic sandwiches." Something wasn't right. First that hug and now, this. . . . She realized suddenly that he was being protective. *Hmm. Wonder what this is about.*

"I'll be in the office having lunch with Kendra," Bert called to Gates.

Kendra hung her coat in her father's office, pulled out his desk chair, and sat down. She looked around at the elegant room, the last thing you'd expect to see in the back of a butcher shop—away from the meat which hung in his huge basement refrigerator and was Bert Richards's livelihood.

He had covered one wall of the room with books on meat, butchering, and the preparation and cooking of meat, and also books on string instruments and music. A handwoven Turkish carpet covered much of the floor, and his desk, desk chair, coffee table, and an occasional table were of walnut wood. A loveseat in brown leather complemented the beige-and-dark-green carpet. On another wall hung two of his prize guitars, a Gibson Masterbuilt acoustic and an Epiphone Les Paul Standard electric. They hung against a sheet of green felt. If he had to discuss anything private with a customer, he did it in his office, and she knew that was his way of letting his customers know who he was.

"What did you want to talk with me about, Papa?" She said it as airily as she could and tried to push back her sense that she was about to hear something unpleasant.

"Let's eat. I sent out for some fresh warm focaccia, and I've got a just-baked ham right out of the oven. I made a salad of tomato, basil, romaine lettuce, fresh mozzarella, and hearts of palm. Coffee will be ready in a minute, and we'll feast." He rubbed his hands together as if in anticipation of something wonderful.

What would have happened to me if he had been a different kind of father? It was no wonder that she loved him. "You must have been Italian in your former life," she said, as a tease.

He covered his desk with a tablecloth, set the "table," and placed the focaccia ham sandwiches, salad, split-pea soup, and coffee on it, sat down, and said the grace. She reached out, patted her father's hand and chided, "You didn't tell me we were having my favorite soup."

"You don't have to know everything," he said, with a gruffness that, to her, spelled unarticulated affection.

So he wasn't going to discuss whatever he'd had in mind until after he finished eating his lunch. She told herself not to second-guess him, but she imagined the worst. After they finished the tasty, enjoyable meal and she sipped coffee in an absentminded way, she heard herself ask him, "Is it about Mama or Sam?"

He ran his fingers back and forth across his jaw, poured himself another cup of coffee, and said, "Both."

She set her cup on the desk with a thud. "What do you mean, *both?* They've never met."

He took her hand. "Don't jump to any conclusions. Just hear me out."

Bert looked at Kendra with eyes that reflected his sadness. "Sam called me minutes after he left you Thanksgiving night. I had noticed that the wonderful spark of new love that I saw between the two of you when we had that picnic was no longer there. Still, his call surprised me. From the outset, he's had a bad reaction to Ginny's treatment of you, because he's protective of you, and it's impossible to protect a person from a mother like Ginny. But when she tried to steal your pocketbook, he became intolerant of her."

"Why didn't he tell *me* this?"

"I asked you to hear me out, Kendra. The day it snowed, he ran into Ginny at a bar where he stopped with a man who teaches at GW. Ginny was there. She flirted with him."

"Oh, Lord. How could she?"

"She didn't know who he was." He decided to let Sam tell her the rest of the story. "Sam is not responsible for Ginny's nasty behavior. He can't bring himself to tell you about it, but when he looks at you, he sees her, and it's killing him. And he told me that until he can clean it out of his head with the help of your knowledge and understanding of it, he can't go further with you."

She was standing then, shaking with a combination of fear and fury. "I only need to know one thing. Did he sleep with her?"

"No, he didn't. And if you make the mistake of asking him that question, I guarantee he won't speak to you again. He detests her."

"I see."

"Do you? This is serious. If a man can't hold the woman he loves without thinking of his distaste for her mother, who looks just like her, what will he do? Does he want that woman to be the grandmother of his children? In some states, grandparents may retain certain legal rights in respect to their grandchildren. And no man would want Ginny for a mother-in-law, keeping his wife—and thus his family—in constant turmoil."

She dropped herself back into the chair. "So it's him or Mama."

Bert stared at her. "For goodness' sake, don't be ridiculous. He deserves better than a comment like that."

"Why didn't he tell me this? Why did he tell you?"

Bert threw up his hands. "I'm your father, so there are things I can't be candid with you about. How did you get to be so naive? The man is frustrated. After a perfect Thanksgiving at his father's house, you couldn't kiss him, because he'd been cool toward you. And why had he been cool? Because of your mother. I suggest you call him, tell him you want to talk with him about his conversation with me. It's important, and it's urgent. Talk with him where you have absolute privacy. I suggest your place, that is, if you love him. If you don't do this soon, you can forget Sam Hayes, and you will regret it for a long time. A woman is blessed if she has the love and caring of a man like Sam, and especially in this town where there are ten women to every eligible man."

"Why did he talk with you rather than his own father?"

"Obviously, because he didn't want to expose you to Jethro. If I were *his* father and he told me that, I would advise him to leave you alone. That's why he came to me."

She tried to digest all that her father had said. After some minutes, she took in the sadness on Bert Richards's face and voiced her understanding of it. "You didn't tell me everything, and what Sam has to add is going to hurt even more.

But as long as she didn't inveigle him into bed with her, I can take it."

"My advice to you is control your temper, and do not accuse him of anything. He does not deserve that."

"You needn't worry, Papa. I trust him far more than I would trust her. Thanks for lunch and for trying to soften the blow. I'll call you."

"Let me check whether the rain has stopped." It hadn't, so he called a taxi for her. "I'll meet you tonight as usual."

She'd get to work too early, but she didn't mind. In the meantime, she could get a lot of studying done. The pounding of rain on the taxi's rear window made her think of sleep, but she shook off the urge to close her eyes and dialed Sam at home, for she knew he wouldn't be at school the day after Thanksgiving.

"Hello, Kendra. How are you?" he said by way of a greeting.

"Hi, Sam. I'm on my way to work. I had lunch with Papa, and he called a taxi for me, because he couldn't get away from the store. Sam, I need to see you and talk with you. Would you have dinner with me at my place tomorrow evening?"

Was he hesitating? "Well, if you'd rather—"

"I was trying to recall whether I've made a commitment for tomorrow, but I think not. So, yes. I'd like that very much, and I'll look forward to seeing you. What time?"

"Seven o'clock. I'll be looking forward to seeing you, too, Sam."

She hated the stilted conversation, and the distance between them that seemed to have stretched endlessly in just one day. But she knew that neither of them was going to pretend anything, and that they would speak and act true to their feelings.

"Sam, neither you nor I is capable of pretending joyful conversation, and I imagine that like me, you're going with your feelings and not make small talk. I respect that in you. Tomorrow, I guess we'll find out if we still have anything going for us."

"We will, and we have, Kendra. Thank you for making this gesture. See you at seven tomorrow."

She didn't say good-bye, because that was not the way she wanted to terminate a conversation with him. When she got out of the taxi in front of the Howell Building, her umbrella was of little use. The rain continued, and the wind was, if anything, stronger. She dashed into the building, but not quickly enough to avoid getting wet. Inside, she shook out her umbrella, pulled off her shoes, left both in the doorman's package room, and padded barefoot to the elevator.

"What's the matter? Don't I pay you enough for you to afford shoes?" Clifton Howell asked when he met her in the corridor. She had learned that, in addition to being charitable, he had a devilish sense of humor.

"You certainly do, sir, but if I buy shoes, how am I going to afford champagne?"

"Touché!" he replied without the semblance of a smile.

To her astonishment, when she stopped by the doorman later to pick up her umbrella and her wet shoes, she found beside them a pair of rain boots that were her size.

"Whose are these?" she asked the doorman.

"The boss ordered them for you, Ms. Richards. He said your shoes wouldn't dry by midnight, and you can see that he was right. Those shoes got soaked."

"That's nice of him, but I don't want him buying my shoes."

"It wasn't personal, ma'am. He would've done the same for me. I've been working this door for twelve years. He even bought a scooter for my son."

"That's different."

"Not really. I told my six-year-old that I couldn't afford a scooter, and the little devil called Mr. Howell and asked him to pay me more so he could have a scooter."

"You're kidding."

"No, ma'am. Everybody who works here has a similar story. Enjoy the boots. His wife probably picked them out." She slipped on the green-dotted black boots and left the building with her shoes in her hands.

Kendra had no difficulty deciding what to cook. She defrosted cutlets that her father gave her and planned a menu around them. She planned to serve a gourmet meal, but she was not going to put on anything sexy. To her way of thinking, sex was the last thing they should be considering. She got her apartment in pristine order, set the table, added white candles and white roses with sprigs of baby's breath, and regarded her handiwork.

"Not bad," she said aloud. "I wasn't born to wealth, but I know how to live, thanks to my father."

Gazing at the warm colors of beige, persimmon, and avocado in her living room, the big picture windows, and the sparks shooting up the chimney, she remembered how happy she was when her father handed her the receipt for her shares in the co-op. No matter what happened this evening, she told herself that she would not let it bring her down, that she would plod on until she reached her goal, and then go on with her life. She chose an avocado-green sheath that just covered her knees and exposed very little cleavage. He couldn't say that she was luring him.

Punctual as usual, he rang the doorbell at seven, and when she was about to open the door, she opened her right fist and saw the prints of her fingernails. *Relax, Kendra. He's only a man!*

She opened the door and gazed up at him. "Hi."

He stared down at her for a few seconds, and then a smile barely touched his lips. "I'm about as uptight as you are. How are you?" He handed her a bunch of pink and purple calla lilies.

A gasp escaped her before she was able to control it. "Sam. These are so beautiful. Thank you so much."

"You may imagine that buying them gave me a lot of pleasure. It meant that I at least was going to see you." He handed her a bag. "Unless we're going to drink the red, please put the white in the refrigerator."

"I guess you'd better have a seat; otherwise, I'll appear inhospitable. I'm glad you agreed to come. You look wonderful. I've always liked you in that navy blue suit, white shirt, and tie of assorted blue colors," she said, embarrassed at resorting to small talk.

"I know. You once told me. That's why I wore it." He'd been walking beside her, but he stopped and looked directly at her, his gaze seeming to pierce her. "Kendra, if we continue this way, saying things just to stave off the silence, I don't think I'll be able to stand it. It's colder in here than it is outside. I care as much for you as I ever did."

"It is not cold in here. I have a fire in the living-room fireplace, and I am not cold." She thought of the cool color she'd chosen to wear, and smiled inwardly.

"But you still don't care to kiss me."

"You don't know that. Have a seat, and I'll bring you something delicious."

He watched her walk away from him and head to the kitchen. She seemed amenable to listening to what he had to say with an open mind. He didn't know what Bert had told her, but he suspected that it was favorable to him. He hoped so. She was back quickly with tiny hot cheese puffs filled with Gruyère cheese sauce. He chose one, bit into it, and with his hand suspended between his mouth and the tray she held, he said, "At the risk of making you mad, let me tell you that if the meal is of this quality, I'll be thoroughly seduced by the time you serve coffee."

"I'm glad you like them," she said with a slow wink. "I made plenty."

He wanted to ask her if she was flirting with him, but he'd better not press his luck. "Where did you put the calla lilies?" he asked when she came back to him with two glasses of white wine.

"In my bedroom. Those are my favorite flowers."

"I'm glad I chose them. I can't wait for dinner. It didn't occur to me that you'd cook this evening. How did you learn to cook so well?"

"My grandmother was a fantastic cook and, while growing up, I watched her, but my dad's also a very good cook, and whenever he'd be doing something in my presence, he'd lecture and teach me how to do it. So I guess I learned mostly from him."

"I've begun to realize that he's a remarkable man. I'm not much of a cook."

"That's because you never had to cook." She got up and tuned the radio to easy listening music. That suited him. He just didn't want to hear any of the song that had a shared meaning for them. "We can eat now," she said, and lit the candles. She would keep a home of which a man could be proud. He wanted to say the grace, but it was her table, so he left the gesture to her. But she reached across the table, took his hand, and said the grace. Then he poured red wine into their glasses and she raised hers.

"I am praying that when you leave here, you and I will both be happy."

He held his glass tilted toward her. "So am I, Kendra. So am I."

She served veal cutlets with madeira sauce and complemented them with an imaginative assortment of vegetable dishes, ending the meal with Brandy Alexander pie; and coffee.

After dinner, he sat in her living room facing the log fire and sipping coffee. If they couldn't mend their relationship, he'd be in for a long stretch of unhappiness. He'd put up a front, just as he'd done when Giselda disappointed him, but this would be worse, and he may as well acknowledge that fact. He followed her to the kitchen.

"I'll help you clean up."

"Sure you want to?"

"Unless it's a matter of life or death, I'm not likely to volunteer to do something I don't want to do. You cooked a wonderful meal. Sit over there in that chair and keep me company." Since he didn't want to talk, he sang "Mariah," one of his favorite songs. "I don't remember all the words," he told her.

"I do. It's a song that deserves a good baritone voice, and you have it." She repeated the words, and he sang them, but he soon tired of it, for he knew they were substituting the singing for the conversation that they needed to have. He finished cleaning, closed the dishwasher, and took her hand.

"Where do you want to talk? We have to stop procrastinating." They walked into the living room, and he waited to see where she would sit. She chose the sofa, and he took comfort in that, but he needed to see her face when they talked, so he sat facing her.

"How much did Bert tell you?"

"He got as far as your reaction to Mama's flirting with you. What *was* your reaction to that?"

"Outrage and disgust. After thinking about it for days, I became anxious about you and me and whether I could handle dealing with a woman like her. Because whether you want to accept it or not, she'd be a fixture in my life for as long as I care deeply about you."

"Papa didn't tell me all of it, did he?"

He took a deep breath and slapped his right fist into the palm of his left hand. He wasn't going to lie. They needed the truth. And as much as it pained him to hurt her, he had to tell her.

"No, he didn't. I stopped at Rooter's Bar and Grill the day of that second big snow, with a professor in my department, and saw a woman sitting at the bar. The bartender was making it clear that she was his woman, but she was casing me." He didn't let her loud gasp stop him. It was what it was, and he didn't intend to mince it.

"She looked so much like you that I asked the bartender her name and nearly got kicked out of there until I told him that she looked exactly like my girlfriend. Then, he got interested and told me her name was Ginny Hunter. Before you know it, they were having words, and she let him have some gutter language. I could even handle that, but when she was strolling out, she stopped and invited me and the man with me to come to her apartment where, she assured me, it would be very warm. I told her that she was not my type."

"That's d-disgusting. And you think I would do things like that?"

"That never occurred to me. The problem is that I can't get it out of my head. I want to put my arms around you and hold you, and the picture of her making that pass at me . . . oh, hell. I don't know how to put it. I couldn't continue without leveling with you about it and knowing that you accept that I can't stand her and don't want her in my life. I'm sorry, but there it is. She owes you a lifetime more than she's given you."

He observed Kendra closely. "You don't seem surprised."

"I told you that when I was in my early teens, I stayed in my room with the door locked, because Mama's men friends made passes at me, and she paid it no attention. But I didn't realize she had such loose morals."

"When did you last see her?"

"I don't remember. Last I heard, she had violated her probation, had a car accident, and was in the hospital with a sprained or broken wrist."

He sat forward. "Did she call you?"

"A nurse called, but I told her to call my uncle, her brother. He refused to help her."

"What had she done?"

"She had an accident while driving a rented car without a license, but she claims that she wasn't driving. The only other person in the car, an older man, had never driven, or so his daughter said. Mama told the policemen a lie. I don't know what will happen to her."

"Do you want me to bail her out?"

"Do I—are you serious? After what you just told me, why would you do that?"

"I'll do it, because I hate knowing that you're unhappy, and . . . and because I love you." She slapped her hand over her mouth, and her eyes widened as she stared at him. "Aren't you going to say anything?"

"You . . . you never told me. I know you care, but . . . that must have really shaken you up."

"It did, more than you can guess. How do you feel about me right now?"

"I'm hurt and embarrassed by Mama's behavior, but that's nothing new. It's just so close this time."

"But what about me?" He had to know. If she blamed him, he was out of there.

"I love you, and I'm not going to let you bail her out. She was driving an unregistered and uninsured car with a suspended license, and well above the speed limit. One day, she will kill someone."

"Are you saying that you love me and can accept that I don't want your mother around me?"

Her eyes blinked rapidly, but not a tear fell. "Don't you realize, Sam, that *I* don't want to be around her? It's the tragedy of my life. Being with you has given me more happiness than I ever expected to have. My father and grandmother have loved and cared for me. If they hadn't, I wouldn't have known what love is. But you've given me so much more. With you, I've known emotional security and belonging, the feeling that someone needed me. When you wanted to slow down, I wasn't sure if you were saying you needed space, a distance between us. I'm still not certain."

"I try not to analyze myself, and it's a good thing. I realized that I was getting in deeper and deeper with you, that the minute I left you, I wanted to go back to you, and I developed a driving, barely controllable need to make love with you. I'd never had such feelings for a woman, and it scared the *bejeebers* out of me.

"I told myself—and with my professional knowledge to back it up—that I didn't know important things about you, things that could wreck a committed relationship, and I confess that your mother's attempt to steal her own child's pocketbook fueled that misgiving. My growing acquaintance with Bert is the only concrete thing that has happened between then and now to alleviate it. I went to him because I needed his advice and support."

She nodded slowly. "He said that if he were your father, he would have told you to forget about me, that Mama is too much baggage."

"If you feel that you have to have her in your life in the role of mother, I . . . I don't think I could handle that. You and I agreed to try and find out if we have anything going for us. That means not dating other people and exploring each other's personalities and interests. Are you still willing?"

He didn't like the sadness in her eyes or her not-quite-certain expression. "I asked you once before if you were sure. I'm asking you again. Are you sure this is what you want?"

"These past weeks have been a great teacher. I'm sure."

She got up, walked over to him, and stood looking down at him. Then, without preliminaries or warning, she sat in his lap, put an arm around his neck, and put her head on his shoulder. "I needed you so badly," she whispered.

He told himself to straighten out his head, that it was not a time for what he was thinking and feeling. "Can we see each other tomorrow? I . . . uh, I think I'd better leave."

She tightened her hold on him. "It's early yet. Do you have to go?" she asked him, twisting around to be able to see his face.

"I'd better," he replied as the pressure of her body against him intensified his need to have her. He started to move her from him, but she obstructed his movements. "Kendra! You're asking for trouble."

"Is that the new name for it?"

"You'd better quit while you're ahead, Kendra."

"You're leaving me? And you call that being ahead?" she asked him. "Not in my book."

"On whose terms am I staying?" he asked, no longer able to pretend a casual, laid-back attitude.

"Ours, Sam. Not yours or mine, but ours." He lifted her and carried her to her bedroom.

Kendra trembled not with fear of Sam, but of herself. Was she like Ginny? Was this the beginning of something that she wouldn't be able to control? Had she inherited a slavishness to sex?

"What is it? What's wrong, Kendra? If you're not sure, we won't do this. I don't want you to have reservations about making love with me. It is the most natural step for a man and woman who love each other. Talk to me."

"I don't want to be like her, Sam. I don't want sex to govern my life."

"Shh. Sex *doesn't* rule her. Greed and want govern her life. Sex for her is a means to an end. Tell me if there is anything I need to know."

"Thanks. I'm practically ignorant about this. Does that disappoint you?"

He leaned over her and began to stroke her bare arms and let his fingers drift over the tips of her breasts. "No. It means I won't have to correct another guy's mistakes." He stretched out on top of her and let her feel his flesh and the bulk of his genitals as he rested his weight on his elbows and shifted slowly and erotically over her. Evidently satisfied that he had awakened her, he rolled off, leaned over her, pulled her nipple into his mouth, and began to apply his talent.

An hour later, she gazed up at him, happy and sated. "Can it be like this all the time?" When he answered in the affirmative, she asked, "If that's so, why do couples split up, sometimes after long years together?"

"If something goes wrong in a relationship, I imagine that the effect shows first when they're in bed, provided they get that far. You didn't want to kiss me, Thanksgiving night. Remember? You certainly didn't want greater intimacy."

"I don't know. If I knew then what I know now, given a little pressure, I might have caved in."

"Don't you believe that. Pride can be very strong in relations between lovers." His lips brushed hers softly and thoroughly as if they were his to do with as he pleased. "I hate to think of what I came close to losing," he said, hardened inside of her and took them on a fast romp to powerful explosions.

Hours later, when he'd gone home and telephoned good night to her, she sat up in bed with the sheet pulled up to her shoulders, wondering about what could come next. Her mother could jettison all that she held dear and would think nothing of it. And if she didn't get professional help for Ginny, she'd either kill herself or someone else. God forbid that Ginny should ever see Sam again. Kendra doubted she'd use discretion even if she were married to him. He'd snubbed Ginny, and she'd get even if it killed her. How did anybody become so asocial, without morals or social conscience? "And Lord, why do I have to look like her?" she asked herself.

She awoke, still discombobulated, the next morning, Sunday, and after alternating moments of joy and anxiety, she telephoned her father. "Good morning, Papa, I thought I'd go to church with you this morning, since I'll be with Sam this afternoon ."

"Really! What brought this on, homage to heaven or contempt for hell? You're volunteering to go to church?"

She wasn't even tempted to be a smart aleck with her father, so she swallowed the clever comment that had settled on the tip of her tongue and said, "It will be the only time I can spend with you today."

"In that case, why don't I pick up some fresh croissants, and you scramble some eggs, fry some bacon or sausage, and make some coffee. I'll be over for breakfast in an hour." He finished the command in a voice filled with laughter.

She wasn't sure that mirth was in order, at least not on her part. If he willingly skipped church, it was because he wanted to know what had transpired between Sam and her. "Give me an hour and fifteen minutes, Papa, I just got up."

"All right. See you then."

She showered, dressed, and set the table. They'd have croissants, but she made biscuits for him to take home. As she tripped around the kitchen in a joyous mood, she suddenly stopped and nearly slipped on the tile floor. *Her father had advised her to talk with Sam in her apartment, provided that she loved him.* Reflecting on that for a few minutes, she realized that he knew they would want to make love if they made up, and he couldn't advise her about that. But it was crystal clear to her that her father wanted her to marry Sam Hayes. She sat down in a chair beside the kitchen table and rubbed her forehead as if that would make everything clear and logical. Marriage in the foreseeable future hadn't been in her plans.

She got up, turned the sausage, and told herself that she'd play it as the cards fell. She loved Sam and, after the loving he'd given her and the way he'd made her feel, she didn't want to think of a life without him. Suddenly, laughter poured out of her. Her papa was skipping church, because he wanted to know what had transpired between her and Sam, but he'd get an edited version.

She rushed to answer the doorbell. "Goodness, Papa. You're looking younger every time I see you. Do you have something to tell me?"

A grin spread over his face, and she reached up and kissed his cheek. "I wish I did. This place smells wonderful." He sniffed. "Why didn't you tell me you'd make biscuits?"

"I made them for you to take home."

"I'll take the croissants home. Let's have the biscuits. Nobody makes them as good as you do."

She poured orange juice, put the food on the table, and they sat down to eat. He said the grace, ending it with, "I don't have to ask, Lord, because I know you answered my prayers. Amen."

"You're still the champion biscuit maker," he said after biting into one. "How are things between you and Sam? Have you talked with him yet?"

"Yes, sir. We talked last night."

He stopped eating, rested the utensils on the side of his plate, and leaned back in the chair. "Where did you talk?"

"Here. I invited him to dinner."

He nodded. "Good. Did you air everything out? I mean, did he tell you the rest of it?"

"Yes, sir. He told me how he met her and what happened."

"Then you know that what's been bothering him is that he doesn't want such a woman for a mother-in-law and definitely not for the grandmother of his children. So don't think you can have it both ways. He won't stand for it."

"We haven't gotten that far, Papa."

"A smart man does not lock the barn door after the horse runs away; he takes care to lock the door while the horse is still in the barn. You understand?"

"Yes, sir. I've been hoping to get her into counseling."

He pulled air through his front teeth, a gesture that she

hadn't known him to make. "Don't waste your time or your money on that. I paid for counseling for Ginny, when we were trying to preserve the marriage, but she took the checks, destroyed them, and didn't go near the counselor. When I didn't see an improvement, I called the man, and he told me he'd seen her only once."

"Then what will I do, Papa.?"

"Leave her to heaven, for goodness' sake. How are you going to redirect somebody who doesn't know she's lost?"

"I guess that's the problem. Did you bail her out?"

"Me? Of what? I didn't know she was in trouble again. Maybe Ed did."

"I don't think so. He said Dot put her foot down, because they have three children to take care of and send to college. Mama already owes Uncle Ed twenty-eight thousand dollars for bailouts and loans."

"It's too bad. I can't imagine what she'll do."

Kendra took a deep breath and told herself once more to be thankful for her father. "How can you eat so much of this fattening stuff and not gain weight, Papa?" she asked him when he took a third helping of biscuits and sausage.

"Simple. I exercise every morning, and I usually have cereal, juice, and coffee for breakfast. This is a treat. Thanks for changing the subject. I spend enough time worrying about the relationship between you and Ginny."

Her relationship with her daughter was not on Ginny's mind. She had avoided indictment for the accident for lack of proof that she was the driver. Because she was wearing leather gloves, she'd left no fingerprints on the steering wheel or elsewhere in the car. The police admitted that the fact that the old man had never had a driver's license was not proof that he couldn't or wouldn't drive.

She sat in her living room staring out the window facing Kalorama Road. What did she have that she could pawn or sell? She didn't want to part with that pair of bronze antique jugs, because the pawn broker wouldn't give her much for them. She could ask Bert if he wanted to buy them, but she had told him at the time of the divorce and property settlement that she didn't know where they were. After considering her options, she stood, walked with wooden legs to her closet, took her grandmother's eighteen-carat-gold blue cameo locket and chain set from the box where it had rested for fifty years, and put it in her purse. Monday morning, she'd sell it wherever she could get the most money.

She felt no remorse for having to part with it. "It's the way the cookie crumbles," she said aloud, lifting her shoulder in a shrug, and heading to the kitchen to open a can of bean soup for her lunch.

Life has a way of screwing some people, and I'm getting more than my share. Kendra's got that high-powered job, so she can just get off some of that money. I don't care what Ed says or does.

Chapter Thirteen

Sam leaned against the wall just inside Kendra's apartment looking at her and musing over the suggestion she'd just made. "You and your father want to have Dad, his date, and me for Christmas Eve dinner?"

"Yes. You don't think it's a good idea?"

"Actually, I do, but that will mean you won't be able to attend the Omega dance with me December the twenty-third. I haven't been in several years, but since I have a beautiful woman to show off, I thought I'd go this year."

"Thanks for the compliment. Maybe I could—"

He interrupted her. "We can go to my alumni dance New Year's Eve. What about WAMA? Will you be working over Christmas?"

"I'm off from the twenty-second to the second, and Mr. Howell is giving me a bonus because I haven't missed a day, not even in blizzard weather."

"And you're leaving for Italy January fourth." He hadn't realized that he would develop a negative attitude about her being alone in Italy for an entire month, but he had. And he knew he'd better keep that to himself. "Be sure that those Italian men don't put their hands on you, and I mean not anywhere."

She bristled and let him see it. "I don't have to go that far in order to engage in hanky-panky. I can do that right here."

He held both hands up, palms out. "All right. That was probably out of place, but I don't feel like apologizing, because I meant it." He ran his hands over his hair, bruising his scalp in frustration. "Do you know the topic you're going to do your research on while you're there?"

"I've been thinking about food in Florence, Milan, and Rome, and how that can be related to differences in the people."

"That's a great topic, because both the food and the people differ among these cities. You've probably guessed that I'm chatting because I don't want to leave you. Kiss me and let me get out of here."

He figured that she made the kiss as brief as her own libido would allow, before stepping back and gazing at him with an expression that said, *Of all the women you've encountered, you want me.* Something flickered in her eyes, and he knew that heat had begun to furl up in her.

"What is it? Don't you want me to leave?"

She turned him to face the door. "Of course I don't, but I can't always have things the way I want them. I have to study." He kissed her again and left.

Kendra got ready for bed, crawled in, and prepared to study. The telephone rang and, not remembering to check the ID, she answered. "Hello."

"Hey kiddo, this is Flo. Sorry to call so late, but when I called earlier, no one answered. You've been out of touch lately, but that's to be expected since you're in school. Us Pace Setters are planning a Christmas Eve shebang at my place. Be sure and come, and bring that guy who's keeping you away from us."

"Oh, Flo, I'd love to, but my papa is having a dinner party that night, and I'm his hostess."

"Oh, crap! Can't you come over after your dinner?"

"Flo, honey, you know I love you guys, but I can't walk out and leave my papa's guests on Christmas Eve. He'd be scandalized. We planned this before Thanksgiving. You'll have to excuse me this time. My papa never lets me down, so you know . . ."

She let it hang. Flo wouldn't think of leaving her parents' guests at a holiday party. It had taken time, she knew, many years, but Kendra was beginning to say no without a feeling of guilt. The knowledge buoyed her, because she would one day be able to stand up to her mother without feelings of remorse or guilt. She'd gotten better at defending herself against Ginny's drama, but she still felt badly about doing it. She hung up as quickly as she could, because she knew that Sam would telephone her before he went to bed.

"I want a word with you, Ms. Richards," Professor Hormel said when Kendra walked into his classroom the next morning. "I like your outline, but remember that your story shouldn't be more than twenty-five double-spaced pages long. And you chose an interesting topic. However, proving your premise ought to cost you some effort. Good luck." He handed her an envelope. "Here are your introductions to establishments in Rome, Florence, and Milan. I'll see you back here February the first." She thanked him and found a seat.

She arrived at work that evening and found a stack of Nat King Cole CDs and a note from the program director advising her that the week of December 6th to December 21st was Nat King Cole week, commemorating the first African American to have a television show, and the last episode of the Nat King Cole Show on NBC. She liked Nat's music, but she didn't see it as especially appropriate for Christmastime, so she played an hour of Nat King Cole and then switched to instrumental jazz. At eight-thirty, the operator told her to pick up the phone. She did.

"Hello out there. KT speaking. Who've I got here?"

"Hi, KT, this is Clarissa Holmes. Remember me? I called in to wish you and that nice man I met with you a very Merry Christmas and a great New Year."

"What a great surprise! I'll tell him, and I wish the same to you and Brock. Come back to see us soon. In a minute, I'm going to play your recording of 'After Sundown.' "

"Thank you. Live life to the hilt, friend. Bye for now," Clarissa said, and hung up.

Yes, Kendra said to herself. *I needed to hear that, and I'm going to begin applying it come January.*

When she went to bed the night before Christmas Eve, every muscle in her body ached. Her father had a reasonably good cleaning woman, but Kendra had polished the place until it glistened. Then, after she and her father had dressed the eight-foot Fraser fir tree, she prepared the turkey, stuffed it, made two lemon chiffon pies, prepared the vegetables for cooking, and put them in the refrigerator.

"You should have let me have the dinner catered," Bert said. "You'll be half-dead when we're ready to eat."

"You got someone to clean up. That's what I hate to do," she said.

Bert looked at the table and shook his head in wonder. "That's the first time I've seen my mother's porcelain on a table since she died. I don't think Ginny set the table properly once in the five years we were married. When you marry, I'll give you my mother's porcelain, silverware, and crystal."

"What if you marry again?"

"If I ever do that, my wife can choose her own tableware." He pointed to the table. "That will be yours."

"Seven is a strange number to have for dinner, Papa. Maybe we should have invited one more person. What about Gates?"

"Gates is married, and it's just as well. He wouldn't know a linen napkin from a handkerchief."

By five o'clock Christmas Eve, Kendra had the dinner ready, except for last minute chores, and was soaking in a sea of pink bubbles in her father's Jacuzzi. She dressed in a red, floor-length silk sheath that displayed all of her assets, combed her hair down below her shoulders, clipped silver hoops to her ears, and applied perfume in strategic places. She noted that she was showing a good deal of cleavage, but what the heck! Cleavage was in.

She answered the door

"Come in. I'm Mr. Richards's daughter. Are you going to help us with the after-dinner cleanup?"

"Yes, ma'am. My name is Emma Barnes, and I'll serve for you, too, if you want. If you're having it in courses, please write out the menu and tell me which serving dishes you want me to use for the different items. I'll take care of the rest." Emma walked into the kitchen and looked it over. "Good. Dishwasher, nice counters, and plenty of space. Don't worry about a thing."

Kendra gave Emma the menu, showed her the serving dishes and utensils, and explained how she wanted the meal served. She had just flicked on the Christmas tree lights and placed two gifts under the tree when the doorbell rang. She opened it and Sam's soft whistle greeted her.

"You look good enough to bite," he said. "I'm engaging in self-restraint."

"Don't knock yourself out with it. We're practically alone."

His eyes sparkled. "Don't tempt me. I have to spend the rest of the evening practicing self-control, and I'm starting the way I can hold out." He kissed her quickly on the mouth. "Where's Bert?"

"He went to pick up two guests. I expect he'll be here any minute."

Sam sniffed. "Hmm. Now this is the way a place should smell on Christmas Eve. Who cooked?"

"I did. Go have a seat while I get us some drinks and hors d'oeuvres."

"Wait till the others come," he said at about the time the doorbell rang.

Kendra imagined that her jaw dropped when she opened the door to Jethro and instead of seeing Edwina with him, she looked into the face of a stunning woman around her own age or a little older.

"Come in," she said, recovering as quickly as she could. "Merry Christmas and welcome."

"Kendra Richards, this is Andrea Lang. Andrea, Kendra is Sam's girl." He looked at Kendra with an amused expression and winked. "Did Sam get here yet?"

"Yes. He just got here. Papa!" she exclaimed when she saw Bert. "Everybody come on in." She let Jethro introduce Andrea to her father.

"Welcome," Bert said. "These are my friends, Jennifer and Hal Underwood, brother and sister. Where's Sam?"

"Right here, Bert. Hi, Da . . . Dad."

Jethro laughed and embraced Sam. "You're looking great, son." He handed Bert a package that contained two bottles of Courvoisier VSOP Cognac.

With the formalities dispensed with, they settled in the living room around the Christmas tree and were soon exchanging tales in a jocular fashion as if they had all known each other for a long time. However, beneath her relaxed and happy façade, Kendra hid a growing anxiety. Tired of guessing, she excused herself, went to the dining room, and called to Sam.

"Could you help me in here for a minute, please, Sam?"

"What is it?" he asked her as he walked into the dining room.

"Look, it's none of my business, but it's driving me up the wall. Did your dad break up with Edwina?"

"Not that I know of. I'm as surprised as you are."

She'd always been told, like father, like son, and she did not care for what seemed like Jethro's casual treatment of his relationship with Edwina. "But . . . does he do things like this?" she asked Sam. "I mean, three weeks ago, they were as tight as two pecan halves. What do you think happened?"

"Your guess is as good as mine. Somehow, I don't think anything's happened to separate them."

"But who is Andrea? Have you met her before?"

"Not as I recall. Who's this lady who's keeping Bert occupied?"

"Your guess is as good as mine. Looks like our papas are doing their own thing tonight."

"Yeah. Tell me about it," he said, walking with her back to the living room.

"After dinner, if you three feel like listening, Jennifer, Hal, and I will play our guitars," Bert said. "The three of us haven't played together for a while, and I'm looking forward to it." He looked at Andrea. "Do you sing?"

"I've been known to," she said, "but not on a full stomach."

"Not to worry," Bert assured her. "We're amateurs. Now, Sam can really sing."

Kendra listened to the pleasant conversation, but it held little interest for her. What had happened between Jethro and Edwina? Had they split? Or was he cheating on her? She didn't want to be unhappy on Christmas Eve, and especially not when her papa had gone to such pains to make it a wonderful occasion. But the story of Jethro and Edwina was such a beautiful tale, strengthening her faith in the power and durability of love.

She checked with Emma, returned to the living room, and announced that dinner was ready. "May I wash my hands?" Andrea asked her. Kendra led her to the guest lavatory, and whirled back to confront Jethro, only to see that Sam had already taken advantage of the opportunity.

"What's going on here, Dad?" Sam asked his father. "What's happened between you and Edwina? I thought she'd be here."

"I guess you did. So, apparently, did Kendra. Edwina is in Florida with her parents. They're getting old and her father isn't well, so she wanted to spend Christmas with them.

This could be his last one. There's nothing between Andrea and me. She's from Eugene, Oregon, and she's here doing research on constitutional law at the Library of Congress."

"What are you going to do with her when Edwina comes back?"

A grin spread over Jethro's face. "Same thing as before Edwina left. Nothing."

As they headed for the dining room, Sam whispered to Kendra, "Everything's straight, and he isn't cheating." He could see relief flood Kendra's being. Immediately, she became the sparkling, wonderful woman that he loved. He'd have to ask her about her reaction to seeing his father with Andrea. To his way of thinking, it had been extreme.

In spite of his few anxious moments at the beginning of the evening, Sam enjoyed the company and the wonderful Christmas dinner. When they finished dessert, he raised his glass. "Kendra, I have never enjoyed a Christmas dinner more. You're a really good cook. Here's to you."

"Thanks, Sam. I admit to having been nervous about the turkey dressing, but everybody ate it."

"It was delicious," Hal said. "It's my favorite thing about a turkey dinner."

In the living room, they drank coffee, and all except Kendra enjoyed the cognac. Sam took her hand, and she leaned back against the sofa and closed her eyes.

He kissed her cheek. "You have every right to be happy," he said, for her ears alone.

Bert got his guitar and two others from a closet, checked the tuning of his own, and said to Hal, "How about a few rounds of 'Let It Go'?" He looked at Jennifer. "You want to play lead?"

She nodded, and they launched into the old jazz tune at a sizzling pace. Sam could barely believe his ears, and they played variations of the tune for ten minutes. Bert Richards and his friends regaled the group with jazz and blues until

Kendra said, "Papa, do you know 'Everything I Have Is Yours'?"

"Of course I do."

"How about the key of G?" Sam asked, and sang along with the guitar rendition.

"Each time I hear you sing," Bert said, "I am amazed that you've never sung professionally."

He'd never had the desire to sing publicly. "I haven't wanted to," Sam said.

"It's a few minutes to twelve," Jethro said, "and as much as I'm enjoying this wonderful evening, I have to take this lady home before I get too sleepy to drive. Merry Christmas to all of you and our thanks, Bert and Kendra, for a wonderful Christmas Eve."

Bert called a taxi for Emma and another for the Underwood siblings. "I don't drive when I've had this much to drink," he explained. "We'll talk tomorrow, Jennifer."

As soon as they left, Kendra cornered her father. "Papa, do you have something to tell me? You and Jennifer did a lot of quiet talking tonight. What's going on?"

"She's nice. I've known Hal for ages. I met Jennifer a couple of months ago. As I said, she's nice."

"Nice? Is that all? Well?"

"She's been divorced for about a year, and she's only now shedding all that angst. Her ex went off with a woman who was a go-go dancer where he worked as the resident pianist. Jennifer is the last person who'd compete with one of those sisters."

But Kendra was tenacious. "I liked her. Are you planning to pursue a relationship with her? She's as different from Mama as wind is from water."

Bert looked steadily at his only child. "What makes you think I'd allow myself to get within a mile of a woman like Ginny? How many times should a man learn the same lesson? Jennifer had never heard of Jimmy Choo. Ed once told me that Ginny was in a snit because she wanted a pair of Jimmy Choo shoes and he wouldn't lend her seven hundred and some dollars to buy them."

When Kendra frowned, Sam asked her, "Who's Jimmy Choo?"

"I have no idea."

Sam didn't say, Thank God, but he certainly thought it. When Bert played Christmas carols on the CD player, Sam reached beneath the tree and removed the two packages that he'd placed there and handed one to Kendra and the other to Bert. He knew Kendra would like her gift, but he wasn't sure about Bert.

"Gee whiz. Just look at this," Kendra said, dropping the pearl necklace in her lap. She threw her arms around him and hugged him. "You're one sweet man. I love it." She showed it to Bert who nodded appreciatively.

"I've always marked you for a man with taste. They're beautiful." Bert opened his gift and released a whistle. "A silver guitar pick with my initials. Hmm. Thank you. I'm not likely to lose this one. I'll be right back." He returned with a box wrapped in gold and red candy cane paper. "The contents are packed for your freezer, so be sure and open it tonight."

Sam opened it right then, though he knew he'd find individual-cut prime filet mignon steaks. He looked at Bert and grinned. "If I had a habit of hugging men, I'd sure hug you for this. Thank you."

"My pleasure."

Sam wasn't sure he should open Kendra's gift to him in her father's presence, so he asked her, "Should I open it now or later?"

"Now, if you want to."

He opened the box with fingers that weren't quite steady, and when he saw the label on the inner box, he quickened his efforts. He knew she couldn't afford it, but she'd bought him a Montblanc Meisterstück Le Grand ballpoint pen. He could feel his face crease into a smile.

"I am definitely in the habit of hugging women," he said, and pulled her into his arms. "You are one sweet woman."

"You two have made a big leap since the three of us were last together and certainly since I last saw you, Sam. I hope you'll work at understanding each other and avoid letting outside forces make you unhappy. If something distresses you, don't let it simmer. Deal with it head-on right then. Little things get bigger with time." Bert looked at Sam. "I was rather expecting some news about Jethro and Edwina, so you may imagine my surprise that he had a different date tonight."

"Edwina's spending Christmas with her parents in Florida, so he brought an associate who'll be returning to Oregon at the end of the year. Edwina still rules."

"I'm glad to hear it," Bert said. "They're an attractive couple."

"I'd better get on home, Papa. I'd stay here tonight, but I want to sleep late tomorrow, and you get up with the sun. It's been wonderful. See you at lunch tomorrow."

"Good night, sir, and thanks again for my steaks. I'm going to have one for breakfast."

"You're having lunch with your dad tomorrow?" Sam asked Kendra as soon as he closed the door.

"It's our custom. We've done it every year since I went to live with Mama. That's when he and I exchange gifts. He wouldn't put a foot in Mama's apartment, so that's how we managed it."

"The more I see of him, the more I like him. I hope he and Jennifer make a go of it. She's very interested in him."

"I noticed that. If she makes him happy, I wouldn't ask for more. He hasn't had much of that."

"Are you going to see your mother tomorrow?" He didn't want to ask her, but he had to.

"No, I'm not. I'd like to call her, but I'm scared I'll open Pandora's box. Isn't it awful?"

"Yes, it is, but sometimes you have to let go."

"I know, and I'm trying." Sam hoped that was enough. He loved Kendra, but he had his limit, and Ginny Hunter was it.

When Kendra got in bed Christmas night, she doubted that she would sleep. Her entire body still tingled from Sam's wild lovemaking Christmas Eve and from his possessiveness and attentiveness Christmas evening and night. Happiness suffused her, but somewhere in the back of her consciousness lurked the fear that her bubble might burst. She was happy for her papa, who had confirmed that he and Jennifer shared an interest in each other, and that the woman brightened his life. But it had been her experience that each time their lives became relatively peaceful and uncomplicated, her mother or incidents in her mother's life disrupted the peace.

Spending a Christmas without any contact with her mother or even knowing where her mother was didn't sit well with her; although Ginny had blighted her life far more often than she had illumined it, the woman was still her mother. After a couple of hours tossing in bed, she slept fitfully.

Sam's call awakened her at eight the next morning. "Good morning, sweetheart. Are you planning anything today that can include me?"

"Hi, love. If you can sew, I'll welcome the help. I'm getting my clothes together for the trip, which is less than two weeks away. Choosing what to wear for an entire month and packing economically requires some ingenuity."

"I imagine it's much more difficult for a woman than for a man. Be sure and carry all the toilet articles and medicines that you're likely to need. Their brands are different from ours."

"Thanks. I don't wear makeup, except occasionally for lipstick, so that's not a problem. We could have dinner together this evening, if you want to, although the weather forecast is for snow."

"I was hoping you'd be free this evening. I want to see you." She agreed.

But early in the afternoon, she received a call from Clifton Howell.

"I know you're on vacation, Kendra, but Tab has the flu, and I'm desperate. Can you fill in on his TV program from seven to eight-thirty tonight? It's just for tonight. By tomorrow, I'll have found a temporary replacement for Tab."

"You know I'll help you in any way that I can, Mr. Howell, but I may not know the guests he's interviewing."

"True. Do you have some friends who could have something important to say about Christmas or New Year's or education or jazz? Whatever. Kendra, that's a prime-time show. I can't give it to just anybody, and I can't do a rerun again tonight."

She thought for a minute. "I've got an idea. I'll call you right back. She hung up, called Sam, and related to him Howell's request. "I'd like to interview you and your father together. I can't interview my papa, because he doesn't close the shop tonight till six-thirty."

"Tell him to close an hour early, and interview the three of us."

"What about?"

"Christmas and the meaning of family. Family can be more than a group of blood relatives, or sexual partners, or relatives by marriage. How about it?"

"Okay. I'd better call my papa and your dad."

"I'll call Dad."

"Thanks. Be at the studio at six o'clock." She hung up, telephoned her father, and couldn't believe his excited response. Figuring that Clifton Howell had begun to bite nails, she dialed his number and told him what she planned.

"You're an angel. I'll make sure that the commercials are for humanitarian causes so as not to embarrass them. Naturally, they'll get an honorarium, and, in addition to my thanks, you'll get paid. See you around six."

So much for dinner with Sam. Still, she didn't doubt that the evening would be exciting.

She went through her closets, and chose garments that she could wear in Europe, but which needed mending, and got to work. However, her thoughts centered on her evening program as questions took shape in her mind. She would lead with a question or two and then let them talk. She didn't doubt that they would relate well to each other.

Minutes before leaving home to go to the studio, she received a call from her father. When she saw his caller ID, she had a moment of fear that he might have called to cancel his appearance on the show.

"What's the matter, Papa?"

"Nothing's the matter. I'm just afraid that if Ginny catches this program, she'll manage to interfere with it."

She let out a long breath in relief. "Good point. I won't take any calls. Thanks for alerting me." She hung up with the thought that she might be the only person in the city of Washington who feared a mother's telephone call.

Her one dislike of anchoring a program was the preprogram makeup sessions. She hated the goo on her face. Dressed in the best suit that she owned, the burnt-orange wool crepe, she walked on camera to the applause of the studio audience, took a seat in a comfortable leather chair, and crossed her knees. A large thermos of coffee, mugs, spoons, milk, and sugar rested on the glass-top coffee table. *Good*, she thought, glancing at the decorated Christmas tree in a corner. *Just the right atmosphere.*

"Hello, everyone. Tab isn't feeling well tonight. I have three wonderful guests, and we're going to talk about family and Christmas. Please meet Herbert Richards, purveyor of the best quality meats to be found in the District of Columbia; Jethro Hayes, attorney at law; and Samuel Hayes, professor of clinical and family psychology at GW. Mr. Richards is my father and, as you have probably observed, Jethro and Samuel Hayes are father and son.

"All four of us have at one Christmas or another been without a complete family. How do you think this affects an individual?" Sam took the question, as she'd known he would, and after a few minutes, the four of them gave the appearance of a group of friends conversing in a living room. The hour and a half passed so swiftly that the producer's five-minute signal surprised her, and they barely had time to wrap up. She had a sense of accomplishment that she'd never experienced as a radio host. *TV is for me*, she thought, but kept it to herself.

As they walked out of the studio, Howell intercepted them. "I'm Clifton Howell. That may have been the best program we've had in this time slot. Thank all of you for coming to our rescue. Mr. Richards, your daughter is an exceptional woman." He handed each of them a gold foil envelope. "Have a Happy New Year. When Kendra comes back from Europe, I hope we can have the three of you on another program. I'm thinking, African American History Month. Think about it." He shook hands with them.

"Kendra?"

She turned around and looked back at Clifton Howell. He took a few steps toward her. "A woman came here about twenty minutes ago. I'm sure it was your mother. Rocky recognized her and had her removed from the building, but she may be around someplace. I'm sorry."

"Thanks. You did the right thing."

She walked back to the three men, looked at Jethro, and said, "My mother is a sociopath. She apparently caught our program and rushed down to make trouble. Mr. Howell took steps to prevent that."

Jethro frowned. "How did he know it was she?"

"She's been here before."

"I see." He put an arm around her shoulders. "We all have our trials, Kendra. It isn't of your making, so try not to let it burden you."

She didn't look at Sam, for she feared she'd see in his demeanor a dispirited reaction to what appeared to be an inability to escape her mother. But he grasped her hand, dropped it, and eased his arm around her waist. "It's all right, sweetheart. She won't win unless we let her."

She nodded, almost as if she hadn't heard him. "I wish I had your faith."

She wanted to believe him. Did he love her more than he detested Ginny? She didn't want to witness the acid test. Every time Kendra had a modicum of success or if something happened to her that gave her a good feeling about herself, Ginny did something, intentionally or not, that weakened her spirit. And it hurt. But Ginny Hunter would never drag her down!

Chapter Fourteen

Kendra removed her shoes, tightened her seat belt, and put her head between her knees, as the captain of the Alitalia flight commanded. She was neither nervous nor scared. After the shock of hearing that her mother had refused food and water for the last two days and threatened suicide if she were forced to return to jail, Kendra doubted that anything could unnerve her. When authorities made it clear to Ginny that, as a repeat offender, she was not entitled to bail, Ginny had reconsidered her efforts at blackmail and accepted food.

After circling around Leonardo da Vinci–Fiumicino Airport for about twenty minutes, the plane touched ground in a blinding rain, bumping with such force that Kendra thought it would come apart. She comforted herself with the thought that the plane was at least on the ground. When it rolled to a halt, she said a prayer of thanks, raised her head, and took a deep breath of stale air.

"That was close," her seatmate, a woman near her age, said. "I fly all the time, but this is the first good scare I've had."

"This is my first flight. I hope the trip back will be easier."

"Have a good time here. As far as I'm concerned, Italy is God's country. And, honey, these Italian men can give you the shivers, so be careful."

An hour and a half later, Kendra stepped out of the shut-tle bus that took her to the di Santi Alberghi, a small bed and board hotel, and looked around. The rain had ceased, the sun shined brightly, and the odor of tomatoes, peppers, and garlic comforted her olfactory senses. She was indeed in Italy. A glance at her watch reminded her that back in Washington it was four-thirty in the morning. She changed her watch to ten-thirty and told herself to make a similar adjustment.

After checking in, she walked into a room that was more attractive than she'd hoped, considering the price. She stepped out on her balcony—and what a sight! Laundry, carpets, mops, buckets, and other things hung from balconies and from clotheslines strung from buildings to posts and balconies above the alley. She sniffed the scent of Italian cooking, which wafted from every window, and went back inside, satisfied that she was in a lower-middle-class section of the Eternal City.

Too excited to sleep, she changed into a pair of pants and Reeboks, went to the kitchen, and asked to see the cook.

"You mean the chef," a waitress, who had been folding napkins, told her. "I'll get him."

The chef appeared, wiping his hands on his white apron, and when he saw Kendra, he removed his chef's hat. "You had a nice dinner last night, yes?" His eyes sparkled and his forty-year-old face brightened with the pleasure of one who had discovered a diamond mine. His gaze darted to her left hand.

What had she gotten into? Even a child could recognize that look as a leer. "I have just arrived, sir." She attempted to explain that she was studying Italian food patterns, but she soon realized that he barely understood what she was saying and pointed repeatedly to his watch.

The amused waitress took pity on her. "He thinks you like him, and he's letting you know what time he gets off."

Kendra tried to explain to the waitress. "You're out of your head, lady," the waitress said. "No chef in Italy will tell you how he boils the eggs. So what you're thinking is crazy. Go to one of the cooking schools. Maybe they help you."

So much for innovation. She hadn't planned to rely on the references that Professor Hormel had given her; she suspected that home economics students from different schools went to those places. She wanted to bring back something that was original and fresh, so she'd use the references only as a last resort.

"Do you know the name of one or two?" she asked the waitress.

"La Buona Cucina is the best, and they have foreign students. My uncle works there." She gave Kendra the address. "Good luck." Kendra thanked her. "And you'd better stay away from this guy. He has the wife and children, but he thinks you want to have fun, and he is willing."

"How can I avoid him? I'm taking my meals here, and he'll—"

The waitress flexed her right shoulder and spread her hands. "You take one step, these men take ten. For a few more lire, you can eat dinner in your room."

It was a lesson she wouldn't have to learn again. But the egotistic chef could take as many steps as he pleased. She didn't intend to pay one extra lira in order to stay at di Santi in peace, and he had better leave her alone.

The next morning after breakfast, she went to La Buona Cucina. When the manager learned that she was an American journalist, he received her with enthusiasm. She explained her project to him and, to add to her chance of success, she asked his advice as to how she should proceed.

Assuming the armor of authority, he said, "You write, but can you cook?"

"I don't want to write about your methods of preparing foods. I want to know what the people eat."

He looked first at his fingernails and then at her. "You spend one week here, or I don't talk to you."

"After a week, will I know about truffles and other delicacies and who's eating them?"

With his mouth ajar, he laid back his head as if greatly put upon. "Signorina, if you write for the rich, you need to know truffles. Otherwise, learn what we do with pomodoro, frutti di mare, cipolla, and formaggio, (tomato, seafood, onion, and cheese)."

Chastened, she knew she couldn't insist on her original idea, and that the information she got would have to guide what she wrote. She admitted that she'd been arrogant in thinking she could go to a strange country—whose language she didn't even speak—and, in one month, understand its people and their food habits well enough to write intelligently about it.

"Thank you, sir. I'll be here tomorrow morning ready for class."

With the help of a woman she met at breakfast the next morning, Kendra changed her plans and obtained appointments at cooking schools in Florence and Milan. However, she wasn't to escape the loving attention of the di Santi chef.

"Eh bella!" the chef said when she walked off the elevator the next morning en route to the cooking school. "Where you goin', *tesorina*?" He took her arm and prepared to walk out of the hotel with her. At the exit, knowing that she was in no physical danger, Kendra stopped, opened her electronic translator, and found the Italian words that she wanted. "*Togliti dai piedi*" she read aloud to him. *Get lost.* She loved the sound of it and repeated it several times with increasing authority.

However, the chef's immediate expression of distress quickly dissolved into a leer. Disgusted, she stamped her foot, raised her voice, and commanded, "*Togliti dai piedi.*"

Indicating that he might be mentally dense, he spread his palms outward, flexed a shoulder, and said, "She did not like the spaghetti *e vongole*?" He shook his head from side to side and walked on.

"Thank God," she said aloud, and let herself breathe.

But at dinner that night, he brought two cannoli to her table, while other diners had sherbet and a cookie for dessert. She loved cannoli, but in sudden awareness that he would chase her until she left Rome, she picked up the dessert and placed it in front of an older woman at a nearby table and left the dining room. She told the hotel manager later, "So you tell him to leave me alone, or I'll tell my university that this hotel is not a safe place for its female students."

The manager rubbed his hands together and then clasped them in a prayerful attitude. "You will have no more problems with him. I promise you. My hotel is the perfect place for university girls."

In her room, Kendra tried to review her notes, but couldn't focus on them. Her thoughts were on the changes in herself after less than one week. She had taken a firm hand against the chef's unwanted attention, and she had not worried about the effect that reporting his behavior to the manager would have on the man.

For once, I didn't equivocate. I didn't like his game, and I've given him no choice but to leave me alone. And she had changed her project's plan as soon as she knew it wasn't going to work and had instituted a better one—learning at the school what a single chef couldn't teach her.

The next morning, with renewed energy and faith in herself, Kendra strode down the corso, and turned into Porta Pia where the cooking school stood one building from the corner.

"What are you so happy about?" Anthony, one of three American men studying at the school, asked Kendra.

"Nothing special." Even if she told him, she doubted that he would understand.

"Want to see some of Rome with me this evening?"

Her immediate reaction was a negative one, but she reconsidered after remembering that Anthony was an American and that they understood the same rules for male–female relations.

"I'd love to, Anthony, because I'd hate to leave Rome without having seen the Piazza del Campidoglio, the Spanish Steps, Trevi Fountain, the Pantheon, and other monuments to the Roman past. I've only seen the Colosseum and the Vatican. I didn't allot enough time for my stay in Rome. But, I have to be honest, if you've got a good-night kiss on your mind, count me out."

"Come now, Kendra, we cross that bridge when we get to it. You can't negotiate that in advance. Who knows? By the time I bring you back to your hotel, you may be crawling all over me. If you've got a guy back in the States, leave him there; you're here."

She probably should have told him to take a hike, but sightseeing alone in Rome in the month of January hadn't proved the most rewarding experience. "It's a good thing you laughed when you said that. I'd like to see the Trevi Fountain, at least. Can we go right after school?"

"Sure, and I can take you to a few other interesting places."

"Like what?"

"The Pantheon and the Campidoglio and, if it's still open, maybe the Church of Saint Peter in Chains where they keep Michelangelo's *Moses*. That's an awesome figure. Okay?"

"That would be wonderful."

Kendra had thought they would use public transportation, but Anthony shuttled them around Rome in his little Fiat.

When they arrived back at the di Santi after eleven o'clock that night, she'd had more fun than she imagined possible with a man she barely knew. Getting out of the Fiat, she slipped, and when he tried to prevent her fall, they both fell. A passerby came to help them, but their laughter apparently discouraged him. Anthony walked into the hotel with her, and although she didn't escape his kiss, she refused to part her lips.

"So that guy's got a hold on you," Anthony said. "I hope he deserves you."

She didn't respond to that. "Thanks for the sightseeing and the fun, Anthony. Good night."

Almost as soon as she walked into her room, the telephone rang. Fearing that the caller was the amorous chef, she allowed it to ring over half a dozen times before answering it.

"Hello," she said in a voice devoid of warmth.

"I thought I'd have to hang up without speaking with you."

"Sam! Sam! Oh, this is wonderful! I'm so glad to hear you."

"How are you, sweetheart? I wanted to reach you before you leave for Florence. I hope it's going well."

"So far, so good, but it certainly is not as easy as I had imagined. Thank goodness they crossed off Egypt! That would probably have been impossible."

"Do you think you can get the story you want?"

"If I can skip Milan and get what I want in Florence and a smaller city, such as Verona, I can write something that justifies this trip. We'll see."

"It's been one long week," he said.

"It sped by for me. I've had to concentrate on my every thought, every move, and every piece of information given me. I've been so busy readjusting, getting my bearings and coping with this language and things I didn't expect, that time has seemed to move too fast. I've felt that the month would be over before I get my story."

"I can imagine. Does that mean you haven't missed me?"

"Of course I've missed you. But I've had to work things out myself, and knowing that I've done that gives me so much satisfaction."

"I like what I'm hearing. Just be certain you're not concentrating on one of those guys."

"Oh, Sam. I haven't even been here a week."

"What does that say? I've spent a lot of time in Italy. If you don't know it already, let me tell you that the average Italian man doesn't need five minutes. Give him a week, and there's no telling what he'll do."

For some reason, that amused her. "Really? I'll keep that in mind."

"I hope you don't think I'm joking. I miss you, and I'd be much happier if you hadn't left here while you were concerned about your mother. There's an acceptable solution to every problem. We only have to find it."

"I guess so. What I can't understand is why a person would be so hell-bent on self-destruction and seem to want to destroy every person in her path."

"Apparently, one thing she has needed is a firm hand. She knows now that she has to remain in jail until her trial and that she can't manipulate the judge, so she's cooperating with the authorities. But that's the answer only for now."

"We'll have to talk about this when I get back, Sam. There isn't much love or sentiment between us, but there are times when I need to talk with a mother, when I want to discuss things, to understand things that a woman would raise in conversation only with her mother. Ginny has cheated me out of that, and I no longer expect it of her. She can't influence me, and her antics no longer hurt me. But I don't know if I'll be able to watch her drown. Have you spoken with my papa?"

"I played chess with him night before last, and I see where you got your powers of concentration. He didn't say ten words during the game. Quite a guy."

"Who won?"

"Need you ask? He was downright vicious. But, he'd just served me a terrific porterhouse steak dinner, so I forgave him. Do you have your phone number in Florence?" She gave it to him.

"Get there safely. If anything should go wrong, remember that Florence is only a eight-hour flight away and call me. I love you."

"I love you, too, Sam. Bye."

At times, Kendra amazed him. Sam propped his feet up on the desk in his den at home, locked his hands behind his head, and let a grin slide over his face. He'd been worried silly about her—whether she'd be able to communicate with the help of her tourist-book Italian and, especially, whether she would convince anyone in the food industry to talk with her about Italian food habits. He'd bet anything that she had a few stories to tell, and not all of them would be amusing. And no matter what she told him, he'd never believe that she hadn't had to fend off the advances of a couple of Italian males.

The Romans were a handsome people, and the men knew it and prided themselves in their looks. And they loved beautiful women of any color. But if he had to worry about a woman's fidelity, he didn't have much going for him. In any case, Kendra was not and never would be a pushover for any man, and that included him.

But something had to be done about Ginny Hunter, because Kendra would never be happy as long as her mother was in trouble. It didn't help that he disliked the woman intensely.

During his first free period at school the next day, Sam phoned a close colleague. "Hi, Dita, this is Sam. Are you free for lunch?"

"Sure. What time?" He told her and they agreed to lunch at La Belle Époque, his favorite restaurant.

Dita's peers considered her an expert in behavioral psychology, and he hoped she could shed some light on Ginny

Hunter's prospects for improvement. He hoped she wouldn't divulge their conversation.

"I'm too close to this to be objective, Dita, and I'd appreciate your confidence in this matter." Without naming names or disclosing his relationship to the characters involved, he described what he knew of Ginny's behavior. "Those close to her think she's a sociopath. I have my own views. Do you think she can be helped, that she can be guided to change her behavior and outlook?"

"Whew! You aren't asking for much! I think a really good therapist can do her some good, but she doesn't seem the type to cooperate with a therapist. If she remains in jail, she'll convince herself that the world owes her plenty and she'll never accept that she wouldn't have been in jail if she hadn't broken the law. If she gets a humanitarian for a judge, she may get forced treatment, which she'll accept in order to get out of prison."

"I hope so. But how do you cure a manipulator who's willing to drag everyone she knows down to the bottom of the pit?"

"Her first and maybe greatest problem is her inability to love and to identify empathetically with another person," Dita said. "She may be slightly autistic."

"I thought of that," Sam said, "but after getting to know her ex-husband, I ruled it out. Still, it's possible. Do you think a social agency can handle this kind of illness?"

"I doubt it. She should go to a private clinic, and the therapist should be a woman. If it's a man, she'll try to seduce him."

He couldn't argue with that.

Finding the crab-cake sandwich as delectable as ever, he savored it along with a plain lettuce salad. "Thanks for letting me pick your brain. I hadn't thought a clinic was the place for her, but it's worth a try. She's not related to me, but she means a lot to one of my dearest friends."

"I wish her the best, Sam, but I know that won't come easily."

How well he knew that. Ginny had not only alienated what would have been her support group; she had made them a part of her problem. If only Kendra would shed that awful burden. As much as he hated Ginny's relationship with Kendra, he understood how difficult it must be to walk away from your own mother when she was obviously in trouble. He was expecting Kendra to do it, but could he if he were in her shoes? It was something to which he had to give serious thought.

Ginny had taken her situation in hand and was applying her special brand of subterfuge. She asked to see the warden, and, after several tries, was granted an audience. "Good afternoon, ma'am," she began. "Since I'm sitting here doing nothing, maybe you could use me to teach these women how to do hair, manicures, facials, and massages. I'm pretty good at things they do in a spa."

The warden looked hard at her with a stern and forbidding expression. "Some of the inmates deserve a break, and they'd probably enjoy learning how to fix themselves up. But you've got a record of ignoring rules and acting like the law is for everybody but you. You've had plenty of breaks, but you always end up back here. So don't try anything clever. I'll see who's interested."

Three days later, having worked ten to twelve hours each day, Ginny had become the darling of the "privileged" inmates. One inmate, a big woman of questionable sexual preference, loaned Ginny the two dollars needed to make a phone call.

She phoned her brother. "Ed, I think I've done enough penance. I've been doing charity work here. If you come and vouch for me in person, I may be able to get out on bail."

"How much is the bail?"

"Practically nothing. The warden said it's been reduced to twenty-five hundred."

"I see. And that's practically nothing. I'd like to know what kind of charity work you've been doing. If I bail you out, I know I've seen the last of my twenty-five hundred. But if you get into trouble again, any kind of trouble, no matter how small, I will testify against you, and I certainly won't bail you out again. Stay out of automobiles, unless you're in the backseat."

She didn't care how much he lectured. He could say whatever he liked. She'd promise him anything in order to get her freedom. When she received word that she could go, she tried not to show jubilation. *After all, if Ed had behaved like any other brother, he wouldn't have allowed her to spend a single night in this snake pit.*

The judge's previous order tied her hands, but, as Houdini proved more than once, one only had to apply a little ingenuity to slip through a few chains. If only she had a bit of lipstick! Going out into the street with her face bare was something she hadn't done since she reached puberty.

Ed met her at the gate and, for reasons she didn't understand, she felt bereft that her own brother didn't hug her. Where had that thought come from?

Hell, I don't need his hug, she told herself. *I just needed to get out of that miserable place.*

"You're out now," were his first words. She stared at him. "But let's get this straight," he went on. "If you get behind the wheel of a car, if you say a word to Kendra, or if you go near her home or her job, you'll go back in jail, and I'm through with you for good. That's my agreement with the authorities when I paid your bail, and I mean to enforce it. If you get into trouble, I'll appear against you as a friend of the court. One of these days, you're going to get behind a wheel and kill somebody, because you can't drive. Furthermore, you don't have a license. So if you can't behave like a reasonable adult, you shouldn't live among reasonable people."

He headed to his car. "Get in, and let's go."

After weeks without an airing, her apartment had a strange, musky odor and smelled of the decayed stems of sunflowers she had bought for the table so as to convince old man Dunner that she was a woman of taste and refinement. She opened her bedroom window, looked out, and her shoulders sagged. *Same old alley.*

A check of her refrigerator with its rotting vegetables and meats served as a reminder that she was broke. It had been a one in fifty chance that she'd have an accident while driving Dunner's rented car, and she'd almost gotten away with it, telling the police that it was Dunner and not she who'd been driving when the car crashed into a wall. But when Dunner recovered sufficiently to be interviewed, he'd sworn that he'd never sat behind the wheel of a car in his life, supporting his daughter's testimony. The police had arrested her on the street as she walked to work. She could have made one call, but what good would it have done to call Phil, the owner of the beauty salon? She'd called Ed, and he'd hung up on her.

Broke! She didn't have the price of a dozen eggs. Pushing her pride aside, she called Phil. "I need work, Phil. Can you get me some appointments?"

"Get you some . . . Where the hell have you been? You left your customers high and dry. I fill your book with appointments, and you don't show. Give me a break!"

She had to level with him or he wouldn't budge. "Phil, I've been in the clinker, and I just got out. I got into an accident while driving a car, and I didn't have a valid driver's license."

"They don't keep you in jail for that, babe."

"You can check it, Phil. It was . . . uh . . . my second offense. I couldn't make my one phone call, because they took away my pocketbook."

"Uh . . . That's a real bummer. Look! I'll give you two days, but if you mess up, you've had it."

"Thanks, Phil. I can be there tomorrow morning." And unless she could find some change somewhere in the apartment, she'd have to walk.

After throwing out all the food in her refrigerator and washing the appliance thoroughly, she sat down and laughed aloud. Except for a half a can of stale coffee, her thousand dollar, stainless-steel, custom-built refrigerator was empty. She sat at her kitchen table for about an hour considering her options and concluded that she didn't like any of them. But she had to eat. So she dressed in a woolen jacket and pants, sweater, and boots, turned a raincoat inside out, and put it on. Then, she took a woolen blanket used for picnicking and threw it over her head and across her shoulders. She conceded that her hands would freeze, but that was a price she had to pay.

As shrewd as ever, Ginny walked over to the corner of Kalorama and Connecticut—where the pedestrian traffic was heavy—sat down on the cold pavement, lowered her head, and held out her hand. Three hours later, she had one hundred and twenty-three dollars and fifteen cents. With her masquerade still in place, she stopped at a small grocery store, bought what she would need for a simple meal, and went home. After shedding the layers of clothing, she cooked, ate, took the first private shower she'd had in three weeks, and went to bed. If she could give at least three massages a day, she could pay her rent, and she'd be fine. She could always pick up a few dollars with her hand out.

She was not a fan of Washington's public transportation, but it served her well the next morning, and she got to the beauty salon on time. "I want you to know," Phil said when she walked in, "that I'm sick and tired of your shenanigans. The first time you mess up, you're outta here. You got that?"

"Don't worry, Phil. I learned my lesson."

"Your first customer doesn't come in till ten, so shampoo for Clara. She's already running behind."

What could she say? He knew she didn't do shit-work. But she'd be back on her feet as soon as she could figure out how to get some money out of Kendra without going back to jail. Then Phil could take his job and shove it.

Ginny couldn't know that with the changes in Kendra's life, she had become a stronger and mentally tougher person. With the experience of having worked, studied, and negotiated with the chefs and managers of cooking schools in Rome, Florence, and Verona behind her, Kendra took a train to Venice for a day trip.

"I may never get back to Italy," she told herself, "and I can't afford to miss Venice." She walked into St. Mark's Square, found a table, and sat down. Even in the damp and chilly weather, she could appreciate the attractiveness of the square to the millions who visited it annually. She had never seen so many pigeons, and after dodging the ones that seemed to want to land on her head, she hoped she never saw another one. She ordered coffee and ice cream and settled back to enjoy the sights.

"Who is sitting here?" a good-looking Italian asked her.

Having learned the ways of the locals, she looked at him with a show of disinterest. "Why?"

He ignored her challenge and sat down. "I'm Mario. You want to go for a ride on a vaporetto? Is very nice."

She'd read about the vaporetti and the use that lovers and tourists often made of them. With a studied glare, she said, "Yeah. But not with you." As if it was no big deal, he spread his hands, flexed his shoulder, and left. *Lesson learned: any female tourist with money would do.*

Two older American women stopped at her table. "Are you from the States?" one of them asked her. She told them she was. "We figured that, since you don't look a bit African," the other said. "If you're by yourself, we know a great restaurant not far from here. Come on and join us."

"I want to," Kendra said, "but I'm on a student's budget."

"Oh, that's all right. I'm Delia and she's Shelia. We're twins, and we'd love it if you'd join us."

"I can't let you pay for my lunch."

"Sure you can. We've been together for fifty years and nine months," Delia said with a twinkle in her eye, "and we don't have anything new to say to each other."

"Is this your first visit to Italy?" Kendra asked, rising to join them for lunch.

"We travel to Italy every year, and we always include Venice in our itinerary."

They ordered the meal in Italian, and she learned that they also spoke French and Spanish and had traveled all over the world. Curious as to their source of income, she asked whether they were retired.

"We both taught for a few years," Shelia said, "but it seemed a shame to take jobs from someone who needed the work, so we established a foundation for children with learning disabilities."

"Are you from anywhere near Washington, D.C.? I host a local radio program, and I'd like to have you as a guest sometime." When Delia's eyebrows shot up in apparent disbelief, Kendra explained. "I'm finishing my degree in communications, and I work nights at WAMA in Washington."

"We'd love to come on your program and talk about our foundation and the children we help." They exchanged information about themselves. "We'll be back in the states mid-March, so give us a call," Delia, the most forward of the two, said. "We'll be looking forward to hearing from you."

That evening, as the train carrying Kendra rolled into Florence, she looked at the card the sisters had given her and gasped. Delia and Shelia belonged to one of the South's wealthiest and better-known families. "I'm going to quit putting all southern white folks into the same barrel of pickles," she promised herself.

With Italy behind her as the big Alitalia jet roared through the skies, Kendra wrote the first draft of her story. "What could you be writing at such a rapid pace?" the man sitting beside her asked.

"A report that's due to my professor Monday morning, three days from now."

"And you'll be ready with it?"

"Absolutely," she said, her voice reflecting both assurance and pride.

"I wish I could say the same. I've been doing research for my dissertation, but I spent too much time enjoying the local culture."

"You can get a lot from the Internet. You've been there, so you can put everything into perspective. I wish you luck. I'd better get on with this."

"Yeah," he said, reflectively. "You're the type who lets nothing get between you and your goals. Thanks for the lesson." He put his drink aside, opened his laptop, and got busy.

At the baggage claim in Ronald Reagan Washington National Airport, Kendra reached for one of her bags, and a hand snatched it off the carousel. "Hey! That's my bag." She whirled around. "Give me my—Sam!"

He picked her up and swung her around. "Sweetheart. Lord. It's so good to see you. I missed you."

"I missed you, too." She looked at him. Could this be the same man? He seemed taller and even better looking. She told him as much.

"You're the one. You're stunning," he told her.

"All right, buddy, you can take care of that when you get her home," an irate male voice said.

"Yeah," Sam said, "and I intend to do just that. How many pieces of luggage do you have?"

"Two, and here comes the other one."

He parked in front of the building in which she lived, put her luggage and several bags of groceries he'd purchased in the lobby. "I'll bring these up, you go on inside," he told her.

She walked into her apartment, dropped her pocketbook and a small bag on a chair, and opened some windows to banish the stale air. Sam soon followed with her bags and the groceries.

"I know you're exhausted, so sit someplace while I put these things away. Then we'll have a welcome home drink and I'll cook us some supper."

She sat on the sofa and fastened her gaze on him. "Can't that wait? I'd rather you came over here and kissed me."

He gazed down at her. "I've wanted this for so long, that I'm afraid if I get started, I might not be able to stop." He leaned down, held her face in his hands, and fastened his lips on hers. But when she tried to deepen the kiss, he broke it off, went to the kitchen, and returned with two glasses of champagne.

"I know you don't drink much, but a month in Italy should have improved your tolerance for alcohol." He handed her a glass and raised his own. "I think this has been the longest month of my adult life. Did you come back because this is home or did you come back to me?"

"In my heart, I came back to you. Thank God you were where home is."

He sipped his drink, placed their glasses on the coffee table, and parted his lips above hers. But he didn't let her start the fire that she needed. He bent, removed her shoes, and turned her head to foot on the sofa. "Rest while I get things in order."

She called her father. "I just got in, Papa. Sam met me at the airport. We've just walked into my apartment. Everything's fine, thanks. I have a million things to tell you. The project? That's right on target. I'll drop by the shop tomorrow. Bye." She knew he'd understand that she wouldn't hold a long conversation while Sam was with her.

After their supper of filet mignon, baked potato, steamed asparagus, and a salad, Sam cleaned the dining room and kitchen.

That will take him about fifteen minutes, Kendra said to herself. Just time enough to get a fast shower. When he rejoined her, he might have commented on her change of clothing had she not presented him with a leather toiletries kit that bore his engraved initials.

"This is fantastic. And you even had it engraved with my initials. I was not expecting a gift, Kendra. This is what I would buy for myself. Thank you. I'll have this for as long as I live." He opened his arms and she dashed into them, eager to lose herself in him. And lose herself she did, as he took them on a hot, mind-bending adventure in the rewards of lovemaking. When he left her just before daybreak, she locked her arms around his pillow and slept at last.

The next morning, she sat up in bed and telephoned her uncle. "I just got back from Italy last night, Uncle Ed. How are you and Aunt Dot?"

"We're fine, except she's mad at me for getting Ginny out of jail."

"She was in jail again?"

"Yeah. The police discovered that she lied. She was driving that car when it crashed. She stayed there about three weeks. I got her out a week ago."

"Something's got to give, Uncle Ed. I wish I knew what that something is."

Chapter Fifteen

Kendra walked into Richards, Inc., Purveyor of Quality Meats, tossed her red woolen cap toward the ceiling, and hugged her father. "I did it, Papa. I'm back. I got what I went for, and I'm twenty years older."

He wrapped her in a loving father's arms. "I expected the first part. Tell me how you got to be twenty years older. Was that before or after Sam met you at the airport?"

"Hmm. I know you're shrewd, Papa, and even wily when need be, but that wasn't even subtle. I negotiated opportunities that I could never have afforded and got them just for showing up. I got in and out of several problem situations and never got a scratch. *I feel as if I can handle just about anything.* I crisscrossed Italy on the ticket the university gave me, and didn't have to add a cent . . . I mean, a *lira*. I learned how to get around on my own."

"I'm proud of you, but I see you missed the one thing I figured you'd learn at the start."

"What's that?"

"A beautiful woman with poise and dignity only has to ask. Italian men must have changed a lot since I was in Italy."

"You were in Italy?"

He nodded. "Uh huh. Don't change the subject."

She had to laugh. "Trust me, those men still like to make

themselves useful, but I found it easier and safer to ignore their free-flowing charm and eager helpfulness."

He produced a delectable lunch, and she told him about her adventures and the report she wrote for class. "I couldn't be happier," he said. "Now tell me how things are with you and Sam."

"We love each other, Papa. I wouldn't be away from him for one second if I could avoid it."

"I'm glad to hear it. Remember that if you want to marry him, keep something for yourself." During the next days, she digested those words over and over.

She returned to the university the following Monday morning, and handed her paper to Professor Hormel.

"Congratulations in getting back here on time. Most students find a reason to stay beyond the agreed time and offer a flimsy reason for having done so. Do you like what you've written?"

"I'm afraid to say yes, sir. If you find that I did a poor job, I'll be terribly disappointed. I did my best, Professor Hormel."

"I'm glad to hear it. That's all I wanted from you."

After worrying over the matter for more than half of the day, Sam slapped his right fist into the palm of his left hand. "That's it," he said, took his cell phone out of his breast pocket, and telephoned Bert Richards.

"Richards, Inc. Bert Richards speaking. How may I help you?"

"Bert, this is Sam. I know you meet Kendra when she gets off from work, but I'd like to meet her tonight."

"Why, sure, provided it's all right with her."

"Thanks. I owe you one." He knew that Bert wouldn't warn Kendra about the change, because he didn't doubt that the man trusted him. "See you soon."

Why was he so nervous?

* * *

It surprised Kendra that Clifton Howell would come to the studio to greet her on her first evening back at work.

"Thanks for keeping your word and coming back here. You've got a lot of mail. I printed it out and saved it, because your box became full. I hope it went well and that it was everything you hoped for."

"It was wonderful, Mr. Howell. I know a lot more about a lot of things than I did when I left here." It took her only a minute to reacquaint herself with the routine and, with Louis Armstrong's "A Kiss to Build a Dream On" making her want to dance, she lifted the phone receiver after the first ring.

"KT speaking. How's your world? Mine's fabulous!"

"You sound happy."

How she loved his voice! "That's because I am. What do you want to hear?"

"Actually, I called because I'm picking you up tonight. I checked with Bert, and he said he didn't mind if you're all right with it."

"Why would I mind? I love being with you. I'll be out front between five and ten after midnight. See you then. Kisses."

"Is this line open?"

"Heavens no. Didn't I say, 'kisses'?"

"Yeah. You did. But you didn't say you love me. I need to hear it, Kendra, because I'm deeply in love with you."

Hmm. Was he feeling down? "Oh, Sam. You're so special to me. I love you so much that it scares me sometimes. Bye."

It seemed as if midnight would never come. Why did Sam want to meet her, and why had he needed reassurance? Surely, he must know that their relationship wouldn't have advanced to such an extent if she didn't love him. She told herself not to second-guess him, that he'd tell her what, if anything, was bothering him.

Kendra stepped out of the Howell Building and saw Sam move away from his car and head toward her. Her steps quickened, but she restrained the impulse to run to him. Before he reached her, a homeless woman intercepted her.

"Can you help me, please?"

Kendra gaped at the woman. She would recognize that voice anywhere. Well, maybe not. The woman wore an old coat inside out and had draped a ragged blanket over her head and shoulders. The blanket covered most of her face.

"Please. You have plenty, and I don't have anything."

Shocked, Kendra grabbed the blanket and pulled it off the woman's head. "Mama! How could you pull a stunt like this?"

"Can you let me have a couple hundred for food?"

Horrified, Kendra asked her, "What do you expect to gain by pretending to be homeless?"

"I didn't pretend anything. You assumed it. I need some money for food. Would you see your own mother starve?"

"You owe me so much money already. Oh, what the hell!" She opened her pocketbook and counted out one hundred and thirty-seven dollars. She kept the seven for herself and gave Ginny the rest.

"Is this all you're giving me? I know you've got more, but you're so damned stingy." She put the money into her pocket, turned to leave, and bumped into Sam. By chance, Kendra looked at Ginny's clothes and then lowered her gaze to the woman's feet.

"You go out begging wearing a Burberry coat turned inside out and Jimmy Choo shoes? Well, I'm the fool."

As if Kendra hadn't said anything, Ginny turned to Sam. "Can you give me a little something, mister?"

"Not even if you crawled along this pavement begging. You disgust me."

It was one thing to know that he felt it and quite another to hear him tell her mother to her face that she was disgusting. Kendra grasped his arm. "Can we leave now, please?"

Something was wrong. She could almost feel the chill coming from him. "Yes. Of course," he said.

He opened the front passenger door for her, helped her in, and hooked her seat belt, but she felt that he was only going through the motions, that his heart wasn't in it. When he headed up Connecticut Avenue and still hadn't said one word, she knew that whatever he'd planned would not happen that night. And when he drove directly to the building in which she lived and stopped, she unhooked her seat belt.

"Thanks for bringing me home." She didn't wait for his response nor did she ask him if he wanted to come in. It gave her a small measure of pride to close the car door softly and strut off without looking back.

You've won again, Ginny, but it won't kill me. Not now. Not ever. And as for you, Sam Hayes, I don't need your brand of love.

Her home phone rang, but she didn't answer it, and after ignoring it, she turned off her cell phone. She'd had enough pain for one night. Pain from her mother's conscienceless, deceitful, and destructive behavior. Pain from Sam's apparent inability to distinguish her from her mother.

"I won't let it bring me down. I've worked too hard, climbed over too many hills, and bucked too many storms," she said aloud. "She gave me life, but she has never been my mother, and I've got to start thinking of her as just a woman I know."

Kendra went to bed, but sunrise found her wide awake. When her phone rang at eight o'clock, she checked the caller ID, saw that the call was from her uncle Ed, and answered the phone.

"I heard your show last night. When did you start back?"

"Friday. How's everybody?"

"Dot's birthday is Sunday. Bert's coming, and I'm calling to invite you to join us. Don't buy any presents. Just come."

She wouldn't be seeing Sam, so why not? "I'd love to come, Uncle Ed. What time?"

"Three o'clock. Bert will pick you up. Whoever had your show while you were gone didn't know a thing about jazz. Yours is much more interesting."

So Ginny heard that show and came out at the end of it for the kill. "Mama must have heard it, too, because she—"

"She what?"

"She was waiting for me when I came out of the building. Imagine, Uncle Ed, she was dressed to look like a beggar or a homeless person, and she was wearing shoes that cost anywhere from five hundred to a thousand dollars."

"Never mind that. Did she say anything to you?"

"She asked me for money. I had a hundred and thirty-seven dollars, and I gave her all but seven. Do you think she thanked me? No. She said I was stingy."

"You're behaving like a masochist. See you Sunday."

"That's it," Ed said aloud. "She's incorrigible." He wrote a letter to the judge on Ginny's case, attached the bill stating the agreed conditions of Ginny's release on bail, and requesting that her bail be revoked. He suggested that a year in a psychiatric treatment facility might help Ginny change her sociopathic behavior.

"But suppose he sends her to jail instead," Dot said when she read his letter.

He stared at his wife. "Are you suggesting that she wouldn't deserve it? The problem is that she'd be as bad as ever when she came out. She won't seek help voluntarily, so this is the best I can do for her." He sliced the air over his head. "I've had it up to here. One day she'll kill somebody, and if I don't get her some help, it will be my fault."

Kendra knew that Sam had tried to get in touch with her on at least four occasions, but she hadn't answered the phone when she saw his ID. At first it was the pain, but later it was more—she couldn't bear to hear him end it. She promised herself that she wouldn't mention Sam's behavior to her father, because he had already told her that no man would want Ginny for a mother-in-law and certainly not for the grandmother of his children.

However, the first thing Bert said to her when she got into

his car the following Sunday afternoon was, "How are things with you and Sam? He seemed awfully anxious to meet you Monday night."

"We're in limbo. I don't know why he wanted to meet me."

"That's odd. Something must have happened."

"Something did." She told him about Ginny's appearance that night and Sam's reaction.

"I see. Either you or Ed is going to have to put her away. She's not rowing with both oars, and she gets worse all the time."

"I doubt Uncle Ed will do anything. When I told him about it Tuesday morning, he barely reacted."

"Then, it may be up to you."

Bert parked in front of Ed's white brick, two-story house on Montague Avenue in Westmoreland Hills, Maryland, a few miles from the District line. Kendra jumped out and started for the front door, but her father stopped her.

"Didn't I teach you not to go anyplace with a man who wouldn't open the door for you? Didn't I? You can accept a man's assistance and still be a modern, independent woman, for Pete's sake."

"Yes, sir."

Ed opened the door. "I thought you guys would never get here. We're all out back. Come on in."

Ed had set up the grill on the enclosed porch and, after the de rigueur greetings to Dot on the fiftieth anniversary of her birth, they devoured his grilled specialties—barbecued steaks, sausages, and pork chops, roast potatoes, onions, asparagus, and zucchini.

Dot rubbed her stomach. "I'm going to pop."

"I'm not," Kendra said, "and I'm taking some of this home with me. That's the great thing about living alone—you can take your meals when and as you please."

Ed laid his grilling tongs on the table beside him, wiped his hands on his apron, and walked over to where Kendra sat beside his teenage daughter. "By the way, Ginny's trial comes up Tuesday morning, and this time she is either going to jail or to a facility for rehabilitation." Kendra's gasp brought only a shrug from him. "I told her that if she approached you by mail, Internet, phone, or in person before you got your degree, I'd turn her in. That was the agreement between her, the judge, and me when I paid her bail the last time. Neither you nor anyone else can help, so don't try to intervene."

"I didn't realize that when I told you what she did."

"I know you didn't. You've been playing masochist to her sadist most of your life, but not anymore."

"Right," Dot said. "A person can't abuse you unless you let them."

Kendra promised her uncle that she wouldn't interfere, but she skipped class and sat in the courtroom while the judge heard the case. At the end, he sentenced Ginny to "one year in an institution for rehabilitation where you will be an inpatient. If you leave there without official permission, you will spend the remainder of the year in jail."

"I can't go now, because I have to feed my cats and close my apartment," Ginny said.

"She doesn't have any cats, Your Honor, because she has been allergic to cats since birth," Ed said.

The judge shook his head slowly. "A policewoman will go with you to pack what you will need in the hospital. If you give her any trouble, she will handcuff you and take you to jail where you will remain for one year. That's all."

Ginny looked around and with head high, she walked over to Kendra. "You came here for the kill, did you? Ed wouldn't have known about this if you hadn't told him. I wish I'd never seen your daddy."

Kendra stared at the woman who gave her life. "I pity you," she said, and she did. With that, she left the courthouse, headed for the subway, and half an hour later walked into her philosophy class. No matter what happened, she'd hold her head up. If she was going to let Ginny Hunter bring her down, it would have happened years earlier.

She got through the school day, ate a ham sandwich with a container of hot cocoa at a fast-food shop on Georgia Avenue, and went to work. For once, she didn't feel like playing jazz or making small talk with callers. When she answered the phone at nine o'clock, Jethro Hayes was on the line.

He identified himself. "I always enjoy your program, KT, and not only the music, but your warm and witty exchanges with the listeners. I notice that you're not feeling too well tonight, and I'm calling to let you know that your listeners always understand. I'd appreciate it if you'd play 'If.' Remember, KT, that there isn't a river on the planet that hasn't been crossed. Thank you."

He hung up before she could thank him for calling in. He had intended to cheer her up, but he had only reminded her of what she'd lost.

When she got into her father's car that night, she asked him, "What would you say if I decided to visit Mama? I don't feel guilty about her having been sent there, because I know she deserved that and more. But I want to be sure that she is being treated for whatever's wrong with her."

"Do what you think best, Kendra. You have to live with yourself. But I don't think it wise for you to allow yourself to become a part of her treatment."

"That won't happen."

"Have you and Sam terminated your relationship?"

"He has telephoned me a number of times since that night, but I don't take the calls. I just can't face it."

"You can't face what? You don't know what he wants to say."

"Papa, he told me more than once that he loved me. That night, when I was so miserably unhappy, was the time for him to demonstrate it."

"And since you're perfect, you don't plan to forgive him. Right? According to you, you gave her a hundred and thirty dollars, and her response was that she knew you had more and that you were stingy. Not a word of thanks. Then she turned to him and asked him for money. I'm sure he thought you shouldn't have given her a dime."

She turned so that she could see his face. "That's what you think, isn't it? Would he have loved me more if I had walked past her, and got into his car? To me, that would have been heartless."

"I divorced Ginny for doing to me what she's doing to you, and I don't blame Sam for being afraid of her and of what would happen to him if he married you. You need to show him that you won't let her use you as she did that night. Have you gotten the result of your story on Italy's food and its people?"

"Professor Hormel told me that he'll have a full report at the end of the week. He's read it, and he likes it."

"Then I don't suppose you need to worry." He parked in front of the building in which she lived. "Think about what I've told you tonight."

"Yes, sir." She hugged him. "Good night, Papa."

Sam sat in the lobby waiting for Kendra. He had telephoned her nearly a dozen times, but she hadn't taken his calls, and he had refused to resort to subterfuge and conceal his caller ID. He wanted her to answer his calls in full knowledge that it was he on the line. She entered the building with her head down, looking neither right nor left. He didn't like that, because he'd never seen her walk with her head bowed. He walked with quick steps to arrive at the elevator when she did.

"Wh . . . what are you doing here?"

"You ask that? I've called you nearly a dozen times, but you won't take my calls. I need to talk with you."

"Oh. Does this mean I'm finally going to know what you wanted to say to me the night you confused me with Mama and clammed up on me? Let me tell you something. You said you loved me, but when you had an opportunity to prove it, you shut down like an engine that had run out of gas."

With his hand at her elbow, he urged her into the elevator, though he knew that in her present frame of mind she was hardly aware of it. "Are you saying that you don't want to hear what I have to say, that you don't care how I felt that night?"

"How could you have felt, compared to what was going on inside of me when you didn't support me?"

The elevator door opened, and he walked with her to her apartment door. "I wanted to see you that night to ask you if we could plan a life together, and if you would be willing for us to get psychiatric help for your mother. I have discussed her case with experts, who say we should never cater to her, because that only encourages her in her self-centeredness. You gave her almost all the money you had. I saw how she acted and heard what she said to you, and I knew she always acted that way, and yet you still pamper her. It was too much for me to accept. I haven't cried since my mother died, but that night I cried for you, for me, and for her."

She stared at him. "Have you thought how you would have felt toward me if I had just walked past her—or any woman who appeared to be homeless—and gotten into your car? I can't deal with this right now, Sam. With the help of my uncle—her brother—the judge in her case committed her for one year to an institution for psychiatric care."

"With your concurrence?"

"I was present at the sentencing, and I have decided to check on her once or twice a month to see that she is indeed receiving treatment. I don't feel responsible for her, but if she gets better, maybe she'll leave me alone."

"I see. What about us?"

"I don't know. This feeling is so raw. I've tried not to think of that night. Maybe it's about her. Maybe it's about you. It could be both. I'll try and sort it out."

"Do you think you can take my phone calls?"

"I don't know. I'll try to. Good night."

"Good night, and thanks for not having me arrested for harassing you."

Her eyes widened. "That never entered my mind. Good night."

The next afternoon, Sam received a text message from his father. "Can you drop by for supper tonight, say, about seven? See you then."

Hmm. That sounded more like a command than an invitation.

He got there a few minutes before seven, and they embraced each other, as usual.

"I brought you a bottle of Hine's fine VSOP Cognac. That stuff you served last week was lousy. So what necessitated your command to dinner?"

Jethro released a hearty laugh. "Feeling testy, huh? How about a beer? I still have some of those great porterhouse steaks Bert gave me. Steak, baked potato, asparagus, and sliced tomato is what you're getting."

"That's hard to beat."

They ate in the kitchen, as they did in the years after Sam's mother died. "What's on your mind, Dad?" His father's silence was getting to him. He hoped that his dad didn't have a health problem.

"What went wrong between you and Kendra? You're both unhappy. I see it in you, and it's evident from the change in her demeanor when she's on the air. What happened? I've been expecting you to tell me that you've asked her to marry you."

"This is a first-class meal. No wonder you don't hire a full-time cook."

"Lacey's here to clean and do the laundry three times a week, and she always cooks dinner. That's more than enough for me. Are you going to answer my question, or are you telling me to butt out? I've got a personal interest in this."

"Such as?"

"I'd like to be a grandfather. Look. Let's cut to the chase. I like that girl. What's wrong with her?"

"It isn't her; it's her mother. A more distasteful woman will be hard to find."

"Have you seen any of that in Kendra?"

"Actually, she's everything that her mother should be, but the thought of having that woman in my life makes me sick."

"Start at the beginning, and don't leave anything out."

They talked until late in the evening. Jethro got a snifter of cognac, inhaled it, and then sipped slowly. "Aren't you proud of Kendra? I can't see how she got where she is with a burden of that measure and significance. She's right that you should have supported her that night. She's not only hurt, but I think she's deflated."

"That's possible. I was listening when you called in during her show, and what you told her touched me. That's the night I waited for her in the lobby of her apartment building."

"You still love her, so get busy before she convinces herself that she can live without you. And you should know that if you meet her needs, she won't need a mother who abuses her."

"I hear you. What about you and Edwina? I had thought you two would be married by now."

"Don't worry about Edwina and me. I'm not foolish enough to lose her again. And if you think you want to spend the rest of your life loving a woman you can't have, let me tell you that you don't. I have time; you don't. When I was your age, you were four years old.

"I'm planning to go fishing the first part of March, and I'm hoping I can persuade Bert to go with me. With a business like his, he must have some reliable workers who can maintain the shop for him."

"He does," Sam said. "Why not wait till spring break, and I can take the boat out?"

"Good idea. I'll see what Bert thinks. I'm glad we had this talk. I don't want to see you lose that woman."

"And I don't want to lose her."

Sam drove home, all the while pondering his next move. Inside his apartment, he reminded himself that he had won Kendra's trust by being straight and honest with her, and that he wouldn't resort to clever tricks. At half past twelve, he telephoned her and held his breath.

"Hi, Sam."

"Hello, Kendra. You can't know how happy I am that you answered the phone. I had dinner with my dad, and we spent the evening talking about you and about you and me. I'm . . . this is so unnatural. I can't say what I'm thinking and feeling. Can you and I be together Sunday after you finish studying?"

"I'd like that, Sam. I ought to be free around one."

"Any news about the story you wrote on your visit to Italy?"

"Oh, yes. Professor Hormel told me today that each of my professors gave me an A, plus I get a semester's credit for it, and that's a bonus that I hadn't expected."

"Congratulations. I'm proud of you and happy for you, Kendra. You deserve every reward that you get."

She wasn't dancing for joy, but she was happier than she had been for a long time. She meant to stand her ground and, for as long as her mother was in that institution for treatment and care, she would discharge her filial responsibility, even though Ginny Hunter did not and never would deserve it. Surely, Sam could live with that. She sent an e-mail to his iPhone.

I'll be studying in the Library of Congress tomorrow, from eleven to five in the main reading room, at First and Independence, SE. The reading room is the best place to study, if I need reference books. It's so good to be in touch. K.

She washed her stockings and underwear, showered, got ready for bed, and went into a sound sleep.

Her father's call awakened her the next morning. "What do you know?" he asked her after they greeted each other. "I hope you've had your coffee."

She hadn't. "I just opened my eyes. Tell me."

"Jethro invited me to go fishing on his boat with him sometime at the end of March or the first week in April, weather permitting."

"No kidding! I'm getting the feeling that he wants to make sure I marry Sam."

"Probably. That's the main reason why I'll leave Gates in charge of my shop for an entire weekend. I expect you and Sam will join us."

"Don't bet on it. No one's mentioned it to me." But Jethro did mention it. He also told her that she'd no doubt prefer to enjoy the boat with Sam rather than with the parents.

By the first week in April, she and Sam were once more constantly together. One evening as he sheltered her from a torrent of rain, she said to him, "Sam, you're spoiling me. What would you do if I began expecting you to guarantee that it wouldn't rain or snow on me? And that I wouldn't get cold?"

"I'd do my best to keep you dry and warm in winter, and cool and dry during vicious summer heat and humidity. You see something wrong with that?"

She hadn't had much nurturing in her life, and she wasn't going to thumb her nose at it. "Not one thing, honey. Not a single thing."

And so it went. Both of them kept a tight rein on the fierce passion that had characterized their relationship in the days before she went to Italy. And although she told herself that she preferred it that way, she knew that their eventual coming together would be explosive.

* * *

Over two months after Ginny was confined to the facility for treatment, she indicated that she recognized her daughter's presence. "Why do you come here? Do you get some satisfaction from knowing that I have to be here unless I want to go to jail?"

Kendra questioned the effect of lying, decided that she wouldn't, and said, "In a way, yes. It comforts me to know that you won't badger me for money or embarrass me at my job, but I hate to know that you have a condition that requires psychiatric treatment. I come here to make sure that these people are giving you the treatment you need. That's my duty."

"I'm glad to know you're not doing it to show how much you love me," Ginny said, and sucked her teeth in apparent disgust.

But she didn't fool Kendra, who had never before heard her mother use the word *love*. "Absolutely not," Kendra replied. "I wouldn't embarrass you or myself by getting into such emotional mush. See you in a few weeks."

Before leaving, she reported the conversation to the therapist. "She's coming along," the woman said, "but she's got a long, hard road ahead. Don't expect miracles."

Who knew whether Ginny would stay there long enough to make genuine progress? She still possessed a hefty share of arrogance and of egotism, and neither bode well for the cure her mother needed. Kendra took comfort in the knowledge that, in less than three months, Ginny had made a small step toward good mental health.

On a Friday morning in mid-April, during spring break, Sam headed his Buick Enclave out of Washington, D.C., full of hope and not a little anxiety. He glanced at the woman beside him, her head resting against the back of the seat and her eyes closed, as she hummed softly. As a singer, she had no skill, but he managed to detect snatches of Stevie Wonder's "I Just Called To Say I Love You." He patted her thigh to let her know, without the benefit of words, that he shared her mood.

Around eleven o'clock, they reached St. Leonard, Maryland, a tiny settlement on the Chesapeake Bay where he moored the boat, a thirty-eight foot schooner that he and his father owned jointly.

"We're lucky that Dad and Bert were down here last weekend," he said, "and we don't have to put her in shape for sailing."

"I know. I don't think my papa has ever raved about anything as much as he did about that boat, the fishing, and the joy of being out on the Chesapeake Bay."

"Dad enjoyed it, too. I hope you enjoy it as much as your father did."

At the boat, he lowered the gangplank by remote control, took her hand, and walked on. "You stay here," he said, pointing to the lounge, "while I get our things."

He was back in fifteen minutes, telling himself that he didn't want to give her head time to start controlling her emotions. "I'll put your bag in the captain's quarters." He turned to go, but she stopped him.

"Where will you put yours?"

"Not to worry. That's a bed." He pointed to the sofa on which she sat. She gave him a long, unfathomable look, picked up her bag, and strolled into the captain's quarters. He stood there for a couple of minutes, reflected that she seemed neither angry nor annoyed, and got busy putting away their supplies. By the time she reappeared in white jeans, blue sneakers, and a blue, collared T-shirt, he thought he'd burst out of his skin.

"You all right?" he asked her.

"Oh, yes. This is one snappy machine. I can't wait to get started."

"You mean the boat?" She nodded. "As soon as we eat a sandwich, we'll take off. I'd like some fresh fish for supper."

They sailed down to Trappe, on Maryland's Eastern Shore and docked upstream. "Dad said the fish here practically competed for a chance to get hooked. We'll see how they treat us."

He baited their hooks, and they sat in deck chairs and waited. "These are more than we need," he said of their fish a couple of hours later.

"I wish life was like this," she said, more to herself than to him, but she knew he heard her.

"Give it a chance, Kendra. Give *me* a chance."

With a look that was level and direct, she said, "That's why I'm here."

"Do you still love me?" he asked, leaning toward her while grasping the tail of a good-size pike.

She stood and faced him. "Yes, I love you. If I tried to stop, I don't know where I'd begin." She didn't want a piece-meal discussion of their relationship, she wanted it all aired out, and when they stopped talking, she'd know whether they would be together forever or would say good-bye forever when they got back to Washington. "We're going to talk, Sam, but let's wait till you dock for the night."

He put the fish into an ice box, closed it, and said, "If I hadn't been handling that fish, I'd try to drown myself in you."

"Everything I'm wearing is washable, including my shoes."

He stepped closer, enclosed her in the warmth of his arms, and held her there. "I've needed you so badly, down deep where the pain stayed. I love you so much. Have you forgiven me, and do you truly trust me?"

"I've forgiven you. It took awhile, but I tried to put my-self in your place, and I had to acknowledge that if it had been your father instead of my mother, I probably would have broken ties with you and wouldn't have renewed them. I never stopped trusting you."

He held her tight without speaking for so long that she stroked the side of his face and asked him, "What's the matter?"

"I haven't prayed much in my life, but I prayed about this, day and night. Will you marry me?"

It was D-Day. If he stood his ground about Ginny, would she do the same and walk away from him? She moved out of his arms and leaned against the door that led to the lower level.

"Do you love me?"

"As I love my life." He walked over and knelt before her. "I will love and care for you and our children and do everything I can to ensure your happiness and well-being."

"What about my mother? I won't allow her ever to abuse me again, and I won't tolerate any of her tricks, but I won't watch her destroy herself, either. I won't bring her to live with me, and if she doesn't change her outlook on life, she won't have access to my children." She eased down until they were face to face. "But Sam, I couldn't ignore her if she were truly in need. I'd lose my self-respect."

"You're offering more than I'm asking. I want you on any terms and without conditions. Will you be my wife?"

"Oh, yes! Yes!"

"Did you really think I was going to let you sleep in the lounge?" she asked him that night as he lay above her, slowly climbing down from the heights of ecstasy.

"After what I'd been through the past three months, I wasn't counting the chicks before they were hatched. I've learned never to do that with you. Wait a minute." He looked at his watch, saw that it was only a quarter of ten, and dialed Bert Richards's phone number.

"Hello, Bert. This is Sam. Kendra just promised to marry me, and I remembered only now that I forgot to ask your permission."

"I figured months ago that it was time. I'm glad to hear it, Sam. You two have my blessings."

"Thank you, sir. I'll take good care of her."

"I have no doubt of that."

"I'll call my dad tomorrow," he said to Kendra. "Right now, I want to enjoy my bride-to-be."

Epilogue

Five years later, Kendra Richards-Hayes and Samuel Hayes sat at home, gazing with pride upon their children, Alex and Ellen Hayes, ages three and one, respectively. Sam had been elevated to dean of psychology at the university, and Jethro and Edwina Hayes were on a perpetual honeymoon. Bert Richards had formed a string quartet which, with performances and record sales, netted him more money in a week than his butcher shop earned in a month. His dream had finally come true, and he had taken on a new life partner, who he married soon after Kendra was graduated from Howard University with a bachelor of arts degree in communications, magna cum laude.

After a year of treatment as an inpatient in a rehabilitation facility, Ginny Hunter had improved to the point that she had a steady relationship with a reasonable man who she appeared to care for, but she had not attempted to affect a normal mother–daughter relationship with Kendra, and Kendra neither expected it nor felt that she needed it. Ginny visited her grandchildren occasionally, but didn't appear to want a close relationship with them.

One summer evening, as they sat around the swimming pool at the back of their seven-room Tudor house in Westmoreland Hills reflecting on their lives, Sam sipped from a glass of lemonade, put it down, lifted little Alex into his arms, and reached for his wife's hand.

"She doesn't care for our stay-at-home lifestyle," he said of Ginny, "and she comes when she thinks she has to. As long as that doesn't bother you, I'm grateful for it."

"So am I."

DISCUSSION QUESTIONS

1. The average student graduates from college at age twenty-two. Why is Kendra struggling to graduate at age thirty-two?
2. What element of Kendra's character is most responsible for her big break as she strives toward her goal?
3. What is the opportunity that enables Kendra to take that big step and register at Howard?
4. What occasion almost wrecked that chance, and who engineered it?
5. Kendra's father buys her an apartment in a good neighborhood. What command does he give his daughter about the apartment?
6. What was at the root of Bert Richards's decision to divorce Kendra's mother?
7. What do you regard as evidence of Kendra's moral fortitude? Her weakness?
8. Do you think Ginny Hunter is mentally impaired?
9. Do you believe she is simply evil? If so, why?
10. Ginny has very sluttish ways, yet she sees herself as being superior to everyone she knows. What is your opinion of such a person?
11. Do you think Ginny's brother should have given Kendra more support?
12. Should he have allowed his sister to remain in jail, since he knew from her childhood that she was a sociopath, or should he have forced her into treatment?
13. Within a few short months, Kendra gets a job she likes, registers in college (after waiting over a decade to complete the last two years), and meets and falls in love with Sam Hayes. What are her main challenges during this time?

14. Name three occasions when Ginny could have destroyed Kendra's relationship with Sam, either directly or indirectly. What do you think of Sam's reaction?

15. What is the first indication that Sam and Kendra's attraction will be a lasting one?

16. Why does Sam invite Bert Richards picnicking in Rock Creek Park with him and Kendra?

17. What is the most important lesson that Kendra learned during her study trip to Italy?

18. Does Bert's attention as a father make up for Ginny's shortcomings?

19. What do you consider to be Ginny's most egregious offense against her daughter?

20. What evidence is there that Ginny can no longer hurt or abuse Kendra, and when is this evident?